Self-published by Guy S

The Smithy

73 High Street

Burbage

Wiltshire

SN8 3AA

thesmithy.gallery

guy@thesmithy.gallery

Instagram: art_forgery_

Facebook: Smithy Art Forgery

First published by Guy Shepherd 2020

To
MY DARLING NATASHA
My friend, my muse, my love.

Circum Navigation

Guy Shepherd

Contents

An Introduction by the Author

My adventures with crop circles began in the summer of 2018. Unbeknown to me it signified a new beginning after a rollicking rollercoaster ride through a devilish decade of retail recession and damaging divorce. I was finding my feet again. It was the start of a miraculous return to my pre-marital cottage. It was the experimental year of its conversion to The Smithy art gallery. It was the first season of holiday rental on my recently completed outbuilding, The Boffy (yes, I know it's spelt wrong). My girlfriend had just returned to Canada. Unbeknown to us, it was the start of over a year of visa wranglings before our reunification. Every day apart was increased agony as we experienced the true depth of our love. It was also the start of my ascent from the quagmire of chain smoking, persistent drinking and occasionally worse.

The catalyst for these changes materialised in human form. Elodie and Marc, a couple from French Polynesia, arrived to stay in the Boffy with their Spanish friend, Consol. The pair had arrived from their south Pacific island paradise for their holiday in the Pewsey Vale. This puzzled me. Their beach home, on photographic inspection, boasted white sand, waterfalls, palm trees, a coral reef, dolphins and whales in the blue beyond. Those that know me personally and those that read my stories will all know that I am a great fan of Pewsey's wonderful valley, nay, this earthly heaven, but I was intrigued nonetheless. Elodie had experienced an extraordinary dream a few months before. When she searched online for the various elements that she remembered from her revelation, she was drawn to the formation of crop circles and, due to the topological distinctions, the southern downs of England in particular. They made plans to visit.

By the end of their week's stay, they were hooked on the field magic. The trio wanted to prolong their Boffy lodgings but it was fully booked for the summer. I already had a very good vibe about them so asked them to stay in my own cottage for a modest fee. A friendship was born. By day they would visit the latest crop circles. By evening they would cook delicious food and tell me tales. I'm a polite chap, so managed to veil my utter disbelief in their hippy dippy stories with lame excuses, drink refills and ashtray emptying. By night, the girls would chat to the resident ghost. They convinced her to leave before they did. It was an extraordinary fortnight.

Despite their continuous insistence, I never visited any crop circles with them. However, my rolling eyes routine only temporarily stalled their attempts to help me. They talked to me in a way that made me wonder about the futility of my current existence and the greatness of our planet and the universe beyond. They saw something in me that I had long lost. They saw my strength. When they left, I decided to find it. This decision was made easier by their encouraging messages in my visitors' book, their 'thank you' card and the crop circle book they gifted me. As a matter of respect for my charming guests, I read it. I was transfixed and mesmerised by the collection of science, facts and stories that Janet Ossebaard had accumulated in "Crop Circles: The Evidence". Admittedly, like every other story, history, film, anecdote, eye witness account, experiment or finding on this subject, she has been ridiculed publicly and brassenly lambasted. But intelligent humans read beyond the fake news that we are spoon fed like naive babies.

The science in the subject was enough to convince me that I had a raison d'etre for my Wiltshire existence. The seemingly selfish life that I had battered myself into, suddenly had a chink of light in the distance. The cathartic process of personal outpouring through writing began in the late autumn. I vowed to cut down on the excesses in my world and concentrate on the work. Alone in my cottage for months on end, I attempted my novel. Wild and sporadic outbursts of my traditional excesses were eventually tempered by mid February 2019. I then vowed to remain sober for a year after thirty three years of not being so. I gave up smoking shortly afterwards. I felt incredible. The writing flowed. I finished the first draft by spring. It was an outpouring of my soul, a romance through others, a study in artistry and a humbling connection to the awesome power beyond.

Having written a fictional work about such a mesmerising subject, I thought I had better go and experience it for myself. I did not have to wait long. The first seasonal sighting was reported relatively locally on 22 May 2019 next to Norridge Wood, near Warminster, Wiltshire. I was buzzing with trepidation on the journey west in my pickup truck a couple of days later. I was slightly disappointed as I parked in the nearby layby and climbed across the detritus of inconsiderate travellers into the green field under grey skies. I immediately met my first enthusiast readying his drone for photography. His eyes danced as he regaled me with tales regarding his previous experiences. I was ready so, carefully following the tractor tracks, I plunged into my first crop circle. Shortly later, I left thoroughly disappointed after all the hullabaloo of the last few months. My overriding emotion was that I could have constructed the simple circles myself using rope and boards. I could not detect the tell tale signs of crop flattening without damage. My enthusiasm wilted like the broken crop.

With my faith in tatters, I half heartedly watched cropcircleconnector.com for the latest artwork. To compound my diminished interest, most of the crop circles reported were appearing in France. Despite riding a World War Two BMW sidecar unit around Normandy for the 75th Anniversary, I did not visit any Gallic crop circles that June. After the glorious distraction of Summer Solstice at Avebury World Heritage Site, I had nearly forgotten my pursuit of crop art, had put the novel to rest and only paid cursory attention to the web news. The only minor positive was that the circles had started appearing in neighbouring counties. Rumours were already spreading locally that the Pewsey Vale had had its day.

On 6 July, with German two wheel drive sidecar technology fresh in mind, I rode my Harley down to Alton, Hampshire, to test the new BMW Scrambler. It was a glorious day of blue skies behind bloated clouds, so I decided to lose myself on the roads beyond Winchester on my way home after the test ride. My nose is substantial but lends itself to directional efficiency which, when coupled with the position of the sun, is ample navigation on a motorbike. Following these simple hunches, I chugged through the picturesque town of Stockbridge, complete with an angling salesman giving a fly rod demo to a client on the High Street near the famous Test river. England really can be bloody marvellous. I throttled uphill to the west and into the sunshine.

A flash on my right was enough for me to slow down then turn in the vague north west direction of Andover and home. The sign claiming Danebury Iron Age Hillfort was sufficient for my subconscious to trigger limited databanks. It was the site of a recent crop circle. A mile or so later, I tripped over a hill crest and saw the green circle for the first time. I parked the bike next to the visitors and amblers, then climbed the hill to look down on the giant ring. It was beautiful. I was overwhelmed by a feeling of calm and peace. These are emotions often experienced by art fans. I walked down and along the winding track to the artwork. It was many hours later, having met curious, interested and enthusiastic patrons, I left with a new warmth in my heart. I had read a passage of my book to a dedicated devotee who had confirmed that I was spot on. That was enough for me.

With a spring in my step, I visited my girlfriend in Canada. It was the first time I had seen her in nearly a year. I returned a few days later with a double spring in my step. A combo of Smithy work and the start of my son's summer holiday kept me away from the new agricultural love I was nurturing but, by 25 July, I was lulled back into its embrace. A seven circled artwork had already appeared at Pepperbox Hill, near West Grimstead, Wiltshire, so I rode off to see. As I gunned the bike along the Salisbury to Southampton road, I missed my opportunity to decelerate at the slip road to the appropriate village. As I prepared to slow and u-turn, a powerful urge to continue straight on overcame me. I did so and, as I climbed a hill, craned my neck to the left. Something told me that I had arrived. I could see no tell tale indentations in the field beyond but a small single track lane appeared which I instinctively took off the main road. Standing on the foot rests, I continued to inspect the crop beyond the hedgerow. Still nothing. I spotted a car parked in a gated entrance and stopped beside it. After dismounting, a large family joined me from the field. They were French and all bore the international signs of joy that crop circles appear to give their visitors, beaming smiles and sparkly eyes. On their departure, I vaulted the barred gate and walked the short distance to the brow of the hill. I was alone. The short hour that I spent with that creation, as the sun dipped towards the horizon, was one of mental exhilaration and an overwhelming peace in my body. It was true beauty.

After my annual vacation to France in early August, I publicly opened The Smithy for the very first time. It featured an exhibition of "Chubby Bathers" oil paintings by Rosy Modet. They were a suitable splash for a glorious summer which had accelerated the harvest by the afternoon of 23 August. Due to the rapidly dwindling supply of agricultural canvas, I had nearly given up on the formation of any more crop circles. However, my subconscious devised a plan to ride my bike down the Pewsey Vale and back again, taking note of any unharvested fields as possible future sites. What happened over the subsequent 72 hours or so can be modestly described as a series of incredible coincidences.

With the greatest respect to the town of Devizes, I decided spontaneously to vere off the A342 to avoid the town's traffic at a junction I had never turned off before. It cut the corner, via the villages of Etchilhampton and Coate, back towards my favourite road along the north edge of the valley. Within a few hundred metres of dribbling along the high hedged lane, I had an inexplicable urge to stop and look at the field hidden to my left. I did. I looked out across the recently harvested field at the combines, tractors and trailers away up the hill. The scene seemed to cement the conclusion of my summer's half hearted research project. In the obvious absence of a crop circle, I decided to bid farewell to the year's seasonal art at the permanent stone version in Avebury. Ten miles or so later, I sat against one of the smaller Sarcens next to the village church at the start of the Avenue, one of the more powerful connection points to our planet's subterranean energy lines. After contemplating both the great and the small, I had a last urge to check the crop circle website. To my surprise, one had been reported a couple of days previously. To my even greater surprise, it was in the Vale of Pewsey. To my astonishment, it was outside the village of Etchilhampton, until an hour previous, a place unknown to me. To my bafflement, the map grid location indicated that the circle was in the field above where I had recently stopped my motorbike. I returned the ten miles immediately.

Walking over the brow of the hill and seeing the artwork for the first time was a joyous feeling. The amiable couple I chatted to on descent to the circle oosed happiness. When I reached the perimeter, I felt a wave of joy envelope me. I joined a small ring of randoms who sat in silence in the centre. I basked in the sunshine and let an arable ocean of calm wash over my body. My mind conjured tricks with the cloud formations above. It was like a beautiful dream. When the sun began to set, the randoms began to peel away; four smiling women, three giggling men, a lady with a video camera and, finally, me. Grins and waves were the only farewell required. I drove east again, stopped the bike, walked up Adam's Grave to watch the sunset and gaze at the last few unharvested fields in the valley below. I felt wonderful.

The feeling did not dissipate the next day. So much so that, after my day's work at the gallery, I had nothing else in mind but to return to Etchilhampton. I was immediately rewarded by the same glow of warmth throughout my very core as I lay with my bare back on the perfect fold of wheat beneath me and my eyes fixed on the blue infinite above. My day dreams were broken by the introduction of a male shadow against the sun, one of the half dozen other visitors present. Chris had recognised me from the evening before and we were both delighted to share our mutual adoration of the artwork for the second time. Chris had been with his two mates the day before but had brought his wife and two year old daughter all the way from Bristol to bask in the experience. We were joined by Graham, a veteran crop circle enthusiast, and much banter was shared. Graham was sporting a t-shirt with a distinctive crop circle design. He explained that it had appeared during the Nineties in the fields below Milk Hill and Adam's Grave. I explained that those fields featured in my literary work and that I had watched the sunset from there the eve before. I explained that there were still some unharvested fields and therefore, some hope. Firm friendships were forged before we all headed different directions home.

On return, I texted Chris a long term invitation to hunt crop circles, ate some supper and went to bed. Before turning in, I checked the Crop Circle Connector website. It contained some strange news. A new circle had just been discovered and photographed by Nick Bull's drone. It had been discovered in one of the same unharvested fields between Milk Hill and Stanton St Bernard and at the exact same time as my newest friends and I had just been discussing it. A strange coincidence for sure. Strange enough to ensure that, after a surprisingly deep sleep, I awoke before dawn with an insatiable urge to go visit.

That morning still feels like a fantasy today. I located the circle quickly from a parallel track, well known and used by me on my long walks through the hills. I have to admit that I was a little spooked. I had written my novel the winter before about a subject I had never actually experienced. Since finishing the story at least half a year before, my physical research took me on a fascinating journey. That navigation had now returned full circle to this surprising local reality. The crop circle was only a few hundred metres across the fields from my fictional version. I'm not sure what the odds on that are?

The sun was rising beside Adam's Grave as I marched towards the field. I met a Dutch couple who had risen early for the same reason but were struggling to find the artwork. I explained that I knew where it was and would wave them up if I was correct. I walked up the field along the tractor track, stopped at the edge, took off my shoes and waved at my future friends. In the five minutes before their arrival, I made a video and took some photos. The crop circle was immaculate in its glory. I have never witnessed such exquisite perfection in nature. Had anybody else, since the artists, visited it the eve or night before? It seemed not. Was I the first person to visit the circle? I don't suppose that really matters. What I do know is that I walked into a wall of extraordinary power and the following two hours were the most blissful terrestrial experience of my life. I will recall that feeling of pure love and total happiness forever.

But that is not quite the end of my little adventure. Yes, we three left at around 10am, numbers and hugs exchanged. Our idyll had been broken by the arrival of a family of three who stared at me menacingly when I proffered a friendly greeting of the morning. The man's size and glare made me assume he was of the farming variety but our circular spell was broken so we left the magic behind. It was Bank Holiday Sunday so there were important tasks to complete. I drove to London where I met my beloved girlfriend, recently returned from Canada, and went for a boogie at Gaz's Rockin' Blues at Notting Hill Carnival. The next day, I went back into the

Bashment, met my ex to collect my son for our last week of the summer holiday together. After a brief boggle to the Soca sounds and Reggae rumbles, we jumped back in the car for the journey home to Wiltshire. We stopped at a supermarket on the way to The Smithy. Having relaxed at home a while, I suggested an evening bike ride, walk and investigation of the beautiful crop circle. After this random series of events, my son and I arrived at the foot of the field at the precise moment that the combine harvester made its very first line through the artwork. It was an extraordinary coincidence of timings. A camera crew was also filming a documentary so we two piggybacked their idea by racing to the centre where we filmed the destruction of my beloved temple. Were we the last people to visit the circle? I don't suppose that really matters. With personal affirmation of the power of the universe and group confirmation of my imagined fictional content, I returned home, edited the following story and awaited your judgement.

Guy Shepherd

The Smithy, near Pewsey, 2019

'Feeling High'

Wiltshire is a queer place. A sparsely populated landlocked island of serene beauty and magnetic charm buried in the West of England. Its gentle undulations of Ice Age escarpments, barren plateaus, curved cliffs, rolling hillocks, distant valleys, saucer shaped fields, lush meadows and clear chalk streams make it a rare jewel of nature.

For a multitude of millenia mankind has been drawn to it. Neolithic hunter gatherers patrolled, then metal Ages farmers settled on the hills. Travellers came in large numbers as pilgrimage to its mighty stone and wood henges along its ancient water courses. European influences from Rome and Scandinavia added fortifications, the natural ridgeways made perfect demarcation points between subsequent kingdoms. After Norman conquest the settlements drifted down into the valleys to create the sturdy villages of today. First timber and straw then warmer brick cottages, before the larger edifices of the triumphant Industrial Revolution were born along the new canal waterways and subsequent steel train tracks.

Perhaps the queerest spot in this strange county is the Vale of Pewsey. If you are travelling south west from Berkshire, there is an obvious topological change when leaving Hungerford for the Vale. It immediately becomes more bleak and mystical as you start to become hemmed in by the gallowed ridge far above Inkpen. The hangman's gibbet overshadows any transgression below. Indeed, if you stray off the beaten track to Vernham Dean and climb the hill to the ancient Fosbury hill fort, you border Hampshire, a third county. There is no doubt where the oddest countryside is as you look across the bleak hill tops to the sharp ridged edges of the valley, as it snakes its way past it's namesake to the distant town of Devizes.

Continuing through this channel, having passed William the Conqueror's hunting forest, Savernake, away to the north, the ground rises dramatically to a relatively high point, Martinsell Hill. It provides the most breathtaking view of the Vale on a clear day. Fields quilt the basin, where Intercity trains appear like toys trickling along its tummy. The soft Downs stretch westward in parallel on both sides, pinching the inhabitants into a cosy pod of sleepy comfort. This is ironic, given that the main body of the county, Salisbury Plain, stretches menacingly south and pays continuous tribute to testing the machinations of war. The Ministry of Defence (MoD) dictates a no go zone when the shells are flying. The distant boom of artillery is a strange reminder that all is not peaceful in the Vale.

Like many men prone to idleness and fantastical thinking, Harry Kitson was walking through this very valley to a favoured public house. Harry had immersed himself wholeheartedly in both saving his dream home from structural collapse and developing his village life as a single man.

"So *you're* the bachelor?" the Colonel's wife had exclaimed when he introduced himself to the couple on a walk shortly after his arrival in the village. "You *must* meet our daughter." Harry Kitson's ongoing love affair with booze, which in England is known as social drinking but in North America is a disease called Alcoholism, meant that he had made far rougher friends than their fragrant offspring at the local pubs since his move to the locality.

Kitson felt even more integrated that autumn after his memorable performance at the local beer festival. The formula for the success of such an event is a simple one. Add one marquee to the local cricket pitch and fill it with casks of beer and cider. Add another tent with hay bales to sit on at one end and build a stage at the other to house the Country and Western or Rock'n'Roll band. In between these two focal points, leave a space for a dancefloor. Then, just add people and see what happens. For things to progress at a measured pace it is also advisable to supply nourishment, for which a hog roast and or a burger bar are the only solutions.

The mention of Harry's memorable performance might have been a misleading introduction. It was not based on his winning the best brewer competition, participating in the band's act or an ability to make a particularly delicious apple sauce. Harry's sometime skill, albeit definitely untrained but always enthusiastic, was for dancing. He had discovered from a youngish age that dance was an artistic liberation that, coupled with his moderately good looks, girls seemed to find most attractive. That knee slide across the polished wooden floor at his friend's twelfth birthday had cemented his dedication to this ongoing pursuit of both loves. The line of female wallflowers that he had nearly collided with had initially giggled at him but then had joined in his vibrant knee shaking. By his mid teens, Kitson had seamlessly integrated the gigantic beer consumption of northern Europe with Elvis' limp wrist into his energetic moves. This amateur performance art really developed its own distinction when he discovered his penchant for Acid House music. His freeform expression exploded further when he introduced the representative rocket fuel that assisted these all night revels.

On this particular local debauch, he possessed no such wobble leveller and the effects of his exclusive beer diet, forsaking the necessary balance with pig fat and bread, proved disastrous. Harry's enthusiasm was undiminished but, with his judgement heavily impaired, he produced a spectacular moment of swoon, stumble and collapse. His neighbours kindly carried him home. He had really made his mark on the village by then.

Some people are slow learners. Others are jolly slow. Harry was just one of those kinds of chap. He just found it easier to ignore the addictions that blighted his decision making process. By doing so, he remained unaware of the damage that he caused to himself and elsewhere. So, without any of his previous drunken crimes in mind, he embarked on another orgy of ignorance by undertaking the walk from his now all conquered village to the local town of Pewsey.

This was previously unchartered territory. It was the ultimate local destination at that particular moment, based on the occurrence of an annual party of the extraordinary. As was his way, Kitson dressed in a mixture of practical and dandy. Firm walking boots, jeans and a navy Guernsey jumper were emboldened by a tan-coloured flasher's mac, a riotously psychedelic Paisley neckerchief and a floppy, tweed shooting cap. To himself and a handful of similarly style minded souls, he appeared quite the dash. To most, he appeared particularly punchable. However dressed, any good walk, especially in the Vale, should be punctuated by the necessity to stop at suitable hostelries for food and drink. Halfway between Harry's home and the aforementioned town is The Bruce Arms. That was the initial goal of this perambulation.

The Bruce is a rare breed of British pub nowadays. With the exception of dry roasted peanuts and pork scratchings, it does not serve food. A briefly successful venture on Saturday lunchtimes, when local chefs cooked the most incredible burgers, was short lived. These dripped in cheese and swiney treats, coleslaw, salad, crisps, but curiously, and strangely satisfactorily, with not a French Fry in sight. Unfortunately for The Bruce, yet happily for the cooks, these most talented burger flippers left and opened a restaurant in nearby Marlborough.

On return to its original basics, the pub is all about beer and chat. The landlord is a biker and the local two wheeled community gravitates there resultantly. There is a popular campsite behind the pub. It is positioned between two of the most lovely villages in the area, Easton Royal and Milton Lilbourne. You can already tell they are lovely villages because of their double barrelled names. As a result of this curious combination of bikers, campers and locals, plus the most excellent beer, it is a hive for all things chatterbox. The tractor driver is at his happiest telling his filthiest joke to the barrister. The barrister, not to be outdone, trumps him with a sickly jape to the biker. And so on. If spit and sawdust still existed, it would be in the Bruce. The brewer continues to stipulate in the lease that the nicotine yellow ceilings and Victorian wall lamps remain, despite a relatively recent historic smoking ban and the invention of electricity some considerable time earlier. It was simply inevitable that Harry would find his new home from home at this bastion of English hospitality.

Harry's village does not have a double barrelled name so could not immediately neighbour the Bruce Arms. However, there are two pub superhighways, each taking approximately forty-five minutes of brisk, beer focused march, which our protagonist had to consider. The one to the south of the valley flirts outrageously with the escarpment below Salisbury Plain. The second legally traverses a combination of roads, tracks, byways and open fields. One has to have a keen nose to attempt this route. Harry was luckily armed with a large one and could sniff his way in blinding sunlight, murky dusk, driving rain, compacted snow or pitch black, if the desire took him. And desire he did. Fortuitously for his amble, he merely basked in the mid afternoon sunshine on that spectacular September day as he strolled west towards his liquid pitstop before the Pewsey Carnival.

Having whooped it up at London's Notting Hill most regularly and even travelled as far as Trinidad for theirs, Harry had been prepared for this particular type of Bashment for a very long time. Indeed, it was only a month since he had returned from the Blackrock desert in Nevada for the Burningman festival. Harry Kitson loved a party. Dancing plus girls equaled his element. But he had been pleasantly surprised when he researched this local revel. Originating from the late Nineteenth Century, the Carnival has been a community focal point for a very long time. Apart from the obligatory funny shaped vegetables and British Royal Family look-alike competitions, the fancy dress wheelbarrow race and illuminated procession were the most fiercely contested. Harry had previously been given the general gist regarding this prestige event from the vivid description by a drinker in the Bruce Arms only a few days before.

"Imagine this," he had started in his soothing local drawl, "A juggernaut was towing an open top articulated trailer as an artistic float. Upon this platform was designed and built the most breathtaking Japanese garden, complete with a small arched bridge, numerous Bonsai trees, cherry blossoms and clipped topiary. Two farmers' wives were dressed as Geisha Girls, complete with clogs, white socks and exotically patterned and brightly coloured Kimonos. Add to that resplendent waist sashes, whitened skin, reddened lips and blackened beehive hairstyles with crossed chop-stick pins and I think you get the picture? The lasses giggled incessantly, clip-clopping, as daintily as possible, across their herbaceous demain whilst furiously fanning themselves with elaborate, delicately corrugated, silk and wooden semi-circles of cooling.

"Real Geisha's allegedly starve their bodies, manipulate their feet with bindings and are subservient to their antiquated male dominated culture. Those buxom Wiltshire lasses were never going to get away with that charade physically and certainly wouldn't bow and curtsy when they got their boys back home, if you get what I mean?" He gesticulated in an obvious smutty manner.

"However, life is often viewed with a distorted perspective." He paused for effect at his descriptive narrative. "The girls' farming spouses, who were already naturally the size of oxen, had commandeered two massive inflatable Sumo suits, which vastly exaggerated their already gargantuan bulk. They were wrestling each other, to the merriment of all, the giddy shrieks of their wives and the struggled bellows of each other. But, all the bloody time, on repeat, again and again over the loud Tannoy system, they played one song and one song only. The Vapours, "Turning Japanese". A wonderful piece of music, but repeated for hours and hours would surely drive you bonkers? They won the Best Float Competition, Category A no less, hands down." As aforementioned, the pub was all about the chat and the beer.

Complete with this background history, Harry set out from home on his walk with gay abandon. He sang or hummed, "I think I'm turning Japanese, I think I'm turning Japanese, I really think so." He repeated the lyrics again and again. The story and song had certainly put him in the swing. He was already keen to seek beer and the merriment beyond.

The bumbling adventurer followed the vague footpath, initially as a diagonal traverse across a stubble field. Only a few weeks earlier, the track had been a distinct canyon through green maize and distinctive yellow cobs, but now, after the harvest, it was merely indicated by posted arrows from stile to kissing gate to tarmac road. After only a hundred yards or so, his predetermined route, much similar to a crow's flight, took him off the road onto a semi-surfaced byway, a convenient cut through for lazy amblers and inebriated motorists. The path was flanked by sparse woodland shrubs and nettle clumps, creating a seemingly intermittent and random hedge, below tall, leafy trees that formed a tantalising tunnel.

This track ran along a ridge with rolling, harvested fields sweeping languorously away on either side. To the south was the trickling source of the River Avon, of trout fishing fame before the water company savaged it, and the barge canal lay to the north, near the village of Wootton Rivers. Yes, definitely a double-barrelled type of local spot. The afternoon light shone intermittently down the reddening tunnel, speckling the leaves on either side. Harry sighed. He was mindful of this catalysing another hallucinogenic flashback so stopped and took in the beauty of this most natural of stroboscopes. He carefully placed his hands between the barbs on the wire fence and looked out across the recently tilled earth, over a wood, beyond the double barrelled village's rooftops to the majesty of Martinsell Hill.

A brief flicker in the light caught his peripheral attention to the west. A figure loomed in the flickering tree tunnel. As the large shape walked slowly towards him, Harry's curiosity was heightened with every step. By the time the tall man stopped a few yards away, Kitson was truly mystified. His hands seemed glued to the fence. Wiltshire is an odd spot. But this man appeared odder still. The County is without a coast. This was certainly a fish out of water.

Firstly, the gentleman was barefoot. The soles of his feet were toughened and dusty by what seemed like a lifetime of wandering. His pale blue fisherman's trousers were cut at the calf, revealing muscular lower legs. They were held at the waist by a piece of rope, frayed at the ends. A coconut shell hung from it. He wore a once white string vest. Australians call this clothing article a 'Wife Beater'. The man before him was of a more single status than marital, Harry surmised. His lean arms were twisted with sinews, leading to powerful hands that were grimy to the nails. One grasped a thick shoulder height staff, slightly spiralled towards the top. It terminated in a large knobule of well handled smoothness. His strong neck was adorned with sandalwood bead and leather thong necklaces. One of these bore a hide pendant in the shape of Africa, triple coloured. Red. Yellow. Green. The colour combination dominated the man's overall style. This was as a result of an enormous woollen cloak draped off his shoulders that nearly reached the ground behind him. The once bright tricolours were faded by time, sun and rain. Its huge pointed hood was pulled over the tall man's head. Only a wiry twisted black beard protruded from its front.

Two hands slowly reached up and pulled the head piece back. An array of wild tubular locks bolted in random directions from the head. Some were long and low, others spiralled sideways and shorter ones ascended with horn-like stubbornness to gravity. They were interspersed by small round knots of hair, like burrs buried in a spaniel's fur. Harry's previous dermatological observations of arms and legs were confirmed by the smooth ebony intensity of facial skin. A bright sheen of sweat glowed across the sallow cheeks, angled cheekbones and large twin holed boxed button nose. His lips curled downwards at the ends in judgemental scorn. The giant's coal black eyes bored into the hapless walker. They were framed by vividly bloodshot wild sclera. Despite this ocular assault, Harry was sufficiently well trained to deal with matters politely.

"Good afternoon!" He started enthusiastically and naturally continued this jovial theme. "What an absolutely splendid day for a stroll? Have you come far?" It sounded like a silly question. Harry had seen Afro-Caribbean soldiers at the army camp towns on occasion but this Nyabinghi warrior on field exercise was certainly a first. The large man averted his gaze upwards to the sky, rolled his head slightly, shut his eyes, took a deep breath in and then slowly and noisily exhaled. He levelled his head, opened his red eyes and stared at Harry again in silence.

Harry was an affable fellow. Peace and love were never far from the front of his simple thought process. He decided to go on the charm offensive. The recesses of his mind stirred. The skills that he had honed and primed long ago as a Comparative Religion Bachelor of Arts graduate bubbled forth.

"All Hail to you, Great Priest of the Twelve Tribes! I & I is off for an enlightening stroll now. It is a most beautiful day, blessings be upon you. Thanks and praise to the all conquering Lion of Judah, King of Kings, Lord Most High, Jah Rastafari!" Harry thought to himself that his monologue to the divine was a sure way to press home his advantage. He was disappointed by his rapid defeat, inflicted by just two sounds of patois rebellion which emanated like melodic bass from the Rasta's throat.

"Tchah!" The first scythed him down. "Babylon!" The second put him in his place.

Unflinching eyes and facial features resumed their pitying analysis of the defeated product of Imperialism. After what can only be described as an uncomfortable silence, the glare dropped and the pressure on Harry's nervous system was alleviated. The traveller reached an arm into a deep cloak pocket and pulled out a long wrapped and crumpled tube of brown greaseproof paper. Laying it along his inner forearm and cupped pink palm, he carefully unravelled it with his free hand. On completion, Harry saw a magnificent marijuana bud curl halfway to the elbow. It's pretty little green leaves sparkled intermittently as the tiny crystals of tetrahydrocannabinol caught the light.

"Ya wan' Lamb's Bread?" the deep voice rolled with transactional enquiry.

"No, thanks. Jolly kind of you though." Harry was mindful of the last time he had consumed the herb. "I'm terribly sorry but I was on a holiday in the French Riviera a couple of years ago and had been blessed with a copious quantity of the local pink beverage. On three separate evenings, staring post dinner at the majestic firmament above, adding mindbending skunk to the drink produced an effect commonly referred to as a 'Whitey'. I'm afraid that the memory of dizziness, nausea and paranoia is still as fresh as your tribesman's bud." Like any closet alcoholic, Kitson had blamed the terrifying result on the weed, not his excess of Provencal wine.

"Tchah! Ya'naa' wanna touch da sky?" The smoker made clear his disgust. Harry concluded that they would never be friends if that type of attitude persisted.

A small piece of the plant was pinched off and placed in the open palm under the paper. The green stalk was then carefully rewrapped and replaced in its wool nest. The coconut was unfastened from the beltline. Harry noticed that it had a clay bowl at the top, rubber tube from the side and a small hole on the other. Liquid could be heard sloshing inside. Matches were passed to Harry. He released his grip on the fence and took them. The man pinched the plant sample and packed it into the ceramic cup. He put his mouth around the hose and finger across the hole. He leant forward to Harry, red eyes stared unblinking inches from his face. The ignitor dutifully struck the red tipped stick, cupped it in both palms with the tried and tested technique of a man that smokes whatever the weather, however drunk.

After the thick fog of repeated tugs on the bong had dissipated, Harry handed back the matchbox and the wanderer repacked his chalice. Still unsmiling, the man stepped back to mutter words of wisdom. Harry was confused and light headed. Maybe he had inhaled a little bit too much of the billowing smoke that had enveloped him? He grabbed the barbed wire fence carefully again to steady himself. He listened as the man began to babble.

"I and I is blessed to be the disciple of Jah Rastafari. Me tribe, one of the Twelve original, 'ave been wandering de eart' for thousand o' year. We escape from slavery back den only to be capture once more by dem monsters of Imperialism again. Babylon!" He scowled directly at Harry and spat at the dusty earth near his boots. Kitson answered with understanding.

"If it is any consolation, my own tribe suffered the same hardship back then too. My Jewish brethren escaped with Moses from the might of the pharaohs after our G*d had brought plague, pestilence, storms and death to the Egyptians. We wandered south and through your Emperor's lands until the Serphadim reached Spain. They too were persecuted by the brutal Inquisition and fled north where they were massacred by the million in the last century."

"True dat. Me sympathy wid ya' people's plight. But you is wrong 'bout ya story. It weren't no Egyptian ya ran from. There is far more powerful forces in da Universe. Five thousand year ago the planet were run by dem Overlords who create the greatest civilisation before mankind ruin it all. Ya don' really tink that dem pyramid, colossal mathematical masterpiece o' scientific an' astrological perfection, were really design by dem pharaoh an' built by our brethren?"

"I had always assumed from my Biblical studies that the slaves built them." Harry was getting confused.

"Nah, ya fool!" The Rasta paused briefly after his cut down, then continued, "Our Bible were created hundred o' year later to fill da void left when dem Overlord disappear. In dere absence, 'uman need 'ope, so dey create dem book to make dem believe in da One God, not d'awesome power of the universe beyon'dis sickly planet. People live in fear wid greed ever since. Dey turn dere back on de intense beauty an' perfection that came before dem and live a lie until now!"

"Oh. I see." Harry Kitson felt distinctly uncomfortable. He was clearly in the company of a raging lunatic whose consumption of marijuana had twisted his brain into a contortion of paranoia. The giant sensed this inquiry.

"Ya doubt me, Buoy?"

"No. No!" Harry stammered, backtracking fast.

"Why ya think I is 'ere? Me striding dese 'ills to pay me respect to dem same Overlord in ya pretty Wiltshire. Ya don't really think dem 'enges of stone like Avebury were really made by mankind all dem thousan' a' year ago?"

"Well, yes, I do actually!" Harry ventured timidly before gaining a modicum of confidence. "It took years for the pagans to perfectly cut, drag and erect Stonehenge into the most perfect of sun and moon dials."

"Pity da fool!" The Nyabinghi man shook his head in despair. "Open dem eye! Look aroun' ya now. Dey is all about ya. Dey have been 'ere, right 'ere, just now, inspectin' a duppy of dere artistic message in dat field the na'. You'll see! Den you'll believe too!" With that the man span on his heels, his tricolour cloak swirling with the drama of an opera maestro, and strode off, his feet padding on the dry earth. Harry Kitson watched the strange figure disappear into the shadows of the tree tunnel to the east. A solitary sound hummed peaceably in his ear long after the dread had muttered it. "Righteous." Harry banked it as a compliment.

A flock of fattened pigeons suddenly got up from their banquet of harvest leftovers in the field's base just below him. They couldn't have spotted the pedestrian pedestrian, camouflaged in his environs, motionless without intent. The Lion of Judah had exited in the opposite direction too. So what had startled them in that vast rolling sea of desolate earth? A strange emptiness overcame Harry and his green eyes narrowed as his mind glazed. A distant sound like an electrical hum, vibrant and warming, buzzed behind the trees drawing closer and resultantly louder. The quiet listener felt his hands tingle on the fence and a soft pulsating charge rippled vibrantly up his arms and into his core. He sighed peaceably.

And then, there it was. Slowly meandering across the undulations of the field was a bright, brilliant ball of light. It's edges were perfect. An orb of precision, the size of his childhood bedroom's spinnable globe. It floated just ten metres in front of him, about one metre above the field, seemingly tracing its delicate contours. Despite the bright sunshine that basked the valley, this miniature sphere exuded a close up intensity, far outshining the Earth's life source millions of miles away behind it. It was hypnotic, mesmerising, calming, enchanting and Harry succumbed submissively to its bondage.

The ball moved slowly and fluidly across a subtle curve in the raked expanse of fine chalk soil, sometimes speeding up slightly, then returning to its previous deliberate and seemingly measured pace. Pausing briefly, it suddenly flashed forward and back, side to side, in a series of erratic and frenetic movements. The actions were like those of a fluid yet calculating drunk dancing with a sound speaker at a village beer festival. As quickly as it started, it stopped, then swept effortlessly around the curvature of the nearby terrain again. Once more, it hastened in an orgy of movement and then stopped again.

It was only then that Harry saw that the sphere was tracking some faint marcations on the stubble. The ground was discoloured by enormous circles and patterns. The circles were composed of fresh green shoots whilst the areas between were the more normal grey brown of the harvested stalks. The outer circumference must have been fifty or sixty metres in diameter. The remnants of the colossal artwork floated like a spectre of the soil. Stranger still, a series of perfect cube shapes, joined by their corners, were imprinted on the earth in a diagonal pattern that veered up and across the entire field to the far hedge some hundred and fifty metres beyond. The stubble appeared to be a different length from the rest of the harvested crop and grew in a contrary direction. How could this be, only a few weeks since the combine had reaped its labour? Harry twisted his body to see more through the meagre gap in the trees. In doing so, he nearly tore his thumb on the steel kiss of the fence.

"Aaaagh, Fuck It!" he yelled at the pain of the bash. Everything around him paused. The round beacon just hovered, motionless. Harry felt a strange sense of embarrassment, like he had walked into a loo when a girl is sitting having a pee. He wanted to apologise. He felt like the eyeless globe was scrutinising him, judging him for his untimely and rude intrusion. The dumbstruck fop held his breath and watched, the bruise in his hand a forgotten inconvenience for now. Then a peace descended on him. He sighed. He smiled. Love overcame him. He beamed. Joy overwhelmed him.

The glowing object moved ever so slightly closer to him. It paused briefly, in taut and energetic limbo, suspended between the firmament, the human and the mystical circular pattern below it. Then it shot away, in the opposite direction to his viewpoint, like a pebble freed from a slingshot. It hugged the field closely along the diagonal line of stubble cube patterns, then suddenly flitted up and over the tree hedge at the far side of the field. It was gone. Harry slumped slowly to the caked mud floor on his backside. He ran his fingers through his hair after dumping his cap between his thighs. The digits tingled. His head seemed hot. He felt incredible. At that point, he noticed that his wounded hand hurt no more.

'A Teenager in Love'

It would be useful to learn how Harry reached this curious state of affairs. Like many previous pilgrims, his journey had been westward too. Born in Buckinghamshire, his charmed life took him to a rather good preparatory school near Oxford where he stayed on and off, holidays permitting, from the age of seven. His loving parents moved west to his mother's previous home in Berkshire. Harry reached adolescence at the same time and started at his second boarding school in Marlborough, Wiltshire, a little further westward again. Despite the distractions of sports and girls (he reached the dizzy heights of County javelin champion and proudly dated whilst in all five academic years), it was the geography of the area that had a lasting effect on the sporty and romantic lad.

Kitson immediately rebelled from these rural environs by moving north where he attended the University of Manchester. He masqueraded in a Bachelor of Arts degree whilst fuelling his desire to rave. By the mid Nineties, Harry was sparsely armed with a Comparative Religion qualification and a recreational diversification into drugs. The Great God Nepot eventually called him to the capital where he settled into his father's diamond business. A James Bond slanted adoration of his patriarch had meant that following in his footsteps had been a fixation since he could remember. It was the easy option and Harry was easily persuaded by a curious combination of protocol and fantasy. A Noughty decade later, having abandoned faiths, swallowed the pills and occasionally thrived at his sparkly vocation, Harry decided that metropolitan life would probably kill him. He sold his Bohemian lair in Clerkenwell and started his search for a peaceful country idyll.

Practicalities to an extent where abandoned. Much as he loved his parents' beautiful Georgian home in West Berkshire and the relative ease to travel into town for work, the area was generally too developed to sate his love for open countryside. His ambient mind quickly reverted to the freedoms of his school days and Wiltshire was quickly game on. Strictly speaking, it is beyond the commuter belt, although the charming Bedwyn train and the high speed from Pewsey provide an almost bearable solution for those tied to the City.

As a devotee and collector of motorcycles, Harry meandered aimlessly along lanes between the horrors of Swindon and the spire of Salisbury. He soon became aware that something was pulling him time and time again to one particularly beautiful little valley in between. Parking up and walking through each village, he noted the thatched cottages for sale. He later checked the specifications and then met estate agents for viewings. It soon became apparent that the remaining money from the sale of his one and a half bedroom London flat would provide the deposit for a stunning three bedroom chocolate box style thatched cottage. Harry already envisioned raising his cap and hollering, "Hullo, there! Isn't it a smashing day?" to the neighbouring Lord of the Manor or retired Colonel. But then he was drawn to a slightly different challenge.

The sales picture of the tired thatched cottage seemed to attract him more and more. There was something enchanting, even magical, about it. After contacting the land agent, Harry saddled up and, accompanied by his wonderfully intelligent, beautiful, blonde, ethereal girlfriend, rode to the village. It had not been on his list of desired locations, due to the relatively unattractive housing estate that had joined four smaller villages and hamlets in the post war decades. The cottage stood at the crossroads to these habitations and, bar a handful of neighbouring houses, was screened off by hedges and gardens. It seemed all alone. An island of serenity.

The dilapidated gate was pushed open, revealing a triangular yard disguised by a wall of six foot high weeds. A small, broken, single storey building flanked the left hand side onto the lane. The long thatched cottage bordered the high street to the right. At the end of this space, a decrepit wall bulged with the force of earth from the raised garden. Garden seemed an extraordinary description for the tangled mess of uncontrolled shrubs, mountainous thickets, ripping brambles, stinging nettles and sagging fruit trees. Beating a path through it all took time but on reaching the next fence, Harry looked back and assessed that this wilderness must be a good thirty metres front to back, side to side. This was a considerable improvement on his window box in London, with a far greater number of neglected flowers too.

The cottage had been a blacksmith's house and workshop historically. The yard originally had two stable blocks to complete the triangle although, as aforementioned, only one remained and that seemed doomed to extinction too. One hundred years ago, the birth of the internal combustion engine provided a rapid death to most blacksmiths' commercial trade. The constant movement of horses from street to yard to stable to yard to smithy to street had long since disappeared.

A century before, local landowners had bought the cottage and the family ran various businesses, including bicycle, electrical, taxi and antique furniture from the shop end of the property. The family had sold the cottage some years later and it had eventually fallen into the hands of a property developer who, having received rejection after rejection for building on the historical site, had given up and placed it on the market for far too much money with the resultant long term expansion of garden to jungle and house to rot'n'recide.

When he first pushed its back door open, Harry should have been scared out of his wits. It was horrid. As he wandered through the small, low ceilinged rooms with corroded pipes, mouldy walls, broken beams and holey floors, he should have walked straight back out. On entering one of the bedrooms, the walls and windows were daubed in blood. The culprit, a large black crow, lay long dead, having bashed its brains in after a bid to escape through the stiff panes and metal construction of the blacksmith's do-it-yourself windows. The bird was identifiable by its distinctive beak, claws and wings but it's body had been devoured by a myriad of hidden vermin sometime before. The original smithy itself was barely recognisable. Its mud floor sloped down the hill in the direction of the road. Rotten ply plank and thin chipboard partitions crawled with fungi and their insectoid residents, the natural replacements when its use for more recent retail enterprises had disappeared. These festering walls disguised the previous sources of heat, from bellows to furnace, over the past three hundred and fifty years. Harry unravelled the history in his mind with practicality combined with imagination. It all seemed magical to the hapless romantic. A soothing voice in Harry's head just repeated, "You're home".

And so it was. The decision was made at a coincidental jewellery client meeting in London. Coincidental because the romantic chap happened to live in the very same Wiltshire village. He just happened to be an estate agent and knew the house intimately, its market history, including previously rejected offers. As far as Harry was concerned, fate clamoured attention. His resultantly low bid was accepted by the owner and the instructive agent's ring purchase was subsequently and most heavily subsidised. Harry and his girlfriend raced to collect the keys, having folded a suitable blow up mattress with additional bedding into the bike's panniers. Kitson turned the rusted key to the cottage for the first time and, armed with some vicious cleaning products, they entered the den of damp to make a small part of the property free from dust, mildew and crow's blood. This building baptism took decidedly longer than expected. As the Spring day grew to a close, the sunlight spilled through the ancient glass panes of the kitchen and alerted them both to their exhaustion and hunger. The local public house beckoned.

The short walk up the hill to the pub on the green seemed like a haze to Harry, already intoxicated by his passion for his purchase. In a few weeks, the girlfriend would leave him due to this devotion to the new house, his unblinkered dedication to alcohol and the resultant addling of his mind. As they approached the pub, Kitson was blissfully unaware of these forecasts which remained veiled in his mist of boozy fumes. The sliding door to the hostelry opened to reveal a neat little bar to the right and some cosy tables clustered around a large, unlit fireplace. There were a handful of patrons supping their drinks and licking their plates.

"Good evening. Isn't it lovely out?" Harry cheerfully announced.

"Good evenin'," muttered the landlord, unflinching and long faced, "Can I 'elp ya'?" His Cockney accent betrayed his diaspora.

"We are absolutely famished and could use a cold draught too. Are you serving food and drinks?" Kitson requested, somewhat predictably given their location.

"Drinks, yeh. We stop servin' food at Nine." The publican glibly retorted. The dozen or so assembled simultaneously glanced at the large clock on the wall, evidently a train station variety to judge by the various pieces of rail memorabilia dotted across the pub walls. It was five minutes past that hour. "Just passing through is ya'?" The landlord continued coldly.

"As a matter of fact, no," Harry replied, "I've just received the keys to my cottage on the hill and moved in this very afternoon."

"Oh?" Came the answer with a deliberately interested raise of the eyebrows and cock of the head, "Which 'ouse?"

"The Smithy on the crossroads."

The governor's face immediately broke into an enormous grin. The response belied his curious nature and cemented the truth about village gossip forever. He thrust out his hand in friendly greeting.

"Harry, my diamond geezer! Welcome to the village! What would ya' like to eat?"

'Boogie in my Bones'

Barrington Knave sat behind the desk in his farm office. The prosperity of the last few years meant that his three piece tweed suit pinched in a couple of spots, especially the waistcoat. He puffed. But the exhalation was not due to his outdated tailoring or the summer heat. He puffed again. This time he undid the top button of his check shirt and pulled his tie south a little. It bore a charming pattern of springing teal, a thoroughly appreciated gift from his wife a few Christmases ago. Looking down he noticed some dried yellow on it. A renegade from the bacon and egg sandwich he had indulged himself in before the early dawn rise. He puffed a third time. He removed the yolk with his nail and flicked it in the direction of the multiple labradors snoozing in the oversized basket nearby. Surprisingly, despite the microscopic presence of food, they continued their dormancy and he looked out of the window at the rain shower. Barry was perplexed.

Sporadic downpours at that time of year were always troubling but the crop was thriving in the general sunshine and harvest would be early this year. Yes, there were plenty of his beloved Pewsey Vale fields to reap but the majority of the crops, destined for that international burger company's baps, would soon be resting to the gentle throb of the drying barn's turbines which blasted warm air through the mountains of grain. Oh, the sweet sound of agricultural profit. A rarity. What's more, the sheep were carefully distributed on the higher slopes of his land. They had bred well earlier in the year and, thanks to the bad yield from his New Zealand competition, had produced a most satisfactory dividend. The European farce that Britain had been part of since his birth in the Seventies, also supplemented his family's income with a subsidy for setting aside land in the valley for development issues. How he prayed that the UK government would replicate the generosity of their continental cousins post EU exit.

The Knaves had owned and managed the farm for a few hundred years. Barry's father had already profited from the lake and pond digging projects. The decimation of the hedgerows during the post war years had obliterated the local bird, bee and bramble populi. Reintroducing water features for crested newts, bull rushes and mallard duck, were biodiversity boxes well worth ticking financially. It also provided Barry and his pals with some excellent wildfowling. It was a far cry from the blackened yarns told by his grandfather of their sweet gorge being obliterated during the Industrial Revolution's grim progress. This was thanks to the coal fired beam engine a dozen miles down the canal that had consistently veiled the low ground in a fetid smog. A score of years earlier, this European windfall had looked in doubt when the United Kingdom had decided not to adopt the continental currency. He thanked his lucky stars that the inevitable ripple effect to leave the Union would take years and his annual Continental gifts would last for a little while at least. By the time the millennia had shifted, Barry had embraced the world of genetically modified crops. Nothing ventured, nothing gained, was a motto that only briefly crossed his mind as he counted the proceeds from his distant European cousins and current political rulers.

"Merci, Bruxelles. Encore une fois, s'il vous plait," he muttered in his schoolboy Franglais. By 2019, the set aside experiments were part meadow and part lavender. A good business but terrible crop no thanks to the chalk soil that made success near impossible. But that didn't really matter now because Barry was at his desk concentrating on fielding emails from his bosses. That's right. Like many self respecting farmers, despite the yield of crops, sheep and subsidy, his life only profited financially thanks to his skill as a land agent and the bigger field beyond his own.

Barry was excellent at his job. His suave charm, rugged good looks, athletic prowess and keen wit made him the most affable sort of fellow. He initially honed his skills at local Pony Club dances, then teenage black tie Gatecrasher balls before he fulfilled his shared passion for Acid House at Manchester University with his old school pal Harry Kitson. There he fine tuned this charisma further with a geographical qualification. His bloodlined farming prowess was later confirmed at Cirencester Agricultural College. This diligent learning path was only slightly marred by occasional blunders. He once tied a primitive kite surfing apparatus to the bumper of his car and watched a friend soar majestically upward. On cessation of the necessary wind requirements, the six foot four daredevil had plummeted forty feet onto the hard field. Icarus had nearly got out of hospital, his punctured lung partially repaired, by the time Knave finally qualified. Immediately hired by local land agents, Barry quickly established a network of trust with the larger estate owners in the area and advised them on how to best manage their hectares wisely and profitably. Barry's natural abilities with rod, gun, horse and hound insured that he worked with his clients in the most sporting manner. They respected and trusted this man of the land.

But Barry was sitting behind his desk, puzzled and puffing because of something far more mystifying. He needed to respond to the in box of client emails but something closer to home was baffling him. In fact, the mystery was directly under his fingertips that drummed with the soft rhythm of horses hooves. The farm archive photograph that he repeatedly tapped and now studied made his mind splinter like a fractal. When it came to the stranger subjects, Harry Kitson had always been his go to man. And this was certainly in the category marked 'Weird'. So it was to Harry that his thoughts now turned.

Both of them, despite being blessed with good looks, easy charm and success on the rugger field, had initially battled ferociously at boarding school. Barry would single out his nemesis' work folder before applying his trademark tippex sheep shagging art to the front cover. Harry would retaliate with carefully aimed butter packs at the back of his rival's tweed jacket. But this tit for tat guerilla warfare was not to last. An eventual respect, then trust, before finally a friendship blossomed, dictated that stationary and dairy weapons were laid down in armistice. They shared a healthy appetite for rugby football, athletics, girls, homebrew beer and rap music. Pop culture was at epidemic levels. How else could you explain the transition from lessons to free time, from privileged, middle classed, white students in uniform to mother fucking 'Niggas With Attitude', complete with pumped up trainers, baggies and the requisite LA caps.

But it was the fusion of Rap or Hip-Hop with Acid House by the late Eighties, that really jolted their rhythm. They turned on pirate radio stations, to listen and record onto cassettes, the incredible sound that was pulsating out of Chicago, Detroit and New York. Mysteriously ignored by Americans, it was entirely embraced by the UK subculture. They were part of a social revolution. But the boys were sensible on occasion. Along with half their gang of friends, they realised that they would never complete their A level examinations if they started taking wild hallucinogens, dancing around fields and warehouses. They were right. The other half all crashed and burned, their eggshell minds fragmented into shattered shards.

Their great day finally came when they put down their pens in the last of their exams. This pivotal moment strangely coincided with the eve of the Summer Solstice. The longest day of the year is a focal point of celebration amongst the abundant local pagan population. A year of freedom awaited the young men before the start of University. That evening a handful of liberated eighteen year olds skipped merrily to Harry's car. It was hidden in the woods behind the school house in readiness for their escape to chaos. The Series One Land Rover was not the most speedy of vessels for this pack of adventurers but, with the canvas top and doors removed plus windshield flattened forward against the spare tyre on the bonnet, none of them gave a jot.

They drove north in the bright early evening. Barry's ear was pressed firmly against the transistor radio whilst his finger and thumb toyed the dial to receive the purest balance of words to static. The technology barked instructions to all their fellow ravers in the south of England. Mile by mile they were joined by other cars until, after half an hour or so, a long snake of automobiles wound slowly through the Wiltshire countryside. The expectant convoy maneuvered towards the junction with the M4 motorway having heard the dance venue directions. It crawled down the slow lane to the service station a few miles to the east.

Service stations in Britain have never been a glamorous affair. Our Gallic neighbours pride themselves on fine food, a glass of wine and a considered smoke before resuming their journeys. The British tend to prefer a fight or scrummage for soggy sandwiches, burnt burgers and fizzy pop. Membury is a fine example of such a horrific place. But on the evening in question, it was transformed as car after car bearing dayglo clad revellers poured into the carpark. The few remaining natural punters realised this was a battle that could never be won and scarpered. Queues swelled in the determined pursuit of chocolate bars, energy drinks and king size smoking papers. Car doors were opened, jagged Jungle and happy House rhythms rattled forth and pockets of dancers started shuffling their feet and swayed their hands in unison with the first ripples of their narcotic supper. Suddenly the general cry went up, "It's on! This way!" and a tidal wave of thousands of euphoric pedestrians moved as one out of the petrol station and along a track towards some farm storage barns.

The lads were born on this human tide with a sense of total freedom and rebellion. Their feelings were justified when the mass of flesh collided, softly and all embracingly, with a police car that was moving very slowly in the opposite direction. It travailed on a laboured mission to evacuate a clearly terrified old lady from her nearby home. The panda car then stopped. It had no choice. A sea of hands enveloped it and gently bumped it up and down. When the upwards momentum was sufficient, they bounced it sideways like a kid's Space Hopper toy into the ditch beside the track. A cheer rippled through the crowd as the wheels on one side spun hopelessly in mid air. The bodies pressed onwards and at the road's end pushed against the huge double doors of the farmer's metallic barn. Bolt cutters appeared and the padlocks were decimated. The sliding doors rumbled to the sides and a second yell of excitement went up as the mob moved into the vast empty expanse of concrete floor.

Before the space was filled, a souped up Ford Cosworth car roared into the depths of the barn, spinning all four wheels in a hypnotic series of circles. The black tyre marks left an acrid stench of rubber smoke. It stopped and opened it's two doors. The sound of more hollers from the crowd was drowned out by a deafening roll of thunderous music which emanated from the boot. The machine seemed more like a showroom for speakers and bass bins than a rally car. The melee pressed next to it, gyrating their crazed bodies to the impetuous volley of sound.

But it was only the amuse bouche of this particular soiree's menu. A large, white lorry, it's cab bearing the name of it's unfortunate hire company, rolled cumbersomely through the doors. It edged its way through the intoxicated crowd to the centre of the enormous closed space. It halted and two dreadlocked raggas descended from the cabin and pulled up the corrugated side of the flatbed truck. It revealed a massive back wall of speakers, black holes of musical promise, with a small table in the front covered in record players, amplifiers and a machine that bore the legend of 303. They climbed aboard. One donned headphones and stood astride the decks. The second nonchalantly plugged in a microphone. He glared aggressively through bloodshot eyes at the throng below him, glanced over at the Cosworth's driver, raised his eyebrows and the car's music ceased.

"Who's ready to rock da House?" he challenged with a deep, gravelly, Bristolian patois. Some half hearted yelps from the crowd affirmed the question but that was not good enough for the master of ceremonies. He angrily bellowed the question again, "Oy said, who's ready to rock da Fuckin' House?" This time he was greeted by a volley of vocal agreement and a piercing scream of whistles. These were planted between the lips of the vast majority of party goers. The music exploded. With it a shattering array of lights and lasers emanated from the back of the vehicle, basking the crowd in a chaotic cascade of pulsating luminescence in the pitch darkness of the barn. The sound jarred the bones in the boys' bodies, vibrated their eardrums and rattled their very souls. The wild eyed protagonist constantly babbled hypnotic rap over the intoxicating mixture of bleep and beat. The sounds and visuals threw the rave virgins into a blindly hysterical void of escape. And, all the while, their first experience of lysergic acid diethylamide came creeping slowly and menacingly up into their psyche.

It is oft forgotten that the birth of Acid House was originally reliant on both these components. LSD and digitally repetitive music. The aforementioned 303 and its relative the 808 were phonetically design compatible with that particular psychedelic chemical formula. It was a match made in laboratory heaven. MDMA or Ecstacy was fast replacing the brutal hallucigen as the raver's choice of Class A but, at that particular moment, half a Purple Ohm was shuddering through the previously innocent boys' minds for the very first time. They were dumbstruck as the artificial construct wreaked havoc on their inquisitive senses. Initially, wild distortions in their sight became evident as loops and swirls enveloped their true forms. The lights splintered like vast fractals before the aural assault exploded in some sort of orchestra of synchronicity with their adjusted visions. They screamed in fear and freedom simultaneously as their perceptions erupted in a kaleidoscope of chaos and colour. They huddled in a group, like some feral pack, protecting each other, hugging and hoping that the barrage would desist. They stared into each others' eyes which shone menacingly amidst startled faces that seemed to ebb and flow like school custard. As quickly as the terror had taken them, it was replaced by the euphoria of anarchy and delusion until they laughed hysterically and danced with the ferocity of a pool of electrified eels. Just when they had reached a height of seeming perfection, pure love and perceived clarity, the music stopped. A ringing silence followed before the voice on the microphone shattered it.

"Which one of you cun's stole moy Special Brew?" boomed the MC through the speakers. There was a pause before he added, "There will be no more fuckin' music until you cun's give me back moy Special Brew". A hand, clutching the super strength lager, held it toward him and the soundsman wildly snatched it back and uttered a phrase that seemed to sum up the strange dichotomy of the event, "Than' you, you cun'". As he glugged it back, the music exploded again and the throng were hurled once more into the melee of madness, seemingly re-energised by the terror at the turn tables.

"Peace and love!" Harry giggled at Barrington as they whooped and leapt and screamed and shouted. Despite the seeming indestructibility of their newfound fortress, the naive revolutionaries were just about to learn a harsh lesson about uprising against any lawful system. Particularly when it involved bouncing police cars, policemen and aged grandmothers into ditches. A black-grey truck, armoured with grills over it's front windows, roared in from the darkness. Its telltale blue flashing light pierced past the comparatively comforting lasers. The back doors of the vehicle burst open and approximately twenty large men jumped out. They were dressed in deep blue with large lace up black boots and bulletproof flak jackets. Their attire was clearly emblazoned with the logo of Her Majesty's law enforcement. Emboldened further by clear visored helmets, they leapt forth brandishing toughened batons. Everybody screamed with a new type of terror. The angry mob of riot police scythed their way through the crush of kids, cracking heads and splintering arms. They dragged the two musical representatives from the white lorry, disappeared them into their own darker model, then destroyed the sound and light equipment with violent kicks of their size twelves and arching swings of their brutal clubs.

The boys ran. Out of the doors, down the track, back to the service station where they hurled themselves into the Land Rover. After a quick head count was confirmed, Barry yelled, "Drive!' and his friend obeyed at speed. The knobble walls of the antiquated tyres screeched against the tarmac, just before the arrival of the next phalanx of authoritarian cars appeared to halt the slower escapees attempts. But they were free. Nobody spoke. The saucer eyed teenagers merely stared ahead as the little four by four trundled down the slow lane of the empty, black motorway towards the next junction at Hungerford, the scene of a far worse massacre just a couple of years before. After leaving the ghostly town, the car ascended the hill and they were back in Wiltshire. There was a collective sigh.

Harry pulled over in a lay-by and turned off the engine and headlights. He tilted his head back and looked up. The moon had a perfect circular rainbow around it. The stars shot in random directions leaving a perfect, pencil thin trace of light behind each and every one of them. The LSD was bubbling in his brain. He dissolved into giggles.

"We can't go back to school like this," he muttered aloud, "What the fuck are we going to do?" The stark realisation of his driving responsibilities began to dawn on him. He started to panic. Harry stared at the apparently wild distortion of his hands on the steering wheel which appeared twisted and menacing. He repeated, "What the fuck are we going to do? We've got to get this car somewhere fast before it gets light." He started drumming his feet and moving sporadically. "What the fuck. What the fuck. What the fuck?" He jabbered almost incoherently.

"Hey, relax, Man! It's Summer Solstice tonight," soothed Barry. He thought for a second then added with the reassuring tone that landowners would draw comfort and strength from in years to come. "We'll go to Silbury Hill. People have been going there on this night for thousands of years. Take it easy. It's only a few miles away. We can take the back roads past school. Everything is going to be perfect."

And so it was for a while, as the little jeep purred along the lanes amidst the rolling hills. The luna light glowed with strange comfort and, a short drive later, they crossed the Ridgeway, then swept down and beheld the bizarre spectacle of Europe's largest man made mound. It's exact purpose has been under investigation for a very long time. Created some four and a half millennia ago, it is clearly linked to Avebury stone circle, a mile or so to the north. The start of it's sarsen stone avenue, only a Wiltshire javelin champion's throw away to the east, forms some sort of symbolic pyramid with the now extinct but not forgotten Sanctuary. Their alignment with the rise and fall of the sun during the calendar year, is certainly not coincidental. The mathematical perfection of such monuments to the universe beggars belief that mankind could possibly have been capable of such precise architecture all those thousands of years ago. The Summer Equinox has attracted a certain type of holistic hero for a very long time. On this morning, if the sky is clear, the tip of the mound casts a perfectly conical shadow up the valley which swings towards the ancient stones as the sun travels from east to west. As the boys drove slowly past it along the A4, in the direction of the car park which was modestly hidden by a scrub of trees, they noticed that a few flickering flames danced on the top of the huge knoll in the dark night.

After a hasty disembarkation and a remarkably short discussion, the other half of the LSD tabs were swallowed and swigged down with Lucozade. The intrepids started the climb. Dotted here and there on the ascent were cavorting couples. As they got closer to the summit they witnessed an increasing orgy of Thai dye clothing, dreadlocks and pale flesh. The angle of the hill was sharp and the rush of blood it caused their bodies seemed to catapult the levels of hallucigen in their brains.

Once more they were at the mercy of the chemist. But the soft earth and warm air, rather than the previous ear splitting audio assault and the subsequent human one, lulled them into a dream of extraordinary and exquisite beauty. When they reached the summit, the gentle dream became a wild fantasy. The fires were bright now, so very bright, and people, wow, such people. The small flat space atop the mount was a carpet of folk, laughing, talking, smoking, kissing, singing and dancing to the melodic charms of musical percussion. Along with these multiple rhythmical hand drums were Spanish guitars, strumming melodies and plucking tunes. A flautist cavorted with his silver pipe in peaceful harmony. The sound was entrancing and the schoolboys were quickly enrolled by the swaying embrace of their earthy compatriots. The depths of the fires seemed to dance with their movements. Occasionally a man in a long cloak and druidical hat would rise from the carpet of humans and yell some ancient gibberish. He wielded an enormous broadsword, bright and dangerous, high above his head like some near forgotten Arthurian legend. Naked white witches cavorted outrageously with the sound, crouching and jumping, arms windmilling sporadically in union with all the nature around them. The boys were lost in a timeless trance of artificial, mystical perfection.

But as the first glimpse of light was spied over the ridge to the east, a bank of clouds rolled steadily and determinedly towards them. The moist vapour in the air dampened their spirits. The rain started. Just a damp, slow summer drizzle but that was enough to let the hope of sunrise and the effects of the drug to be dissipated. They were left feeling slightly cheated but happy that they had enjoyed such a spectacular evening. They climbed slowly down the severe slope, a necessary speed as the grass was now sleek and slippery.

Looking down they suddenly halted. In the first light of the grey morning, two curious circles leered in the wheat field below them, one tiny and one much larger, about forty metres across. The bigger form had two distinct mini ovulars towards the top. A semi-circular line with stoppered ends ran in parallel with the base of the circle. The separate smaller circle was positioned just to the side of the larger perimeter. It was level with the stoppered end of the semicircular line. The boys giggled as they recognised the symbolic emblem. The smiley face of Acid House stared back at them in the half light as it contemplated eating its next pill.

After admiring the artwork hunched on his haunches, Harry had got up and ambled down the slope to the edge of the picture and studied it. The ingenious creators of the cereal picture had been careful to walk down the rows of crop, only stamping them flat at the pill, perimeter, eyes and mouth. They must have used a rope as a central fulcrum to make the perfect circle and correspondingly symmetrical facial forms. Harry chuckled at the prankster's innovative joke.

"I don't know why you're laughing?" Barry had cut in, "Think about the poor bloody farmer and the shameful destruction of his precious business". Harry had been joined by his friend and realised that his own rurally reliant family, just a couple of miles away, had to put up with this type of surreal vandalism every now and again. Their party was over, for now.

It was with this in mind, over twenty five years later, and Harry's extraordinary story from the more recent autumn before concerning a Rasta, a flying orb and a ghost crop circle, that Barry adjusted his three piece tweed suit, looked at the picture in front of him, puffed again, then called his old mate.

"Hello, you Gay." He automatically announced himself using the distinct parlance that Harry had reluctantly adopted for the past thirty years. As outside centre for the first fifteen rugger team, this simple nickname had been further developed with linguistic nuance. It was cunningly adapted for sporting bravado into his proud title, 'The Flying Queen'. It had certainly stopped those beefs from Wellington College tackling him too low during a most rare victory.

"Hullo, you Bender." Harry answered in the same vernacular that had ensured that none of their contemporaries had come out of the closet until they had safely left their public school. Harry had only believed one chap, who claimed he batted for the other side, after he had failed to force him to snog or finger a girl at a neighbouring school's dance. Kitson had been stunned by this revelation, despite the fellow's insistence that he was the reincarnation of Vita Sackville-West, smoked from a cigarette holder and wore a velvet dressing gown. Harry was a very slow learner.

"Hey, Cute Cheeks. Get your hot little butt over here to the farm. I've got something to show you." Barry teased. "Now!" He barked like a teacher and settled into his role play, "Oh, and tuck your shirt in, Kitson. Please present yourself at my farm, shoes shined, ASAP. I have a most circular conundrum for your earnest consideration. Bye Bye." Barrington Knave then placed the phone back on the receiver. After a second or two, he picked it up, held the cord and let the already spiralled form slowly unwind until he felt that all the excess twists were eradicated. He put the phone back down and the cord immediately jumped back to its previously chaotic rebellion. He puffed once more but, knowing that expert help in other, more pressing, matters was at hand, he closed the email page on his computer, settled deeply into his swingy office chair, laid his arms along the detachable armrests and shut his eyes to snooze. His snores soon met, matched and mated with those of his nearby canine companions who still had not detected his renegade egg yolk.

'Hurt So Good'

All great men, like Barry, and especially some lesser minded souls, like Harry, have their problems. Human beings are far from perfect. They tend to learn from their supposed betters and superiors. They have even more to garner from those that are tested, troubled, tormented and tortured. Because they rarely listen to these testaments, they predominantly act in ways that were pre-ordained to them, often over multiple generations. This predictable reaction is often reflective on their mere geography on the planet. Despite contrasting tales of which son of God, prophet of God, reincarnation of God, monkey related to God or simple science of God, mankind mostly believes that there is something better, superior out there. They tend to stick to their guns on this subject. It gives people weak hope when the stronger stamp their feet and thump their chests. It is this status quo, between hope and fear, that is the cause of the vast majority of the millions and millions of deaths that have occured in war over human history.

It is even reprinted incessantly in the Holy books that we still use as examples to live our impossible lives. In the Old and New Testaments of Judaism and Christianity, after those strange long lists of names, brothers and begats, the Zealots really kicked up a fight against the Romans on Masada until it became much easier for the invaders than mass slaughter to just nail hands and feet to a cross. In the Quran, Mohammed was no shrinking violet when it came to conquest. Centuries later, the Crusaders retaliated with further bloodshed. They travelled across continents for the honour to prove that the higher power they believed in, had a different name to that of the people who also believed in the same higher power. In the earlier Hindu pantheon, the romantic hero and god, Lord Krsna, chariots

Arjuna into a colossal battle in the epic Mahabharata. Religious champions of slaughter. Thousands of years later, millions of innocent subcontinental people lost their lives based on the same dividing presets when an alien Empire crumbled and a line was drawn across a map. Millions continue to die and suffer on these principles around the globe. And, while it does, war remains the most excellent of businesses.

Major Montgomery de Crecy Conrad-Pickles was a believer in this business. England is a funny old place to defend geographically and historically. The de Crecy family had arrived, as their name suggests, with the Normans nearly a thousand years ago. What part of the successful invasion they played remains entirely unclear. Maybe they weren't even there until the latter colonisation of the previously Anglo-Saxon south coast, which was already unsure of its racial heritage having welcomed cohorts from La Bella Italia in the south, Viking long ships in the East and Celtic fans from the North and West. Britain has always been a melting pot for all sorts. The next time you meet somebody that says they're English, just humour them and agree because they tend to get very aggressive about their frequent loss of identity. The next time you meet somebody Welsh, Scottish or Irish, just humour them and agree because they tend to get very aggressive about their constant gain of identity. C'est la vie, as a Norman might say.

Apart from forcing the locals, who wished to get ahead, to speak French, a dedication that clearly irks the inhabitants of both sides of La Manche to this day, the Normans did a fabulous job of civilising the south of England. So much so that, as the centuries drifted by, the de Crecy family entered into a historic union with the more localised Conrad family. The Conrads were a hardy bunch and proved so, with great distinctinction, when they contributed wholeheartedly to the re-invasion and then defeat of their short-term family at the battle that bore the same name. These heroic bludgeons demanded to keep the Gallic title, along with the spoils of their dastardly chevauchee, and thus returned to the rolling downs of their homeland with untold riches and heavily pregnant girls. Theft and rape have always seemed to be shielded in war by man's greater desire to kill. Having a religious cause has always made it so much simpler, even when the warring parties followed the same religion, just with very slightly different interpretations. But let's not pick too many holes in theology at this particular point.

The military and financial prowess of the de Crecy Conrad family grew over the next cluster of centuries. You see, the two go hand in hand. War and money. If there was ever a lull in the storms between the other emerging European Empires, which admittedly was rare, the Conrad Militia were always for hire for any buccaneering and profiting adventure. Their major commercial break was in Africa. Their first independent commission was to protect tribal chieftains who had sold their own kin to slavery. Governments then hired them to protect the slaves from trans Atlantic pirates. In turn, hired thugs were employed by these waystral brigands as extra fortification against these zealous governments. These greedy institutions then needed help guarding the proceeds of the plunder they had seized from the pirates. It was all good business.

Few slaves survived this battle for power and money but opiates were easier to maintain and just as profitable so provided the next boon in the family business portfolio. The poppy based drug was then liberally spooned out to the people of Britain. This kept them very quietly comatose. The Conrad Militia made money from every angle of the venture. When the government started going direct to the drug's source, with their own armies and homeland finance, the wealthy privateers merely adapted their business model. Before long, all the non-profit workers (slaves) and the middle tier management (pirates) were producing all kinds of new and interesting things to smash civilised society into a pulp. All this excess cash was syphoned to a few increasingly wealthy male individuals, particularly the de Crecy Conrad's.

It was around this time that one of Montgomery's ancestors, on a business trip to Jamaica, stumbled across an exotic creature by the name of Miss Monah Pickles. When the bump in her belly proved the extent of his stumblings, he married her and a fresh branch of the family emerged as de Crecy Conrad-Pickles. Meanwhile, their commercial structure was honed to perfection, guaranteeing that most people were dependent on something or other, whether molasses rum from the Caribbean, bitter tobacco from Virginia or the much stronger stuff from the East. As the years went by, the Conrad Militia even safeguarded, then distributed, the refined versions of previous products. When the world started getting bored of opium, but was still addicted, they talked to their chemistry chums at Bayer, a fine tax free pharmaceutical practice, who promptly invented heroin. That really shook everybody up even more.

In more recent times, they did the same to cocaine, an already highly addictive drug. Made famous as a recreational piece of hoity toity fun in the 1920s then at 1980s decadent cocktail parties, it was then refined to chemically addictive perfection. Crack was produced and it was clearly evident how many individuals, groups, communities and societies were reduced to a bunch of blue lipped, demented desperados over the last few decades. When people are this desperate, they do silly things. Sometimes they hurt or murder each other with guns and knives. They steal. They lie. There is often no escape from poverty, addiction and violence once submerged within their murky quagmire. Unless you join the army.

War is the perfect completion of this ongoing circle of profit. It suppresses people who are desperate to make drugs for a living. It suppresses people who are desperate to consume drugs then stop living. Conflict gives those powerful few an opportunity to decimate parts of the globe using very expensive weaponry. It is the perfect win, win situation for those rich and powerful few. They can sell to the oppressed side who can thus retaliate. This gives governments a further excuse to sell weapons to the other side too because it is now they who are oppressed. When everything is destroyed and the people are either dead or have fled their homes, the same authorities pat themselves on the back and award themselves reconstruction contracts before moving on to the next defenceless populus. Sometimes they just wait for the redevelopment process to be completed before starting the same evil plot in exactly the same place. This makes people very angry, unless they are dead or profiting from it.

Thanks to the previous few hundred years, Montgomery de Crecy Conrad-Pickles did not need to profit too much from it. The blood of soldiery still trickled slowly through his veins. His father, after a little slap and tickle on home leave in Wiltshire, had dashed off to Ulster to give the Irish Republican Army (IRA) a good shoeing. On his return, his second son, Montgomery, was born and naming him after the general was significantly easier than the actual birth.

"A stubborn little sod", the midwife had remarked after the breach was diagnosed. There had been grunts and screams from both ends of the operation. His mother's were for obvious reasons but the nurse's resulted from her failure to make any of the vast array of tongs and instruments extract the babe in the way of their intended design. After everybody had given up, the doctor just cut his mother open in the Roman style. At that point there had been a collective shriek as the child was held up. On not such a close examination, the boy's scrotum was larger than his head. It was also blue. The scrotum that is, not the head. The sack had been so badly bashed in the breech birth that it had swollen and discoloured. This fact caused a cessation of alarm and immediate switch to hilarity for all present in surgery, except his mother who was unconscious. It was the precursor of many events in a life that would often result in ridicule.

Monty had a very normal childhood for a lad of his genre. His father was away most of the time, a soldier for life like generations of de

Crecy Conrad-Pickles before him. His mother was indifferent to her second born. This was not out of malice for the bloody battlefield the baby had created in hospital, for she was a kind woman at heart. It was mainly due to her husband's randy temperament. Like Monty's own creation, there was a distinct time pattern between his infrequent visits, a nine and a bit month gestation period and the arrival of another sibling. By the time Monty was sent to boarding school at seven years young, they numbered five. Given that his father had two long military tours of duty abroad during this timespan, any calculator can testify that his dear mama had little time to rest while his Pater wasn't killing people for Queen and Country.

Preparatory school was brutal. The daily routine of cold showers, bland breakfasts, endless lessons, lardy lunches, hours of sports, precious freetime, delicious tuck, revolting suppers, tedious extra work and regimental bedtime continued for five years. Monty did not really excel at anything. In the essentials, English and Maths, he floundered like the Cod Mornay that passed as food in the school kitchen. However, in classes that taught a brand of history, which celebrants of Britain and Empire could be proud of, or a Mediterranean language or two that had been dead for thousands of years, he seemed to come to life a little. The combination of Empire and language meant that Monty's halfhearted interests were in the ancient Egyptian, Greek and Roman varieties.

Sports didn't really bother him. Rugby tackling practice on the rock hard, snow strewn playing fields, was more of a mere inconvenience for him. This was apparent when he compared his emotions to the tears on many a bloody kneed childs' cheeks. He certainly felt no jealousy towards the sports heroes who were awarded school colours for their daring on pitch and track. The headmaster would present this award when everybody was tucked up in bed, reading quietly. He would walk into the hat trick hero's dormitory and, after a very brief congratulatory speech, would throw the appropriate scarf or cap at the boy. This was the cue for every other boy in the school to offer their unanimous congratulations. This was achieved by a ripple effect of news spreading down the entire school corridor, which motivated all the pupils to shout, run and pile onto his solitary bed. Monty didn't much like the crush so would wait until most of the boys were atop before joining in. The writhing mass of boys gave him a warm and cosy sensation which he assumed was similar to the non-existent embrace of his mother. He cuddled up.

The headmaster ran a jolly tight ship and had briefed his teachers to act accordingly as well. His own liberal use of the cane, and occasional cricket bat, to the more badly behaved boys' buttocks, seemed to scare the little blighters enough to ensure that he could proudly state to any prospective parents that he had never had to expel a pupil in all his tenure. His loyal and equally violent masters would dispense a second, lower level of torture on the undisciplined. The Latin teacher took delight in having his pupils spread their hands open atop the fliptop wooden desks whilst they conjugated verbs. Sadly for him, they were remarkably quick learners, after initial failures earned a wrap across the knuckles with his metal ruler. The edge of this makeshift sword, not the harmless flat, was his chosen method of assault which accelerated the speed of learning, "Amo, Amas, Amat". If the boys were careless enough to bleed, they were sent to the vastly bossommed matron for sticking plasters and a most welcome nussle, on condition they returned during free time to write out the offending ancient grammar one hundred times.

Sport was an arena that a child had to be on his toes. Monty would never forget the day when he was mindlessly staring at the woodland below the playing fields. He was pondering his most successful stick camp to date. It was aggressively brought to his attention that he was actually at slip catching practice when the coach threw a well aimed red cricket ball at his head. The resultant egg on his forehead was a colourful reminder over the following weeks, first angry red through purple, black, blue, green and yellow, that catches win matches.

Monty didn't drop many cricket balls again. However, he did start failing those little Latin tests much more than most of his fellow pupils. On occasion, his indiscipline even reached a level that warranted a visit to the headmaster. In short, Monty had discovered at a very young age that he liked being spanked.

Which was lucky for him when he attended Public School. In essence, the regime was the same as before. The daily routine of cold showers, bland breakfasts, endless lessons, lardy lunches, hours of sports, precious freetime, delicious tuck, revolting suppers, tedious extra work and regimental bedtime continued for a further five years. But there were some additional extras that made it much more pleasurable for Monty's maturing tastes. For starters, the school had been founded on military principles. As a result, armed forces officers were heavily subsidised by the government to send their offspring to the red brick children's barracks in Berkshire in the hope of nurturing future warmongers. Its curricular affiliation and geographical closeness with Sandhurst, Britain's leading officer cadet school, guaranteed that as many young chaps as possible could be herded efficiently towards the training of war. Given his long standing family history and victorious mediaeval name, Monty was one of those chosen few. It suited him greatly to dress up once a week in combat gear and pretend to be a soldier. He realised that aside from playing with guns and things that go bang, he just liked being around men in uniform.

From an early age Monty learnt the importance and urgency to keep a uniform pressed, starched and polished. This was mainly thanks to the sixth former to whom he was unofficially assigned as fag. This history does not record what happened to Wilberforce Waverling before or beyond Wellington College but what is perfectly clear is that he was an utter swine at the boys' alma mater. Willy was a rugby legend by then, decimating other school's packs with a malice and disdain that he never really could control on or off the field. He was just nasty. So much so that the teachers all concurred that he would bully his way to colonel but would never make brigadier or general. It was considered a bad draw of sticks when Monty pulled Willy as his fag. Waverling liked both his school and military uniforms just so. The eighteen year old enjoyed watching the youngster polishing his shoes and boots. It wasn't long before he introduced his enraged cock into the cleaning ceremony.

"Spit and polish" he would urge. "I want to be able to see my handsome face in it, Pickle Pot, you little slut!", he would moan aggressively before pushing his submissive's head down again. Monty proved most adept at his cleaning duties and it wasn't long into the second term before Willy bent him over the drying rack then ironing board. Such important pieces of apparatus in the build up to threading a needle in a button hole. This servile life seemed to suit the young trainee. As previously mentioned, Monty had a very normal childhood for a lad of his genre.

By the time Monty reached the same age as his depraved, long departed, kink master, he had adjusted his sexuality to within the boundaries acceptable to the antiquated laws of society. At black tie dances, he made a jolly good fist of chatting up plain, more boyish, girls. On presentation, he developed an uncanny charade of relative humour in their presence. He would sign the requisite dance cards, Foxtrot as best he could, skip a Gay Gordon, force a smile and return the strange object of femininity to their respective chaperones. This was a necessary heterosexual charade if one was going to get ahead in a homophobic world. On returning to his school house, Montgomery let off steam by ordering the entire junior dormitory to strip naked for a game of Slippery Pig. For those who don't know the rules, one boy, the swine of the game, is basted in goose fat and the other blindfolded boys have to catch the naughty, greasy, little piggy wiggy. This game gave Monty such blissful relief after the tedium of entertaining girls.

By the time Monty finished school, he was sparsely armed with some mediocre qualifications and joined the preordained conveyor belt to Sandhurst. He was turned into a leader of soldiers within a few short months at the military academy. The subsequent interview with the colonel of his cavalry regiment was a shoe in too.

"Wellington, Hey?" muttered the mustachioed walrus behind the desk, somewhere near Saffron Walden.

"Errrrr...... Yes, Sir." Second Lieutenant Conrad-Pickles managed the first question after a brief cerebral pause.

"Splendid, splendid," continued the orifice hidden by bushy bristles. "Bloody good school. I can only assume that they have equipped you with a satisfactory skill set for the cruel world beyond the golf courses of the Home Counties? Can you ski?"

"Oh, yes, Sir. I was quite the whizz on school trips, what, what." The senior soldier seemed to pique at the youngster's last turn of phrase.

"Excellent news," he continued regardless. " You see, this regiment prides itself on its skiing. Oh, and it's polo, of course."

"Of course, Sir."

"We are looking to stick another one up those Guardsmen's arses for the third winter in succession. Bloody important for our morale, skiing, you know. I would very much like you to spend your first six months with my officers in Verbier, Switzerland. Is that agreeable to you?"

"Oh, yes, Sir. Thank you, Sir!"

"Don't thank me. Toughens us soldiers up. It gets so damned cold in those Alps." The Colonel shivered.

"I'm sure it's marvellous training, Sir, for when we make the Big Push against the Russians or Chinese?", stammered the imbecile trainee. It was with this in mind that the Colonel glared back at him.

"The Russians? The Chinese? Don't be so bloody ridiculous, you ignoramus! Our bloody business won't be fought in Russia or China. We have all too much money and power at stake to risk anything daft like that. Consider it as a 'Gentlemen's Agreement' between the new superpowers that we only inflict our brutal damage using third party countries or states as our business playgrounds. Think about Iraq and Afghanistan. We all pick an opposing side and make pots of cash by aiding our relative allies, selling them our weapons, using our own troops as little as possible and then awarding ourselves lucrative redevelopment programs in the aftermath desolation. That is our business in a nutshell. As a result, you've got more chances of visiting Mars than bloomin' Russia, m'Lad! No. No. No. It's the slippery streets and hard pistes of Verbier for you." He paused, before adding pensively, "What are you going to do for income?" Monty seemed a little taken aback by this question so answered with a question of his own.

"I rather thought that you were giving me a job in the regiment, Sir? You know, with a salary, what, what?"

"Please desist from bloomin' 'What, what?'ing me, m'Lad! You sound like a bloody bitter lemon." The tank chief roared. Monty had clearly touched a nerve for the second time. The colonel calmed then continued, "I mean your additional income. You know, for Swiss nightclubs, charming the fillies with buckets of Bolly, buying flash sportscars, those sorts of important extracurricular regimental activities. You can't survive on the pittance we pay you for mere soldiery. That's only your first six months sorted over the winter too. By the time you get back here, the season will be well underway and you'll need to buy at least four polo ponies plus all the wretched kit. Well? What have you got in your piggy bank?"

"My forefathers have been in the business of war for sometime, Sir." Monty answered with a knowing smile. "I will be provided for most comfortably, Sir, I can assure you." The old soldier raised a monocle from lap to eye and studied the paperwork on his desk as if it were the form guide in the Racing Post. A beaming smile curled out from the edges of his magnificent 'tache and he added,

"Ah, de Crecy Conrad-Pickles. Why didn't you say, Man? Welcome to my Lancers!"

"Much obliged, Sir, what, what!" The Colonel winced slightly before he recovered his happy demeanour, wrapped a paternal arm around his young charge's shoulders and introduced him to a rather fruity little glass of port by way of celebration.

'My Boy Lollipop'

This was pretty much the pattern that military life dictated for the young, then, not so young, then middle aged, Monty. A dazzling life of regimental dances, debauched dinners in the officers' mess, winters schussing down slopes, reckless apres ski, spring pony auctions, galloping down goal lines and, very occasionally, mucking about with very small tanks. Despite some brief inconveniences chasing Taliban in the Himalayas and ISIS around Mesopotamia, Monty managed to avoid most direct combat, almost entirely maintaining his gadd about lifestyle. There had been a couple of hairy moments on these support tours but his expert soldiers ensured that he returned alive and as a supposed hero, despite never actually killing anybody personally. This he kept to himself. He also kept his sexuality secret too. It didn't do one any favours being a soft pussy or a roaring bugger in Her Majesty's Forces.

Apart from discreet visits to a little club in London's Soho called 'Madame Arthur's', Monty just led a heterosexual lie. He was an excellent liar. He seemed quite the horny little devil while he quaffed champagne with his fellow officers accompanied by a constant gaggle of girls that crushed them, kissed them and galloped atop them, wherever they were in the world. On one visit to Egypt over the New Year holiday, Monty and his brothers in arms had some leave from their Libyan desert 'training'. The Nile side town provided a most clement alternative to their more natural, winter, Alpine environment and they had walked along the river bank and watched the low sun disappear behind the majestic triangles of pharaoh's burial. Monty was comforted by the recall to one of his more beloved school subjects. His mind drifted quickly to oiled slaves and neatly tunic clad overseers. After a little supper, the horny bucks decided to chance their luck at the local nightclub. To their surprise, their Mohammadan cousins had temporarily discarded their religious beliefs and swathes of drunken people, mainly men to Monty's secret delight, whirled like dervishes to the North African beats. When the club shut, after heralding in the next year, the drunken officers staggered back to their hotel, disappointingly alone.

The first day of the Christian calendar was greeted rather late in the day and with eyes most bleary. After shaking off their hangovers with a bracing walk around the monuments to space, time and human death, large quantities of couscous were consumed, drenched in meaty stew and washed down with epic volumes of locally produced alcoholic grape juice. The emboldened soldiers decided to chance their luck at the same 'Boite de Nuit' again. They were quickly disappointed. There were more staff than punters on entry, a direct contrast to the previous evening soiree. The military mob were just about to give up when one of the soldiers spotted a deliciously attractive girl. She was clad in a thigh length fur coat and dangled her seemingly endless legs out of a microscopic skirt from a stool at the bar. She seductively sucked on her cocktail straw.

"Fuck me", remarked the sometime killer of men pertinently, "She's staring at us! No, hang on a bloody minute. She's not staring at us at all. Fuck my old marchers, she's staring at Monty. Monty, you terrible cunt!" He paused briefly then continued to speak through gritted teeth that he had forced to resemble a smile in the direction of the goddess, "You lucky fucker. Go on, go and talk to her".

Despite his internal loathing to chat up this beautiful example of the sex he liked least, Monty got up and ambled, seemingly calmly, over to the seat next to the goddess. He briefly looked back at his compatriots en route with a confident wink and grin. She smiled and nodded at his request to join her and buy her a drink so he settled in, waving the bartender over. She was half Moroccan, half French, lived in Paris and stank of wealth and sexuality. Against his will, but in keeping with his denial, Monty chatted affably to the vixen. Before long, she yawned, stretched out her slender arms above her head, and muttered in an accent that sounded as charged as an Arrondissement riot,

"Y'ur frien's 'ave gone. I am a little bit too drunk now. Pleassse, will you take me back to my 'otel?"

Without waiting for his reply, she got up and walked slowly towards the club door but paused and turned when she reached the centre of the empty dance floor. Her subsequent actions shocked Monty but the staff of the venue reacted to her performance far more dramatically. Opening her mink coat, she flicked it back behind her shoulders, revealing the most delightful breasts which she proceeded to wiggle gently from side to side, whilst fixing her demure glare on Monty. The Islamic workforce were initially mortified, then screamed at her in an angry cacophony. They ran over to the Jezebel, pulled the coat back over her naked flesh and forcibly ejected her from the premises. Monty sprinted after them and pushed his way through the throng, levering his body as a shield between them and her. He pushed them away and apologised, in the way that Englishmen have perfected. He then explained that they had nothing to worry about, hailed a taxi and bundled the drunken hussie into the back seat.

"My 'ero", she breathed a font of gin based fumes at her awkward saviour, "Take me to my 'otel maintenant". Monty relaxed his grip on her but, no sooner had he done so, she pulled open her coat again, bearing her perfect orbs once more whilst laughing hysterically. The taxi driver, having rescued his eyeballs from the rear view mirror, went apoplectic with rage, cursing the harlot. On frantic restoration of the coat to its designed position, Monty once again apologised profusely and ordered the driver to continue his work.

On arrival at the hotel, Monty paid the irate cabby, whilst the damsel stumbled into the enormous marble foyer where she dropped the coat to her ankles. She stood topless and giggled with drunken abandon. Predictably, the staff went berserk and once again Monty vaulted to her rescue. He covered her naked torso with his own clothed one. She then collapsed in his arms. The shouting staff led him up one side of the regal double staircase to the first floor landing and then to her room, which they opened. Monty carried her limp body inside. He carefully laid her on the bed, then left her boudoir, shutting the door quietly behind him. An exhalation of breath revealed the relief that the ordeal was over, particularly as he had not had to perform any, personally unnatural, sexual duties.

The next morning, he recounted these strange nocturnal revelations to his captivated colleagues over a substantial and late breakfast. A waiter arrived at the table asking which gentleman was Monsieur de Crecy Conrad-Pickles. On answering in the affirmative, the drinks bearer relayed a simple message to Monty.

"Blessings be upon you, Sir! Your friend at 'Le Grand 'Otel' would like to apologise for "'er be'aviour" last night and has invited you to join her this afternoon at her hotel's cocktail bar for a drink to say sorry personally. The prophet forbids our imbibement, Sir, but, Inshallah, you take my blessings with you."

This news was met with catcalls and wolf whistles by the assembled pillars of the British Army.

"A second bite at that juicy cherry, eh, Monty? You Lucky Twat!" one defender of the realm pipped. Not exactly what Monty had been thinking but, in the interests of keeping up appearances, he smiled and replied to the messenger.

"Thank you, Waiter. Please relay my thanks to Mademoiselle and I look forward to accepting her kind invitation."

There had been frenzied excitement amongst his fellow combatants, much giving of luck on his important regimental mission and tactical advice had been dished out liberally.

"Give her one from me, Monty!" was perhaps the most useful and eloquent. So he had set out, heterosexual pressure fizzing in his ears, to her hotel where he sat at the cocktail bar in the very same foyer that had been the scene of many bare crimes the night previous. He ordered a drink and perched, uncomfortable with his predicament as well as the stool. He nursed his glass of something emboldening and waited. And waited. At last, he was approached by a similarly tight lipped and polite waiter.

"Monsieur Conrad-Pickles?", he enquired and, on Monty's positive and personal assurance that it was he, continued, "Mademoiselle regrets that she is unable to join you at this time but has asked for your attendance in 'er room instead. I understand that you know the way?", he added with a poorly disguised smirk.

Internally cursing his predicament at the hands of this seeming slave to sex, Monty thanked the waiter, attempted to pay the bartender who mentioned that the financial requisites had already been taken care of. He ascended the enormous semi spiral staircase for the second time in as many days. He reached the top, pivoted towards her familiar door, breathed a deep sigh, accepted his fate and knocked firmly on the white painted wood before him.

The door opened, revealing a familiar sight. This time her breasts were wet, as was her long straight dark hair that was combed after a recent shower. A white towel was wrapped around her slim waist. Her elegant arms reached forward, grabbed him by the neck and pulled him into the room. She thrust her lips then tongue onto his own and slammed the door shut behind them with a violent swing of her knee. She grabbed frenziedly at his shirt buttons so he helped her remove the garment until their naked torsos locked against each other. They staggered back and onto the balcony. Monty winced as he saw all too familiar staff members look up at them so pushed her back onto the vast bed inside. She dominated again, kneeling on the bed, levering him onto his back and grabbed at his belt and trouser buttons. She freed them, gripping then pulling them and his boxer shorts down over his buttocks, thighs and ankles. Having ripped off his shoes and socks, she pulled these clothes over his feet. She paused, looked up at his naked body, smiled and started crawling, panther like, towards his surprisingly engorged penis.

She sighed contentedly, then gripped his shaft firmly with one hand and gave his swollen balls a gentle tug with the other. She pulled each hand expertly in synchronicity, massaging his erection. She then looked him in the eyes, smiled, licked her lips and flashed her tongue across the enraged tip of his penis. He moaned with raw carnal pleasure, which encouraged her to do it again, then again, and she worked her hands and tongue until he wanted to scream. She lowered her hot mouth down his shaft, just the end at first, then rhymically descended lower and lower, faster and faster. As she did so her movements became more sporadic and she slurped, gurgled and spluttered up and down his rigid stave. Monty was elevated to a plateau of bliss and, forgetting his sexual preference, resolved to penetrate her whichever way she demanded. He sat up, her face still buried in his lap and reached a hand behind her buttocks, pulled the towel up and searched for her wet vulva. He stopped short when his hand met her own enormous cock and balls.

The ending to their encounter was almost entirely happy. The exception being that she, or rather he, or in socially correct parlance, they, had been mildly disappointed that Monty had not reacted like most heterosexual gentleman. At the very least they had expected some embarrassed reaction but what they really enjoyed was being beaten to a pulp in some homophobic rage. Having confessed this sado-masochistic preference, Monty reassured them that he was game for whatever they wanted and that he would have absolutely no problem with thrashing them during any future erotic dalliances. So long as they agreed to administer a similar punishment to him too. Once their mutual ambitions had been ascertained, they spent a gloriously violent afternoon practicing their saucy talents. An understanding was negotiated, addresses and phone numbers exchanged and another merciless spanking was administered to both their and his raw buttocks. Monty had met his perfect nemesis. The Major returned to his own hotel with a skip in his step and the perfect story for his workmates, who eagerly demanded every sordid detail which he enthusiastically recounted with one obviously large omission.

Monty's lie had been perfected that autumn previous. On army leave between work missions or just for weekends when he was back at base on Salisbury Plain, Montgomery, the conqueror of north Africa, would fly or take the train to the French capital to meet his sometime girlfriend, sometime boyfriend, always Babylonian Temptress, at her flat. Publicly, they were a stunningly beautiful woman that he could proudly show photographs of or introduce to the friends who they rarely bumped into in Parisian bistros and restaurants. Privately, they released themselves in an erotic and romantic world of sexual debauchery. They amassed an extraordinary collection of apparatus. A hobby horse, manacles, plugs, handcuffs, masks, chains, whips, bats, dildos, gags, ticklers, grips, gas masks and vices, to name but a few. An enormous wardrobe contained a vast array of costumes dependent on which character they wished to violate and punish that particular day. Their life together was most satisfactory in this manner and it had continued for the last few months in the same pulsating vein.

The summer was now upon them. The weekend was now fast approaching and it was with this in mind that Monty, by now a Major consigned to mostly desk duties back at his Wiltshire base, stared blankly at the strange photographs in front of him. The office was simple and tidy in general. A wooden chair and desk stood before a metal three tier filing cabinet against one wall. A door hung in another, a picture of Her Majesty The Queen proudly gazed from the third. A metal, corrugated blind covered the window on the fourth wall, to obscure the drab tarmac parade ground outside. The top of the table was the exception to the tidy rule. It was littered with papers, photographs and files emblazoned with red stamps warning of, 'Top Secret', 'Highly Classified', 'For Your Eyes Only' and 'Codename: Circum Navigation', contents.

Monty sighed and reshuffled the wedge of photographs in front of him. He stared at the images. Despite the inexplicable and extraordinary nature of the evidence before him, his professional conclusions tended towards fake news. Surely these images were the product of Russian or Chinese mischief, simply to feed his own beloved army and the secretive circles of espionage beyond with an artistic diversion whilst they hacked and corrupted through social media and the dark web? He found all this arable work most tedious. To a large extent, all the images were very similar. They were all night shots taken from his army's low flying helicopters of local land using a combination of infrared and thermal imaging cameras. The dark backgrounds all had a greenish tint to them. They all had a bright digital code specifying the exact time, date and location of the shot in the top left hand corner. The times were nearly all 0000 to 0400 hours, the dead of night. The dates were spread throughout the year. The locations were varied in name but most specifically geographical. Devizes, Bishops Cannings, Allington, Silbury Hill, Avebury, East and West Kennet, Stanton St Bernard, Alton Barnes, Alton Priors, Huish, Bottlesford, Wilcot, Manningford Bruce, Oare, Pewsey, Martinsell, Clench, Milton Lilbourne, Easton Royal, Ram Alley and Burbage were all in, or very close to, the Vale of Pewsey.

But one thing was entirely different in every single photograph. Each one displayed a unique linear image that seemingly glowed in the darkness of the rolling fields and hills of the area. Some were simple patterns, others incredibly complicated. Some were elongated, others circular. Some were clearly definable emblems such as hearts, stars, butterflies and crosses, others were just stunning patterns like complicated fractals or geometric forms. All of them were serenely beautiful. The Major's major puzzle was that they did not actually physically exist. By day these forms just could not be detected. They were a mere trick of light, a result of energy sensitive technologies. Then, seemingly randomly, a relatively small quantity of these nocturnal blueprints would appear physically in the crops during the summer months, from June to September, naturally disappearing at harvest time. That very morning's moment of excitement, an actual helicopter recce down the Vale, had revealed an incredible spectacle. However, the daylight photographs were currently being developed by his female assistant, Captain Kitty Parker, so the results would just have to wait until the following Monday. It was these bizarre secrets that Monty had been tasked with to research and report to his military superiors and government. After years of covering up his personal truths, Monty was the perfect white liar for the job but, for the time being, his conclusions would have to be withheld. The weekend beckoned and he had some stimulating spanking to look forward to.

"Kitty!" he yelled in the direction of the door. It was opened a few seconds later by an attractive young woman, three facts barely appreciated by the Major who was predisposed with thrashing thoughts and Parisian pain.

"Sir?" responded Captain Kitty Parker politely and efficiently.

"Kitty. I'll be damned if I can deal with this clap-trap for a moment longer, what, what."

"What, what, Sir?" His subordinate responded.

"Don't be insolent to your superior officer, if you may."

"Apologies, Sir!"

" That's better. Now, the top brass want us to study, evaluate, process and report on this bloody nonsense."

"Nonsense, Sir?" the Captain enquired.

"Of course it's bloody nonsense, Parker! What, what."

"What, what, Sir?" Kitty ventured a grin.

"I've told you before. Mimic me at your peril."

"Sorry, Sir!" The woman retracted her smirk.

"I'm damned if I can believe that these images are artworks, messages or codes created by Russkie or Tiddlywink infiltrators. Surely they are created by a bunch of pissed up artists having a prank in the fields whilst they smoke a bundle of spliffs, what, what?" Kitty bit her tongue then answered more diplomatically, yet with enquiry.

"If it is all about a bunch of guerilla brigand artists, Sir, why have they only been discovered on the rarest of occasions?"

"Stealth and guile, Captain. Stealth and guile, what, what. They are committing trespass and vandalisation crimes. That's why they rarely get bloody caught."

"But what if it is neither dictatorially based democracy infiltration or trippy dippy hippy pranksters, Sir? What if it is something else?" Kitty, for various reasons, had a mind that demanded further inquiry.

"What are you suggesting, Kitty?" The Major added with a sigh. He sensed longer term paperwork accumulation.

"Well, given the evidence accumulated beyond our own environs, there is a high likelihood that there is intelligent life somewhere in this vast universe beyond the limitations of our tiny planet. Can we open our investigation just a little, or rather a lot, please?" De Crecy Conrad-Pickles stared disbelievingly at his assistant. He was silent for a few moments before he answered with a bewilderment similar to that day that his head had collided with a cricket ball all those years before.

"You are a crank crack, Kitty! That is the most ridiculous suggestion I've ever heard, what, what! Retract that nonsense immediately!"

"But, Sir! Judging by these photos, we are stationed right next to the epicentre of the very essence of pagan planetary and natural universal beliefs. We are studying temporal phenomena that appear right next to permanent constructs that have been unmoved for thousands of years. We cannot discard the argument that mankind received help from, or even just observed, more intelligent sources five or so millenia ago. Two examples, near and far. One. The perfect order of astrological exquisiteness at Stonehenge. How could these primitive people have possibly calculated these interplanetary alignments? We have been taught that humans thought the world was flat until only a few hundred years ago, for God's sake! The math just doesn't add up! Two. The microscopic accuracy of the vectors and angles in line with the earth's core and the sun and moon at the ancient Egyptian pyramids...."

"Enough!" The Major interrupted with a rare venom. "How dare you suggest such a monstrous thing about my beloved pyramids. They are the envy of subsequent civilisations since their creation. They were painstakingly calculated by the pharaohs' architects and painfully erected by the slave populus of the day."

"With respect, Sir, modern scientists still argue about the way and means of building such colossal constructions. They still don't actually *know*. Isn't it just easier to open your mind and question that a higher intelligence, with superior tools at their disposal, could have created the aforementioned edifices?"

"Poppycock!" The former venom turned into the worst linguistic strike the sheltered military pen pusher could summon. "Have you gone stark raving mad, Captain Parker? I've never heard such unmitigated balderdash in my whole life, what, what!"

"What, what, Sir?"

"Right, that's it! If I do not have a full apology for this ridiculous train of inquiry on Monday, you will be reported to the top brass and your pathetic attempt at soldiery will be terminated!" The Major was flustered by his own reaction, let alone this insolent rebellion against his long substantiated beliefs and learnings. He paused and composed himself with a brief repeated mantra of selfish ignorance. "Enough. Enough. That's it, I've had enough. Enough's enough for this week." He jerked his thoughts back towards his own bubble as it was on the verge of pop. "I need to catch my train to London sharpish otherwise I will miss my connection from St Pancras to gay Paris." He announced the end of the sentence with a camp flourish that Kitty felt suited him rather too well. He sighed and returned to his former flaccid persona. "Would you be an angel and tidy up this mess?" he asked, waving towards the sea of photographs.

"Of course, Sir. It won't take me long and I have no immediate plans tonight anyway." She responded with an easy smile.

"Many thanks, Kitty." The Major replied, "Have a fab weekend."

"You too, Sir" she added as Monty shimmied, his head slowly shaking side to side, out of the door, shutting her inside the office. The Captain waited for his footsteps to recede down the corridor, heard the building door open and close, then settled down at his desk. Now was her chance.

'Sister Big Stuff'

Captain Kitty Parker picked up those same photographs that the Major had recently rejected to the table top and held them close to her pretty face. She sighed quietly and put them down again before rolling up one sleeve of her khaki shirt, then another, immaculately above her elbows. Using her delicate, long fingers, she smoothed the folds flat and pinched the ironed crease that rose towards her shoulder back into its former sharpness. Her arms were surprisingly slender, although the subtle sinuous definitions belied a hidden strength as she lay them back on the jumbled mountain of pictures.

She carefully spread out about two dozen of the aerial night photos, making sure that the extraordinary patterns displayed were as varied as possible. She stood up, walked briskly to and locked the door before she continued to the window, where she obliterated all sight, in or out of de Crecy Conrad-Pickles' office, with a swish of her wrist to the blind cord. She strode back in front of the table, reached her right hand behind her pistol holster, plunged it into the back pocket of her green military fatigues and retrieved her phone from the warm nest of her full and firm buttock. Swiping it on, she chose the camera setting and, with her narrow arms extended, slowly and systematically held the device above each picture, checking the viewfinder for light and clarity before gently tapping the button and moving on to the next image. The simplicity of the act was not lost on the Captain whose extensive training over the last few years, especially in the secret art of photography and surveillance, had been made increasingly easy by quantum leaps in technology.

When she had finished, she swiped through each picture to double check that they were perfect. She then selected them all and forwarded them to her encrypted WhatsApp friend, "Uncle Max". On sending, she noticed that her friend was not just one mobile number, as on previous occasions, but several. A group was metamorphosing. Kitty smiled, Uncle Max was clearly taking her 'Codename: Circum Navigation' research and findings seriously if other parties were now involved.

She deleted the pictures from her normal photo file, sat back down in the chair and scooped the night photos back together. She turned them vertically, tap tapped the ends of the card on the desktop, until they were all perfectly aligned, and returned them, all bar one, to the 'Codename: Circum Navigation' file sub-sectioned 'Blueprints'. She then lay the outcast image atop the file. It was no less intriguing than any of the others but Kitty was particularly fascinated by the geometry of this glowing nocturnal design and its corresponding history.

A small seven pointed star was the central focus of the pattern. On closer inspection, the star was actually eight small circles, one in the middle of seven others. At each point of the star were another seven small circles, beyond them seven slightly larger circles and, at the perimeter of the design, seven even bigger circles. What had singled out this blueprint, beyond all the others, on July 19th? The answer lay somewhere in the multiple photographs that she knew lay within the 'Codename' file marked 'Evidence 19.07.2019'. She knew the contents because she had developed them after that morning's helicopter sortie. She just hadn't told her boss yet. She opened it.

Kitty's smooth, pale olive skin crumpled gently on her brow as she scrutinised the contents, a long waving strand of her light hair fell forward from its army regulation housing. She brushed it absentmindedly backwards, leaving her hand slightly cupped above her enchanting green eyes, which dissolved the information before them. The outline of her angled nose and full pouting lips made her appear more like an Olympian goddess than a British Army officer but it confirmed the distantly Mediterranean roots of her family.

The aerial photographs she now studied were of wheat fields in daylight. They were exactly the same pattern as the simpler nighttime blueprint outline. More intriguing were the detailed swirling patterns that each and every one of the twenty nine graduating circles identically contained. Further fascination was in the seeming background pattern which resembled a perfect weave. The last extraordinary fact, that the officer had to consider, was that it was exactly the same pattern, form, scale and location as a crop circle formation that had been photographed near Bishops Cannings in 1999. It had been appropriately named 'The Basket'.

There were multiple assumptions to be made from the evidence before her but very few plausible answers and certainly no firm conclusions. She decided to start with the historical so reached for and opened a third file sub sectioned '1999: The Basket'. The original crop circle had been destroyed by the farmer, a cantankerous killjoy by the name of Knave, whose family had farmed in the Vale for centuries. It was the estate policy to immediately cut down any of the agricultural artworks that occasionally appeared on their land over the summer months. This decision was based on a furious acceptance that these seasonal vandals could and would defile their land but, under no circumstances, would they entertain the increasing swathes of voyeurs and tourists that would trample across their acres of undamaged and harvestable fields, over the following days and weeks. They, quite literally, had nipped it in the bud ever since.

It had been most fortuitous, for both the ever swelling ranks of crop circle enthusiastics and for the increasingly secret information gathering departments within the military, that a civilian pilot had managed to photograph the breathtaking formation, those twenty years previous. Knave had butchered this horticultural perfection within hours but the evidence was there in those simple snaps. Kitty now handled them with the affection of an over-sensitive lover. In direct contrast to the Knave estate attitude, these original photos were clear evidence that it would be impossible for a group of determined artists or vandals, dependent on your point of view, to create this vision of such complexity and unique perfection, however many of them tried, between the hours of a midsummer's dusk and dawn. How on earth could such a large group of people create an image, hundreds of square metres in size, in such a short space of nighttime? Not only were they entirely undetected or without witness but their creation had been performed on the undulating surface of a Wiltshire wheat field with a mathematical precision and symmetry more likely to be performed with accuracy on the home of calculus, a two dimensional sheet of A4 sized paper.

The next anomaly was the actual manner in which this extraordinary swirl and weave pattern had been created. When a human walks through a crop, he or she leaves a trail, whether by flattening the crop or by snapping it. Kitty had subsequently experimented with this concept over a period of some weeks. She had taken a strand or two of wheat from the side of a random field, in the clear interests of research for Her Majesty, of course. However many times she tried, whether along the shaft of the blade or at the growth joints or nodes of the plant, Kitty could never bend the stem, only break or damage it. Furthermore, she had conducted her test to a few strands, in daylight, and failed. 'The Basket' had appeared overnight, as had most historical examples, and consisted of hundreds of thousands of bent, woven, unbroken stems.

Some weeks earlier, having had Major Conrad-Pickles sign it off with the disinterested nonchalance that was his norm, she had taken this puzzle, some samples from a circle earlier that year, down the road to the regimentally affiliated laboratory at Porton Down. This infamous hive of once chemical and always secret weaponry was the perfect facility for such a dilemma. Its scientists were thoroughly overqualified. The results had been couriered back by a dispatch rider. She had timed the journey when the lab announced the motorcycle's departure. Twenty five minutes. That left no chance for the rider to have stopped, carefully opened the envelope, read or photographed the contents, resealed the paper and resumed the journey. The soldier had given Captain Parker an awkward salute to the side of his helmet and, with a splutter of ignition, roared back to his deviant base. Kitty had locked the door to the office, opened the seal, pulled out the contents and read them.

She had been mildly disappointed by the findings. It wasn't that they weren't incredible, on the contrary, but they were exactly the same results that amateur civilian researchers had consistently produced over many years. These had been systematically ridiculed by the powers that be and their findings buried by the press from the public domain. The report confirmed that the bending of crop nodes is achievable using heat of six to eight hundred degrees centigrade, equivalent to a microwave oven. Simple science. But the heat generated by this sort of power would burn. Crop circles sometimes had evidence of the plant ears being slightly singed but there had never been any fires reported on any of the sites. What is more, the heat affects the alkalinity of the soil which in turn can make the crop grow faster or slower compared to the unaffected plants around them.

Stranger still, this brutal heat seems to have little or no effect on the wildlife either. One would surely expect the insect, rodent and bird populations to be massacred? Even nests containing eggs had been discovered entirely undamaged. Mass evacuation seems to be a precursor to these enormous energy surges. A number of reports, both local and international, indicated that farm animals such as cows had made a significant rumpus in the nights when crop circles were discovered the following mornings. This phenomenal power is not just effective on wheat or barley. A tree circle was discovered in the Netherlands in 2007 and, more bizarrely, a three inch deep geometric pattern appeared in the mud of a dry river bed in Oregon,

USA, in the early Nineteen Nineties. It was photographed from a plane at three thousand metres and was estimated to have twenty one thousand metres of lines in the intricately symmetrical design.

Breaking her focus, Kitty's mind wandered back to the autumn past, before any of her new covert escapades had begun. She smiled at that memory of innocence and freedom because the American riverbed had triggered a fantastic memory. Kitty had always been a free spirited girl. She suspected it was a natural reaction, in the most positive and loving way to all concerned, against the old school environment of religious, business and family misogyny that she had grown up in. She was expected to find a nice fella, settle down, have kids, go to church, have ladies' lunches, obey her husband and eventually die. As an intelligent and determined girl of the 21st century, she decided that expressing herself with art and feminism, coupled with a mildly nonchalant disregard for men, was a far more progressive and stimulating way forward.

So it was that Kitty and her then girlfriend had flown from Heathrow to San Francisco, joined up with other girl friends, jumped aboard a huge Winnebago recreational vehicle and driven east, passed the sins of Reno and out into the Nevada desert to the Burningman Festival. Viewed from the air, the precision of the forty thousand revellers' camp looks like a crop circle. Unlike the powerful imprint the latter leaves on the land, 'ghost' crop circles impact the soil for months, sometimes years to come, the annual party has a 'leave no trace' policy. The enormous salt flat and nature reserve is returned after the carnival carnage to its simple natural purity. It is also a non commercial event. The ticket price goes towards the clean up operation, the showers and loos, a coffee stand and, most importantly in the searing desert heat, an ice stall. Everything else, most notably food, water, drugs and alcohol, have to be taken to the site by the participants. No money changes hands. These and other commodities are traded amongst the revellers for the week-long party. Art installations, bars and clubs are lovingly constructed, admired and appreciated, before everything is disassembled or, more heartbreakingly, burnt at the close of festivities. The burning of the man effigy is the high, or low, light of the drama. The girls had revelled in this temporary city of freedom and fun.

It was at one of these temporary clubs that the two lovers had found themselves as the sun rose on the edge of the thirty mile long expanse of dust, gyrating to the sounds of House Music. They had been attracted to this particular revel by a carnal instinct to look at and party with extraordinarily beautiful women. 'The One Hundred Brides Party' was an apt description. A Las Vegas casino owner had brought his own art form up state and recreated a lavish nightclub, complete with towering podiums, cocktail bar and DJ booth, in the sand. It was also furnished with a century of the most exotic women, all in various stages of white bridal dress and undress. A combination of all these factors, plus a thousand or so goggling guys and gals, made for the most Bacchanalian of parties. Kitty and her girlfriend, having discarded all clothing bar bras and knickers, bucked and weaved, kissed and heaved to the pulsating rhythms of music and against near naked flesh.

Oddly for her, Kitty's attention was drawn to two men, moving spasmodically beneath one of the dance towers. They were about twice her age but appeared to be behaving like teenagers, clearly very high on some forbidden cocktail. One staggered dramatically to the weight of a half empty whisky bottle, the other wielded a sword. They were dressed differently to most and this made Ms Parker giggle. The lover of Scottish distillers was reeling about in the garb of an ancient Visigoth, enveloped in a huge, shaggy skin cloak with a close matching, furry and horned helmet. The other armoury expert was clad as a Roman gladiator, complete with sandals, armoured shin guards, short tunic, muscled breast plate, plumed helmet, small round shield and the aforementioned stout blade. His suntanned skin seemed slightly oiled and it glowed in the early morning sunshine. Kitty looked at his face. He looked up and caught her inquisitive gaze. She noticed that he had the same intense green eyes as her. He smiled and she felt a strange comfort. He exuded friendliness. She felt warm in a way that she was unused to from his kind.

But the moment was broken by a shriek uttered by the man in bear skins, clearly audible from their close proximity on the dancefloor. He had turned his horned head skywards to see what had disrupted him. A few feet above him, an Oriental girl with the remnants of a bridal gown hitched around her thighs, was sitting on the edge of the podium, peeing on him. She was laughing hysterically, her eyes rolling in her head under the intoxication of some wild, fungal, hallucinogen. She leant back on one arm for support whilst her other was between her naked thighs, her fingers spreading her shaven labia this way and that to direct the piss left and right, covering the hapless barbarian.

He moved sharply out of the line of fire and retreated with his gladiatorial consort towards the cocktail bar. There he stood, drunk, puzzled but slightly bemused, in the fine jetted spray of mist that the bar gently pumped out from its canopy over the drinkers and dancers beneath. Before long, his cloak was a bedraggled combination of whisky, water and urine and he excused himself to his friend before staggering off in the rough direction of his camp. Seeing the Roman alone, clearly still undecided whether he was shocked or amused, Kitty skipped up to him.

"Your poor friend!" she began. "I'm so sorry for him. That was one of the weirdest things I've seen for a very long time."

"I usually pay a lot of money for that in Soho!" The man quipped. "Don't worry about my friend, Barry, though. He can look after himself."

"Hah! I'm sure he can! He seemed to be able to simultaneously juggle whisky and pee perfectly! You're from London?" She questioned. His English accent was decidedly Port out, Starboard home. She was surprised not to hear the more familiar West Coast drawl of the majority assembly. "I've come from England too! I'm with a bunch of my best gals on a uni reunion holiday. That's my GF over there." Waves and smiles were exchanged.

"I'm from a little further west, from Wiltshire," the man continued. He thrust out his right hand, "Hello. My name's Harry."

"Wow! What a fab coincidence! I live and work in Wiltshire too! Totes cool to meet you too! Hi, Harry. I'm Kitty.

"A pleasure to meet you, Kitty." The gentleman replied in a soothing baritone. He proffered a hand which she took, appreciating that his strength was considerate not punishing like so many of his bullying sex. She noticed that strange warmth again, this time physically. She slowly shook it, he leaned forward and kissed her gently on the cheek. It flushed with heat and colour. She smiled at him and he returned a similar sign in a way that calmed and comforted her.

That day had turned into a crazy blur. After introducing Harry to her girlfriend formally, he had produced a little bag of Ecstacy tablets and proffered them.

"Hey, You Two! Have one of these little beauties between you. Half is more than enough to rave the next couple of hours away with me." The girls cracked then swallowed the MDMA tablet. "Tell me a little bit about yourselves?" Kitty logged the question. A boy that did not just want to talk about himself was a rarity. Kitty looked at her girlfriend with understanding. She wasn't prepared to share her military background in this scene of peace and love.

"This gorgeous girl works for a clothes retailer in Andover and I coordinate photography and design projects nearby."

"I should have known that you would be a fellow artist! I'm always drawn to those that are more creative."

"Oh, great. What do you do?"

" I'm a jeweller specialising in precious metals and gemstones, recycled wherever possible to contribute as little as possible to the mining process in my bid to save our beloved planet. I do all the talking, schmoozing and selling. My brother does all the designing. He is a technological wizard so all our work is digital using a combination of modern metal printing techniques and then reverting to the time honoured artisan skills of gold preparation, stone setting and metal polishing. My clients are all over the world but, due to the digital nature of our work, I usually can limit my travel to London to see this International fan club or see them at my studio in Wiltshire. The Smithy, of the traditional black variety, is now one that glitters in gold. I also represent other artists; oil painters, photographers, blacksmiths, wood sculptures and garden art. I pride myself on immersing myself in the beauty of art and the transcendental voyage of love to the universe." After this monologue, Kitty retracted her previous assumption that this boy didn't like to talk about himself. Despite this, he fascinated her. He seemed so innocent, naive and vulnerable.

They continued to dance the day away with an air of carefree abandon. They chatted incessantly. They wobbled up to the bar. He had produced another bag, this one containing miniscule diamonds. He had explained that each one was worth about one pound but that it was a fun thing to barter with at the money free event. He was clearly a hopeless romantic, seemingly lost in his various passions and he was gladly guided by the girls and their new found friendship.

Kitty caught Harry staring at her, kissing her lover. She whispered her thoughts and hatched a naughty plan with her girlfriend in secret. They both giggled. She took Harry's hand and pulled him gently towards them. She kissed him, just letting her tongue flash briefly between his lips. Her friend then muscled in and kissed him too. Having stopped their titillation, they both watched him squirm awkwardly and squealed at his gentlemanly discomfort.

"Harry," Kitty purred languorously, "We were just wondering whether you would like to come back to our tent now that the sun is setting? It is going to get freezing cold soon, you are decidedly underdressed and we thought it might be fun to warm each other up?" The part time warrior stood and stared. He opened his mouth and shut it again. His eyes had seemingly popped. "C'mon, Goldfish Boy! What do you say?"

"Yer, Yer, Yes, please," he had weakly stammered, after a long pause, before continuing with increased confidence at his perceived predicament, "I would love to!"

"Terrific! Great choice! Let's get going then!" Kitty beamed at him. The girls flanked him and linked their arms in his. "This way." She added, "It's about a twenty minute walk across the Playa."

"Lead on, Dear Ladies of My Dreams. Lead on." Harry exclaimed. He shivered to her touch. She knew not whether from the cold or excitement or both. Kitty remembered a distant history lesson at her secondary school in which the King of England, Charles the First, had done the same on his way to execution. She smiled to herself and hoped that the conclusion of their day would not be quite so dramatic. The sun disappeared behind the distant mountains. Kitty introduced the next stage of her kinky plan with a knowing look and a contrived wink behind Harry's shoulders at her fellow female conspirator.

"Harry," she questioned, "Would you mind if we made this a little more exciting for you?"

"How?" he replied. "This is about as exciting as my little life gets."

"We can do more." Kitty teased. "Can I tie a blindfold over your eyes and lead you the last couple of minutes to our love nest? We don't wish to remove it when we get there either." She had provoked him but still thought that his affirmative answer had been rather quick.

"Bring it on! I can't think of anything more exciting, right now. Life is a journey to be experimented on to the limits of decency and desire. Feel free to conduct your experiments on me!" Kitty thought that his reaction had been a little too wholehearted but, then again, who could blame him for fantasising about such a delicious menage? She looked about, pilfered a fluttering pennant from a neighbouring tent and removed his helmet. She tucked it under his bare armpit, pushed his strong, thick, dark hair back with both her hands and then tied the ribbon around his handsome face. When she had done so, she leaned forward and gave him a warm kiss on the lips until her girlfriend had giggled and pointed at the front of his tunic which had flinched. They then took his hands and led him on. Literally.

"Oh!" the girlfriend had ventured on cue, "I'm a little lost, Kitty. Do you know where our base camp is? I'm sure we're close?"

"I think we are really very close but let's not wander in circles," answered the plan's machinator. "Let's leave Our Big Brave Warrior here for two seconds while we orientate ourselves. Harry, you stay here by this roaring fire to keep warm please, Darling? You'll be nice and toasty here until we come back to heat you up even more, you sexy beast!"

"OK." said the hopelessly trusting and increasingly randy chap. "Don't be too long though please. I don't think I can take much more of this excitement!"

The girls wandered off and hid behind a tent some twenty metres away to watch their dastardly plot unfold. They had indeed left Harry by a roaring fire. What they failed to mention was that he was standing at the epicentre of the all male orgy camp. All around the fire lay, mainly naked, but exclusively men kissing, sucking and fucking each other. Alone and unaware in their writhing midst, stood a very good looking, Roman gladiator. His heavily oiled skin glistened in the dancing fire light. Within seconds those gentlemen, that weren't already engaged in their preferred form of coitus, were forming an orderly queue next to the fresh Latin meat. Very shortly afterwards, Harry was bored of waiting for the girls to return and was increasingly curious about the aural assault of slurping and slapping by lips and flesh all around him. He removed the blindfold, paused briefly to survey the homoerotic carnage, before he sprinted off into the cold darkness at great speed. The wolf pack had lost their prey.

Kitty had initially roared with laughter, her feminist plot completed to perfection and the two girls had rolled into bed. They promised each other that they would find Harry over the next couple of days to apologise and laugh it off with him and try to hook up with him back in Wiltshire. Nearly a year later, back at the Major's army desk, staring at top secret pictures of crop circles, she sighed with a twinge of melancholy for her lost friend. She actually felt sadder now not to have seen him again, more than the nearly forgotten ex-girlfriend. Harry had made an important impact on Kitty that dusty day.

The desert is a forbidding place. Roasting by day, freezing by night, she had been unaware that the wind would whip up a storm that night, making finding Harry impossible. Visibility was down to about ten metres and seeing and breathing was difficult even with the requisite ski goggles, builder's respirators, handkerchiefs or more practical gas masks. She sighed again and tidied up the papers on the Colonel's desk, filed them, turned out the light, shut the door and walked slowly out of the building. She had research to complete on both her professional and personal lives. She didn't want to do this alone. Decision made. An evening at The Bruce Arms beckoned.

'Cathy's Clown'

Despite the decibel level, there is something distinctly soothing for devotees of sedate motorcycle touring about the simple throb of a Harley Davidson's twin cylinder engine, thumping along the open road. It is said that the company patented the sound. It was with this simple audible pleasure in ear that Harry pulled the clutch lever with his left hand, tweaked the Road King's throttle with his right and clicked the peg at his left foot down into third gear, simultaneous to the start of his ascent up the steep road which curled up the north edge of his beloved valley. At the top of the one hundred metre incline, he repeated the process to second gear before applying the brakes gently, clicked into neutral and guided the heavy machine to a smooth halt at the entrance to a track off the main road.

Leaving the engine to sputter, then idle, he looked back over his shoulder and down at the enormous field below. All was calm in the Vale. The early morning's shower had been replaced by hot sunshine that had steamed, then caked, any moisture. He breathed deeply as he soaked up the sight of the breathtaking Ice Age escarpments around him, worn smooth by farmers for thousands of years. Clicking the bike back into gear, he throttled gently up the track, carefully weaving up the chalk and grass surface to avoid any sharper flints. This was not the livestock highway the 'Hog' had been designed for.

Creeping to the top of the natural incline, Harry looked across at the ancient Wansdyke before descending again, away from the force of wind and weather, into the sheltered bowl where a farm's buildings clustered cosily. On entering the stone courtyard, he directed the front wheel towards his friend's office, came to a standstill, throttled the engine in a brief but deafening roar, shut off the ignition and carefully put the side stand down. He slowly lowered the machine onto the cobbled surface until he felt sure it was balanced and then let it go. He pulled off his gloves and placed them behind the clear wind fairing, unclipped his helmet at the chin, removed it, reclipped it and hung it from the higher of the two twisted handlebars. His black leather jacket and trousers creaked as he swung his leg over the petrol tank and stood on terra firma. As he did so, the farm office door opened and a myriad of yellow dogs bounced enthusiastically out to greet him, tails wagging. Their owner was less cordial.

"Thanks a lot, you fucking twat! You'll wake the kids making a racket like that." Barrington Knave noisily exclaimed as he yawned and rubbed the sleep out of his eyes.

"I think I know which child was asleep, you knob end?" Harry retorted with well practised ease. "Another tough day on the farm then, hey? No hunting, shooting or fishing today?" They shook hands. At this contact point, Harry was reminded that Barry was the sort of chap that could shake the last few stubborn baked beans out of a tin can with extraordinary ease.

"Actually, I've got a little date with a sexy piece of chalk stream later this evening. Anyway, everybody that's anybody knows that the grouse shooting up north doesn't start until next month and our pretty little partridges and fat pheasants aren't legal until September and sportingly presentable until a month later. But I forgive you because you are clearly a nobody." Barry boasted of his intricate sporting knowledge and taunted with a knowing grin. "But first to work and then possibly back to breakfast," he added as he licked his finger and made a second attempt at the yolk removal from his favoured wildfowling tie. "C'mon, Harry. You've got my work to do. In you jump." He beckoned to his nearby pickup truck.

"You're such a fucking redneck, Barry." Kitson nodded towards the vehicle.

"Rednecks don't wear tailored three piece suits, do they, you dick?"

"Tailored when you were seven, judging by that popping waistcoat." Harry had gone for the jugular but it was too early for the kill and his prey was keen of wit and superior in strength.

"Farmers need pickup trucks, Harry, Old Chum" Barry played the soft yet slightly sarcastic tact before launching his own calculated offensive. ""When in Rome, Monsignor Kitson. When in Rome." He paused for effect. "And you do know what they drive in Rome, Harry?"

"Chariots?" Kitson knew where this was going.

"Correct. And do you know what Romans like to wear the most, Harry?"

"Togas?" was Harry's half hearted attempt at defense.

"No, no, no, no, No! They wear gladiator outfits, Harry, and they lube up and go to homosexualist orgy parties for painful sodomy, don't they, you twat?"

"I thought I was going to have a threesome with two sexy girls." Kitson glumly replied with a gulp.

"But you didn't, did you, you naive prick!" Barry pushed the metaphorical blade in deep and, clenching a fist with the central finger joint expertly raised, gave his friend a real dead arm for good measure. Harry did not retaliate. He had learnt over many years that resistance would be futile and the inevitable wrestle would result in his head being rolled in a muddy farmyard puddle of slurry. They clambered aboard the 4x4 which trundled out of the yard and the men sat stoically in silence. A little way up the field, Barry added proudly, "AND I got pissed on. Stuff of dreams." He sighed happily.

It was late July and the men were thoroughly entertained, despite their temporary lack of conversation, by the glorious natural world around them. The rolling hillocks on the high ground, once the defence systems for warring peoples, were now a lazy haze of free trading meadow flowers and drunken insects. The grass was short, nibbled by the masticating mandibles of docile sheep, so the landowner directed his vehicle easily across the dry terrain in the hot sun. The exposed areas of chalk sent up wafting waves of fine white dust, like slowly swirling smoke in an opium den, as the knobbled tyres scrunched softly across them.

The truck reached the crest of the hill and, as one after the other wheel went over the top, it lolloped and waggled slowly from side to side. The bodies of the friends followed in rhythmical time, before their heads finally caught up with the same momentum too. They stopped. Sloping away from them in a gentle bowl to the valley bottom, seemingly waving up and down with the gentle undulations of the drift downhill, which would eventually lead to the Avon stream and Kennet canal, was an enormous wheatfield. It glowed with the fire of a treasure chest in the bright light, gently swaying to the faintest of breezes. The crop was tall and the ears were full. It promised to be an early and profitable harvest.

Harry sat still in the passenger seat and gazed across the expanse of slowly heaving golden wheat, apparently hypnotised by its rise and fall, lull and ripple. His friend opened the driver door, stepped onto the running board and dropped down onto the dusty deck. He removed his tweed suit jacket and his teal tie before he threw them on the backseat. He undid a further brace of buttons on his checked shirt and rolled the sleeves messily over his forearms. They were scarred with angry red scratches from tossing hay bales into the horses' stables the evening before. He left the door ajar and walked to the back of the pickup, flipping its lid down to reveal his adoring gaggle of blond girlfriends who wagged their tails enthusiastically at the prospect of an order. They were not disappointed. With a well practised wigeon whistle, they were summoned and dutifully leapt from the flatbed to their master's side who bent down slightly to affectionately rub each one's neck in turn as they jostled for his attention.

Barry then walked up to the lowered passenger window and looked at his friend who, despite the twinkle of his bright green eyes in the sunshine, seemed lost in some distant place or thought. He smiled. Harry had never been the man for mental heavy lifting but this mysterious job had all the trappings for his simple companions, canine and comrad alike. He snapped a finger and thumb beside his chum's tanned face. Nothing. He leant in a little and gently slapped the nearest cheek, in a caring way, unlike the brutal arm treatment of a few minutes previous. Harry blinked out of his reverie.

"Hey, Weirdo." Knave whispered, "Are you having another one of those Acid flashbacks?" He paused. "Take your time, we're just going to go for a little walk whenever you're ready." Harry turned towards his pal and smiled. It was moments like this that he recognised what a lucky fellow he was having such a terrific ally. They had been through much together in over thirty years but a true friend knows which moments are best to jape and jest or sooth and supplicate. Barrington was also most handy on a pal's side during a ruck or scrap.

"Holy Hallucinogens, Batman!" Harry laughed, "I'm fine, thank you. I just got this wonderfully powerful sense of beauty and brilliance just then. It felt like some powerful magnet pulling me gently yet with strength and determination. It was stunning. So peaceful." He seemed to drift briefly again before snapping too. "C'mon then. Let's get whatever nonsense you have planned over and done with. Caped

Crusaders to the rescue!" He flattened one hand open before he lightly and quickly punched it with the rolled fist of his other, just as the red, yellow, green and black masked sidekick of a nocturnal superhero might do. Opening the door, he leapt down onto the chalk and grass terra firma, before swishing his imaginary shawl and proclaiming, "Atomic batteries to power! Turbines to speed! To the Batmobile, let's go!"

Barry walked along the edge of the field. A low brush hedge to one side, the tall crop on the other and a ten metre wide strip of unplanted stubble between them, worn by the semi circular turns of gigantic machines. They walked, breaking and bursting the dry sods beneath their size tens and a light haze of brown dust drifted away behind the pack. Every twenty metres or so, the field edge would have a clear double line disappearing ruler straight into the depths of the crop. Barry counted them aloud and when he got to the fifth he stopped and turned. He looked at his besotted fan club with his kind hazel brown eyes. When he had their attention, he pursed his lips, whistled his familiar duck call, pointed his arm down the tractor's tracks and the four hounds leapt obediently down the narrow double tunnel of huge tyre marks. He then jerked his thumb in the same direction and Harry dutifully followed the dogs. Barrington Knave took the parallel track and the two compadres strode, waist deep in gold, a couple of metres apart into the heart of lightness.

Harry's mind drifted again. Easily done for such an absent minded and relaxed individual but this seemed strangely different. The further he walked down this seemingly endless Roman road of agriculture, the more he felt the same bewitching pull to peace and calm. What was pulling him forward in this trance? What was happening to him? He was jolted out of his trance, this time not by Barry's slap but by the yelping of a dog some distance ahead, hidden by the sea of burnt yellow. The eldest of the pack soon honed into view, her mouth open, tongue lolling and a thick foam of spittle encased her gums. Her eyes were wide as she sought her master and her tail was curled submissively back between her legs. She stopped and sat on the same appendage behind Barry's knees, whining pleadingly, looking up at him whilst occasionally glancing nervously in the direction she had bolted from.

"Hey, Tinker." He soothed. "What's the matter? Have those others been bullying you again? Come on, You Silly Sausage. You'll be fine. Heal." Barry continued his amble but the dog did not follow as commanded. It sat. "C'mon, Tinker!" He added louder this time. The dog turned its snout away and whimpered. "Tinker!" Barry now shouted but the animal just started to bark at him and got up and feigned movement in the opposite direction. When the barking had subsided, Barry addressed his old schoolmate with concern. "She's really freaked out, Harry. You carry on. I'll catch up with you in ten minutes after I've dropped her back at the car." He turned and walked in the other direction. "C'mon, Girl! Heal!" The aged mutt bounced to his side, the tail extended in its more natural direction then resumed its former wagging with gusto and gladness. The pair returned up the track.

Harry watched them go. He turned around again and was immediately hit by the soothing wave of emotion that had preceded the canine cacophony. He walked forward. After thirty metres or so, he noticed that the track opened up and saw, waiting quietly at the entrance, the other three labradors, one sitting and two laying on the arable floor, lazing calmly in the warm sunshine. He stopped at this gateway and surveyed the scene. It surprised him greatly.

He stood on the edge of a large, maybe ten metre wide circle, bordered by a near upright wall of wheat. The crop had been flattened from the centre to the wall in a dramatic spiralling clockwise pattern. It was as if a tornado had just touched down and left its twisted print. He stepped inward. As he did so, he was hit by a surge of energy that pulsated through his body, similar but far stronger than the recent car then walk experiences.

He felt joy. It seemed to massage him to the core and he felt alive, more vibrantly than he had ever considered before. He glowed with the power and warmth that enveloped him. This pressure was not claustrophobic. It made him feel free. It reminded him of the sensation he had experienced when he encountered the glowing ball of energy on his walk to Pewsey Carnival the year before. This was just far stronger. He raised his arms above his head and very slowly pirouetted in the direction of the spiral movement. He was overcome by a harmonious force rippling through his very soul. It felt incredible.

Something was drawing him in and it felt peaceful. He sensed liberation. He walked, mesmerised and intoxicated, forward, carefully treading onto the swirls, over the centre and to the far wall which he looked over. There was a similar yet smaller circle, with an identical spiral pattern adjoining his and, tiptoeing, he thought he could see another one beyond it. He looked to his left. He looked to his right. Both confirmed his previous assumptions. At a distance of ten metres or so from him on either side were the wheat walls of three identical circles that were decreasing in size to a centre point. He was gobsmacked. But then something else drew his attention and he stared in awe and wonder. The crop between the circles had been flattened too. But this was entirely different to the cyclone swishes within them. The stems of about twenty to thirty plants had been grouped into straight lines and flaxed in a seemingly endless interwoven criss cross of perfect weave. It looked like a basket. Unlike an object of raffia work, the area Harry was looking at must have been ten metres long and wide.

He sank to his knees dumbfounded by the immensity of the form. Harry held his hands to his head and let the tidal wave of euphoria overcome him. He shut his eyes, threw his arms forward and placed his hands carefully in front of him, like a supplicant to a familiar Eastern religion. His fingers began to tingle. He opened his eyes and looked at his hands. The skin had darkened and felt numb. It felt marvellous and he let them seemingly mesh with the earth beneath him. He studied the stems around him. Nothing was broken. The thousands and thousands of plants around him were bent into these extraordinary shapes. Just bent. He mused aloud to himself and chuckled, "How in a world of commercial cereals and business bakeries could this possibly happen?" It was unimaginable to his fragmented mind. But there was more to confuse the hapless soul. Deposited amongst the swirls, were piles of snow white powder. Harry lay back and stared at the blue skies above as his mind catapulted into a quantum leap of confusion and chaos. Where was Barry? Where was his journeyman, his buddy, his partner in crime? He shivered at the sight of the white powder.

'Blue Boy'

The boys had started their mission into debauchery together when they were at school. The few underage alcoholic tinnies they had innocently enjoyed during the first sprouts of puberty had escalated over time and circumstance. The defining feature of this early adventure into toxicity was that it was innocent fun. Everybody smoked cigarettes. It was legal, a bonanza of taxation for governance, but nobody warned them that nicotine is significantly stronger than heroin by volume and it will kill you very, very slowly. The 1980s can be remembered by some for glue sniffing. Most that indulged can't though. Trichloromethane, smuggled from the chemistry lab, seemed a far more pure and sophisticated alternative for our schoolboy anti heroes. Those were the days when the lads inadvertently punched massive holes in the ozone layer and their briefly intelligent brains, breathed in deodorant aerosol gases through a towel, convulsed into giggles.This resulted in wild heat rushes and sometimes collapse, before they repeated the cycle of planetary and mental destruction. The next conundrum they faced was whether to smoke slate or grass when they cycled up to the Ridgeway to score dope from the local travelling community. After purchase, hair was grown, drain pipes were shinned down at night, expert reefer rolling was mastered and more school grades were expensively flushed down the proverbial plughole.

Alcohol, particularly the 'Yard of Ale' initiation ceremony after First XV rugby matches or the '18th Birthday Beer Challenge', probably tipped them over the edge at an early age. The latter rite of passage was particularly galling. The birthday boy had to secretly consume a case of beer, twenty four cans, during the day. A couple before breakfast, a couple after, a couple more at break. Et cetera. Ad infinitum. All day. Add it up. It's a lot. Especially when one was trying to read Shakespeare in a play rehearsal or flick a penalty in a hockey match. Drinking was seen as a social must, not the start of an addiction that ruins lives. It has been previously mentioned that Harry and Barry, despite their obvious propensity for the wilder things in life, did actually complete their A levels before they hurled themselves at the mercy of Lysergic Acid. The only saving grace for both these towers of Bacchanalian strength was that they did not appear to let their parents down, now significantly more impoverished by the previous ten years of school fees, and achieved respectable grades. They had learnt to live a lie.

After a brief separation during gap years, the formidable friends teamed up again for their assault on Manchester University. Despite the occasional come down session at Severe, a Fallowfield dive where beer bottles were a pound on student night, alcohol took a back seat whilst increasingly complicated concoctions of far more dangerous chemicals were created. The LSD came in various strengths and a kaleidoscope of pictures on the cardboard tabs warned the buyer of their impending trip. A Purple Ohm was the standard bearer with the Hindu symbol in deep pink. Easy. At the other end of the psychedelic spectrum, the druidical Getafix picture was perforated into four quarters. Nobody digested all four corners of the wizard and resumed a lifetime of sanity.

Throw into the mixture some raw amphetamin and the boys could stay up for a weekend. A dab here of white Billy Whizz or another there of Pink Champagne and the dance frenesity was accelerated in synchronicity with the intensity of the acid trip in the brain. Slate and grass had been replaced by a myriad choice of exotic and far stronger high breds. Moroccan Gold, Red Lebanese and Kashmiri Charice helped the lads chill out after days of decadent exertion. Just in case a further pick me up was required, weed had been tuned up, like a race car engine, into mind bending super skunk varieties, like Northern Lights and Cross Haze, and, coupled with a few shots of dirty, filthy Mexican tequila, dance floors could be reconquered with devastating efficiency.

The not so ancient proverb, "What goes up, must come down," is true to a degree, especially if referenced to one in Geography and the other in Comparative Religion. Maybe the minds of Classics or Science students are made of sterner stuff but on a trip to Trip in the Peak District, too much was taken. The previously indestructible Barrington had been reduced to a naked shivering wreck, cocooned in an embryonic pose, who questioned the very substance of everything he loved. He snapped out of his foetal state shortly before the hallucinating, stand in, driver and devoted friend, Harry, had arrived at the hospital. Once home, all was well again after a nice cup of empire building sweet tea and an episode of their favourite Aussie soap on TV. The mind is like a Slinky toy. Once it is bent out of shape, it never quite slides along as smoothly and efficiently ever again. It hiccups on the staircase and stops. The boys gave up LSD then and there. They had escaped the heaven and the hell that let so many others sore high and so many more dive so very low.

Another not so ancient proverb is, " You can't keep a good man down." These two fellows were no exception. Rationalising correctly that the cocktail of acid, speed, skunk and alcohol was not going to provide a stable future backdrop for their all night revels, they retreated to safer ground. Ecstasy, for those that are uninitiated, is the greatest drug ever created. Or that's what the boys felt when they started popping pills in the early 1990s. Whether at a regular club night at the 'Hacienda', a sporadic student 'Pollen' party or an enormous free rave in the countryside, one thing was a beautiful constant. Methylenedioxy-methamphetamine, MDMA or Ecstasy. For obvious reasons, Barry and Harry gravitated to the latter two names more suited to their simplistic vocabulary. In the same linguistic vein, they eventually settled on 'E'. In reactionary terms, it was the perfect drug. It was the best of all their worlds.

Approximately forty-five minutes after oral ingestion, the Class A creates the first ripples and shivers through the body. A warmth spreads from fingers and toes, down the limbs, through the body, tickles the back of the neck, flushes the cheeks and explodes the brain into a dystopian euphoria. Movements become a fluid extension of loving thoughts. Dancing is suddenly the sexiest, asexual, manifestation of pure truth (and therefore lies) as the false composite grips the mind and body. Music fuels it. Stroboscopic lights, laser beams and rainbow filters influence it in a hallucinogenic way that seems blissful, yet controllable, unlike the rollercoaster chaos of acid. These energy rushes ebb and flow like a powerful riptide in knee deep water. The celebrant soars and flies, briefly stoops and falls, gradually getting higher and higher, gyrating in a rhythm of perceived passion and energetic movement. This can last for hours and hours then, slowly slowly, this elongated process of time and reaction is reversed back to a state of relative normality. Unless one took another one.

Kitson and Knave quite often had another one. And another one. Weekends were mostly lost to the memory in the fog of Ecstasy. This was a behavioural pattern that would continue for the best part of their lifetimes. Sure, post student inconveniences, such as work, marriage and children, eventually slowed the ingestion rate significantly but fun is fun. The short term effects of MDMA are still a multiple hour commitment and those time slots just got fewer and shorter. Alcohol reared its ugly head once more. It bared its teeth briefly and then skulked back to the shadows from where it dominated. This socially accepted brand of self destruction was far easier to get away with, especially when coupled with the more occasional pulsating bliss of an E. This dynamic duo of debauch, whether at Old Trafford football or Twickenham rugby or Lords cricket matches, Stone Roses pop or Rolling Stones blues or Lee Scratch Perry ska concerts, Glade or Glastonbury or Burningman festivals, Pewsey or Notting Hill or Trinidad carnivals, fizzed and popped. Boom.

Mankind's shape shifts to adapt to circumstances. When not partaking in these longer events, a shorter term high was required by our erstwhile revellers for a regular night out. The first time Barry and Harry witnessed cocaine consumption, they were still studying for their Bachelor of Arts. Another schoolmate, also then at The Victoria University, had invested fifty pounds in this rare form of exotica. At the time, 'Columbian Marching Powder' was the staple diet of over worked, over paid, jumped up London and New York City traders. Clad in blue pinstripe suits, shirts with plain white fronts, collars and cuffs yet with multi-coloured and multi-patterned mismatching sleeves, shoulders and back sections. In addition they wore requisite red braces or suspenders, a hideously bright tie and an oversized, brick shaped, newly invented, mobile telephone completed the ensemble. The cocaine fiend was easy to spot.

This rare and aggressive financial animal was not present at that particular student house party in Manchester. Which was why Barry, when he saw the enormous chopped out line of white powder winking at him beneath a cheap floral shaded lamp on a grotty side table, thought, firstly, that it must be cheap Billy and, secondly, it funny to grab a note and hoof the whole firework party up his greedy nostril in one. The results were spectacular. Barry, already tipsy, frisky, jumpy and rushy, was elevated to a new state of Nirvana as fast as a medieval trebuchet launches a skipping unicorn over an enchanted castle. His friend Julio, already tipsy, frisky, jumpy and rushy, was subjugated to a new state of bankruptcy as fast as a medieval trebuchet launches a dead, diseased horse over broken battlements. Within two heartbeats, both seriously accelerated, one was incredibly high on drugs, the other was low on meagre student funds.

Throughout their twenties and thirties, both men continued to enjoy a lively social relationship with copious quantities of booze, a liberal supplement of Gianluca Vialli and the occasional wobbly egg(E).

Despite these occasional over exertions, they generally led balanced lives. Sport and work gave their bodies and brains a counter to the weekend chaos. They both reached relative peaks of responsibility in their chosen vocations, making good money, one managing grand estates and a farm, after his father's retirement, the other his family's jewellery business. Harry's devotion to the Great God Nepot has already been referred to. During this time, it became apparent that the two were made of the same metal. If we use a goldsmith's analogy, they both had very different purities. Barry could be seen as eighteen carat white gold. Pure gold is twenty four carat. Eighteen carat white gold is eighteen parts gold and six parts alloy, including palladium for colour and titanium for strength. Barry's metaphorical composite was handsome, white and strong. Harry was pure gold. Hopelessly romantic but far too soft.

In happy times, this was a useful blend. At the Millenium, they joined thirty four other friends, hired six boats and sailed around Antigua for two weeks. There was very limited sailing experience between the three dozen voyagers, or rather pirates as their devotion to fancy dress so proved. The picture postcards of Caribbean beaches are very true. White sands, palm trees, tranquil turquoise lagoons. Antiguas' tourist board boasts a beach for every day of the year. It is beautiful. Unfortunately, for this party of brigands, to access these paradisiacal hotspots by sail, the rocky reef had to be navigated and the worryingly tempestuous swell of the sea had to be conquered. For the uninitiated, this is frankly terrifying. Barry took to the helm. Harry took to the cocktails. Despite a few narrow escapes and scraped hulls, it was a miracle that the miniature fleet arrived safely into port at Nelson's old stomping ground, English Harbour.

The pirate's dinghy raid on the distinguished, colonial yacht club was met with great celebration and mirth by the resident expat community on Millenium night. The renegades laid down their plastic weapons and an alliance was made with the nautical fraternity in the mutual interest of celebrating wildly. One of Harry's most lasting memories of the night, indeed one of his last memories, was his dear University chum, Byron, chatting to the Club Commissar and his wife. She was about fifty five years old with hair that she had given up trying to dye. The sun seemed to have given her greying blond shoulder length locks a most elegant lift. She wore a sleeveless, pale, floral long dress with pretty, strapped, white, kitten heeled shoes. Her husband was probably ten years older and was dressed exactly as a gentleman of his esteemed position should do. Blue double breasted blazer, white slacks, deck shoes and shirt, a natty cravate and a splendid captain's hat complete with gold embroidered anchor emblem above the stiff peak. They were engaged in a seemingly polite and protracted conversation with 'Lord' B. He pinched a red Marlboro in the fingers of one hand and clutched a bottle of French fizz in the other. He was dressed in nothing. Despite his decision to enjoy welcoming in the next thousand years naked, the charming couple did not even bat an eyelid. Harry laughed. His mirth would be short lived though.

Harry sat down on a high stool next to a female friend who's metiers were film production and outlandish fun. He ordered them both a sweet, fruit and rum based shot to drink. They downed them. She ordered another pair and suggested that they laid some money on who could drink the most. Despite his many vices, Harry was not a gambling man. However, the emboldening strength of the alcohol, one of his genuine crutches, made him forget and he accepted. In the blink of an eye, the shots competition had aroused considerable interest from the sailing community. A book was opened and the bar descended into the sort of bedlam akin to a bear pit with bank notes hastily changing hands. In a world of sexual equality, it should not matter when a girl drinks a boy under the table. But when Harry awoke twenty four hours later, it did to him.

What mattered even more was that he had lost a whole day of his life for the most ridiculous and banal of reasons. The rapid progression from drunken semi-twilight to that black space, that nothingness, that meaningless hulk of vapid emptiness, is something that alcoholics often experience. It did produce, for what is also frequent in those that drink themselves into a dark stupor, a rare moment of clarity. Harry Kitson languished in the quagmire of hopelessness that his rash actions had resulted in. After a decimation of all comparative religions at university, Harry craved more than the texts and dictats he had been told to follow in childhood, studies, society and news. He looked out over the turquoise lagoon where the boats were moored, thanked the powers of nature for this beauty and his life and thought as deeply as he could that there must be more to it all than the recent loss of time and the pounding headache that he experienced at that exact moment. He pondered more. He looked beyond the reef and up into the perfect blue skies above. Surely there was something infinitely more perfect in the universe beyond than his personal insular sorrow and the seeming perfection of the Caribbean cove immediately surrounding his pain?

Harry had previously been proud of his drinking skills. His fellow pirates took great pleasure in recounting his spectacular nose dive from the stool. The double cuts in his forehead, that still throbbed so badly, were explained by his broken sunglasses that had embedded in his head in connection with the concrete floor. Initial attempts to slap him back to consciousness were abandoned. One rational genius built a thick, white, train track of Bogata Express and blew it up Harry's nose with a drinks straw. It had apparently worked spectacularly. The drunkard had reared off the deck, eyes bulging, roared like a wounded tiger and dashed out of the club bar, straight into the swimming pool where he sank like a stone. In the blink of an eye, Barry had dived to the bottom and pulled out his once more unconscious friend. It was decided that sleep would be a better long term revival technique, rather than the previous illegal pharmaceutical one. So the limp fop was hoisted from beach to dinghy to yacht to bunk. In human terms, Barry's heroics and Harry's stupidity exemplify the difference between eighteen and twenty four carat gold. Harry Kitson was a rare and vulnerable precious product of this earth. But that was not enough for him. There must be more than all this he questioned? Like so many artists trying to perfect their fragile qualities, Harry would only start learning about his true destiny after he had plunged further into the hellish pit of human entrapment, despair and depression. For the meantime, the infinite beauty and love beyond would have to wait.

'Barbwire'

The Noughties saw the two Naughties grow up a little bit. Marriage and children entered the fray. Apart from the occasional hoof of coke after dinner with friends and the even rarer E at middle aged raves in the garden, everything was far more settled. Quite right too. A healthy adoration of finer wines smoothed the rougher edges of their lives of privilege whenever necessary. But good and bad marriages affect a chap differently. Barry's was a happy one. Harry's was not. He began drinking heavily, making sure he was semi-inebriated before he got home. It seemed to cushion the barrage of constant shouting and verbal abuse. But what did come first, the chicken or the egg? He knew it was time to leave her after an evening with another alcoholic friend, to whom he poured his heart out and poured multiple bottles of vin rouge in. When Harry awoke the next day, he was cold. This was explained by his lack of any clothing and his location on the wrong side of the house door. His clothes were draped over walls and shrubs. They were purple and brown. Harry hoped that it was he that had hung them there, after he had simultaineously puked and shat himself in his unconscious delirium. That was the nail in the coffin of that brief marital experience. He walked away to face the inevitable consequences.

The slightly longer divorce period was an even tougher test of Harry's metal. Due to his previously discussed pliable and soft composite, he failed this legal test miserably. He was now broke and drunk, his former existence in tatters around him. His friends and clients took pity on him, offering sofa surfing and brand loyalty. As settlements were agreed, the housing market collapsed and the cottage was plunged into negative equity. Deals were made regarding property, finances and the child. By a miracle, Harry kept his beloved home and access to its heir. This was the glimmer of hope he needed.

But Harry was a slow witted and irrational fellow, as we have witnessed on multiple occasions already, so it took him rather a long time to fully understand this blinding chink of light. In the meantime, his classic mid life crisis was in full swing. He resurrected his Harley. Frugal home cooking and walking to work on visits to London, justified Harry's financial expenditure, in his own vapid mind, on Filthy Dirty Martinis and filthy dirty cocaine, physically on filthy dirty dancing and filthy dirty sex. Mayfair nights were initially fuelled by cheap booze and token quantities of bolstering food in local hostelries, before the descent to his private members clubs' lavish dance floor for cocktails and cha cha cha. His innocent nature and propensity to overindulge made mornings a blur of hangovers and kinkiness at the mercy of Russian oligarchs' wives, European industrialists' daughters or Indian entrepreneurs' heiresses.

But it was a wild escape from the reality of his various addictions and was also entirely unsustainable in money and mental terms. Harry's finances buckled and his brain melted. Before long, Harry was holed up, alone, at home in Wiltshire, a far cry from the decadence of central London. He split his life into an extraordinary juxtaposition. For two or three days a week, he detoxed due to his commitments to his son, the true love of his life. The rest of the time, his toxic routine seemed a natural progression as he slunk closer and closer to the jaws of total dependence and unassailable depression.

The night before Barry's singular circular distress call to Harry, the latter had drowned himself in his, now usual, devotion to the merciless demons of self pity. Harry had already been touched by the divine in the stubble that previous autumn but he could not break the bondages of his addictions. A normal night at home started with the purchase of some often untouched food, twelve cans of cheap, strong cider, a box of matches, a pouch of tobacco, some rolling papers, menthol filters and a couple of grams of cocaine. Cider was poured over ice into a glass and placed on the table in front of the television. Minty cigarettes were rolled, the window was opened ajar and a seat and ashtray were placed nearby. A plate was heated in the microwave and, on removal, one of the drug wraps was carefully unfolded, its contents emptied atop the warm surface and placed on the dining table. This helped dry the sometimes moist Class A chalk. A card of worthless function, never a bank, credit or driving licence for paranoid fear of detection, was used to separate a sizable section from the small white mountain of powder. The flat side of the plastic was used to crush any rocks within the compound. Then the edge of the card scraped a mini mound to one side which in turn was racked into half a dozen lines or so. A new receipt was rolled into a tube. Never banknotes because paranoid fear also dictates that they all have traces of other users' blood which might contain hepatitis. Two of the more sizable lines were initially selected and double barrels were administered up each nostril . That initial hit was the relief that a drug fiend demands and needs. A cigarette was lit. Cider was sipped. The TV was turned on.

In the absence of glamorous girls from the club, Harry had adapted his rampant sexual appetite, heightened by the drug, with glamorous girls from an alternate reality, of the two dimensional kind. The adult section of the televisual menu provided a good selection of near naked women of various dubious to false to beautiful constructs. Their profession was to entice viewers to call the telephone number at the base of the screen, at vast expense, so that they could talk dirty to them whilst the callers wanked themselves blind and the porn and mobile companies robbed them similarly.

Harry was daft. But not that daft. He didn't call. Besides, they never showed anything too revealing beyond their often plasticised breasts and crossed legs. Harry was an experienced fellow. He needed more than that. After listening to an array of regional British girls begging him to call, Harry turned down the volume. He then had a glug of cold alcoholic apple juice, walked to the table, hoofed two more lines of Charlie, walked to the window, sat down and smoked another cigarette whilst watching a delectable creature called Alice on Babestation. He felt the first tentative twitch from the depths of his boxer shorts.

He returned to the sofa having hoiked his jeans down over his ankles and removed his socks. He flipped open his laptop and turned it on, checking out Alice whilst the computer warmed up. He loaded Safari and clicked on File then New Private Window. He typed in You Porn and waited for the site to load. Once it had, he clicked on Categories and sat back in earnest consideration. He needed to think so, had a slug of drink, a line of coke and lit a cigarette taking the dilemma with him on the short journey to the window via the table. He racked his brain. Anal, Big Butt, Big Tits, Blonde, Blowjob, Bondage, Brunette, Creampie, Double Penetration, Face Sitting, Femdom, Fingering, Fisting, Footjob, Foreplay, Hairy, Kissing, Masterbation, Orgy, Panties, Penetration, Pissing, Public, Pussy Licking, Redhead, Rimming, Rough Sex, Shaved, Small Tits, Squirting, Striptease, Teen, Threesome and Young/Old. All had to be carefully considered. Harry went back to A. That was always the simplest for a chap of limited intellect. He briefly marvelled at how anal sex had become part of his own erotic pantheon thanks to the world wide web. It certainly hadn't been a consideration after school dances thirty years before.

With all the porno pieces of his chess set assembled, Harry reached inside his chequerboard boxer shorts, pulled out the King, glanced at all the Pawns, raised the Castle drawbridge with the sole intent to bash the Bishop far into the Knight. One of the main disadvantages of cocaine abuse, apart from likening the adventure to a board game, is erectile malfunction. Despite feeling like a rampant sex god, this message is often lost in translation by the time it reaches the cock and balls. There are two ways to play the game. One is all out assault. With the right quantity of perverse thought, coupled with a furious wrist tempo, the semi flaccid appendage can be briefly man handled to a state of near full erection and premature ejaculation. The other method is the long game. This takes enormous amounts of discipline and self control as it requires a near constant grip on the situation. Concentration is integral as frequent missions to the loo, fridge, table or window to pee, drink, snort or puff tend to put one off one's stroke. Harry always played the long game.

It took him approximately eight and a half hours to finish the two grams of cocaine. He rarely finished the cider cans or tobacco pouch, which was a good thing because, if he had, he would have climbed the walls before getting into his car and driven off on an ill advised trip to the closest twenty four hour convenience store. Apart from the television stations, Harry had flitted joyfully, high on a plateau of his own deviant concoction, between the unholy trinity of You Porn, Porn Hub and Porn Tube on his computer.

Sharp and alert in the depths of the night, the quick witted fool engaged his smartphone into proceedings so that he had three devices which simultaineously displayed the erotica that helped him maintain a mediocre, half blooded erection. His near continuous efforts were ably assisted by some luxurious organic lavender oil for the duration of this masterbatory marathon. Harry felt a mixture of panic and relief on the final consumption of every spec of white powder. The addict always cleaned up thoroughly. The receipt was unrolled and licked. The two card drug packets were unfolded and licked. A dampened finger was run caressingly around the plate and licked. All gone. Panic over, for now.

Relief time. Having carefully maintained a semi erect cock for the previous third of the clock, he turned out the lights downstairs and settled into his bed after an ascent up the short flight of spiralled, wooden, rickerty steps in the Smithy. One of the best things about taking loads of coke is that, as the effects dissipate, the male penis engorges to rock hard perfection. For Harry, this was playtime. His mind was splintered by the drug and pornography in a wild mesh of fantasy that he grouped together into this brief window of physical self punishment. His stale, sweet mouth cried out and moaned with pleasure as his nicotine stained fingers slid their dirty oily mastery up and down his solid shaft, faster and faster, until he exploded. All the sexual frustrations that he had accumulated burst from the depths of his swollen balls. He lay panting on the sweat drenched sheets until his body shivered as the moisture on his skin cooled and the drug wormed its way out of his mind.

He pulled up the duvet. He looked at the clock on his phone. 05:37. He swiped his finger to the calendar. He witnessed his earliest morning agenda. '10:00 Philly Bagshawe - ring fitting.'

"Bollocks." Harry muttered aloud and fittingly. He thumbed the screen out of Calender and back to Clock where he pressed Alarm and selected 09:20, having mentally worked out the timing of his journey backwards from studio to coffee to bath to bed. "Fuck" he added sagedly, "Four hours of Captain Kippage".

But that was wishful thinking. Like all cocaine devotees, he had temporarily forgotten the horror of the dive that inevitably follows the soaring flight. It was getting light so he jumped up and shut the door to the bedroom and sealed the curtains tight. The normally quiet high street outside was a fulcrum of traffic through the village and the rush hour for hardworking folk had already started in earnest. Every gentle engine hum, or the sedate dawn birdsong chorus between, seemed vastly amplified in his accelerated delirium. The cacophony of racing cars and squawking crows terrified him. He wrapped the duvet around his ears and eyes, just allowing his sizable proboscis to poke out to sift the air to breathe.

Having dampened the sound of the big bad world, Harry then focused on his tortured self. The doubts then came into his eggshell mind. His shattered life. His job. His home. His son. Smoking. Drinking. Drugs. He heard every breath in his throat. He felt sick.

His head throbbed. He could feel his blood pulse. He panicked at the wildly accelerated rate of his fast beating heart. His skin burst open in a torrent of sweat until the pillow beneath his head and duvet that wrapped his body were drenched. He pulled the goose down cover off his bedraggled torso and the exaggerated perceptions of bright light and deafening noise assaulted him once more. As the cool air hit his soaking body, he shivered violently.

Class A users refer to this moment as 'The 4am Luge'. You are freezing cold. You metaphorically launch yourself down an ice track, feet first on a tiny sled. You lift your head to try and see each corner that rushes towards you. Your eyes pop. Your heart races. Your body shakes uncontrollably to the chatter of the packed ice beneath you. You try to steer a course, to slow down, but you are at the mercy of the mountain. Tears stream from your eyes. Your hands, feet and limbs go numb. You are out of control. Suddenly the incline changes. You start slowing down. You dig your heels in. Your legs wobble. You stop. You are drenched in sweat. You shiver as the liquid condenses. You thank a greater power that you are still alive.

At the lowest of ebbs, Harry Kitson reached out for that higher force. The artificial deconstructs of the drug seesawed crazily with the perfect nature of the universe. The very powers of good and evil battled within his fragmented mind. His very self destruction at this point, even that of his once beautiful planet, just seemed like some horrific inevitability, a foregone conclusion, despite the clear cut warnings that shouted within his skull.

"You can do this! Free yourself! Free your slave masters! Free their people! Free your planet! Listen to the signs. Everything is now in your peoples' hands. Release them from their bondage. Throw aside their captors!"

Harry grasped wildly at the memory of the light orb that had touched him in the stubble field the year before, submitting himself to the inevitable truth.

"Thank you for saving me! Show me the way! Save us from this misery!"

Harry was wide awake and shaking uncontrollably. He had been in these moments of confused delirium before. He got up, staggered to the bathroom, waverly peed in the porcelain then gulped down a glass of water in one. He filled up the receptacle again and, sipping it slowly, took a double strength ibuprofen pink pill to sooth his aching head and body. He returned to bed. He deliberately slowed his breathing down. Deep and slow, measured and controlled. His heart slowed. His cock grew. Splashing some oil on his hands, he rubbed his hardening shaft and massaged his balls and arsehole. He gently worked his pole, letting his mind slip into the realms of fantasy once more. He marvelled at it's rigidity, such a short time since he had last exploded, and revelled in the delights that his brain conjured. Slowly, slowly he continued his tender manual caresses until his hips bucked and his throat moaned in the shuddering grip of orgasm. He sighed. He panted softly. He shut his eyes. He felt the comforting wave of painkillers sooth his core. He relaxed. He slept.

'Cupid'

Harry was awakened from his deep slumber by a gentle prodding to his groin which he realised was rock hard and straining at the confines of his black leather motorcycle jeans. He felt the soft mattress of folded wheat against his back. He opened his eyes. He was staring directly up into the blue skies of a perfect July afternoon. The drug induced horrors of the night before seemed like a distant memory. The sun away to the west warmed his tanned face. Harry was distracted by something in the sky above him. Fifty metres up he saw an object hovering. That seemed weird. He looked down at his trouser flies. A yellow labrador hound lay next to him, it's heavy head resting on his balls. He sat up. His cock softened. He laughed aloud. That was weirder.

"Hello, Handsome", said a familiar voice behind him. "It looks like somebody is well up for a spot of bestiality. If you try to make love to my beautiful blond girlfriend, I'll kill you." Knave was pulling and pushing the controls of a radio control unit. Within seconds, he had skillfully dropped the four rotor drone to a few feet in front of him, hovering, before he shut it slowly down and landed it gently on their flattened tapestry of interwoven plant stalks.

"Jesus, Barry!" Harry ejaculated, "What the fuck is going on. I didn't sleep much last night. I went to Hell and back. Now I wake up and feel as if I have just been to Heaven on a one way ticket. Everything is weird but perfect. How are you feeling?" He sat up and turned towards his friend.

"Fine." Knave answered before explaining, "I was up at the truck looking after Tinker and when she had calmed down I came back here and you were fast asleep. You have been slumbering like a sloth for about the last five hours and I've been pottering around taking pictures of this beauty with my son's drone. What about you? How do you feel? What do you think of her?" He waved his arm in a large circle at their immediate surroundings.

"I'm dumbstruck", answered Kitson.

"You always are, you useless dreamer", Barry answered, quick as a flash, before he paused, then apologised. "I'm sorry, Mate. Old habits die hard, like my dog and your prick. Really? Tell me? How do you feel?"

"I feel incredible", Harry sighed. "I have prided myself in pushing the borders of my body and soul to their extremities and the last few hours, five you say, have been like a seamless run up, hop, skip and jump that has cleared all the sand in the triple jump pit and I'm still flying and observing it from above."

"Gosh. That good?"

"That good." Harry paused, deep in thought. He exhaled softly and calmly. " Bazza? I know you know me better than most, so hope that you can understand what this is all about for me? I feel like I am at a crossroads in my life at this very second. All the fun and naughtiness of my past has been driving me towards this time and place. This experience comes just twelve hours after I reached rock bottom of the St Moritz Cresta Run."

" You mean the 4am Luge again? You stupid bloody idiot! You can't keep destroying yourself. It's time to pull yourself together, Man!" There was heartfelt affection in the farmer's tone.

"I agree, Barry. I'm not sure that I believe in fate but being drawn to my Smithy originally, losing it and my mind in divorce, regaining it through recession and sadness, establishing myself in this Vale and having that extraordinary experience with the burning light ball, now suddenly all have a reason.

"Today has been an epiphany in my life. As I sat in the car earlier, looking over this field, I physically could not see this creation but I felt the warmth of its energy from afar. I was being pulled to its source. When Tinker bolted, I still felt no fear. Everything can react differently to forces in nature. She was scared. When I got to this circle and saw the other dogs in a state of calm, I willingly stepped inside and was enveloped by the most mind blowing power surge. To feel my body numb and brain relax, at the very heart of this perfect art, was unbelievable. Maybe it was just the after effects from a crazy night? Maybe it was something far greater?

"Its stalk swirls and wiry weaves are like the most beautiful moments in a hallucinogenic trip. The tidal wave of energy that soothed my limbs was better than any Ecstacy rush. The eroticism of my dreams and the subsequent physical result were more sensual and harder than that conjured by any blue diamond shaped pill. The peace in my slumber was more tranquil and lucid than one imagined in an opium den. The only time I freaked out was seeing the little piles of white powder and I now understand that it was just my fear of something else. Something I have a big problem with. But this is all natural! This has nothing to do with the drugs that we use to accelerate or heighten our emotions. This is the raw power of the universe and I am inextricably bound to it now."

"Hallelujah! Praise the Lord, Brother!" Barry mocked and briefly raised his hands in supplication. "How come I do not feel the same thing then? Sure, it is one of the most beautiful things I have ever seen but why haven't I felt those sensations?"

"I don't know, Barry." His friend answered, then paused, before continuing with some effort, due to the recent brain overload. "I'm guessing that, like Tinker's negative and my positive reaction, yours is a neutral one because we are all different. One thing is for sure. We have a new hobby to learn about! Or maybe we could call it a new religion, if the ultimate power throughout the universe in nature could be called God?"

Harry had come a long way, very slowly, over a minefield of misunderstanding, retracing his steps and following new and often misleading paths, to come to such a dramatic divine and cosmic conclusion. Baptised as a son of Middle England he was groomed into the native church from an early age. Sunday school taught him to love one's neighbour and the beauty of storytelling. The epic tale of war, slavery, passion and forgiveness, justified its position at the top of the all time best sellers list. Traipsing to church or chapel, whatever the weather, between the ages of seven and eighteen had cemented his faith in the God of his Hebrew and Christian forefathers. Such was his dedication to the cause that, after some heightened training in matters beyond us, as an early teeenager he was confirmed into the fold by the Bishop of Salisbury. Taking this truth for granted, Harry just initially enjoyed singing a hymn or two, reading from that book and immersing himself in thought during prayer. It was comforting and gave him hope.

His gradual fall, at his Satanic Majesty's request, has already been documented but you do not need to be a scientist to work out that falsely elevating yourself to a higher sense of consciousness, using an amalgamation of man made chemicals, is not the route to divine liberation. Harry's stumblings were exasperated when he went to college to study Arabic and Comparative Religion. The Arabic did not last long. Having acquired a moderate interest in the Middle East on his gap year travels, the basic language course, coupled with the religious, was the perfect gateway into the Acid House scene that he coveted most in Manchester.

Naturally expecting to be taught his A, B, Cs, 1, 2, 3s, Kitson was nonplussed to discover that ninety five percent of the course participants were already fluent Arabic speakers. The weak lecturer was manipulated by the brethren into reading the Quran from day one. Harry floundered and dropped out under the linguistic, political and religious pressures. The students were a hotbed of fundamental thinking Islamists and, when the young, sometime Christian, Englishman refused to join them for American flag burning and twisted prayer, he was ostracised. This was nearly ten years before like minded thinkers flew planes into New York towers. Even then, secret interest was being shown in their activities. As one of very few native Britons in the class, Harry was approached by a recruiter for one of the MIs. Sadly for our intelligent services, the agent quickly ascertained that Harry did not possess the correct linguistic skills or covert temperament. His long hair, untucked floral shirt, baggy jeans and wild, drug addled eyes did not make him company material either. The FO told him to FO.

And so it came to pass that Harry settled into the other half of his joint honours degree, Comparative Religion. Two became one. I and I. Which would eventually prove relevant. It was packed full of people like him. He relaxed into the interlocking web of spiritual history and philosophy. Keeping a close and steady eye on Islam, he realised that its message was a far cry from the distorted vision of his previous classmates. Mates was not a suitable title.

Harry jumped head first into the realms of mystical Sufi poets, the ancient Hebrew Torah, bloodthirsty Hindu epics, Zarathustran fire worshippers' consumption by vultures, proud battles of Sikh warriors, peaceful Bodhisattvas meditating under trees, wild Aghori Sannyasin resorting to cannibalism and maintained motorcycle Zen. He was transported on a confusing intellectual quest that ran parallel to his rampant drug taking. By the time he wrote his dissertation, Harry had managed to fuse these two fundamental pillars of his dystopian dream into an essay on the All Conquering Lion of Judah, Jah Rastafari. Smoking bongs with the dreads of Moss Side proved his perfect research project. Back to I and I.

And what pearls of wisdom did our dim witted protagonist emerge with? Common sense luckily prevailed. Peace and love became his creed. He began to draw his life into a simple cocoon of basic principles. Don't cheat, steal, harm. Show love and compassion for people and most will do the same. Steer clear of people that do the opposite. They will hurt you. Be in awe of the higher power that governs our universe. We have a brief history in time. Make the most of it. Having fun and creating beauty became the mantra for his perceived legacy. Art and love are the ultimate expressions of this. His post student years were committed to this in his career as a jeweller.

Harry Kitson thrived in this environment. The vast majority of the people commissioning him professionally were doing so for the happiest of reasons. They demanded his and his brother's metallic and crystal art at birthdays, engagements, Christmas, marriage, child births, Christianings, anniversaries and whims. Harry, the hopeless romantic lapped up the emotion, sentiment and occasion of all and sundry. Even the few sadder events, whether through robbery, divorce or death, were spun in his positive world to be celebrations of our roller coaster existence. These two poles of his business rarely collided, but Harry found joy in all their creations. One fella took the ashes of his girlfriend's father, with his widow's permission, and had them carbonised as a diamond which the brothers then forged gold around into an insect styled engagement ring come mausoleum. Dragonflies had been father and daughter's favourite so, with tears for most conflicting passions, she said yes to his proposal. Surrealism through the beauty of occasion and art.

Around this time, Harry was introduced to Richard Dawkins' book, 'The God Delusion' and his religious construct immediately vapourised as he faced the scientific truth of our universe. But Harry is a simple soul and quickly drew the positives of one and all into his own focus. Big Bang theories wrestled with a supposed Creationist clap trap. Basic life rules, whether in faith, hope or common sense, could be explained by the bigger picture. Thankfully researched and proven by scientists, the previously unexplainable forces of nature on our own planet and those in the darkness of the universe beyond suddenly made sense to him.

Simultaneously, the Kepler telescope had started to discover the thousands of planets that surround other more distant stars than our own sun. This search into history, as light years dictate, made the existence of life beyond our own planet's entirely plausible, if not probable. The unknown provokes fear in those only living in hope through relatively recent political doctrines and religious laws. The voyage of discovery that astrophysicists travel brings excitement and joy. Billions have been spent travelling to and probing into space to find out how and why it all ticks. Harry was fascinated by this pursuit of truth in the name of universal harmony.

"Oooooo Aaaaaagh." Barry broke his friend's stellar reminisce with the type of expressive sound enjoyed by farmers. "Well, while you've been enjoying interplanetary intercourse, I've been busy recording this little circular conundrum. I gave this drone," he held up the four rotor contraption from it's wheat nest, "to my eleven year old boy in the clear knowledge that he wouldn't be able to master it until the fourteen plus age recommendation. Daddy is the drone lord now. I have Jedi powers when it comes to handling this baby. 'But with the blast shield down I can't even see! How am I expected to fight?'" He quipped in the manner of the cinematographic intergalactic struggle of their childhood.

"'This is our most desperate hour. Help me, Obi-Wan Kenobi, you're my only hope.'" Kitson replied, warming to the theme by bunching his hands at the side of his head in mimic of an infamous Princesses' hairdo. "How cool are these drones! Well, if in the right hands. We don't want to be using it to shut down international air traffic, do we Bazza, like the Old Bill did at Gatwick a few months ago?"

"It's funny that you should say that, Harry," the agricultural aviator replied, "because that is exactly the reason why I called you early this morning. I would never have even known so quickly about this crop circle without being alerted to it by the forces strongest with Her Majesty."

"I'm intrigued. Tell me," replied his trustworthy confidant. Knave continued with this blessing in mind.

"My story starts yesterday evening, just before dark at about 10pm. I walked up the hill, a little way beyond where we parked the truck, because I wanted to fetch in the horses which had been grazing beyond it. They love the warmth in the sun and chomping on the meadow grass and flowers at this time of year, but I had heard on the weather forecast of showers arriving early today so thought it best to bring them in. When I got to the top, I paused a while and smoked a cigarette. I looked down at my full crop in the fields at the valley's bottom. Unblemished and ripe. It has been predominantly dry over the past couple of months and with fast growth and high grain prices, it should be a bumper year despite all our concerns about our exit from Europe."

"Oh, Christ! Don't start all that again, please, Barry! We have been politically punished by democratic deviance and legal lies for too many years now!" interrupted his friend.

"Agreed. This is not the time or place for those Westminster wranglings, Amigo." Barry continued, simultaneously demonstrating the full extent of his continental language skills. "We have far greater issues to discuss right now. On On! By the time I had led the nags back down to the farm, given them all fresh straw, locked up the stables and gone to bed, it was getting close to midnight. I remember the time because I had tried to scuttle the missus, even bringing foreplay into the suggested equation, but she had looked at the clock and reminded me that it was over forty eight hours until Sunday and it was not my birthday."

"You're such a romantic, Barry." Harry broke in sarcastically, a poor form of wit that he was heavily reliant on. "That poor darling girl. Making love with you must be like wrestling with an aggravated and randy bison."

"Don't mock it until you've tried it, Ducky?" retorted Knave, adding a wink and pouted kiss for good measure. "I slept and awoke to the usual dawn chorus of farmyard chatter. The cockrell did what cocks do. The chickens, peacock, guinea fowl, geese and pond ducks all then joined him in an aural orgy. No, not oral before you start all your usual smut." He raised one eyebrow and continued when his friend had refocused. "It is quite a sound. I have to be up most mornings at day break and have not set an alarm in years. I got dressed into the three piece that you were so damned rude about earlier, popped downstairs, fed the dogs and made some coffee. It's an alternative Colombian pick me up in liquid form to the powdered one you're more familiar with. I then flipped a couple of Es and some B in a frying pan, and plonked them in a sarnie. I ate and drank them whilst I listened to Farming Today and the Weather forecast. I listened to the 6am news pips and headlines, then went outside to shit the dogs, chuck some grain at the birds and check the horses.

"All was quiet. Fowl are incredibly sedate once they have noisily reminded you and you have responded with their request for grub. I was just about to go into the office when I heard a strange hum away to the north. It got louder and louder and eventually became a repeated, pulsating 'WhaWhaWhaWhaWha' noise really quite close by."

"How did it sound? Harry asked, shielding his grin.

"'WhaWhaWhaWhaWha'....Oh, fuck off, you twat." Barry had been temporarily off his guard for this childish comeback. "So, I started running, yes, running, before you make any more clever dick comments, in the direction of the sound. It was coming from the same hill that I fetched the horses from the night before. As I rapidly climbed it, the decibel level of the 'WhaWhaWha's rose until it was deafening but I still could not see anything.

"All was revealed when I reached the crest of the ridge. A massive helicopter was hovering below the hill line above this field. It was jet black, evil looking, menacing in its ferocious style and sound. It had no markings or registration numbers. Army. As I just mentioned, the Force is strong with Her Majesty. I then got my first glimpse of our beautiful woven friend below it. I was stunned for multiple reasons which I will try to elucidate on one by one. My first thought was why the army was building a crop circle in my field? But even then, before I came down here with you to inspect it at close quarters, I thought that an army of hundreds of men could not have created that intricate form in the handful of hours since I had last visited it. Let alone a couple of helicopter pilots and their crew. Besides, there were none of them on the ground. It was then that I realised that they were studying it, not building it. The base of the craft was covered in all sorts of dishes and aerials suited to reconnaissance. It was very slowly, nose pointed to the centre of the form, circling it, at a distance of about twenty metres from the perimeter. It seemed to be slowly and meticulously digesting everything about the phenomenon.

"Given my geographical degree and topological expertise," he winked at his chum, "plus my simple mathematics skills, when I'm allowed to use my fingers, I deduced the following. The hill is approximately two hundred and ninety five metres above sea level. My crop, given its excellent growth and undulating nature, is between one hundred and eighty to one hundred and fifty metres above sea level. The aircraft, being lower than the hill and with an approximate depth of five metres itself, could therefore be assumed to be flying at a height of between fifty and one hundred metres. This is a clear breach of the recommended flight height of two hundred metres." Harry clapped slowly after his friend's presentation.

"Bravo, Holmes! Most intriguing! Please continue with your stunning powers of deduction, I pray you."

"You are kind, Watson, but be patient, Doctor, and all will become as crystal as your meth!" the landowner, come sleuth, replied. "I've been puzzled for years why the MOD practice their low level flying manoeuvres down the belly of our tiny little valley when they already have most of Wiltshire to play their wargames over Salisbury Plain. That is until I saw them hovering above our symmetrical friend. I have surmised that they have been doing recce missions concerning crop circles for years and years, accumulating information which, given the official secrets act, won't be released for twenty years or so. They don't want the information in the public domain until they have to. They know something which we don't and they don't want us to know."

"That is an incredibly paranoid notion, Bazza!" Harry interrupted, "That's the sort of crazy shit that I come up with after a session."

"Hear me out, please?" Barry barrelled on, "As the helicopter slowly circled our circle, digesting knowledge, it eventually reached the opposite side to me. It paused briefly, before quickly banking first left, then right, around the formation before it headed straight for me! I'd been spotted! The noise was thunderous. I stood on the hill top and the chopper slowed, then hovered, right in front of me. The wind from its blades rushed beside me but I stood my ground. Afterall I thought, Knaves own this damned land. We have farmed these fields for centuries. How dare they intimidate me! Peering into the dark mass of metallic weaponry, surveillance and menace, the sun shone through the darkened glass windows and I saw a slender, boyish face raise a camera and click it at me. Well, that was the last straw for Barrington Knave, BA(Hons). Kid soldiers taking pics of me on my mountain! Damn and blast them all! I sound like my father. Fuck 'em, is how I would say it!

"I thought fast. A position of strength was required. Looking at my onetime immaculate tweed ensemble, I first placed my hands on my hips, legs planted firmly astride, puffed out my chest and flung my head back in a sure rebuke of defiance. I then unbuttoned my trousers and yanked them to my ankles. Pulling my recently redundant sexual nerve from its Marks & Sparks housing and being careful to aim the old chap down wind, I proceeded to urinate. I made sure that I slowly rotated the trouser snake like a windmill to achieve the most dramatic arc of pee. That should teach the rotters, I'd thought. But no, oh no, they were not finished. They just kept a'hoverin' the helicopter and a'clickin' the camera shutter. Never one to take a scrap lightly, I turned around, bent over and hoiked down my underwear. That got them. The craft rotored up and away, south across the valley and back to the safety of their military playground. They clearly were not as interested in my moon face as the real one!"

"Barry? Are you not a little bit concerned that you have flashed, then moonied, at a military helicopter whilst it performed an illegal flight and covert recce mission on a crop circle?" The concern was clear in Kitson's tone.

"Haor!" Barry snorted like the porcine contents of his breakfast sandwich before it died. "Nobody will ever know for the next twenty years. Besides, if things get sticky, I'm the Chair of the Village Council."

Harry marvelled at his pal's naive bravery. Nevertheless, he thought it ill advised to remind Barry that the fate of volunteer soldiers had been buried from the public eye after the LSD tests on them at Porton Down back in the 1950s. They were Royal Marines. Barry was a mooning farmer and moaning councillor. Their only commonality was his voluntary participation in acid tests. He didn't fancy Knave's chances against the top brass. With this in mind, he decided to change tact.

"An incredible tale, Barry. Thank you. What an extraordinary dimension the military interest gives our crop conundrum. I'm glad that we are not the only ones with a fascination for this unexplained art and power. Speaking of which, please can you show me your creative contribution to the art of drone photography?"

"Indeedy, I willy." Knave reached down and unbuckled his smartphone from the undercarriage of the quadruple blade remote controlled big boy's toy. Putting the drone back down on the nest of bent stalks, he walked over to his friend and planted his bum firmly down next to him. He grimaced, farted, paused and then muttered, "Aliens!", looking slowly left and right, up and down, as if blaming his flatulence on something from afar. He then resumed his technology tour and swiped through the pictures that he had amassed over the last few hours of intermittent flying. They were really most impressive. Some were from way up on high, others eerily close or immaculately focussed on the detailed patterns of standing walls, swirling circles and woven backgrounds. Occasionally, the pictures were blurred or blank. Harry looked quisicaly at the photographer.

"I have a theory," Barry started, "Which is very much aligned with the army helicopter's behaviour earlier. You explained to me about this all empowering energy that affected your body and my dogs? Well, the same force seems to affect technology too. It seems there is a vertical column of the stuff through the art form, whether from the earth's crust or the sky's heavens, I know not. But all the drone photographs from directly above the circle are incomplete or nonexistent. It would also explain why the helicopter was completing its survey from just outside the edge of the cylinder of power."

"That makes sense, Baz." Kitson contemplated. "Although the mists of confusion are only just beginning to clear in this world of nonsense that we have stumbled upon. The orb of bright light energy I saw last year, this extraordinary artistic print on your field, the army's reaction to it and to you this morning are all very mysterious. We have research to do. I really want to know what those little piles of white powder are too." He shuddered at the parallel memory of addiction and discovery. "There's something very fishy about all this."

"Speaking of which," Barry started, after considering his watch, "It's high time I got going. I have a date with a trout pool soon. The perfect opportunity for peace, quiet and contemplation. I will make a few calls to some of the big wigs while I'm casting a fly too. I know people in very high, extremely low and sometimes both simultaneously, places! C'mon. Let's get back to the car. I have something to show you there which will fog your grey matter even more. You can then start your own investigations."

The befuddled men started back along the tractor tracks. The sun was getting lower although there was plenty of daylight left for Knave to catch supper in a local stream. The wheat had changed colour from the bright yellow of midday to a rich orange in the late afternoon glow. They got back to the truck where an excited Tinker was repatriated with her correspondingly wagging clan. Once all were settled in the pickup, canines to the flatbed, humans to the seats, Knave lent across his friend's knees and opened the glove compartment. He pulled out an A5 brown envelope, flipped open its flap and removed a solitary photograph. He passed it to Harry who digested the image.

"How come you have already had this picture developed and printed? You haven't been back to your farm printer since my arrival, have you?" Harry said, staring at the crisp image of the art that he had left a few minutes before.

"Correct, Doctor Watson." The driver replied. "This picture was taken by a German aviator, Ulrich Kox, on 19 July 1999, exactly twenty years ago to the day. Our crop circle is in exactly the same place and has been reproduced for a second time in near identical perfection to the original. It is known as 'The Basket' for obvious reasons. Herr Kox's photos are the only proof of it because my father, in his fury at the vandalisation of his product and the expected invasion by enthusiasts, cut it down immediately. I am not going to do the same. The MoD have proven to me that there is far more to this than meets the eye. I called you over because of your previous experience. Now that you have spent a day channeling this extraordinary energy, which has been corroborated with my detailed then blurred pictures, I'm convinced that we are onto something of the utmost importance."

"I have never been so excited or enthralled by anything in my life as this, Barry." Kitson's eyes gleaned over once more as he stared forward over the slowly rippling field. "Whilst you go and contemplate the infinite on a river bank, I'm going to ride home via The Bruce Arms and do the same over a couple of mind expanding pints of Waddies Six."

"Go easy please, Jelly Brain. I think you had more than enough last night, didn't you? Promise you'll keep today a little calmer?" Barry reluctantly nodded his agreement.

"I promise. Thanks for everything, Baz. Today has been very important to me. Between the motorbike and our little conundrum here, I have more than enough reason to behave myself at the pub. Don't worry. "

The boys stared out over the valley. At that moment, they simultaneously heard a low hum from the West and looked along the gorge. A plane approached from the direction of Devizes, the home of Harry's beloved beer. As the spec loomed closer, they saw that it was heading straight towards them. They made out its four huge propellor engines. It was dropping in height all the time. It was enormous. Travelling at a height of about two hundred metres by the time it passed them, deafeningly loud and languorously slow, the slate grey Hercules army plane, complete with radars and dishes on its underbelly, flew directly passed the crop circle before banking right to avoid the escarpment and then left and up and North. It's thunderous noise dissipated with its distance as it climbed to a height more appropriate to a heavy reconnaissance plane. It eventually was lost as it headed back towards one of the Oxfordshire airbases. The men turned slowly towards each other, unblinking and lost for words. Barry eventually broke the spell. He turned the ignition of the truck, put it into gear and started for home, briefly turning to Harry.

"We have work to do."

'Love Is Strange'

The rectangular wooden table, with built in benches either side, provided the most comfortable late afternoon office. To the left was the low pub door, a convenient gateway to the next glass of ice, slice, tonic and London gin. The field to the right was packed full of caravans and a cluster of motorbikes were parked next to a huddle of smaller tents. Their owners lazed in shorts and t-shirts atop their makeshift rugs of leather clothing, enjoying the warm rays after their long ride. Behind Kitty's back, the covered smoking shack provided nicotine addicts with an occasional hit and shelter from the bright sun. The full benefits of its soothing power were still angled a little way above the trees to the West and her skin relished them face on.

Kitty Parker's slatted desktop had little decoration beyond her cold beverage. An upturned terracotta flower pot provided an ashtray which she had pushed aside as redundant to her needs. A glass jam jar had followed suit as its floral contents had dried, wilted and were not the splendour they must have recently been. Her laptop was open in front of her, tilted to maximise the shadow on the screen. The WiFi signal was weak but enough to crack on with her tasks in hand. She had giggled when she acquired the password from the bar. TheGammon. Very Wiltshire. The computer's browser bar displayed a few of her current dilemmas. They ranged from a Dutch scientist's recent crop circle report, a Porton Down memorandum from the 1980s on the same subject, an article of similar theme from Farmers Weekly magazine and, lastly, an online dating site. It was on the latter that she clicked. It was the start of the weekend after all.

As a Millennial and one in tune with the generation, Captain Kitty Parker had a number of issues with it. These could be fine tuned to a simple personal fact. She didn't want to be labelled. She never wanted to be put in a specific box. She was many things simultaneously: a libertine, an artist, a bisexual feminist, a soldier, a spy and hopelessly alone. She had innocently enjoyed liaisons with her own fairer sex. This had always been by natural persuasion, enjoyable circumstances and with a spirit of freedom. Despite the increasingly modern outlook of the British army and intelligence services, this was not something that should be shared in her work place. Private lives should not be shared in the workplace, particularly not her private life. Her recent knowledge of covert operations, confirmed that the facts concerning her sexual and artistic preferences, would be very easily accessed by her superiors and would be used against her, if they ever needed to. Indeed, the Parisian fact finding mission she had been sent on by Uncle Max, only a few weeks previously, was testimony to this fact.

The MI boss', plus her own work was being unwittingly undermined by the vapid ignorance to glaring facts that Major de Crecy Conrad-Pickles was deliberately bypassing in their designated agricultural research. He just didn't want the hassle of all this seeming "poppycock". He would write meaningless reports to his own superiors, postulating on worthless leads involving rumours of underground vandal crop artists or new Russian weapon espionage. He seemed totally obsessed by the partly proven theories or those that sparked memories of the Cold War. They were leads that went little or nowhere. The Major totally discounted the seemingly endless evidence regarding an alternative power that was being harnessed to create these images of incredible beauty. But here was another one of her dilemmas. The artist inside her was conflicted with the questions she asked herself rather than with the spy craft that she was paid for. Uncle Max wanted to harness this energy for greedy future destruction in weapon development. Monty would rather bury the information. He was far more interested in preserving his historical family business, an ongoing source of private wealth. Kitty saw the beauty in the crop circles but also that there was an extraordinary quantity of information that was still unanalysed and unanswered. Not only in the consistently peaceful imagery that was displayed but in the healing and wellbeing powers that were regularly reported by enthusiasts and visitors. Whoever or whatever was creating these beacons of notable interest was doing so with peace not war in theme. She felt an overwhelming urge to respect this message.

It had not been difficult for Kitty to remove the limp threat of the Major from the ongoing investigations. He just didn't know it yet. A few weeks back, she had dressed in a chic two piece navy blue Chanel suit inherited from her Grandmother, seamed nylons, high heels, oversized tortoise shell glasses and a smart silk headscarf. Kitty looked like a silver screen actress, rather than a soldier, when she boarded the same carriage as her work colleague at St Pancras International. Montgomery had no idea that she was sitting a few rows away from him as they sped on the train beneath La Manche.

On arrival in Paris, she wiggled elegantly behind him at a suitable distance to remain undetected on Metro and boulevard. She had sat in a cafe opposite the apartment building he had disappeared into and, when he had emerged a few moments later, with his surprisingly enchanting girlfriend, she had watched them walk down the street to a little brasserie where they had settled in for lunch. On Kitty's return to their block, it had been the easiest task to find the letter box emblazoned MdeCC-P and the corresponding flat which she had opened. Once inside, she headed for the bedroom. Despite the initial shock of the part dungeon part theatre decor, it was in a trice that she was outside again, having installed the simple filming device.

She had returned to the cafe and waited. This was not such a chore. Anybody interested in people is in heaven watching Parisians float by. Locals and tourists alike even pay extra for having front row seats on the pavement. This direct performance was not in Captain Parker's secretive interests so she had settled into a corner inside by the window with her back to the wall. Having ordered a large cafe au lait, she flipped open her computer on the small round table, angled it so that voyeurs and waiters could not see the screen, plugged in her headphones and checked the live images of the Major's lust nest. All was quiet so she sipped her coffee and watched the world go by.

Forty five minutes later, the couple returned through the front doors of their building, amorously reeling from the effects of some bottle of Burgundian delight. A minute or so later, they hove into view on Kitty's laptop and the slam of the door reassured her that the audio link through her headphones was complete too. The woman was dressed in a tight black and white polka dot dress which highlighted the voluptuous curves of her thighs, bottom and breasts. These features were not lost on and were thoroughly appreciated by the spy. She couldn't help wonder how on earth her lily livered boss had managed to attract this vision of female sexuality. The Major stood before her, dressed in a simple white shirt, blue chinos and pair of brown leather brogues. They kissed, first tenderly and then surprisingly ferociously. She stopped. He moaned, and looked at her pleadingly. She took a step back and, in the blink of an eye, slapped him hard across the cheek.

"You are a very bad boy." She sternly rebuked him. She spoke English with a delicious French accent.

"Yes. Yes, I am. I am a very bad boy, what, what." He answered sincerely.

"You are a very naughty boy." She continued.

"Yes. I am a very, very naughty boy." He lowered his sparkling eyes to the ground like a chastised dog.

"You know why you 'ave been a very bad and naughty boy?" She commanded.

"Yes. I have been in England for a whole week looking at big brave soldiers whilst Daddy has been waiting here at home all alone. What, what?"

"Correct!" She snapped. "Bad, naughty boys are punished aren't they?" She added, walking to and opening the enormous wardrobe, stepping behind the door and out of sight of Kitty's lens.

"Yes, please!" The Major replied, then begged. "I have been very, very naughty! Punish me accordingly, please!"

"Very well. Get ready to be disciplined," came the voice from the closet. "Quickly!"

It soon became apparent to Captain Parker that her superior had been well drilled for these preparatory measures. Unnervingly close to her camera, he removed all his clothes, fastened a leather strap around his head, inserted a red snooker ball gag into his mouth and tightened it. Reaching forward, he grabbed a plastic bottle and squeezed the opalescent lubricant onto his hand before reaching back and slapping it between his buttocks. He prostrated himself, face forward, bum up, on the leather vaulting horse. He clicked half a pair of handcuffs on one wrist, reached below the gymnastic apparatus and secured the manacle to the other side. It was at this point that his girlfriend emerged from the cupboard.

Her lower half was scantily clad in seemingly endless pointed heeled stilettos, black fishnet stockings and suspenders. Her upper half sported a large pair of mirrored aviator sunglasses, a grey-green collarless jacket and matching peaked hat, both of which bore the emblems of the local conquerors of 1940. She carried a black cane with a silver skull handle. In the middle of this unnerving decortage, she wore what seemed, at first glance, to be an enormous strap on dildo. As she strode towards the British army officer's spread arse

121

cheeks, it then became obvious to Kitty why Monty had referred to his girlfriend as Daddy.

Kitty was normally of romantic temperament but she certainly loved a little bit of kink. Her own adventures into the sexual underworld were based more on the purity of ideology in Leopold von Sacher-Masoch's "Venus in Furs" than the brutal violations and shocking punishments that these two men administered to each other over the next couple of hours. Much of the action had been far too close to the camera for her personal liking, indeed the mental scars would take time to heal, especially those concerning the ruthless application of the skeletal staff. But, from a professional standpoint, it represented a job very well done. She downloaded the full movie and then emailed Uncle Max the contents. His response proved that they now had the Major over a barrel, literally. Kitty had packed up, paid the bill and was back on the train sous La Manche shortly afterwards. She had been instructed to leave the camera in situ. It might continue to prove useful and, if detected, would maintain the right level of paranoia for the bondage masters until their eventual exposure to blackmail.

It was with this recent memory in mind that Captain Parker now considered the online dating site. It was a lonely life for a young, beautiful, single woman, as an artist, soldier and spy. She also lived in one of the remotest parts of Britain. The vibrant, free, artistic and Bohemian lifestyle that she craved in her downtime just didn't exist around Salisbury Plain. Her trips to civilisation were rare and sporadic. On visits to London, she invariably relieved her sexual tension with gorgeous girls at the gay scenes myriad of dancefloors and in their random flats afterwards. But this was not enough. One night stand after one night stand proved entirely unfulfilling for her soul. What did she really want? Did she know? She did know a few things. She wanted to meet somebody special. She wanted to meet somebody that understood her. She wanted somebody to respect her. She wanted to meet somebody she found fascinating. She wanted somebody to share her passionate carnality. She wanted somebody to love, possibly even forever.

Grasping these thoughts, she tried to make sense of them. She tried to put them into the context of her dating profile. It was so frustrating. Box after box to tick so that some pervert could judge her and place her in the box that she or he imagined. Ghastly. She would never be tied down. "Well, metaphorically speaking," she thought to herself. She was reminded of the Major's kinks which, firstly, pushed her boundaries a little too far but, secondly, made her feel a pang of jealousy for Monty's liberty and happiness in these extraordinary circumstances. A trashy 1980s pop film sprang to mind. She used to watch it, as a teen in the early Noughties, with her school girlfriends while they discussed boys, clothes and makeup. Yuck. She thought about how far she had come since then. However, she pulled out a small notepad and pen from her bag on the bench and wrote, 'Desperately Seeking....' She then proceeded to pen all the thoughts, dreams and aspirations that she was looking for in a partner. Some minutes later she surveyed the scribbled and edited project before her.

'Female (usually) but would consider male (rarely) partner 25-50 to share love of photography, art, theatre, dance, fine food, poetry, literature, passionate sex, mild bondage and then freedom. Applicants must have a keen sense of humour, be a good listener, a great storyteller, strong lover and romantic fool. No spys or addicts.'

She read it, sighed, paused, then tore off the page. She crumpled the sheet of paper into a ball and placed it delicately on the table. This was not going to work. She clicked back onto the computer and shut down the page.

"Oh, joy! Just the three work assignments to digest now," she thought to herself. She surveyed the triplicate of scientific reports on crop circles. This subject seemed to stress her far less than dating. It was a strangely calming subject.

At that moment the peace of the beer garden was momentarily shattered. A large green motorcycle lumbered into the parking area. It's noisy engine spluttered in the afternoon heat. The tank bore the transfer sticker of the Harley Davidson company. The solid back pannier wall confessed its type, 'Road King', in chrome. This bright white metal was strangely absent from the rest of the bike, replaced by a menacing matt black on spokes, exhausts and engine mountings. Resultantly the bike looked well used, if not lovingly maintained. A third advert was written in black at the base of the fly splattered clear windshield. 'M.C.M.C.'

The biker was obscured from identity by blackness too. Boots, leather jeans and jacket, gloves, a faceless helmet, large bug eye sunglasses and a skull and crossbones pirate bandanna that was wrapped over the lower half of the face. Kitty noticed that the other two wheeled fanatics sat up from their sunbathing to soak up their most favoured spectacle. The bike came to a halt to the right of Kitty's workstation. She watched the rider kick the stand out from under the left side and tilt the bike onto it. The engine was revved once, which was loud and aggressive, then shut down. This audio addition was totally unnecessary in the Captain's opinion. This attitude was not shared with the enthusiasts in the field who grinned toothless and gesticulated with thumbs aloft. As the biker dismounted, Kitty turned away. She didn't want the 'show off' getting more attention than had already been mustered. She gambled in her brain that it was a man. Prick.

She turned away, sipped her G&T and returned her green eyed gaze to her computer. She clicked onto the Farmers Weekly page. It featured a debate between a group of crop circle scientists with a selection of farmers from southern England. The landowners mainly argued that the existence was nothing more than an outlandish hoax and a scourge on their livelihoods. What was more, the tourism it brought with it was an illegal invasion of their precious turf. The scientists countered that only 5-10% could be proven to be man made. The rest were unaccounted for and research was fundamental for a full understanding of the incredible unexplained forces at large. They added that this would only be possible with the cooperation of the farmers. The farmers wanted an organised method of compensation but the government was not willing to discuss the matter. Both parties agreed that the obvious aerial investigation conducted by the military was strange, given the official denials. Kitty pitied them. The circles were sending all parties concerned in circles.

Her attention was distracted by a figure blocking the sun in front of her. She glanced up and recognised the dark outline to be the biker less a helmet.

"Kitty?" She was slightly taken aback by the deep voice that asked the nominal question. The last thing she wanted right now was one of those macho idiot officers from base ruining her time out. She cupped her hand over her eyes and peered. Noticing her discomfort to the light, the man stepped to the side and she was able to focus. The smiling face she saw was out of context, out of place and out of time. It flummoxed her.

"Harry?" She eventually answered with confusion. "What the hell are you doing here?"

"More to the point," he continued, "What the bloody hell are you doing here at my favourite biking local? I'll forgive you for forgetting that I live here. Is nothing sacred? However hard I tried, I did not forget that you are from this area. I was praying that I would not have to endure the humiliation of meeting you again. Unless you've grown up a little since your days as a ruthless prankster?" He added the last bit with a twinge of bitterness as the desert festival memory came back to haunt him, not for the first time that day.

"I live about five and work about fifteen miles from here too!" She answered enthusiastically. She couldn't help but be happy to see him again. "I'm a professional photographer." The half truth was her standard response for obvious reasons. "How's the jewellery, you hopeless romantic?" He smiled. He too was happy to see her and his initial temper was rapidly dissipating.

"I go to town a couple of days a week to see my son and London clients. The rest of the time I'm down here in my home, come, art gallery about three miles from here." Kitty noticed a sadness in his tone. He seemed far more deflated than at their last brief rendez-vous.

"I didn't even know you were married?"

"How would you? You and I had a whirlwind twenty four hour relationship before you dumped me at the mercy of butch men. I went to Burningman to recover from divorce. I nearly got buggered in a more literal way instead. My ex and I met, married, procreated, separated and divorced in a handful of years. We made each other very unhappy. It was sad but for the best." He paused, seemingly lost in a memory that clearly pained him. Eventually, he forced a smile and attempted to be more cheery. "How about you? How are you and your girlfriend enjoying Wiltshire life?"

"Huh. We split up a short time after Burningman. It was no biggy. We just weren't right for each other. End of." She too paused for thought before adding, "I'm single and as for enjoying Wiltshire life, I do, but it's totes tricky trying to meet people when you work too hard in this desolate place. It does get very lonely sometimes." Her voice trailed off.

"Ho, hum." Harry felt awkward in the moment. "Well. It's been nice to see you again. I guess we will be seeing each other from time to time in the good ol' Bruce. It was good to bump into you again, Kitty. Take care." He started to move off towards the pub door.

"Harry!?" She interrupted his progress and he stopped. "You can go if you want to but, before you do, I just want to tell you something." He turned to listen to her once more. "That day and night on the Playa was probably one of the best days of my life. I have never forgotten the fun we all had. Firstly, I want to apologise for playing that ghastly trick on you. Secondly, I need you to know that we had every intention of finding you the next day to say sorry. But that sandstorm came in and it was just impossible to move anywhere. We never even saw the 'Man' burn. I have always regretted that chance to see you again. Please don't just run away now. It would be great if you could join me now for a long overdue catch up and have a drink or two?" She looked into his eyes, which visibly softened and sparkled at her news.

"Once bitten, twice shy." Kitson responded, flashing his teeth in a relieved smile. "I would love to," he added before pointing at the lemon peel remnants of her glass. "Mother's Ruin with a splash of quinine based mosquito repellant?"

"Marvellous!" Kitty replied with a grin that outstretched his own.

"Back in a mo." Kitson strode in the direction of the refreshments. Miss Parker looked at her laptop screen and shut down the debate, spy and science pages, before closing down the power. She sighed. She was not going to have anything more to do with crop circles for the rest of the evening, she thought to herself. It was time to concentrate on somebody, not something that made her feel happy right now. She was surprised how good she felt at their spontaneous reunion. Harry returned with her drink and a pint of brown still beer. He sat down opposite her just as the sun dipped below the tall trees behind him. He got straight to the point.

"So," he started, "the inevitable question that any red blooded man, promised a threesome by two gorgeous girls, who was then led into a den of sodomy as a hilarious joke, but who has since learnt that the girls intended to find him the next day, must ask. Would we have had a menage a trois if we had met up again?" Kitty squirmed in her seat as the giggles took over her.

"What sort of question is that?!" She exclaimed, still laughing.

"The sort of question that any middle aged, mid life crisis, English gentleman would ask given the same circumstances? You could always lie." Harry retorted.

"Lie? I wouldn't ever lie to you!" She lied.

"Go on, humour me. Pleeeeease!" He begged. Kitty sat silently, considering her subsequent answer.

"I'm not sure," she started, "but we certainly had enjoyed a lot of fun before we left you at the mercy of the male orgy anyway. I can't answer for my then girlfriend but, what I can say is, at the time, I would have loved to be intimate with you with or without her." A shot of beer escaped Harry's nostril due to the unfortunate timings of her answer and his sip. This made her laugh even more. After Kitty calmed down and he had wiped away the evidence with a spotted hanky from his back pocket, she continued. "It was very, very funny seeing your reaction when you took off the blindfold though!"

"You swine!" Harry reacted before he too dissolved into laughter. "You're right though. It was a top class wind up. The irony is that I have always attracted more men than girls. I certainly get chatted up by men far more frequently than advanced on by lasses. I would describe myself as the most homosexual heterosexual ever."

"Ha! Don't try to pigeon hole your sexuality, Harry. You never quite know. There is a little gay in everybody. There is a lot of gay in the type of man that goes to a near naked festival, heavily oiled and dressed as a Roman gladiator. It is far more natural to follow male or female or otherly impulses naturally when they manifest themselves. So many people are bound in the chains of oppression that their souls are knotted. There is usually some religious reason or other than stamps on our freedoms."

"Fair enough," Kitson combated, "but there must be a God if Beautiful You is available to mankind too. You've certainly doubled your chances of pulling, for sure." He paused. After a moment or two, the mirth subsided and he added with a calm and considered tone. "I had more or less given up on love, whichever way I choose to swing, until today when I had an experience which transcended everything I have ever had before it in that sensual domain."

"Today?" Kitty replied. The twinge of jealousy that she felt at his revelation of fresh love was disguised from the hapless romantic seated before her. His eyes seemed suddenly glazed as if caught in a mist of passion. She didn't like this effect in the context.

"Yes. Today. It hit me like a freight train. Full impact. Pure love. On this very day." He briefly halted, which just amplified the girl's dismay, before he dreamily added, "I fell in love with something so beautiful, so very artistic. Earlier today, I fell in love with a crop circle."

"With a what?! What the fu....?!" Kitty stopped herself from concluding the ancient English expletive. This control saved her from revealing her two true emotions. Firstly, the shock at hearing that his innocent passion was for her new secret passion. Secondly, the relief at hearing that his love was not for somebody else but was for something else. After she had stabilised the haste of her breath, she resumed. "That sounds incredible, Harry, as you saw from my reaction! Please tell me all about it."

And so he did. Everything. For some reason, this relative stranger provided the most cathartic outlet for his extraordinary passion. He felt that he could tell this woman everything. They sat, he talked and she listened. She hungrily digested all the information of the day that she too, unbeknown to Harry, had had such a fundamental role in. But her new friend was at the frontline of the battle on the ground, not her own airborne assault. He had experienced what she knew to be true. He had even previously witnessed the glowing orbs that the military had linked to the 'Blueprints' file. Having photographed the 'Basket' that day, she was fascinated by his intimate and romantic descriptions of the swirls and weaves of the design plus his confirmation that the lay of the crop was unbroken.

She had laughed aloud when she found out that the farm owner, Barrington Knave, was the same Barbarian that was responsible for Kitty first meeting Harry when the farmer took an unscheduled golden shower. He now was responsible for the second time too, so it seemed. The army captain also remained shtum that she had already established the identity of the tweed clad gentleman that had urinated at her helicopter. Harry had only confirmed why she had recognised him whilst taking the piss shots. His pee fetish should have been enough intel for the spy if she had been on her toes. Kitty didn't tell Harry what she already knew about the white powder but promised that she would research it for him that evening if he in turn promised to take her to the circle the next day. He did promise. They exchanged numbers and planned to meet in the Bruce carpark at 10:00 hours.

Kitty got up from the table. She excused herself for Barry's same lavatorial forte, a pee, and took their now empty glasses to the bar on her way. Harry sat, glowing with the excitement of sharing this love with somebody he really felt was intrigued by his new loving cause.

He was strangely fascinated by her raison d'etre and she was in his, he felt. It seemed wonderful to share this passion with somebody so infinitely more sensitive than Barrington. Harry saw a rolled up ball of paper on the table, opened it and started to read, 'Desperately Seeking...' The pretty photographer returned before he could continue so he stuffed the paper into his leather jeans pocket. She picked up her bag and computer and he walked her to her car, a pretty little classic MG. They embraced formally but tenderly on both cheeks, he opened her door, she hopped in, started the engine, he slammed the door firmly shut, she gave a cute wave and the sportscar skipped away. Harry was left in a light cloud of dust and a state of bewildered bliss. She was wonderful. He reached back into his pocket, un-crumpled the paper and read the note in full. Once concluded, he grinned at the missive.

"Result!" He thought to himself and punched the air with his fist. "I'm nearly perfect! Only the last word to work on!"

'El Pussy Cat Ska'

The following morning Harry was in the carpark ten minutes early, even though he only lived five away. He had called Barrington Knave earlier and recounted his extraordinary meeting with his lost Playa Princess and that they were heading over to the farm together for a pitch inspection. He had prepared a modest but well considered picnic and popped it in one of the flip lid lock boxes on the Harley. He had rinsed the previous day's dusty exploits off the bike, then sensually shampooed her, tenderly toweled her and perfectly polished her. He donned clothing more suitable to a first date than a dirty bike ride. Polished boots, clean blue jeans and a crisp white shirt, fastened at the cuffs with the rose gold fox head accoutrements of his trade. The links' little red ruby eyes seemed to wink encouragement at him.

He had hung his own helmet, gloves, pirate bandana and bug eyed shades from the clutch lever before considering some suitable attire for Kitty. He settled on a matching lid and gloves, a blue and white spotty handkerchief and some ski goggles, in case she did not have shades. He selected a black leather jacket that he had not been able to fit into comfortably since his late teens. It was a classic '50s design, all zips and collars, and had his own yellow hand painted artwork on the back. 'Acid Rocker' was a momentary tribute to his love of a mate's house night at Manchester's Hacienda, 'Acid Rock', and the sublime Sunbeam S7 motorcycle that he had ridden at the time. The front of the 'R' of 'Rocker' had been elongated below the other five letters in the style of many period Brit motorcycle logos. The dot on the 'i' of 'Acid' was the same smiley face emblem that the crop circle artists of Silbury Hill had used all those years before. Harry reflected on these themes, bikes and dance, and realised just how important they had remained to his liberties throughout his life.

By the time her little convertible pulled up in the yard, Harry had settled on the Jimmy Dean 'Rebel Without a Cause' pose rather than Marlon Brando's 'The Wild One'. Both required a snarl. However, the standing, ableek leaning, next to the Harley, one foot crossed over the other with the lit cigarette hand's index finger pointing across the hip like a pistol, seemed the obvious choice at the time. Primed and ready to go he waited for the imaginary film director to signal for the clapper board. 'And.... Action!'

"Disgusting habit," Kitty immediately vocalised after she had jumped out of the car and then added, "Filthy addict. You stink," after she had kissed his cheek. She looked at the two helmets on the bike, reached back inside the car and pulled out her camera bag which contained some chewing gum amongst many other more high tech contents. "If we are going for a ride on that thing and I'm breathing the fresh air behind you, you'd better have some of these?" She proffered the sweets.

"It's lovely to see you too, Kitty." Harry ventured, stubbing his cigarette out beneath his sole before he took the breath freshener. His script had definitely gone awry early. The Rock'n'Roll Legend routine had temporarily backfired. He hoped the bike wouldn't do the same. "I've got you a few bits and bobs to keep the wind out of your hair and grit out of your teeth." He said with heartfelt concern. "Do you have sunglasses?" He regretted his question as soon as he spotted her tortoise shells perched atop her head. "Oh, sorry," he apologised and added with quickly resumed enthusiasm, "and you can have this old favourite of mine." He passed his prized leathers to the secret soldier. She gripped the shoulder lapels, pulled them apart and read the yellow words on the reverse of the straightened cow skin. Parker looked away, seemingly disinterested, then she pointed at the windshield logo, before she asked him a question.

"What does 'M.C.M.C.' stand for? No, wait, let me guess? M.C. is Motorcycle Club, that's easy," she pressed her slender fingers to each side of her temples in serious contemplation, "so," she paused, "I'm hoping and praying that it is not 'Motorcycle Club Motorcycle Club'." The biker shook his head. "It must be something really nasty," she thought aloud, until she finally exclaimed, "I've got it! 'Maniac Cannibal Motorcycle Club'? That sounds rough, tough and roady! Am I right?" Harry didn't answer for a while. When he did, he did so sheepishly.

"Errrr." He paused before whispering, "It stands for the 'Marlborough College Motorcycle Club'......" His voice tailed off as he said the words.

"What?" She answered incredulously. "Please tell me you didn't just say the 'Marlborough College Motorcycle Club'? You must be joking? That is the softest, most pathetic, name I could imagine. What's more, I've never heard of anything so toffee nosed and pompous in all my life. How many of you public school fools are part of this club?" Harry squirmed at her question.

"Errrr," he repeated once more in the way that simple souls do. He was trapped like the proverbial rabbit in full beam. "O-O-O-One." He eventually stuttered.

"Huh!" Kitty scoffed. "I've heard of private school elitism, Harry, but you've rewritten the entire rule book with that one. The sole member? C'mon?"

"It wasn't my fault!" interjected the deflated member. "It was a joke! A school chum of mine, Fruit Sheldon, stuck it on without my knowing and after all the mirth and enjoyment it caused, it just stayed on."

"You have a friend called 'Fruit'?" Kitty seemed a little disturbed now.

"Yes," Harry continued his underground digging descent, "Fruit and I were dormitory buddies in the Shell. It's not his real name." Harry could not help but think that this initial scene could have gone considerably better. "I'm very glad I removed the other sticker from the back of the pannier now. You would have dined out on that one."

"What other sticker?" Kitty replied with a sigh more of pity than tiredness.

"Fruit found it at a kid's music festival and thought it appropriate. It was pink and sparkly and read, 'Fairy on Board' with an appropriate accompanying picture, you know, Tinkerbell, wand and all. I drove around with it totally unknowingly for weeks before I finally twigged that it was there. Some amorous gentleman wound down his driver window and asked me for a date whilst I waited at some traffic lights."

"Dear, Oh, dear." Kitty was somehow touched by the naive sincerity and innocent tenderness of the humbled man in front of her. After the previous evening, thinking how charming and handsome she found him, these attributes had conflicted with her professional interests. Her predetermined charade to play it cool and subsequently hard to get was already evaporating rapidly. She just thought he was lovely. He made her feel comfortable. "The most homosexual heterosexual ever, for sure." She added with a kindly roll of her eyes.

"Hah! I'm glad you remembered that! Sticking to the theme, I got my own back though." Harry added gleefully. "I was giving Fruit a lift through London a few weeks later on the bike. It was a really hot summer and we were in shorts and t-shirts. I grabbed my revenge by detouring to Old Compton Street. I stuck this baby into first gear and curb crawled all the way down the road, revving my engine on the half clutch. All the fellas were loving it, wolf whistling and shouting sweet things at us. Fruit didn't see the funny side. I told him that jokes were about give and take. He pointed out that this wasn't a moment that he wished to give or take. After a very short negotiation, regarding who was responsible for the imminent purchase of alcoholic refreshments, we motored off to indulge his wallet."

"Bravo, Harry!" Kitty smiled and clapped her hands enthusiastically. "You'd make a splendid army general with longterm battle tactics like that!" She stopped herself, clicking her subconscious shutter back from soldier to photographer mode before adding with a cheery countenance, "C'mon! Let's get these two wheels up and running! I can't wait for our adventure to paradise!" After Harry had lectured her on the fine art of pillion passengering, they popped her bag into the box not inhabited by pic and nic, togged up, jumped on, started up and roared off. Harry felt a flood of relief as the tone headed back towards his preplanned theatrics. The James Dean bad boy from a good family was back on the right track.

The sun was already just shy of its full vertical. Its beams from afar pulsated their life giving energy and the artists lapped them up on their tanning cheeks. Harry's mouth was fixed in a broad grin although years of touring had trained him, despite the windshield, to keep his teeth clenched against the threat of bumble bees. The impact of such a beast at sixty miles per hour on the face is dramatic enough. The ingestion of this stinging creature is at best agonising and at worst fatal. But this thought had drifted slowly back through the vapid mists of the automatic pilot's brain. He was distracted by all things heavenly. The bone of her chin on his left shoulder felt like the warmest cushion and her small breasts pressed to his back seemed to fuse and melt with his very core. Her arms, wrapped around his midriff, seemed to pull him in to the supplication of their oneness. They seemingly floated down the winding hedged road on the luxurious machine. It felt to him like they had been locked together forever.

Kitty sensed something similar. The surging energy that flowed through their leather shells fused them in an intense heat of glowing warmth and total comfort. In keeping with her sexy feline appearance, she felt like a contented cat basking in the sunshine at the window of some cosy cottage. He stirred her inside. Sure, he gave the outward impression that he was a little dim but she threw that notion up into the air as just atypical English self deprecation. He seemed kind, giving, honest and interesting. Whilst his chat was gay and light, she sensed some dark conflict in his past that saddened him and thus her. The little of his life that she knew, must have been painful and damaging to his sweet soul. She wanted to comfort him. In her own rational mind the world was far too overpopulated. Coupled with the brutality of childbirth that she didn't want to inflict on her slight body, this fact had helped her ongoing attitude not to have children. Harry seemed at times to be a vulnerable oversized baby. She had an urge to look after him. In an adult, not motherly, way. She saw that he needed pulling out of the quagmire of mistrust and pain that he wallowed in. He was too fine a fellow to let slip deeper under the mud. Like the line in a tragic play, he then nearly blew it when he tilted his face to the left and shouted against the wind back towards her.

"You can hold onto the gear stick if you like?" He grinned and nodded towards the petrol tank.

"Gear stick?" She replied, "I didn't think bikes had them?"

"Grip it like a tennis racket," the fool continued above the whistle of the wind. "We're in third now. Slip it into fourth." As the penile penny dropped, Kitty initially was outraged and then, luckily for Harry, saw the funny side.

"You dick!" She exclaimed between giggles, squeezing his chest momentarily tight like a bear cub.

"Exactly!" replied the juvenile comedian, before adding with a sideways smile, "I'm sorry, Kitty Cat, I couldn't resist that timeless quip!" Kitty Cat? She loved that. That made all the previous warmth come flooding back. She smiled in the Cheshire style, purred to herself and lazed contentedly in the sunshine once more.

Halfway through Pewsey, Kitson steered the bike left up a narrow lane, skillfully gliding the machine between the ferrous bollards and dormant road constabulary up the hill. Approaching the school, the traffic lights sensed their presence so switched to green, they crossed the railway bridge and throttled out of town. The rugby club drifted past and a little further down the road they slowed and successfully negotiated a wooded crossroads. The trees formed a hallowed arch above them as they headed down the hill, then slowed to bank right at the pretty little pub on the corner. The Golden Swan was nominally a reference to the earthly depiction of the Sun God in Ages of Stone. The fine ale provided a more recent focal point of reverence.

Lolloping over the canal bridge, the sheer cliff of the downs loomed ahead of them. Knapp Hill, the home of Neolithic settlers, soared dominant and proud to their left whilst Golden Ball Hill was directly in front of the bike's respectfully lit head and fog lights. The glowing orbs of light energy swooping across the fields that had been witnessed by many, including Harry Kitson, for centuries was assumed to be this hillock's unholy christening. The aforementioned clicked the gears into third as they banked around a sharp lefthander and then back up to fourth. He giggled to himself at his recent attempt at mechanical cock humour. At least she had seen the funny side. He usually was the only celebrant of his own attempts at mirth.

They headed west with the dramatic ridge to their right. The road swept languorously up and from side to side and at the highpoint of the valley's floor the pilot coasted the bike into a dusty agricultural layby and cut the engine. Once halted, he balanced the bike with the legs which had been strengthened by straddling American iron over many years. He waved a hand across the enormous field between the road and cliff.

"This is the East Field," he began, "and from my limited grey celled knowledge," he tapped the brow of his helmet, crossed his eyes and stuck his tongue out of his mouth's side, an action that prompted a giggle then shake of the head from his pretty passenger, "it is arguably the global epicentre of recent crop circle activity." Kitty nodded encouragingly at him to continue. She feigned this initial interest in the location that she had secretly studied in minute detail. Apart from the unsung heroes of research, public enthusiasts who were constantly ridiculed by the machinations of power, she could be considered a leading expert in the field. Especially this particular field. Dozens upon dozens of daylight aerial photographs, hundreds of glowing nocturnal blueprints and reams of scientific data flashed through her sharp mind. Innocent of this topical encyclopedia, Harry continued. "There have been as many as four circles per annum here. Who or whatever is creating them, certainly wants the message to be seen by as many as possible. The hills provide the perfect viewpoint and focal distance for these rural canvases. Make sure you look over your right shoulder when the Hog climbs up. It is stunning, even without any current circular artworks in nature's gallery. Hold tight. Next stop, chez Baz!"

After pushing the starter button with the expected result, Harry scuffed the bike through the dust and back onto the tarmac. He gazed across the valley floor at the twin nipples of Pickled and Woodborough hills, smiled like a naughty schoolboy at his geographical perversion, then started the fluid descent to Alton Priors. Halfway through the village, opposite the spectacular thatched barn, Harry briefly glanced right at the unassuming track that is the start of the climb to the ninety mile long Ridgeway. It is the east west geographical vertebra of Britain used by mankind since prehistory. Leaving the tiny village, the couple stopped at the blind junction before easing tentatively right and up the enormous bank. The chalk White Horse majestically dominated their view to the port and the gigantic East Field stretched away to the starboard. Kitson felt the passenger's helmet shift in the latter direction as she followed his previous suggestion. He relished and shared the sharp intake of breath and soft exhalation as she sighed at the serene beauty below her. Togetherness. Oneness. I and I. That dissertation had come in useful after all.

Over the crest of the hill, Harry slowed then pitched the motorcycle left up the familiar farm track of the Knave estate. A minute or two later he tilted the handlebars into the cobbled yard, narrowly missed a hissing goose that lunged an orange beak at his front tyre before it retreated with pronounced wiggle and waddle to its brethren. He stopped the bike in front of the farm office and revved the engine once with the same exaggeration as on the previous day. He straightened his legs in a brace position and asked Kitty to dismount. The disappointment of her release from him and subsequent loss of her vibrant warmth was quickly forgotten and replaced as her enchanting bum brushed across his shoulder when she stood on the pillion pads and swung her lithe body over to step onto the stoney ground. Despite the involuntary twitch of his manly gearstick, he selected neutral, in box and boxers alike, tipped the bike onto the side stand and dismounted.

Having removed and hung their headgear on the handlebars, with the excess accessories buried within them, Kitty looked at Harry, her sparkling green eyes mirrored his kindly variety, and said,

"Thank you so much, Harry. That was utterly beautiful. I enjoyed every last second of our fabulous journey. I felt like some movie starlet from the silver screen behind my leading man."

"Bingo." Harry answered with his own brand of simplicity. A surge of restored pride was replaced in his James Dean pastiche performance. The girl placed each of her hands on his shoulders, tilted her elegant face upwards and tippy toed to reach his. She planted her lips on his, quickly and softly, in a momentary kiss which, to the boy, would last for an eternity in his single mindedly romantic revu . After she had returned her heels to the ground, their gazes still in hypnosis, he proffered his ultimate compliment with a smile and a whisper, "Double Bingo."

"Get a room!" Their bliss was interrupted by the outburst that came from the direction of the opening office door. On completing its traverse, it revealed the bullish frame of a familiar farmer bedecked in the cloth of Harris. The hulk lumbered forward, a host of ochre waggers overtook his heels as he thrust out his hand to Kitty. "Barrington Knave, Esquire, at your service, Ma'am. Landlord, estates manager, farmer, local councillor and best friend to this unseemly imbecile." As Kitty shook his hand, Kitson stared at his old friend in a manner that begged him not to spill any unnecessary beans. This really was not the moment in his performance to drive his 'Little Bastard' Porsche Spyder into a headlong fatal road accident. He was actually rather keen to cut that scene from his fantasy movie entirely. Meanwhile, Kitty was hoping that Barry's formal greeting would become less so when they met again. If not, she predicted a very premature onset of arthritis in her right hand. She massaged it discreetly with the functioning left when the clench had dissipated.

"Kitty Parker," she smiled warmly despite the deep bone bruising, "Photographer, general lover of the arts and vehement supporter of your wonderful friend. He is no imbecile. He is a fabulous chap and I won't hear a bad word said about him please." She was stern. Barry was chastised. Harry was jubilant. The latter mentally canned the racing car crash scene with a proud smile. His female champion continued, "It is a pleasure to finally meet you. The last time I saw you," she lied, "You were caught in a torrential typhoon of urine! I hope you weren't too traumatised? Having said that, Harry told me all about your pee protest against a certain military helicopter yesterday? Very brave but there's definitely a lavatory based theme developing around you."

"Why, thank you." Knave answered, flashing the smile that had broken so many hearts at Pony Club dances, "I thought by wiggling them a sausage of Cumberland character they would learn that this land owner would stand firm against their violations, however intrusive. I merely fertilised my dominion with all curing urine. An old mate of ours swears by it. Climbed the Himalayas on the stuff apparently. A glass a day keeps the witch doctor away. Helps prevent acne, viral infections and cancer allegedly. As a result, I was absolutely over the moon when that little Jap spread her legs and pissed on me at Burningman. Yummy!"

"Eee-uw! Yuck!" Kitty replied, wrinkling her nose. She was desperate to give the farmer a taste of his own medicine. Not the pee kind, but the stuffed offal type. Her wide angle lens had clearly focused from the chopper earlier that morning on the more chubby chipolata variety of genitalia. The camera never lies. But the owner had to. She bit her tongue for the time being. Official Secrets Act, and all that. She had work to do. Besides it had been early in the morning yesterday and the light rain and cool air might have accounted for any shrinkage. She would give Barry the benefit of the doubt for now. The undercover army officer decided to take charge of this ridiculous chat and steered the conversation back to the conundrum in hand. "Enough of this pissy nonsense now, Barry. We have important work to do. Let's get into your office and discuss what we've all found out overnight." She led the way inside. The men followed. Whilst her back was to them, Barry raised his eyebrows to Harry a couple of times in quick succession, punched him lightly on the arm and mouthed the words, 'You Twat!' Harry beamed with pride. This was indeed decidedly rare and high praise from his esteemed colleague. He banked it.

'(Til) I Kissed You'

The Pow Wow was of little import to Kitty. She was as keen as Colemans to see the spiral and woven field in person. But she bade her time in the interests of remaining hidden from her serious spy work. She listened to the men, soaking up all their information. The facts were nothing new to her extensive knowledge of the circular conundrum but their different points of view fascinated her. Barrington Knave opened proceedings.

" I recognise that farmers still angrily reject the need to research the phenomenon. They should have been confronted about this decades ago. They need an education on this topic, sharpish. The premature culling of crops when circles appear just does not make sense to me anymore. My morning's research has confirmed what we saw yesterday. The stalks are bent, not broken and thus plant growth can continue. This should be a major breakthrough for most farmers' paranoid fear that they are going to suffer a loss of yield.

"Once they are aware of this fact, their main issue remains policing researchers and tourists to access their land in a safe and sympathetic manner. I've already spoken to a handful of my larger landowning clients from my stunning little chalk stream office last night. I didn't catch a thing!" Harry rolled his eyes and spoke.

"Now there's a surprise." Barry ignored his old friend's interjection.

"They are all encouraged by their most trusted land agent's news regarding the crop growth and subsequent yield. However, they remain adamant that some form of financial compensation should be available before the public can be given access. As things stand, they are not insured for any liabilities concerning crop circles. You know, some nutter has a heart attack on the land and sues. They need cover. We must try and bridge this gap. Farmers may be as greedy as the next folk but they are canny too and have responsibilities for their properties and the welfare of those on them."

"I totes agree, Barry." Kitty briefly piped up. "I read an article in Farmers Weekly after meeting Harry last night. This access and legal matter is of primary importance if we are to get the gumboots on side."

"Gumboots?" Barry looked hurt. "I think you'll find the majority of my bigwigs prefer a stylish brogue."

"Soz for the fashion faux pas, Barry. Please carry on."

"I'm meeting one of my most serious bigwig brogue boys this afternoon to discuss everything in greater detail. He knows people in the highest places and I want to butter him up with that infamous Knave charm. Most of these aristos are connected historically with big business and power politics. He could be very helpful, if on our side. He's absolutely loaded too. Cash is king. We may have to grease a few palms on this journey."

"Barrington Knave!" Harry was appalled by his friends last suggestion. "This purist needs purity. I thank you most sincerely for your intent to help the cause using your most influential contacts but may I please stress, at this very moment, that a dark cloud hangs over this crazy subject in the public domain. This cumulus needs to be lifted for clarity, not darkened further with cash corruption." Kitson's eyes then glazed over again. He spoke with passion and intensity, about the life changing experience of the day before, in an almost evangelical manner. "It is clear to me that the powers used to create these artworks are of enormous benefit to mankind. Unity between scientists and researchers from the agricultural, medical, business, tourist, energy and military communities, to name but a few, will provide safe information that the public can trust." He eulogised further, "This energy appears to be entirely clean and might provide life giving longevity for sustainable farming, the fight against disease plus non polluting defense and power systems. No more burying uranium! Yippee! What is more," he added with his distinctive passion, "Britain is at the start of a new political and economic journey into the relative unknown, alone in the world once more. To make dear old Blighty the hub of this important research and potentially environment saving project, might bring stability and prosperity to our shores once more."

Kitty glowed for her friend. He was one of those rare breeds of people that genuinely cared about others, whether for his nearest and dearest or for mankind as a whole. She wanted him to care for her, although she already knew in her heart that he did. She wanted to care for him too. Ironically, the only person he didn't seem to look after, was himself. The sadness in him seemed to be a waste of a great soul. She suspected that he had led a self destructive existence. His carefree abandon in the desert had alerted her. Smoking cigarettes was another vital clue. The speed with which his pint had disappeared in the Bruce was further evidence. Her psychoanalysis was confirmed when it was her turn to contribute to the discussion.

"I've been researching the curious piles of white powder." Harry visibly juddered at the mention of her own pre-promised topic. "Fret not, Harry," she soothed, "but be prepared for a couple of pieces of extraordinary information. The first was analysed by the Burke, Levengood & Talbott (BLT) Research Team in Massachusetts, USA. The second by the Foundation for Fundamental Research on Matter (FOM) in Amsterdam, the Netherlands. Our white powder could be one of two things. The first produced laboratory results of an extraordinary nature. The crop circle studied had produced minute spheres of silicon or glass which confirms the presence of intense heat. Even weirder, the grains contained striae which result from temperatures of approx 3,000 degrees. Mind blowing! Or should I say glass blowing!" Kitty smirked with minor embarrassment before returning to sincerity, "How no burning occurs where they appear is entirely baffling." Captain Parker paused for breath and for her audience to digest this wonder. "The second type of powder, discovered in small piles usually in the centre of formations, is of a flakier crystal structure. Tests proved that this variety was magnesium carbonate hydrate. It is used in fire extinguishers. How it was deposited in the crop circles and by what remains as unanswered as the artworks themselves."

There was a triplicate intake of breaths and resultant sighs. All three, the farmer, the artist and the spy, recognised that they had an opportunity to make a difference to the planet, albeit the latter in secrecy. Like Barry, Kitty was already formulating a plan to win over the top tier of her powerful establishment. The greater good for mankind was not usually in the interests of warmongers. Her task was a perilous one. She put the thought aside for the time being. If she had any chance of convincing the top brass, she would need first hand experience. She would gain that very soon.

Not that he needed much help, but Kitson gave Knave a short lesson in sales tactics before his meeting with the prominent landlord. Verbal lesson accomplished, he then pumped some enthusiasm into his schoolmate with the use of the dusty full length wooden framed flip mirror in the corner. He placed Barry in front of it.

"You are the King of the Jungle, Baz," the jeweller proclaimed, "You are creeping undetected through the thick foliage. Your great feet pad gently on the moist earth. Not a sound. You pause. You spot an enormous buck deer grazing peacefully in a clearing. It looks up, gazing towards the impenetrable thicket in which you hide, still and lithe. Your stripes blend seamlessly with your surroundings. You note the multiple prongs of its majestic antlers. Your attack must be carefully calculated to avoid them. The noble beast resumes its feeding on the rich plantation. You creep with guile and stealth, stopping and recalibrating your plan every few feet, until you are just a few yards behind it's flank. You peer out of the last stalks of your forest cover. You lay on the cool firm mud and coil your hind legs, ready to spring. You pounce. You're a tiger, Barry! Let me hear you roar?!"

"Grrrrrrrr." The farmer's half hearted response did not merit the enthusiasm of the scene setting. The narrator told him so.

"You're a fucking tiger, you twat! Tiger's don't say, 'Grrrrrrrr', they fucking 'ROAR'!" He demonstrated the last word of his speech with the impassioned dramatic delivery that had made him the toast of his Sunday School nativity play forty years before. "Now it's your turn. Roar!"

"ROAR!" Barry was warming to the theme at last so Kitson capitalised on the vocal improvement by introducing some action into the choreography.

"Very good, Your Highness!" he flattered, "Now, show me your rapier claws and sabre teeth?" The farmer did with a snarl and a swipe. "Excellent! Now use them! You are a stone cold killer! You are the King of the fucking Jungle!" Knave curled his fingers and slashed wildly at his reflection, baring his teeth so much so that his gums made it clear that he had eaten muesli for breakfast. "Brilliant! Now let me hear you 'Roar'!"

"ROOOAAAAARRRR!" Barry put enough spunk into his fierce theatrical ejaculation that it could have convinced a Chinese homeopathic doctor to bottle it. The men celebrated in a high ten body slam style that, in their youth, had been on a par with Michael Jordan's. On this occasion their toes barely left the ground, no thanks to soft middle aged bellies and general gravitational pull. Kitty clapped her appreciation too before bringing the drama to a close.

"You are ready, Barrington 'The Tiger' Knave. Go get 'em, Wild Cat! The very best of British, Barry. Remember, you can be the catalyst for wonderful change, if you can sell hard to your most affluent clientele. We'll touch base later." Barry advanced towards the girl. He placed his hands on either side of her upper arms and kissed her on both cheeks. Kitty was touched by the sincerity of his action and also relieved that she had already graduated beyond his cripplingly formal handshake.

"Good luck yourselves," he answered, "And let's try to make some sense of all this insanity. Give me a call this evening when I'm back." He turned to his friend and wrapped his arms around him. Harry did the same and they patted each other's back in a well practised ritual of genuine affection. Kitson planted a kiss on the nape of Knave's neck before they parted.

"Gay." Barry deducted.

"You know it, Ducky." Harry smiled at his chum warmly, turned and walked to the door. He collected Kitty en route, with a gentle arm around her waist, and they exited stage left. The audience of wild and domestic fowl greeted them with a cacophony of quacks, hisses, squawks, crows and clucks and they basked in the sunshine's applause. They mounted the motorcycle and throttled slowly out of the yard, leaving their helmets and accessories within them swinging lazily from the handlebars. Harry skillfully wound the heavy lump up the hill, along a sheep track of grass that had been nibbled short to the hard chalk soil. The gentle breeze ruffled their locks the higher they climbed. He was comforted and relieved by the little girl's slender arms wrapped around his waist. Oneness again. He was catapulted into the mental firmament when he felt her head turn to the left and her right cheek was lain across his upper back. She squeezed him gently in the moment. Heaven.

Ignoring the previous day's parking area at the entrance to the wheat field, Harry toiled the machine towards the summit of the hill and halted it next to the steep upturned turf nipple on its top. With unusually sage-like foresight, he thought it was romantically unwise to disclose at that particular moment that it was one of the thousands of ancient barrows scattered across Wiltshire's ridges. These neolithic mausoleums were once packed white chalk, which glowed white in the night when the moon, who's Goddess man worshipped, shone. The couple dismounted, Harry unclipped the pannier and removed Kitty's bag. She thanked him with a smile and crouched on the floor. She opened it and removed the photographic apparatus she required. Harry jumped up the mini mound, turned and offered her his hand. She took it, revelling in his courteous care. She felt like a warrior queen being pulled into her chariot by her brave consort. Holding her eye with his own for the journey upwards, Harry made sure she was safe before he released his grip, cast his arm in an arch across the valley beyond, and announced.

"I thought this the best place to start your survey, Kitty. From this vantage point you will be able to get an initial sense and perspective of this wondrous place and circular happening." The army captain and spy thought it best that her familiarity of the place, after her aerial assault on the Basket's crop formation and Barry's cock malformation, would remain a secret. The photographer and artist gauped in awe at the world around her. The sky was a perfect blue. The sun shone fiercely above. The circle radiated its beauty from the enormous waving wheat field around it. The steps and promenentaries of the cliffs and ridges cast vivid dark shadows. The valley of patchwork fields, woods and villages shimmered in the summer haze. On the opposite side of the valley, some three or four miles away, an undulating wall of peaks and bowls rose spectacularly to the enormous plateau of bleak wilderness beyond. The Plain stretched out to the horizon beyond, veiled in a heated mystery of wavering air.

"God's Country," she whispered, then added, "Or whatever power from the heavens has created this infinite beauty on our earth." She liked to keep her divine options open. She swung her slung camera from under her arm and set it to the panoramic function. She started her slow and graceful sweep of all she surveyed from the left ridge. Her lens passed the dazzling sun's rays then was guided back into the blue and gold of high and low. It absorbed the scientific signature below, the cliff and plain afar, the barns and dwellings in mid range and the steep bank away to her right. Then it stopped. Whilst she examined the picture on the view finder, Harry stood and gulped in the spectacular view. As she moved, he digested every curve and nuance of her perfect form. The gentle slope of her neck, the pinch of her waist, the small peeks of her breasts, the roll of her hips, the plump mounds of her bum, the flowing undulations of her thighs and calves and then back to her bottom. Oh! That bottom! It looked so tasty! He imagined kneeling behind her, holding her neat hips and biting it! Softly, of course, but enough to make her yelp.

His fantasy was interrupted by a distant call. He recognised the sound to be his name. It was repeated, softly, again and again. Suddenly he was acutely aware that the source of this Siren was remarkably close. Harry blinked and followed the sound north from his previous transfixation. Approximately two feet into this ocular ascent, his eyes stopped at a pair of luscious lips that appeared to be mouthing his name. As his focus intensified, he saw pale skin to softly sharpened cheek bone, a proud regal nose, arched eyebrows atop green pools of sparkle and mystery. These were hooded by blinking long lashes and all were occasionally veiled in long wildly wavy tresses in the breeze.

"Haaaaa-rrrrry, Haaaarrrrry," whispered the voice. "Haaarrrry, Haarrry, Harry. Harry!" The exclamation mark finally broke the spell. He looked Kitty in the eyes then guiltily shifted his attention to his shuffling toes. He blushed. "Harry?" She commanded attention. He raised his eyes once more. "Were you checking me out?" He nodded slowly. The last downward direction of his head movement gave him an excuse to resume the study of his feet. "Harry?!" Her tone was mildly sharp but it had the desired effect. His chin snapped off its breastbone hideout. "Do you like what you see, you perv?" she teased, giving the object of his fascination a little wiggle and accompanied it with a bigger giggle. He nodded, this time with relieved enthusiasm thanks to her joviality. "You dirty old bugger!" she laughed, then beseeched, "Come here." She outstretched her arms, hands open, palms up. Kitson lumbered forward, more in the trance like style of a zombie than his favoured silver screen movie heroes. He took her hands and stared into the green pools of sparkle that were the root cause of his hypnosis. He plunged deep into their shining aura. He was lost.

Kitty released his hands. They swung like weightless pendulums back and forth, ever slowing until they halted at his side. The stillness of the moment was met and matched by the emptiness that Harry felt at the severed contact from his warmest dream. His disappointment was short-lived. The girl reached her hands up and clasped his neck on either side, bracing her toes up so that her enchanting face reached his. She planted her lips against his. But this time she did not flee. She held him there for a brief moment before they dissolved into each other. He turned his head, opened his mouth, wet his lips and wiped them slowly across her own. She opened them invitingly and their tongues met, first softly and tenderly, then eagerly and earnestly. As the kiss became more impassioned, Harry pulled her body to his and their bodies were fused in a warm waterfall of fluidity and love. He wrapped his strong arms around her as they embraced harder and deeper, their heads rhythmically rocking from side to side as they lustily explored each other's mouths. Kitty moaned lightly. It sounded similar to the meow of a cat. Harry was defenceless against his wanton desire and his trouser twitched in surrender. Kitty stopped, panting very slightly. She looked at him in the eye, smiled lovingly, then glanced down and giggled.

"Have you got a telescopic lens in your pocket," she asked coyly, "Or are you just pleased to see me." Harry squirmed in embarrassment.

"S..S..Sorry!" He started to apologise but she hushed him by placing her index finger over his lips.

"Shuuush, Silly! I love that you are so turned on by our kiss. It is wonderful!" In affirmation, she removed her finger and replanted her lips there instead, holding their wet warmth on his for a few seconds more. She pulled back, sighed contentedly, then added, "Come along, Handsome. We've got work to do!" She pulled him to the brink of the barrow and they stood there looking down the short incline. "By the way," she added, "I think it is the most wonderfully romantic place in the whole wide world to share such a fab kiss with such a fun man. It is made even sexier for me that it happened on a mound of homage to the ancient moon goddess. Call me a naughty white witch but I adore that sort of dark love!" She laughed, then jumped. Harry seemingly floated down next to her. He had met his match at last. She was clearly omnipotent. He basked in her glory.

He straddled the Harley and offered his hand to her. She took it, smiled at him, curtsied gracefully, giggled childishly then let him pull her up where she sat with both sets of booted toes on one rest in the side saddle position. She waved her arm forward and ordered,

"Onward now, my King of the Road!"

"Your wish is my command, Oh, Great Queen Kitty Cat!" The recently inaugurated biker answered with a grin, "To the palace and do save the horsepower!" In answer to his confusing wordplay, he let the bike roll down the incline, engine off, gently squeezing the brakes so that his precious yet precariously perched prize remained in the upper most comfort. He slid their temporal state carriage to a soft stop and kicked the side stand down. Having descended in an already natural royal demeanor, Kitty awaited her charge who bowed low and long with a flourish of his hand when he planted his boots back on his kingdom. Kitty squeaked in appreciation of his gallant gesture before she started to walk towards the field. "My Lady?" Harry too was warming to his new role, "Dally awhile please? I must instruct the footman to bring forth our banquet." He clapped his hands quickly twice then, on the realisation that no such servant was forthcoming, adopted the part for himself. Luckily, it came very naturally to him. He unclipped the pannier and removed an elegant little wicker basket. Holding the object's handle in his left hand, he scurried to Kitty's side obediantly. Switching back to his regal role, he raised his significant nose high in the air. He used his right hand to first adjust his imaginary crown, then secondly offered it, raised with a limp wrist, for his consort to take in a similar manner. Thus regaled, they set forth.

'Words Of Love'

Historically, the downfall of most monarchies has been due to a lack of understanding about the wants and needs of the people and powers over which they unwittingly rule. The dynasty of King Harry and Queen Kitty would prove that lessons can be learnt from the past to avoid such a catastrophe. Although their kingdom was imaginary, a sense of duty and purpose hung heavily from their shoulders. It spurred them on towards their goal of discovery and adventure, albeit one of them in open innocence, the other in covert discretion.

Hand in hand they sailed along the edge of the field and then down the tractor tracks. As they neared the circle, Harry felt the now familiar pulse of energy. When they entered the formation they were silent, soaking up the atmosphere. Harry noted that the power was not as great as the day before. But even dissipated, it was awesome. The virgin did not know this. The breaking of her crop hymen was one of the most beautiful experiences that Kitty had ever enjoyed. Her body tingled, especially her slender hands and elegant feet. She felt hot, flushed and aroused, similar sensations to those when she was starting to menstruate. Her femininity oozed. She felt delirious with pleasure and squeaked occasionally in her distinctive manner as she digested every minute detail of the masterpiece.

She hunched over the white powder, glanced at Harry to check he was watching, pretended to snort it up one nostril, giggled and then apologised.

"Sorry! I couldn't resist. That was mean and cruel of me. One day, when you are ready, I want you to tell me all about your past application of the Devil's Dandruff please?" Harry looked away. He was not ready. In fact, he was in a right old pickle about his Columbian lover and alcoholic slave master. Sensing his acute discomfort, Kitty returned to the point in fact. "This is definitely the fire hydrant variety of white crystal in my humble opinion. It is much flakier than the glass variety." She paused in thought for a while then continued, "Whoever made this crop circle must have needed it to put out a blaze, I guess?"

"Whoever?" Harry questioned. "Surely we have ascertained that it would be impossible for even a large group of people to create this between dusk and dawn? Barry was here at both the set and rise of the sun. He saw nobody except the army. The helicopter crew couldn't have done it. Unless they have been hiding a secret power pack to make extraordinarily beautiful artwork instead of utilising it for their damned weaponry?" Kitty feigned surprise as her apostle chuntered on. "What's more, what burning? This wheat is bent and unbroken, not burnt. My online research informs me that it takes temperatures of hundreds of degrees to bend these plants. That kind of heat would surely ignite them and all the wildlife inhabiting them. This crop is fine and healthy. Nothing is burnt. Nothing is dead.

"It's not about 'Who' did this. It's about 'What' did this. Circles have been appearing for centuries and people have been reporting glowing orbs of light around their locations for just as long. We have only really started to register them, documenting them more accurately and increasingly, thanks to aerial developments. From the birth of balloons, then to planes, helicopters and drones. Whatever is creating them is doing so almost invisibly. The rare film footage that exists, proves that these forms appear in minutes, sometimes in just a handful of seconds. Whatever is mapping and plotting them is doing so with calculated intelligence. The designs are all highly complicated patterns, mathematical puzzles or carefully considered images. They are a message in a pictorial language that is understood by the multilingual inhabitants of our planet. They are a signature for mankind to decipher and learn from."

"Are you really suggesting that they are formed by an intelligence from outside Earth?" Kitty came straight to the point.

"Why on Earth not, if you'll excuse the pun?" Harry quickly struck back before he continued his intergalactic rant. "Scientific evidence points to the high likelihood that there could be other life out there in the universe beyond. So why not intelligent life? Whatever is sending these messages is probably warning us about our own inevitable collapse and imminent destruction as we wring the resources of our very lives dry from beneath our toes and from the air we breathe. Maybe, whatever it is could have sent the messages light years ago before its own habitation was destroyed? It is trying to help us. This awesome power, that you can still feel all around you, could have been used for destruction but it hasn't been. It has been used to show us that this power can cure and nurture, not kill and maim. Art and love is the perfect antidote for ignorance and hatred. We must learn and we must react quickly for all our sakes."

Kitty stared at the man she was rapidly falling in love with. Whether he was right or wrong, his passion for nature, his freethinking liberalism, his scientific objectivity and his chivalrous romanticism made him interesting, intimate and approachable to her. She trusted him completely. Trust was the most important thing to her in a personal relationship. That was the reason why she could never be close to anybody at her conniving workplace. She was struck by a desire, a want, a need, to tell him everything about herself for the very first time. She did not want to lie to him. She believed his ideology far more than the ridiculous veil that the MoD were hiding behind amongst their own. The heavy curtain that shrouded any information from the general public now seemed nonsense to her.

Even if Major de Crecy Conrad-Pickles' vaugeries were released into the media domain, it would garner sufficient interest for positive progress. The initial fear generated by his strange Russian or Chinese communist conspiracy theories would quickly evaporate when the press realised that they were absolute rubbish. However, the exposure generated from even the release of the most simple facts about the phenomenon would push most intelligent people to demand the truth, share information, learn the science and make objective and rational assumptions. Knowledge is strength. This could only be a benefit to mankind. Kitty was on the verge of confessing all when the subject was changed by the most thoughtful fellow she had ever come across.

"Are you as hungry as I am?" Kitson enquired. She immediately answered his question with an enthusiastic nod and smile.

"I could eat a horse!" He laughed.

"Luckily, for Beautiful You, Queen Kitty Cat, we are not in the Gallic land of snail, frog, songbird and equine delicacies. We are in Wiltshire. We tend to do things a little simpler over here. Which suits the simpleton in me!" Captain Parker was frustrated at his self depreciation but not shy of the local fare so prepared herself for the inevitable ham, cheese, tomatoes, pickles and bread. Once more this man's thought and care astonished her. He was a girly boy. Having laid their motorcycle jackets on the bouncing 'Basket', they sat side by side and he flipped open the little wicker portable version. The weave of both seemed a perfect union. He pulled out a little blue and white checked cloth and spread it in front of them. Matching napkins appeared, two plates from inside the lid followed and an assortment of cutlery that had been neatly buckled to the inside lid were added to the ensemble.

"What a gorgeous little picnic set!" Kitty exclaimed, clapping her hands briefly in appreciation.

"Isn't it fab?" answered the waiter with punchy pleasure, "Fruit gave it to me as a housewarming present many years ago. I think he was still smarting from the batty boy revenge I inflicted on him after his fairy fiasco. He said it would prove more useful to me than the sticker had been." He paused then added with aplomb, "And, by Jingo, he was right! Useful? That's the understatement of the century. I'm having lunch with the most gorgeous little cat in the whole wide world. Bingo!" He grinned broadly before confirming his joy with a lean and a kiss. They both smiled and gazed at each other before the maitre d' snapped back to his duties.

"For zee premier plat," Harry's Franglais was of an interesting mix but his accent was passable, "We 'ave des prawns et avocados dans une sauce magnifique de Marie Rose." He produced a flip blade from its suitably French branded wooden handle and proceeded to cut then peel the fruits. He flung the husks and stones into the field beyond the artwork's perimeter. Noticing her momentary horror, he pacified, "Entirely biodegradable, I assure you. Unlike zis little beauty." He flipped the supermarket plastic lid off the premixed crustacean cocktail. "Excusez moi, Mademoiselle. Not every morceau is 'andmade." He curled his mouth sulkily down and stuck his nose arrogantly up as he said so, clearly in disgust at his chef. He added a nonchalant shrug and dramatic, "Buff!" for good measure. With a theatrical flourish, he dispensed the pink contents onto the soft green pears. He then spoke with disdain for his previous lack of consideration, "A am terribly sorry, Miss Parker, mais maintenant, desirez-vous quelque chose a boire? Maybe something a little fizzy?" Kitty nodded with enthusiasm at the prospect of the product of Epernay. She covered her disappointment convincingly when he produced a bottle of sparkling elderflower and two plastic stemmed glasses and poured. She was impressed that it was cold. Another magical trick from the smaller of the two baskets present.

"Harry?" Her intrigue got the better of her. "Why have you chosen not to have your beloved alcohol to wash down this delicious food?" Despite his aversion to this style of questioning, he sighed and paused to consider the answer that he had been mentally preparing himself for. They ate their starter in silence for a brief time. Then, he manned up.

"Yesterday was a turning point in my life. I have been conflicted in myself, like any human, by positive and negative forces for many years. During all those times, I often turned to alcohol and sometimes cocaine to boost my body with fake energy and shelter my soul from reality. This was terrific fun during the good times but, when the party slowed down, the Dark Ages rolled in. They were ruthless. As was my way, I jumped on the devil's back and he took me on a rapid spiral towards his underground lair. Once I was there, I thought I was too weak to pull myself out. Besides, el diablo made that as difficult as possible. He made sure that my love of dance and girls was perverted with an orgy of one night stands, mountains of coke and barrels of booze. It was all too easy. I failed to see the effect it was having on my parents, my family, my son, my love life, my friends, my business. Most importantly, I had failed myself.

"Two fundamental changes occurred yesterday. My arrival here in the morning put me in my place. I was overwhelmed by the physical beauty, the vibrant energy and the mystical enchantment of this perplexing puzzle. It's majesty made me realise who I was. I am Nobody. Despite my addled mind, I have often thought about legacy. The goal of leaving something behind for others to remember you by after your death. Death." He whispered the word, "I suddenly realised that I would be dead in five to ten years if I carried on that demonic lifestyle. And when I died, my friends would say, 'He was a good bloke but he didn't half cane it.' My parents would be distraught. A wasted life after all their love and support. My business would collapse and jewellery clients would say, 'By jingo, they made fabulous stuff but now he's carked it, we'll just have to find somebody else.' My house would be sold and the pathetic profit beyond the mortgage would go on death duties. My son would inherit nothing and when he was older would ask, 'Who was my father?' The honest would reply, "He was a wonderfully kind man that loved all good people, especially you, but threw it all away on drink and drugs.' A brief rotten legacy, quickly forgotten." Kitson wiped a tear from his eye and Kitty tried to put an arm around him but he gently pushed it away. He smiled sheepishly at her, tasted his tears, then continued.

"Sorry, Kitty. I just need to say these things without anybody's support." He tempered himself before he continued. "The power of this circle awakened me. It seemed to shout at me, 'Hey, Nobody! Be somebody! Do something!' And so I am. Since the first time I got drunk when I was thirteen years old and my parents started driving me to the hospital to have my stomach pumped, through the 'good' times when I lost the first day of this Millenia unconscious after a Caribbean drinking contest, to necking so much red wine that I soiled myself in the really bad days, there has never been an 'off' button. Add to that the countless nights high on cocaine and, with hangovers and recovery times, there has barely been a day of clarity in thirty two years. So I am going to do something. Our jewellery is sensational and I am going to sing that from the rooftops. Wouldn't it be fab to have somebody look at our stuff in two hundred years and say, 'Wow! Look at this! Is it really from those brothers in The Smithy?' Similarly, this crop art is incredible and I believe that mankind should learn all about it so that we can better ourselves. I will shout that to the heavens! Let them all remember us for selling this beautiful truth in art?

"I drove back from here yesterday and stopped at the pub. I didn't understand what I had to do at that point. Then the second happening occurred and that catalysed this change. I bumped into you, Kitty. Please don't take this the wrong way, Darling Cat. I do not know where your, my or our destinies lie. We only just re-met each other, for God's sake! But what I do know is simple. When we met each other on the Playa, I felt an immediate attraction to you. I trusted you too. Well, until your misunderstood joke. But yesterday, when you called me back and explained your real intentions, I immediately felt that trust again. As soon as that happened, I relaxed and enjoyed the wonderful woman that you are. After you had left, I read this by chance." Harry reached into his jeans pocket and pulled out a neatly folded piece of previously crumpled paper. He unfolded it, cleared his throat and read, "Desperately Seeking..."

"Oh, Ffffffff...... Fiddle Sticks!" Having expelled her long missed grandmother's favourite words when the F swear variety loomed largest, Kitty grabbed her lonely hearts missive. "Where did you find this? This is sooooooo embarrassing! I can barely look at you!"

"Please don't be embarrassed!" Harry soothed, "It was on the table when you went to pee and take the drinks in. It has helped me to see who you are and, more selfishly, who I am. I genuinely think I am the man that you are describing. I admit, I can't help with your female preference but I am in touch with my more effeminate side. Except for the very last request, I'm your man. Go on, read it." Parker scanned the document with a thoroughness that belied her officer standing. He was right. It could be him. She read the last sentence, then giggled.

"Your reference is to the last word but, given your incredibly thorough investigations over the last two days, I think the whole last sentence is relevant. 'No spies or addicts.'"

"An astute observation, Kitty Cat. It takes one to know one after all your probing today!" The spy winced at how close he was to the truth. How could she tell him now? She was temporarily reprieved when he changed the subject. He smiled with relief from his psychological download and returned to his servile duties. "Now, for the main course!"

He dived back into the basket and produced an array of delicacies that he had lovingly prepared. A tupperware of rice with sweetcorn and almonds appeared. Another contained enormous slithers of beef tomatoes, fresh basil and mini buffalo mozzarella balls. Olive oil was drizzled sparingly over both. The captain's own meticulous efficiency was matched when the jeweller pulled out a small thermos flask, twisted the two lids off and tipped some piping hot halloumi slices onto their plates. Harry had evidently got up and grilled them that morning. She beamed. A man after her own heart. Let him feast on it. Usually a pescatarian, Kitty only rarely strayed into the world of carnivores. The exception was slow roasted lamb. As if by magic, he produced some generously cut pink slices. This was the perfect picnic for her. Was this fragile flower really the perfect man for her? Judging by the smug grin on his face as he registered her delight, he certainly thought so.

They munched through their feast. There was no need to engage in conversation merely for politeness. They were comfortable and just needed to eat. They were both content with their newfound love for crop circles. They were joyous in their love for each other. It all seemed so dashed simple. One set of green eyes gazed adoringly into another set of green eyes with complimentary adoration. Two Mediterranean style noses twitched in the hazy heat of the field. One terse and tight pair of lips grinned at the other's luscious full pair which smiled lovingly back. Harry even felt comfortable enough not to apologise in that jolly English way when she removed a little piece of green basil from the corner of his mouth. She must be a keeper if she could achieve such a Herculean task without him feeling awkward or embarrassed. On repletion, Kitson resumed his waitering role by holding onto the plates and cutlery tightly whilst jettisoning the last edible scraps into the field beyond with a strong flick of the wrist. Harry grinned at his simultaneous thought to this action. The once Wiltshire javelin champion had still got it. Contrarily, Kitty thought that the poor man must have been single for far too long to have developed such a localised strength in his wrist and arm.

Harry muttered another curse at supermarkets under his breath. The girl recognised the plastic theme of his whispers when he produced three different punets of berry. He tore off the transparent seal from the solid clear base of them, each literally prefixed with 'blue', 'straw' and 'rasp'. As she popped the delicious fruits into her mouth, Kitty linked the first two words with the sky and crop. Her search for a rasp was unfortunately forthcoming as her host wiped the knives and forks clean on a stone.

"Harry?!" She interrupted the rasper, "Not now, please! That noise is so ghastly. It was so peaceful here. Can you do that when we get home please?"

"We? Home?" stammered the man on receipt of Hermes' marvellous tidings from Aphrodite. He quickly recomposed himself after this stunning revelation, "Sure. I'll clean then when we get home." He resumed his gravelly tone, rather than actions, and gently placed a strawberry between her lips before nibbling one himself. He watched her eat hers slowly and replaced it adoringly with another when she had finished. This time he leant forward and kissed her on the lips, biting the bulbous red flesh between them in half. They both ate their demi rations and then kissed without the juicy obstacle.

Cupid's bolt hit them. The food had seemed like mana. The sparkling soft had tasted like champagne. The heat of the sun pulsated on their foreheads. Their kisses seemed electrically charged. The energy of their circular environment pulsated through their bodies. Their vision blurred in the intensity of the moment. They reeled like dervishes intoxicated by all that is mystical about them. The polarity of their sexes meshed in a single union of delirious bliss.

He rolled her onto her back on their mattress of leather, check and straw. He pulled a blade of the latter from her locks and smoothed the rest behind her temples before he kissed her again. Her body rose to meet his in their tantalysing tangle of tantra. She fumbled briefly with his shirt before thanking the powers of heaven and tailoring that boy and girl buttons are opposed for this very reason. On successful completion, Kitty ran a hand inside between his smooth strong shoulders and down his chest. Leaving his mouth, she traced her hand's steps with her lips. She kissed his neck behind the ear, his hard collarbone then his pectoral.

Harry was overcome by the eroticism of this swirling vortex of love and passion. As is often man's downfall in moments of heightened arousal, he attempted a more direct approach. He gently tugged her blouse from the beltline of her skinny jeans. He popped the button of the leg wear and carefully unzipped them. Half cupping his hand, he pushed it beneath the now visible small white triangle of knicker and down between her thighs. He gasped. Her heat was intense. So hot! And wet! She was so wet! As his fingers teased her, Kitty moaned, the sound seemingly resonated from the very core of her soul. His fingers were enveloped in her lustful warmth and inviting moisture. He worked them back and forth as if they were magnetised. She moaned more. He had an overwhelming desire to taste her.

But Kitty had other plans. She first pulled his hand away from her panties then pushed him forcibly away and onto his back. She sprang up and onto him, pinning him to the ground. She hungrily undressed him until he lay at her mercy with just his white opened chemise guarding his back from the straw. Kitty seemed ecstatic by the eager reaction of his manhood. She grasped it in strong fingers, making it the man's turn to moan. Whilst slowly pulling her clenched hand repeatedly up and down, Kitty stood up slowly and with bent knees smiled at her future lover. She released her grasp of him temporarily. She removed her own shirt and Harry gasped as he stared up at the perfection of his preconceived fantasy. The saucer curve from her hip to the undulations of her small breasts were his twin heaven confirmed. She discarded with her remaining clothes and resumed her leg stance either side of Harry's torso. The devotee stared up at his goddess. Her naked olive skin bathed in the brilliant sun's glory. Her long hair waved gently in the breeze, framed by a sea of azure. In that wonderful moment, he soaked up every detail as his dream became reality. The wanton look in her eyes, her slightly panting breath, the corresponding rise and fall of her breasts. He felt an overwhelming desire to taste her once more. He groaned when he saw the result of his previous foray there glint in the sunlight, beads of opaque lust clinging to her gateway. The triangle of her long slender legs and his chest seemed like some divine geometric perfection.

Once more, Kitty took command. She pushed him back to his previous position with one hand. She bent her legs. She reached behind her with her other hand and resumed her former grip before she pushed her body back. She hovered on her haunches before she sat down very slowly upon him. Her bottom stopped at his thighs. She held herself there and moaned. It was a primeval sound which made the man beneath her shiver with delight. She looked skyward and Harry gazed up and marvelled at her long waving locks cascade over her breasts, her bullet nipples poked aggressively through the folds of hair. He gripped either side of her hips and pulled her down firmly.

They held this capture, twitching against each other, locked inside. Eventually, the shuddering girl released her eyes from their solar searching and returned her gaze to her prisoner. She placed her hands on his taught shoulders, leant forward and kissed him. She opened her mouth to his and tasted their love. Nose to nose, eye to eye, they kissed again and again. She lay her breasts to his and both were comforted by the bond inside their baking bodies.

Despite his defensive position, Harry turned on the erotic offensive. He flexed and slowly pushed himself upwards. Their dampened frames slipped rhymically together as they passionately kissed and rampantly loved. There was no hurry. There was just a completeness within each other that seemed to buck and fall for an eternity. Oneness. Her knees gripped his sides, her arms his neck as they pushed and panted deeper and louder. He rotated his massaging fingers and thumbs from the small of her back to the heavenly hillocks of her bum. As their bodies slapped faster and harder, their groans and moans turned to screams and yells. They pumped and squeezed each other onwards towards a frenzy and climax. The seeming earthquake ripped through their limbs, jarred their minds and sent them into fractals of delirious dreams. As he released, her body exploded in complement. They cried, nibbled and scratched each other as they contorted in the throes of shared orgasm.

At last, all was still. Their two bodies lay drenched against the other. Her body went limp atop his. His head lolled sideways, her hair followed his wet brow's movement. Her face lay on his matted chest. She locked her arms over and under each of his. He held her back firmly with them. They wrapped their legs inside and out of the others. They were bound by a writhing sea of limbs that resembled amorous serpents sinking after their dance of love. They shut their eyes, suddenly exhausted by the emotions of the day. The power of the circle, the strength of their shared trust, the revelations of their love, the intimacy of their lust, all amalgamated at that very moment. The soft breeze tickled their skins dry. The hot sun soothed their replete souls and bones. The day lulled. The circle rejoiced. The lovers slept.

'Sunday Morning'

For a most sharp witted lass, Kitty was extremely confused when she awoke. The noise of strange snoring is often disconcerting but when it emanates from a proximity of mere inches, it produces a far more panicking effect. She opened her eyes. This did not help. Optical assurance was demanded and the fact that it was dark merely hindered her investigation. Her extra sensory perception was further confused by her realisation that she was naked. What's more, she appeared to have been sleeping atop the pink skin of a farmyard pig that issued the repetitive sound. As her eyes started adjusting to the lack of light and her memory filtered back to the delirium of the recent food and sex orgy, her mood lightened. The outline of a large nose rather than a porcine snout and the object's bony lack of bacon meat confirmed her reasons for increased calm. The frightful noise emanated from the throat of one Harry Kitson, Esquire.

"Haaarrrry," she whispered in his ear, "Haarrry. Harry!" On remembering how long it had taken her to get his attention earlier while he was awake, she resorted to the louder nomination far quicker in these new slumbering circumstances. The effect produced a dramatic nasal intake of breath that sounded more like the contented sound of an oversized boar dreaming of being in a sty with an overabundance of sows.

"Quuuu-aaaahhhhh!" rattled the nose, before it resumed its previous metronomic sound. Kitty was reminded of the word 'rasp' once more.

"HARRY!" This was no time to dawdle so the army captain put some extra vim and volume into her next salvo. The effects were as desired.

The hog was awakened and immediately replaced by a bumbling Englishman.

"Er? What? Er? Er? Er? I'm terribly sorry, I appear to have nodded off? What the heck? It's dark!" The man scratched his neck then rubbed his eyes. After a quick assessment of the situation, he came to an obvious solution. "Let's get dressed and go home, My Darling Kitty Cat?" In the soft light of the three quarter moon above, the photographer saw the flash of his teeth in full smile. He was clearly far happier with the predicament he had awoken to than she had initially been. He gave her an affectionate peck on the cheek to clarify her assumption concerning his joviality.

"Your snoring woke me up!" Kitty exclaimed. "What the hell is that all about?"

"Oh, it's far worse if I've been smoking and drinking," replied Harry, "but I hope these are the sorts of things that I will improve on at the earliest opportunity. No addicts." He reminded her of their shared goal and she discerned a corresponding wink in the semi darkness. "In the meantime, the trick is to roll me over onto my side or front. I'll stop then."

"Oh, thanks for the advice," she answered meekly. She wasn't really very convinced that he would be able to control his addictions or whether she could shift his dead weight during sleep. Luckily for Kitson, she was in the mood for trial by error and benefit of the doubt. "Great advice, Harry," she added more cheerfully, "Let's get the heck out of here. What time is it?" Harry fished his phone from his jean's pocket nearby.

"Strike a light! It's just after midnight!" He paused and she clearly saw that same grin in the glow of the mobile device as he added, "And not a pumpkin or witch in sight? You really are an Enigma!" The dressing of clothes, packing of culinary remains, plus the walking to and mounting of motorcycle took about as long as lardons to crisp in a frying pan. After carefully negotiating the hill and farm track by the lights of full beams and fattened crescent on high, they reached the road and within a further twenty minutes they had made the journey east where they pulled up outside Harry's Smithy.

It was dark inside, bar the light from a single lamp in the kitchen. Having kicked off their footwear, the ancient ceramic tiles were cooling and refreshed their toes. He pulled her to and up the spiral wooden staircase. Halfway up, he considerately tapped the lintel to the floor above before standing with head stooped, back bent and shoulders against it. His lesson in 1650's average height and matching architecture complete, they resumed the ascent and turned left into a dressing room. It too had a night light burning for direction. The bedroom opened up before them and the bathroom was to the right. All the gnarled floor boards were covered in cosy kilims and rugs of Turkish and Persian origin. A mystifying mixture of wild British landscapes and Hindu love portraits adorned the walls. It was a comfortable nest of art and romance.

Harry switched on the bathroom light and disappeared behind the open door inside. A couple of seconds later Kitty heard the hiss of the shower and her lover reappeared already in the process of rapid undress. His nudity complete, he turned his attention to his feline lover and assisted her, thus doubling the speed with which she disrobed. He coaxed her into the already steaming room. The walled shower was to the left, loo, central basin and free standing Victorian bath to the right. They were shrouded by walls of light blue paint, white border tiles and mosaic panels of deep lapis lazuli cobalt colours. Gilded mirrors adorned the walls. It was like a miniature bath house from antiquity. She smiled at the thought of her one time Roman gladiator, now naked in front of her. They held each other close. They kissed, lustfully and longingly. When she felt him harden against her tummy, she reached her hand down and rubbed him.

They darted for the shower, letting the hot stream gush over their bodies whilst they kissed and played. Remembering his hilltop fantasy, Harry spun the woman around. He gripped her wrists and held them against the far wall. He knelt behind her and pulled her bottom onto his face. She sighed and widened her legs. The hot water cascaded through his hair and down his cheeks as he lapped at her repeatedly. Kitty purred with delight and, when she could take no more, she wriggled her hands free from his vice, reached round and pulled him upwards by his elbow. He resumed his grip on her wrists with one hand, placing them high above her head against the streaming wall. He used his other to guide himself inside her. He pushed forward, she back and then they both paused. Guidance complete, Harry used his free hand to grasp and twist her chin carefully sideways so that their mouths could conjoin. They rhythmically pushed against, then away, from each other, passionately kissing all the while.

Harry shuddered. Before he lost all control, he stopped then smiled like a naughty schoolboy at the clearly disappointed reaction from his recently moaning lover. After a quick rinse, he turned off the shower and reached for a large towel. He briefly flashed it over his limbs and hair before opening it wide for Kitty to step into. He then wrapped her shoulders in its fronds and led her to the bedroom. He sat on the enormous super king and watched her dry her body then hair. She found his comb by the dressing table and ran it through her long locks. The light pine four poster dominated the room. It was bedecked in a beautiful silk embroidered lotus pattern cover and pillows which smelt of some exotic Eastern musk. It was crowned by a translucent damasc curtain that was tied by large golden ropes with tassels. This gave Kitty an idea for beautiful dominatrix revenge.

She pushed the man back bedwards with a reassuringly sultry smile. She reached for one of the ropes which formerly made the muslin curtain drift dreamily shut. She wrapped the cord around his wrists then, having raised his arms above his head, knotted it to the slatted wooden headboard. She untied another drape fastener and repeated the action with ankles and footboard. Before he had time to doubt his submission, she first knelt beside and lovingly licked him before she swung one leg over his face and sat down to urge his lust on.

For a second time, the man reigned back on his climax. Kitty was nonetheless reassured by his desire to titillate and tantalyse her for longer than they might have if unharnessed. She relinquished her bondage of him and the unfettered man tilted her off him before lifting her writhing torso with one arm, balancing on the mattress with the other, and lowered her gently onto her back. Her head sunk deep into the soft Indian cushions and her body was enveloped amidst cosy goose down. He placed his knees between her own and straightened his arms beneath her smooth armpits. He arched his back and pushed his pelvis forward. She pushed herself to greet him, bending her legs high and back so her thighs gripped him. She held the back of his neck as he let his weight guide him deeper on his repeated and increasingly rapid downstroke.

Coming together was reason, both physical and mental, for the couples' ecstatic celebrations. They moaned and panted, thrust and bucked, screamed and shouted, licked and bit, kissed and nibbled. Their slippery torsos simultaneously spasmed and their sexes gripped and twitched inside the other. As the convulsions lessened, they held their position, locked in their love making. Their eyes gazed adoringly at each other, they smiled, then giggled, then laughed before they rolled onto their sides, still entwined, and nuzzled into the opposing neck napes.

"Harry?" whispered the army captain. She was tired but in an inquisitorial mood. "That was dreamy. Thank you. You are my quintessential hunk." She teased.

"Ha!" he recognised her jape but returned the compliment more sincerely. "That was so much fun, you gorgeous Little Cat! You give me strength everytime I touch you. You make me feel like dynamite when you make love to me. There is an understanding and trust, even when we are playing fun and naughty games, in everything we do. I think you are the most wonderful girl I've ever met." He smiled lovingly before continuing, "Not to mention the damndest cleverest researcher that we could possibly ask for on our circular navigations. How on earth did you find out all that stuff about the white powder compounds?"

Kitty was not ready to share the extent of her former research, let alone the military and covert organisations that she officially and unofficially did the work for. The innocent romance of her new friend was a far cry from the bewildering ineptitude of Major de Crecy Conrad-Pickles. She thought that it would be merely a matter of time, thanks to her Parisian pornography film footage, that Monty's pathetic smokescreen would be removed by her other bosses. What really upset her was that until then he would continue to type his dictats regarding local artists or more distant communist factions purely to keep his familial warmongering operations in profit. Laziness and greed were vices she couldn't condone. But how was she going to bridge the gap between the opposing poles of truths and lies that she now found herself betwixt? With these thoughts in mind, she answered Harry's question with her own lie in mind.

"Same as you, you soppy sod! I just research it all online."

"But so much information has been lost, covered up and disappeared by the powers that be," moaned Harry. "It is a minefield of false information, fake news and perverted distortions of the truth."

"Yes. But those times are a changin'! We are both testimony to the incredible power of the earth within the circles. It made us feel strong, healthy and horny. We slept in that forcefield for hours. The various emotions that I feel now, add up to the grand total of freakin' fabulous! Now that we know it can do all these things, it is so important to find out how, before why, by whom or by what."

"I was transfixed by this subject last year when I saw the glowing orb at the ghost crop circle. The healing of my bashed hand was one of the oddest but most pleasurable experiences in my life." Harry paused for a moment before recollecting, "In fact, I think I was fascinated by the topic way back when Barry and I came across a manmade one at the Summer Solstice once upon a long ago. That morning was a hallucinogenic blur but I still remember how upset my farming friend had been at the vandalisation of another agricultural ally's field."

"For a burly bloke, he is remarkably sensitive to the ways of the land." Kitty agreed.

"You are right, Little Cat. He's always been a great friend to me. Barry is a wonderful combination of fun, brawn and mindfulness. I can't wait to hear how he got on with his bigwig power client though. It is the sort of situation where his calming influence, however out of control the subject matter seems, can shine through and make his client sit up and listen. It will be even better if he can enlist his help."

"We all have a small part to play in this big adventure, Harry. Thank you for providing the mystical vision and belief in the limitless possibilities that these beautiful artworks conjure. I want to take pictures of them, study them, along with historical texts so that we can make a valuable contribution to the scientific research of this incredible subject. How we can bridge the gap between the general public and army is of primary importance. The military are clearly interested in something extraordinary. Let's hope that we can come up with a better plan than Barry's chopper flash!" They laughed together before she continued, "I'm quite sure that his more professional approach to his client was far less physically and much more intellectually exposing earlier!"

174

The laughter soon reverted to giggles. A brace of "Goodnights" were exchanged with tender kisses, then smiles, then sighs, then lazy breaths, then the measured contentment of slumber. Kitty managed a last smile as she heard her partner exhale purely. His sideways snoring advice was true.

Later that day, Kitty awoke in puzzlement for the second time in a few hours. It was no longer dark. The bright light that streamed through the cream curtains, which were loosely pelmetted with a bronze and gold woven sari material, indicated that it was already late that Sunday morning. Contrary to her previously porky presumptions, she immediately identified her manly lover laying next to her. His heavy arm lay protectively across her shoulder and back. She drew comfort in the heavy security. It seemed strange, given the flavour of her former lovers, but she was meant to be with him. She smiled. She loved him. The reason for her bewilderment was nothing to do with Harry Kitson. It was sourced at the emergency tone of her hidden phone. On careful dismount from the acrous bed, she located the buzzing, flashing object from the jumble of discarded cloth at the entrance to dressing and bath rooms. When she clicked into messages, the text it revealed, confirmed that her confusing weekend continued.

"My Darling Niece. Urgent spontaneity dictates that I must take you out for Sunday lunch. Meet me off the Paddington to Bedwyn train at 12:24. All love, Uncle Max."

'Redskin Rumba'

It had been easy to lie to Harry. She just didn't like doing it. Kitty had already lost her moment for honesty at the picnic the day before. Waiting for one of the highest ranking spymasters in the United Kingdom was definitely not the most suitable moment either. As a result, she had kept her fib to Harry simple.

"A slight change of plan, Harry Darling. My Uncle Max is coming down to Wiltshire. Could I please cadge a ride four short miles to Great Bedwyn?"

"Of course you can. Your charioteer would be honoured, Great Goddess." On Harry's answer, Kitty squirmed.

"You're so gorgeous! If we can meet up later on, I can try and wriggle out of work early the following day so we can laze in bed together for a little longer."

"Laze? I had other ideas!" Harry winked.

"Of course! We can touch base with Barry and take our plans to the next stage too!"

"That's not what I had in mind, My Lover. But I guess that you are right. We have got some serious research to complete as soon as poss." Kitson begrudgingly accepted her suggestion. His atypical male one track mind had previously assumed that their adventures would not stray beyond his quadruple post sex den that day. She was sad after their brief road trip when he throttled away from her waving hand and warm smile. Sad because she already missed him.

Sad because she had lied. She sighed and looked at her mobile's clock. Ten minutes early. She texted Uncle Max to confirm her punctuality.

Seated in the front carriage of three, somewhere between Kintbury and Hungerford, the recipient was awakened by a gentle digital massage to his left breast from the inside pocket of his jacket. Years of field work had trained him not to jump with a start but to adjust subconsciously and then open his eyes very slowly. Situations could be assessed far more thoroughly this way. Besides, it drew far less attention to oneself. This seemed ironic given his attitude to clothing. It was seasonal, for sure, but certainly couldn't be described as discreet.

The wide brim of his navy blue felt fedora hat had provided ample eye protection, when tilted forward, against the morning's sun rays whilst he had snoozed aboard the train. The electric blue and emerald green peacock feather that protruded from the hat's band was most decidedly inconspicuous due to colour and length. The pink shirt that he wore under his three piece cream linen suit perfectly complimented his ruddy cheeks and nose. The minute capillaries that criss crossed both these distinctive features, mirrored both the international patterns of his travels and the more localised stumblings between those destinations' bars. A lifetime of gorging, whoring and vomiting across the globe meant that his skin hung slack and as a result he looked more like a seventy year old, than his actual fifty years young.

This summertime style combo was rounded off by a plain tie of blue and pocket square of green. Both had been carefully chosen to match the outrageous plume that waved above his head. He crossed his legs. This action made the turn ups on his trous climb to mid calf. This elevation did not reveal his blanched skin, thanks to his dark navy knee socks and suspenders. Soft calfskin brogues, of the brown and

white variety, dangled elegantly from his feet. This model of
indiscretion was highlighted further by his clear love of jewels.

His more gentlemanly accoutrements, cufflinks and a signet ring
which bore some family emblem that he had long lied about
dependent on whom he was discussing them with, were eclipsed by
his significant sparkles. Victoriana was clearly his foible. His fingers
dripped with old and rose cut diamonds. The garish gold carved head
rings were stacked and packed together on both ring fingers. An
enormous yellow gold, ruby and diamond starburst brooch adorned
his suit lapel. It flamed wildly in the dazzling light of the large train
window. Even the heavy gold watch tucked into his waistcoat pocket
sparkled with adamantine splendour and the matching fob chain and
T bar seemed more suited to medieval battle than chronological
usage.

Most of the skin on his face was subtly concealed. The Victorian
sunglasses he wore looked more like miniature welders goggles. He
had replaced the lenses with those of a blue mirrored variety.
Between his bloodshot nose and nicotine stained upper lip, lived a
small, well groomed, light brown mouse whose whiskers and tail had
been waxed into long horizontal points. Or so it seemed. Max liked to
call it his little 'Demi Dali'. He flipped the lids of his shaded eyewear
upwards, revealing his small dark eyes behind secondary
prescription reading lenses. He flipped the lid of his pocketed
timepiece. He observed that both hands had reached the XII and the
longer had dashed ahead to the III. He sighed. It was fifteen minutes
after his self imposed curfew already. He reached inside his right
hand jacket pocket and produced a slender little silver and leather
hip flask. He unscrewed the cap and tilted its attached arm against
the neck. He raised it to his lips. The rich partially viscous treacle
gurgled into his mouth. On filling his greedy orifice he tilted the
receptacle downwards and refastened the top. He worked the brown
spirit around his mouth, washing it across his furred tongue and

receding gums then swallowed. He sighed happily and then muttered aloud.

"A delicious Bajan filly of sixteen sweet sugar years; a right little poppet. Yum. Rum".

Uncle Max looked around him. Although most of the carriage was full-ish, nobody was directly seated next to or opposite him. He briefly wondered why? It could not have been the booze flask and appreciation speech because it had only just appeared. He looked at the seat beside him and found the answer. His worn yet well maintained brown leather briefcase lay dormant. Despite the secret classified contents, it had remained well guarded whilst he slept. Another little trick he had picked up on his professional travels. This ruse was always a guarantee to give security to both snoozer and luggage. The magazine laid atop the valise was of the vintage variety. The spread legged lady with limited clothing fashion who adorned the front cover could be described as displaying a growler most hairy. As if the picture needed further explanation, the title and accompanying catchphrase gave indication of an underfunded advertising department at the publisher. 'Razzle - Makes Your Cock Big.'

Uncle Max smiled to himself as he picked up the prop, opened the double double zero seven combination code catches on his case, another double bluff, and slid the offending article inside. It always did the trick. On rare occasions some over politically correct, right-on, do-gooder thought it necessary to politely ignore the jazz mag and sit beside the stinking loathsome toad of a man. A poisonous toad at that. These space invaders were soon repelled with a few vile puffs and pants, one of Uncle Max's hands carefully turned the porno pages whilst the other delved deep into a trouser pocket to enact a frenzied game of billiards. As far as the spy was concerned, fighting fire with fire was far more normal to most people than trying to slip around secretly. Nobody would have believed that this flamboyant dandy and raging pervert was actually trying to conceal his identity. Mine's a double double. Bluff.

Like most humans, Uncle Max had inherited a vast swathe of his personality from his parents. Some say you are a third your mother, a third your father and a third yourself. As one may have expected, Max's kin were queer fish. In fact, his dear old Mum was more funny bird than queer fish thanks to her sex and profession. A relative female anomaly, she had worked for the Avro company on the Vulcan bomber project during the Fifties. When the beast finally took to the air for official duty in the next decade, she retired from the Royal Air Force to marry and raise her only son. Her husband was a spy and a jolly good one at that. So good in fact that even his brilliantly minded son did not work out that he was actually working for the Soviets until he disappeared during Glasnost. Various snippets of Cold War information were traded in the interests of freedom. Max's father's liberty was to be exclusively hidden in Russia. Max, by then a university student and Foreign Office recruit, never saw him again post 1986. It was testimony to his own individual excellence that Max was able to climb the ranks in the dark corridors of Ministry, despite his father's previous double dealings.

Secrecy was part of growing up for the young Max. As the son of a retired secret weapon technician and a USSR double agent, a nice quiet backwater of the United Kingdom was required during the revolutionary Swinging Sixties. His parents settled on West Belfast. This proved to be a mistake. How the IRA had discovered his mother's military past remains unknown. The resultant incident was unofficially considered by The Royal Ulster Constabulary to be in retaliation for the recent 'Bloody Sunday' massacre. A group of British Army Paratroopers had opened fire and killed a number of civilians attending a band march in broad daylight. The IRA were understandably infuriated. They left a pile of Semtex, a recently marketed plastic explosive, at Max's home. It remained unfound. This was mainly due to its detonation at the family's front door. It instantly removed the entire fascia of their two up two down terraced home. It blew the sleeping three, in the two up half, straight across the room and into the thankfully forgiving back wall. How the first floor floor remained intact also remained a mystery. Cursing their luck and thanking their lucky stars, the family upped sticks to the British capital across the water.

Before they left, Max had learnt a couple of invaluable lessons that would serve him well in the future. They involved the devastating effects of alcohol and lies. Britain was under the cosh from the Irish terrorists and it was unprepared in legal terms. New anti terror legislation decreed that property damaged as a result of a bomb would only be covered on insurance if a witness could confirm the sighting of at least three assailants. The invention of Semtex and timers meant that this was impossible. The devices could have been planted anytime before detonation and the era of CCTV was still in its infancy. In short, Max's family stood to lose everything. As they began preparing to return to their native England, his father did the rounds of the local shops to pay his outstanding accounts. His son accompanied him on this farewell tour of baker, newsagent, mini market and finally butcher. On entering the last premise, the proprietor expressed his sympathy and condolence in the distinctively twanging brogue of north east Ireland.

"Ahhh. A terrible business, Sir. These're frightening tames, for sure?"

"Indeed they are. We are going back to live in England where my family and I are from originally."

"Safest place for yous, I'd say, especially for the wee man?" The butcher indicated towards Max before he added, "Just take the insurance money and run. There's nuthin' here the now but hatred." He shook his head despairingly.

"Well, that's just the problem," Max's father started, "we can't claim the insurance because it was an unwitnessed act of terror. We needed somebody to have witnessed three terrorists plant and detonate the bomb." Max's father hung his head and sighed. "It's going to be tough to start all over again but, ho hum."

And ho hum is exactly what the meat seller did. He paused in deep thought. He announced his mental conclusion with a dramatic physical prelude. The butcher raised his mighty meat cleaver above his shoulder then slammed it down, straight through a leg of lamb and deep into the wooden board behind, where it lodged firm.

"I saws them three men, Sir." He began.

"What?"

"I saws them three men, Sir." He added a smile and a wink for good measure this time.

"What do you mean, you saw those three men?" Max's father was still perplexed.

"I saws them three men plant a bomb at your house. I saw them as clear as day. I'd recognise them anywhere. Bastard I.R.A. Catholic scumbags the three of them. Fenian Fuckers for sure. Excuse ma' language, Wee Man." Max's father could hardly suppress his delight at meeting this bigoted Protestant lunatic. However, before he could celebrate, he needed to confirm some fundamental logistics.

"Let me be clear, My Good Man," he began, "You are willing to falsely testify for me, a relative stranger who merely purchases his meats from you, that you witnessed this act of terror, if need be, in Her Majesty's court with your hand raised in promise to the Lord God Almighty?"

"It is the will of God." The Orange fanatic replied.

And so it was. Some weeks later, Max's family received their insurance cheque. The butcher had saved them from destitution and this required a very special thank you gift. In this day and age, we are conscious of the damage that food and drink can cause our fragile bodies. If we say thank you or gift somebody, we do so with wine and chocolates if we are feeling a little naughty. Organic biscuits or gift tokens are more considerate though. Back in the 1970s, a bottle of plonk was a new and rare fad for the beer guzzling Brits. Social norm for the generous and sophisticated involved taking a bottle of spirits, usually gin, vodka or whisky, to a dinner party. Driving home after a skinful was also socially acceptable. It was with this spirit of drink in mind that Max's father carefully considered his gift. A large case was needed. Twelve bottles was the ultimate gift. Whisky was the local preference. The Scottish variety was purchased so as not to make any sectarian faux pas with the Ulster Unionist. The butcher was beside himself with gratitude on delivery and, with tears in eyes from giver and taker, the family left the shop and then set out for Blighty shortly after.

A few weeks later, Max accompanied his father to Northern Ireland to resolve a few outstanding business and insurance concerns. Once the adult had completed these chores successfully, he thought they should go and pay their respects to his old friend the butcher. When the little bell above the door tinkled as they walked in, Max's father sensed that something was amiss. For starters, there was remarkably little meat on display amidst the sea of bright green plastic cress in the glass cabinets. The second absentee appeared to be the man himself. The butcher was nowhere to be seen. He had been replaced by a large lady, her hair in curlers and her arms folded across an overly ample bosom which was covered by the tradesman's striped apron over a brown and yellow large floral print polyester dress. The butcher's wife. She looked tired. On enquiry about his whereabouts, he understood why she looked so fatigued and attired. She sighed and answered.

"It's a terrible thing, so it is, Sir." Max's father gulped. Had the IRA inflicted their merciless revenge? "My husband is a recovering alcoholic and some bloody idiot gave him a large case of whisky a few weeks back. I haven't seen him since. The Lord Jesus Christ forgive me if I ever lay hands on the fucker that did this." Max and his father had left quickly without expanding on their secret story. Alcohol and treachery played a strong role in Max's life from an early age. To eventually metamorphosize into a poisonous toad in human form was surely an inevitability?

'Sorry But I'm Gonna Have To Pass'

Uncle Max sat back and smiled at his childhood remembrance as he stared out of the train window. His mother was long dead after a brief battle with The Big C. His father might as well be, even if he was not. The strangely elegant soak had an entirely new family now. They were dependable substitutes and he reached for the closest member of his clan inside his jacket and took another swig. He sighed. His mind then turned to another side of his fantasy ancestral tree. This branch was far more complicated but, at this particular stage, he just had to concentrate on his little 'niece'. The train slowed through Little Bedwyn, crossed the lushly flowered water meadow below the canal and slid to a halt at the tiny platform of the Great neighbour. Having pushed a filterless Turkish into his long ebony cigarette holder, Uncle Max stood up, walked to the door and stepped down onto the thick yellow line which bisected the long rectangular tarmac concourse. He rummaged in his side pockets and emerged with his heavy silver Art Deco Cartier lighter. He ignited the end of the contraption now gripped by his molars. As the blue smoke engulfed him, he saw a familiar girl slink out of the modest weather shelter.

"Uncle Max!" Kitty forced a smile, "How wonderful to see you," she lied, "I hope you had a comfortable journey?" Secretly, she hoped that he had not. In the short time since her enlistment, she had never liked or trusted this bastion of power and perversion. In fact, she loathed him and his misogynistic attitudes.

"Hullo! My Darling Girl!" Uncle Max started, he was a natural at the game of charade. "A most agreeable preamble through the home counties to the wild west, thank you. How the devil are you?" He asked the question with feigned interest, another twisted attribute of his deceitful profession. He liked his girls a little beefier. Captain Parker was of the slighter, more boyish variety. He did not like boys. He loved girls. Especially bigger ones. The girl hugged him awkwardly and she noticed that he stank of stale cigarettes and fresh booze. She noticed his fellow passengers look with pity at her as they wandered off the platform. She made a series of deductions during this nauseating embrace.

"Disgusting habit," she whispered her familiar smoking mantra, "and you've already started drinking, you hopeless old lush. You are the most useless uncle a girl could have. What's more, judging by the wide berth all those train travellers are giving you, I'm guessing you played your vile magazine trick on them, didn't you? You are a disgusting pervert!" Kitty maintained her false grin despite catching her rising bile. She knew the dangers that vintage pornography weaponary could inflict on innocent bystanders.

"Of course I bloody well did," replied the stinker, "I needed a jolly good kip before all this wretched weekend work. And what's more, how dare you question my choice of living. Post snooze, equals booze. The very fabric of life, right there, You Naughty Little Scrumpet." He was so pleased with himself that he risked a well aimed smack on his false relative's real behind. All part of the charade he would claim under cross examination. This did not go down well with the slap's recipient. Within this short rendez-vous, Uncle Max had already managed to violate everything sacred to Kitty. Both mentally and physically. Why did men in positions of power still think that they could get away with this type of horror show? The reeking wreck before her represented everything she hated in man. Here was the living proof for her love for the serene island of Lesbos. It wasn't just about the sex. That's all these dirty blighters thought of. She even remembered the disappointment on Harry's face that morning just before he left. It resembled a different type of smacked arse.

"Men. You're all the bloody same." She grimaced through her grin, before adding with a whisper, "I'll only say this to you once, you dirty fucker. Touch me again and I'll fucking kick you in the balls."

"My Dearest Little Strumpet!" He proclaimed this loud enough for the last stragglers on the platform to hear before they hurried away, up the little kinked path to the red brick railway bridge and their awaiting transits. The letch knew that he had wound her up. Just as he intended. "Promises, promises, you little slut! I dare you to aim one of your dainty little feet at my massive Methusalars. I pay damned good money for a good ball kick in my regular rub and tug parlour whenever I fancy. With you pummelling my fun bags, I could get quite turned on, despite you not having enough fucking meat on you to really deliver. Come to think of it, while you're down there....?" He paused, then nodded towards his groin.

"Don't be so fucking disgusting!" She spat back. "I will kick you in the balls then kill you if you ever insinuate that again, you fucking pig!" He leered in reply as her anger excited him.

"Don't try and bite the cock that feeds you, You Little Tart!" He continued in more hushed terms, "You'll be sat behind a desk in Whitehall for the rest of your insignificant life if you carry on making ridiculous threats like that." He paused again for effect. He knew that Kitty was bright enough and scared enough of this professional mediocrity to pipe down. "I wonder how much you really want this job?" She did pipe down, so he continued, "We have much to discuss so let's forget your sexy flirtations for now. We need some solitude followed by a generous portion of claret, roast beef and Yorkshire puddings, dripping in gravy. What do you suggest?" Kitty had guessed that the selfish oaf would require these ingredients for his luncheon. She had tried to think positively about the meeting. The only positive certainty she had selected from the very shortlist was that he would charge the meal to the business. A plus only if she could stomach the pub's delicious food in his grotesque company.

"We can walk west along the canal and then hang a left towards Wilton. The Swan pub will cater for your intricate demands perfectly. It's about a half hour walk, probably forty five for a decrepit sloth like you."

"On On, Dear Girl!" Her paymaster winked an eye and licked his lips at her. She charged off in disgust.

The odd pair marched up to the railway bridge, turned left, crossed another bricked canal bridge, then diverted immediately right to the boat club yard and onto the waterway. They walked in silence, the slower man in front, a decision that Kitty had insisted on with a sarcastic sweeping bow on arrival at the towpath. The last thing she wanted was the lewd letch watching her luscious bottom lasciviously all the way. They walked past the line of gaily painted long barges tethered to the bank, weaving between seasonally recreational obstacles. Bicycles, deck chairs and barbeques were quiet but when their aquatic owners offered a 'Lovely day for it' or 'How do?', they were answered with one sneer and another smile by the contrasting spies. After they had stooped beneath a couple of Victorian red brick arched bridges on their perambulation, the boating population dwindled away. Uncle Max cleared his phlegm filled throat, spat a repulsive brown example into the similarly coloured water and spoke in his posh gravelled tone.

"Congratulations on your 'Codename: Circum Navigation' research, Captain Parker." He paused for effect. Praise did not come easily to him but he knew that his accomplice would need bolstering if she was going to keep the sensational flow of crop circle information forthcoming. He needed her close to the centre of his imaginary radar scope. He was loathe to admit more candidly that she was an excellent field operative. One of his very best. He watched her shoulders drop a little with relief and her face relaxed in appreciation of the compliment. Satisfied with his success, he continued. "The powers in Westminster have been formulating the data. They have decided that a new pattern is emerging, based on previous activity but strengthened by Friday's repetition of 'The Basket'. They now want to catch the people responsible for these imprints, whether the Russians or Chinese, as your fucking Major Conrad-Pickles keeps saying, or scientists, artists or whoever. The technology that they are using is highly sophisticated and we need to get our hands on it, sharpish."

"'Whoever?'" Kitty decided this was her moment to put forward the more far thinking theory that her new trio of amateur sleuths had investigated. "Surely we should be considering forces beyond the shortsighted ideas of Major de Crecy Conrad-Pickles, Sir? The scientific results of crystal structure, plant growth, mathematical precision and heat intensity indicate that this could be created by something else? Something unknown to us?" The red beacon of Uncle Max's imaginary mental radar flashed brightly on and off. He needed to keep the girl on the grid. In his heart, having assessed the vast array of surveillance that the military and home office had accumulated over the years, plus the far reaching probes of space discovery whether telescopic or expeditionary, she might be correct. However it remained in the interests of national security to disregard such prognosis. He decided on a policy of appeasement.

"Actually, you may bloody well be right. Or you may not be, Kitty?" He used her first name in a further attempt to pacify the soldier. He already knew that the planned mission might well confirm either direction of their thought processes. "Given the probability studies that HQ have been conducting, it seems highly likely that these seemingly random events are not so. Given the vast aerial array of nocturnal blueprints using night vision and thermal imaging, the significantly lesser number of actual patterns appearing and the mathematical messages displayed, we now think that we can accurately pinpoint future locations. Decades of data have been loaded into computers and algorithm coding has enabled us to best

189

guess at time and space. I am giving you the heads up today because the program has predicted a very local incursion tomorrow night. We all need to be onside now. Especially you!

"That is why you are going to be our commanding boots on the ground for the mission. That bloody numpty, Major de Wanker Agincourt Pickled Heart of Darkness, will get his version of these orders when he returns from having his slack hole pumped by his Parisian Lady Boy. How those gaylords can stick their cocks up each others' shit holes, baffles me." He paused, seemingly lost in the imagery, before he conceded gingerly, "At least Montgomery has chosen a fella that looks like a curvy bint. Huh!" Uncle Max snorted in disgust. "As far as we're concerned, Kitty, you're our officer in charge. Just let that limp dick think he is. We've planned everything in advance to the most miniscule detail. We don't need the fucking Major screwing it up because he's got his nancy eyes on all those cute little soldier boys."

As they walked along the canal, a gigantic brick chimney loomed into view on the far bank. Crofton's coal fired beam engine was used from the early 19th century to pump water into the canal. It raised the water level over a high point in the valley, negating the need to build a very long and expensive tunnel. This fantastic tribute to the engineering prowess of the Industrial Revolution was still in occasional operation, although Lottery Funds and local philanthropy were in desperate need for it to continue so. Luckily for the surrounding countryside and the two passing amblers, the thick black smoke that impressively belched from way on high on selective Bank Holiday weekends was currently dormant. They turned left over a narrow metal footbridge next to a sluice gate. It filtered algae and weed from the large expanse of Wilton Water that hovered in the bottom of three small ravines. They continued down the well worn footpath along the east bank, passed a kopse that hung to the steep bank and out onto the long field towards pub, meat and red. Puffing another gasper, Uncle Max continued his pant rant of instruction.

"This mission has been thoroughly thought through up in London. We've pre-selected a dozen of the best chaps from your Major's little Company. Sergeant Major Grimley has helped and will lead his chaps. A good choice, I'm told?" He glanced at Captain Parker who nodded the affirmative. She knew that the bloke was a bastard and thus an excellent choice. The strategy instructor took another weeze from the tip of his holder, then continued. "He's chosen most of the older, harder fellows. Soldiers that know how to bite when bitten. None of those namby pamby scally sixteen year old babies that have only just graduated from twocking hub caps off crap cars on their estates. We're adding a couple of Specials to the group. They will be there, just in case things get a little hairy. We're going to tell de Crecy that they are specialist observers.

"Everybody will have night vision, thermal sensing goggles and scopes. SA80A2 assault weapons will be deployed for your team. The exceptions? Our two sassy boys who will carry silenced L115A3 sniper rifles and combat semi-automatic shotguns. They will be concealed in large map tubes en route to maintain their observancy disguise. On arrival at the rendezvous point, they will split and position themselves high up on the ridge above the forecasted site. We have to be prepared for these supposed Russian or Chinese infiltrators to be armed to the teeth to protect their intense energy equipment. From their vantage point, they will be omnipotent and be able to take out any aggressive threats unseen with their rifles. If things get really dicey, they can descend and be able to use the twelve gauges plus pistols at close range. Their vile knife skills will come in handy if they end up staring into the whites of Ivan the Terrible's eyes."

"With the greatest respect, Sir," Kitty interjected, "this is Wiltshire. I hardly think it likely that there will be any Russians loitering about?"

"Why? The Cossacks managed to poison one of their own in Salisbury recently. That's the cathedral town of Wiltshire last time I checked.

Never underestimate your enemies and assume that all eventualities must be covered. You are there to make sure the plan goes accordingly. You will be armed with your faithful little Glock by your side, Captain Parker, but it is your camera equipment that will be our greatest ally during this agricultural raid. Your documentation of the perpetrators is key to the ongoing investigation into this plasma weaponry. I needn't remind you that your FLIR cost us over one hundred K, so please fucking look after it." The state of the art camera was Kitty's pride and joy. In the absence of her desire to breed and contribute to the world's exploding population problem, the camera was her baby. She did not need reminding how to wipe it's bottom. The masterplanner continued, "We will be taking no heavies. Machine guns and mortars are too indiscreet despite the area being a good mile from the closest village, Stanton St Bernard."

"I'm rather hoping that the need for any weaponry, let alone the heavy duty stuff, will be unnecessary, Sir. I repeat, this is Wiltshire, for God's sake." Kitty did not ask a question, she made a statement. "The evidence that I have accumulated, regarding this peaceful art, is that it does not pose any threat whatsoever to Britain's internal security as far as I am concerned. I have extreme doubts that the soldiers will encounter resistance on a par with that of the Commies' Ho Chi Minh trail." The spymaster halted and looked at her suspiciously.

"Don't go fucking peace and soppy love on me, Captain Cowardice!" He growled with a tacky rasp, "Be Prepared. That's what they taught me in the bloody Boy Scouts. I hope you learnt the same at the softy Brownies? If not, I know that your extensive Army and Secret Service training did. Now is your moment to coordinate your military and surveillance skills for your blessed Queen and your damned Country. Don't you fucking forget that. Now, when you have quite recovered your sense of duty, I will give you a little lesson in the relevant geography." Kitty bit her tongue. It would stop her from tasting the poison on this toad's back.

"I'm ready to continue the brief now, Sir."

Uncle Max plucked his pocket square from beside his left lapel and dabbed the nearly neat alcohol that seeped from the pores on his brow. He took the four corners of the emerald green silk and wafted it flamboyantly in the air before he carefully tucked them back into their previous housing. The excess ballooned drapery bulged out of the flat opening. He peered up and down the lake. On confirmation of their privacy, he stooped and lay his leather case flat on the short dry grass. He clicked the Fleming inspired combination code catches and opened the lid. Pornography glared offensively forth. He ignored it, rummaged the papers beneath, then pulled out two Ordnance Survey charts. He unfolded them entirely, then refolded them both in turn, revealing the areas of interest only. He laid them horizontally on the turf, one above the other, and mated the relevant roads from both. The white border and black titled line declaring 'OS Explorer Map 130 - Salisbury & Stonehenge' made this marriage of cartography slightly disjointed.

"Right then," he started, "You snuggle up here next to Uncle." He patted the earth. Kitty shivered but obediently sat, cross legged in front of the maps beside him. He hovered on his haunches and pointed his yellow stained finger at the lower section. "Here is your base near Tidworth. This mission doesn't demand any tanks or helicopters. The platoon will drive in three Land Rovers, panel backs with space for men, all the camo and light artillery. We need to be in position, here," he struck his digit on the northern carte, "by 23:00 hours. The sun won't set until about 21:00 hours. You will be able to undertake most of the journey in daylight across Salisbury Plain," he reverted his finger to the lower map, "along these two byways. We have guarantees that there will be no live firing on the artillery ranges that evening. Shortly before nine pm you will arrive at this escarpment above Wedhampton. Here is a small wood, the Redhorn Plantation, that will provide ample cover.

"At dusk, having checked that the last dog walkers have vacated the White Horse Trail, you will proceed east for approximately a mile and a half to this point, here, and drop off the plateau, on this byway to Wilsford. From here on, you're off the tracks and onto minor roads so the least dwellings you pass the better. At least it will be dark. We have planned your final approach with this in mind. You can turn right, a few yards down the main road, before the village and skirt it before resuming your northerly direction to this junction at Broad Street. Turn right up this road called The Sands and proceed over the bridge at Honeystreet. Some bloody jokers put an alien spacecraft on one of the road signs there, it being the epicentre of crop circle activity, of course. There is a museum dedicated to this art by the canal there. Have you visited it?"

"Yes, Sir. It is one of the most historically interesting and beautiful visual accounts of the phenomenon so far exhibited. I hope that our own research can vastly improve understanding of the subject matter for all enthusiasts. Oh, and by the way, wearing my photographer's hat for a mo, I'm most impressed that you referred to it as 'art'." She flashed him a smile and he returned a scowl.

"Remember, Parker. Don't get fucking artsy fartsy on me. We have a job of national importance to do before we can even consider that bullshit." Her grin subsided and he pressed on. "Ignoring the Alton villages of Barnes and Priors on the right, turn left towards Stanton St Bernard. After a mile, forget the left turn into the village but immediately turn right up this farm track. Proceed north then east until its end. There is a footpath to the base of the hill, its summit is the highest point in Wiltshire. The Landies can easily reach the border of hill and field. Leave them there.

"At this point, as previously mentioned the two specials will climb to their vantage point, one hundred and thirty metres above the site. You, or rather Major Fucking Bender, will lead the platoon around the bluff into the target zone which is nestled into the valley between Clifford's, Tan and Milk hills. You will all fan out in a semi circle from south to east to north. From here, around to here." His nicotine stained finger traced the ambush on the map's two dimensional contours. "Once in position, everybody can sound off with their radio mikes and briefly illuminate their head torches so you all know the others' locations. The last thing we need is a friendly fire situation if the crossfire gets confusing."

"Let's hope it doesn't come to that, Sir. I must remind you again that this is the Vale of Pewsey." Kitty answered before cannily continuing, " But we will be prepared for any eventuality just as you commanded. A question, Sir?"

"On with it, Scrumpet."

"What about the farmer? He's not going to be very happy about three army Land Rovers rocking up on his land with sixteen heavily armed soldiers hiding next to his fields!" Having seen, photographed, before she actually met one of them recently, she knew that they could be a breed most stubborn and confrontational.

"What he won't see, won't hurt him." Uncle Max prophesied. "Besides, the farm is up and over yonder." He waved his hand over the expanse of paper at the valley that stretched away beyond Milk Hill to the north east. Kitty stiffened in momentary recognition. "You already have a pretty intimate relationship with him, judging by the wizened cock shots you so very kindly sent me on Friday. Barrington Knave will be sleeping soundly with his labradors and, possibly, his wife. We've been keeping an eye on him, and his father before him. Two key components in this little game for many a year, thanks to the annual evidence that appears on their farm. The father used to harvest the crop immediately when a circle appeared, which made collecting surveillance far more difficult. At least his son seems to have a greater appreciation of what is what. Tomorrow night, if it all kicks off and he hears a battle, we will have cleared off by the time he's even pulled on his Plus Fours. We've got enough on him to claim insanity if he releases his story. Despite his high standing in the local community, we've dug up some high behaviour of a more sordid nature, don't you know?"

Kitty really hoped that it would not come to Class A blackmail. Much as she had come to appreciate Barry's polite charm and steadfast determination, it was his best friend, Harry's dubious psychedelic past that haunted her more within this candid threat by her spymaster. Forgiving her friends once more for being merely immature middle aged men, she noted that same wonderful twinge in her soft heart for the only man she had ever fallen for. He was much too sensitive and fragile to withstand a press smeer orchestrated by the Home and Foreign Offices and their most deviant servant. Uncle Max would surely slaughter her lover. She sensed that Harry walked a tightrope of limitless length, held aloft by his innocence and love. If he tumbled, the demons below would strangle and destroy him.

That very devil folded up the maps, placed them in his case and they continued their walk to the village. They wound their way past a delightful duck pond and various charming homesteads before pitching into the pub at the road junction by a bubbling brook. Kitty refrained from telling Max about the pub's history. It would only titillate him. The previous landlord and his wife used to hold weekend lock-ins with a difference. The local men, from solicitor to shepherd, would take turns performing lewd sexual acts on the aforementioned wife for her husband's voyeuristic pleasure and her nymphomaniac delight. A national red top newspaper had scooped the story and the outrageous orgy had ceased. Luckily, a couple of decades later, the new governor had turned it into the best gastronomic public house for miles around.

It was with the latter in mind that the flamboyant 'uncle' and elegant 'niece' made their orders at the wooden bar. Kitty noticed a small party that she recognised from the train look over, mutter to each other and shake their heads. On the bartender's request, their reactions confirmed her decision to choose one of the outside tables in a single line beside the pub car park. Besides, the bar, two restaurant rooms and beer garden were packed with culinary devotees already enjoying the Sunday fare. The young woman behind the bar, pad in hand, then confirmed Kitty's choice of baked local trout, new potatoes, salad and a glass of Sancerre, adding that it was a great choice on such a hot day. She was not so complimentary to the dirty dandy after his initial requests.

"Roast beef with trimmings is fine, Sir, but are you sure you really want a whole bottle of claret to yourself along with an extra jug of gravy?"

"I'm not sure why I have to repeat myself twice, Girl!" Max snarled. "You are here to serve me. Do as I demand!" The waitress winced.

"I'm so sorry, Sir. Is there anything else I can get you?"

"That's more like it, Girl! I am fine for now but maybe I will take you up on your kind offer after I have dined." He leered at her. The waitress turned away in disgust at this ugly man and walked away. Kitty wasn't sure whether the server also heard the letch mutter, "Great tits. What a buxom lass." Either way, after his disgustingly vile behaviour, Kitty secretly hoped that the waitress would seek retribution in the kitchen by asking the chef to prepare his 'Special Sauce' for the awaiting pervert. Sadly for the dreaming agent, this was not the place it once was and the chance of white globules appearing in his gravy was highly unlikely, nay impossible.

Carrying her glass and his bottle outside through the reassuringly large and heavy front door, Kitty and Max settled at the end table under a beer sponsored parasol. They booked taxis individually on Kitty's suggestion. Country living had taught her that they were a rare and distant service, thus governed plenty of advanced planning. They drank, one happily, the other desperately, and discussed the plan with appropriate further detail. As their stomachs started to grumble, the food arrived. They ate, one slowly and politely, the other noisily and brazenly. Both were thoroughly contented by the treats from stream and pasture.

Waiving pudding, coffee and the spy's insistence on another glass of white aside, Kitty jumped at his rare flicker of chivalry when he offered her the first hansom cab. She wished him a safe journey back to the metropolis and he wished her luck for the morrow. She staged another awkward hug and climbed into the backseat of the awaiting car. He watched her lean forward between the front seats and lip read, 'Collingbourne Ducis, please.'

"Ah hah. That's where my skinny little protege has been hiding. She is a very good spy but no match for this old bloodhound." He muttered to himself. He waved her cheerily bye as the car reversed out of the gravel yard and backed onto the tarmac. She returned the farewell similarly.

He gulped his rouge and refilled the glass. A spot of pudd, another bottle of Bordeaux, both accompanied by the Sunday rags was his real plan. Uncle Max had no intention of commandeering a taxi for the station. He prepared then puffed his cigarette ensemble. He pressed redial on his mobile phone and cancelled his cab.

"Does my army photographer really think that I am going to miss all the fun tomorrow night? Not bloody likely. I will observe all and not have to don a camouflage suit either. Not really my style." He tilted his feather plumed hat back a little in affirmation of this defiance. Secrecy was an art. He flaunted his skill. That was exactly the reason why he hadn't told Kitty that he had been disappointed by the barmaid's earlier attitude. "It must be twenty odd years since I've been to this pub." He rasped drunkenly to himself. "There was much better service back then. I pummelled and pumped the landlord's wife against that very bar in front of a roaring fire and an even more heated crowd. At least the food and wine is significantly better now." He leered through the window at the terrified staff member and rampant memories as his alcoholic afternoon took bleary form both real and fantasy.

'Cold Weather'

Harry was initially disappointed by Kitty's call. She apologised profusely for not being able to meet up as planned but work was work. An important photography assignment had come up and she was going to have to work through around the clock for a few days to meet the deadline. She had improved her lying. This was the truth after all. Partially. The inner demons of despair had been temporary for Harry and it was not long before he had mentally forgiven her and was looking forward to seeing her again later in the week. He called Barry with news of the absentee and was summoned to join his friend back on the farm the following afternoon. They had much to research and discuss, plans to be made and executed on. With the joy of love for both his circular craze and wonderful woman pattering his happy heart, Harry skipped towards his motorcycle that Monday afternoon like a spring lamb.

On arrival at the familiar farmyard, Harry Kitson was surprised to find his old chum bustling busily around his office. He had expected the more customary snoozer. The extent of his travails were plain to see. One wall had been stripped of its portrait heroes. The three or four oil paintings of beloved deceased labradors rested, lovingly stacked against the side panel of Barrington's wooden desk. They had been replaced with a collage of seeming insanity.

The centrepiece was a detailed map of the farmland. It appeared to be an oversized Ordnance Survey variety which, judging by the arrow of the north south east west cross key, was skewed for squared symmetry by about forty five degrees. Its southern border was governed by the road from near Allington, past the turning to Stanton St Bernard to the junction at Alton Barnes. The chart then followed the north to north westerly road, up the escarpment, passed the farm track entrance, up to the crossing with the Wansdyke. The upper line of the map crossed Downs east to west, Harestown, All Cannings and Allington. The western border rejoined the starter village via the downward cliff from plateau to Pewsey's valley.

The large map had some additional homemade features. The most obvious was the red felt tip line that marked the actual boundary of the Knave estate. Two sides straightforwardly followed the roads but the north and west were a more curious meandre between hill tops and valley bottoms where hedges often gave demarcation lines between neighbours. In addition, Harry noted that Knave had added a key using black marker pen with corresponding artwork to various farming products. The homestead was represented by a bird. It's specific identity, a duck, would have remained a mystery to the art world if Barry hadn't added a sound bubble 'Quack!'. The large fields above and below the escarpment were indicated by hamburger and dollar signs. The experimental pastures of lavender were marked with bottles labelled 'Old Spice' which spoke volumes about the farmer's knowledge of the perfume industry. The more gnarly slopes on the map were officially clarified by close gradient lines. Their use was unofficially scrawled with detailed artwork in the style that Harry recognised from the covers of his school ring binders. A man gripped the hindquarters of a fluffy sheep in an act of bestial sodomy. Harry was impressed by the details of trousers rolled low over gumboots and the shocked wide eye and sound bubble bleat of the ewe. This sound was indicated 'bleat' or 'BLEAT!' dependent on whether the man's hips were back or forward. Barrington had clearly spent dedicated time to the repeated imagery over several miles of scaled mapping.

All around the cartography, plastered to the wall, were hundreds and hundreds of photographs, press clippings and handwritten notes. The latter all displayed a title and date but often had other useful information relevant to their detective work such as 'wheat' or 'barley' inscribed. Each cluster of information was joined by an orange cord to a relevant spot on the map. There were a few dotted about on the downs in the north, but the vast majority of the lines terminated to the south, along the base of the near shere bank on the valley fields. It was a writhing mass of previous crop circle locations. Harry was initially impressed with the detailed and meticulous work that to him seemed worthy of a meeting room in Scotland Yard. On closer inspection, he noticed that a hammer, roofing nails and crudely wrapped bailing twine had been employed. Most fitting for his robust friend. In fairness, it was a thorough piece of morning's work. Harry told him so.

"My dearest Barrington," he began, "This is a most excellent piece of amateur sleuthing. I can almost imagine your brow beaded with sweat, tongue sticking out of the side of your gob, in total and utter concentration for hours and hours. Bravo, Jelly Brain!"

"Why, thank you!" Knave accepted the compliment with a shrug and a grin, "Although I wish my fingers thought the same." He brandished his left hand digits, revealing their new black and blue status, no thanks to the poor aim of those on his right. "I've spent a long time creating this masterpiece." He stood back to modestly admire his handiwork, "And I have come to some very interesting conclusions regarding the Knave estate's crop circle history."

"I'm all ears," responded the newcomer to these lines of enquiry, "What can you summarise from this tagliatelle of twine? What can you ascertain from this collage of crops? What can you deduce from this mosaic of madness? What....."

"Oh, shut the fuck up, you twat, before I shut you up!" Barry shouted. As if to make his point more salient, he grabbed a leather scabbard laying on his desk and unsheathed the rapier within. He waggled it at Kitson's chin. Harry knew better than to carry on. The research project had clearly been undertaken far too early in the day and at a pace that had not allowed for Knave's standard mid morn siesta. After a pause which was long enough for the farmer to calm down and thus forget slashing the irritant, he continued. "I went through the family archives and arranged decades of crop circle appearances in chronological order. I then arranged them in order on the wall, as you can now see. I noted that they appeared in different places but that a repeating pattern, albeit never exact, returned to the same places approximately twenty years later. The only perfect replica, like the one you saw near Wootton-Rivers, or 'Ghost' image as I have learnt they are called amongst enthusiasts, to date on our farm is our sexy little bitch dog, 'The Basket'. The timings are converging closer and closer each time. Here is the location." He stabbed the fine sword point into the map above Stanton St Bernard. Harry was relieved to see that the weapon had a more practical purpose than as a means to stop him ranting.

"What's more," the fencer continued, "the circles seem to appear in a close sequence of location." Harry looked puzzled so Knave spelt it out for his friend of slow wits. "The circles appear one after the other in a gradual progression of geographical order. For example here one appears at this date and then, a couple of fields away and a few days later, the next one appears, and so on. It's as though it is easier to recalibrate the plasma power application using minimal adjustment even if the actual artwork is wildly different to the previous one. It seems that blueprints could be pre programmed for each new design but the actual implementation is easier if the rough area, gradient and height above sea level are already known and calculated for. This would account for the perfection of the art on the undulating surfaces."

"And you have deduced this by sticking pretty pictures and sheep string to your office wall?" Harry blurted out. The pointed foil whistled through the air and stopped short of his cheek. It waggled briefly then stopped. "Sorry. Carry on." It has already been noted that Harry was not a fast learner.

"Yes, I bloody well did, you stupid idiot." Barry was not the most patient of men. "If you had just spent the last ten fucking hours doing the same, you might have come to the same conclusions. Even with your obvious lack of cerebral assistance." He added the latter for good measure and maintained his intellectual highground. "I have literally been going around in circles geographically and chronologically, pinning circles within those circles. I think I am entitled to a little bloody credit, you dumb arse?"

"Agreed." Harry was meekened.

"So," Knave breathed in before exhaling during his conclusion, "That would mean that the next crop circle to appear should be round about," he paused whilst he homed in, "here." He tapped the lethal pointer at an arable inlet at the base of Tan Hill. "And, if my calculations are correct," he tucked the blade under his arm, grinned and used all ten fingers for his mathematical deduction, "It will appear on this very night!"

"Tonight!" Harry could not conceal his glee. "Yippeeeeee! That is the most exciting news I've heard in ages!" His happy smile turned southwards almost instantaneously as he realised, "But, Oh No! Kitty is busy tonight doing a photo assignment. She can't miss it?"

"Don't be daft, you soppy rag," Knave rallied, "If my theory is correct, we'll be visiting crop circles whenever we damned well please soon. She has work to do tonight. We have some fun to enjoy tonight. I'm sorry that your love can't join us this time. However, I think it is fitting that you and I can welcome the artists in our own inimitable style."

"We have an inimitable style?" Kitson questioned, "Dare I ask what it is?"

"Think about it, you daft brush," Barry smiled, "We are the two most qualified people on the planet to welcome Tom, Dick and Harry, or cutesy wootsy E.T., for that matter." Kitson looked blank. His friend had surely lost it, he thought to himself. The head of the welcoming committee continued regardless. "Whatever is producing these crop messages is doing so using plasma energy, a degree of intelligence and a peaceful theme. We are equipped with our own limited versions of these same three attributes. We will be ready to greet them, fighting fire with fire, so to speak, whether they have travelled from another sodding solar system or from Wootton bloody Bassett. We are going to throw them a party!" He announced grandly.

"A party?" Harry's ears pricked and his eyes widened at the mention of his specialist subject.

"Yes! A party!" Barry exclaimed. "C'mon! Follow me! We have a busy afternoon, evening and night ahead! I'll tell all over a sandwich in the house then we'll roll up our sleeves and get busy. On! On!"

Barrington Knave had left no stone unturned in his mental planning for this historic event. The two men finished the physical work shortly before sunset and stepped back to admire their handiwork. Barry's pickup truck had been transformed. The flatbed had been simply extended by folding the tailgate down. Beyond that initial respect for the manufacturer, the design was all their own. Having spent the earlier part of the afternoon trawling through various barns, attics and bedrooms for apparatus, the early evening had whizzed by with their dedication to assembly.

The cab had a ski rack strapped to its roof. Two theatrical lighting rigs were lashed to it. The parallel grids had multiple spots and directional gears bolted to them. The front section's pointed directly upwards. The back one was angled low and flat across the truck's rear. Between them was secured a wooden board that had a swirl of glass tubes fitted to it. A sturdy fishing rod, Harry had been told of the salmon variety, arched from this cab construction above the flat back. Suspended from a short strong wire, Harry had been told of the sailfish variety, hung a large multifaceted glittering ball. Harry had been told this was of the disco variety. He pointed out that he was aware of its use but thanked his friend for the fishing lesson.

Along the top of the rear windscreen and both upper sides of the boot ran long glass strip lights. Inside the confines of the flatbed, a small formica topped desk was pushed against the cab. On its surface were assembled various lighting controls, amplifiers, wires and a rather retro looking original iPod. The wires had been grouped and taped together. They ran in various directions like a mass of seething serpents. Some wound to the lighting rigs above, others under the table to a small cluster of tweeters and bass bins stacked between the four thin metal legs. The remainder snaked forward to two ginormous six foot high speakers, which were strapped together back to back facing the wheel arches. One large cable led to a sizable petrol generator at the back. A jerry can of gasoline was buckled to the low wall opposite. All of the above, despite having their own harnesses, were wedged apart by two hay bales. One between the power unit and giant speakers, the other between them and the table. Barry clearly had not factored in a visit from Wiltshire Council's health and safety inspectors in his design. Another wooden board, similar to that on the cab roof, was strapped atop the lowered lid which extended a couple of feet beyond the vehicle's rear. It too had a curious collection of twisted glass tubes attached to it.

Having ascertained the party mechanics, the middle aged revellers had also resurrected some decorations which they now admired in situ. They were a collection of simple party paraphernalia amassed over twenty five years. Millennial field raves and middle aged barn bashments had warranted the purchase of the more serious kit including the 3K sound system and lighting rigs. Most of the car exterior had a jagged skirt of black and white Jolly Roger bunting. Tied intermittently to the pennants' white cord were silver helium balloons with floated and darted dependent on the mildly gusting wind. These were contributions from more recent kids' New Year discos. But the crowning glory was Vintage Kitson Knave. Four large double bed white sheets fluttered from long, slowly bending bamboo poles which were tied to the four corners of the open cargo area. They were decorated with wild splashes of day-glo paint of vivid pink, orange, yellow and green hues. They had been created at a Manchester student house party and, despite their obvious Jackson Pollock style, were more tribute to the artwork of local musician John Squire. Oh! Oh! Acid House!

"Bravo, you old bastard!" Barrington could not conceal his delight. "We've done it! And only just in the nick of time. Phew!" He looked at the pinking crest of the hills and then further up at the increasingly darkening clouds. "Looks like rain a little later but, fear not, Barry has thought of everything! Before I come to that, let's fire her up and give everything a good check over? You climb up there," he pointed to a nearby straw bale mountain inside an open sided corrugated iron roofed barn, "and have a goosey gander at our creation." Harry started to move off but Knave halted him with a bullying bark, "Stop! I nearly forgot! What type of party would it be without a few of these?" He reached inside the front pouch of his tweed waistcoat and pulled out a small see-through plastic bag. He broke the parallel seal with a roll of his forefinger and thumb and shook out a couple of round white pills onto his other palm. He proffered them to Harry, who mechanically took one, popped it to the back of his tongue and swallowed without question. Barry did the same and grinned. "I've got a few of these left over from that Beatrix Potter party we had earlier in the summer. Judging by the grin in the picture I've got of Mrs Tiggy Winkle, you rather enjoyed them?" Kitson smarted. He had certainly embraced them wholeheartedly when he had wriggled around in his prickly washerwoman fancy dress that June evening.

The friends hugged each other warmly, parted and both cleared their throats in mock embarrassment. They laughed and hugged again.

"Like a Mighty Wind, come Rushin' in!" Harry quoted fondly an Acid anthem, while Barry added some vocal beatbox accompaniments. After the brief joint performance, Knave added, "Right! To positions!"

The two men bolted in opposite directions, one scaling the enormous rectangles of yellow straw, the other vaulting into the back of the truck and settling his behind on another one. Harry reached the top, sat on the edge with legs dangling and looked down. Knave pulled the rope starter on the generator and it spluttered noisily into life. When he was content with the engine's tick over, he stood atop the bale and maneuvered around the giant speakers via the wheel arch covers and sat on the other. He turned on the lights.

The vehicle exploded in optical chaos. The Stone Roses flags and pirate pennants burst into purple white and coloured life under the glowing intensity of the now blue fluorescent tube lights. Search lights swept the clouds above, rhythmically swaying left and right on their whirring precision gearings. Primary coloured spots did the same over the conductor, his face turning every colour as the beams met, meshed and moved on. An oil based filter threw an ever changing fluid of light and colour over the flags. Another slowly twisting lens projected perfectly symmetrical fractals onto the glowing sheets which grew and shrunk with the ebb of the breaze. Two lasers, one red, the other green, shot forward and danced in multiple directions, correctly coloured port and starboard, as they hit the rod and line suspended, randomly moving glitterball. This tribute to illumination was crowned by the neon signage which buzzed angrily as the sweeping bulbs warmed up. The tail design was of the Soho variety. A blinking scarlet light of scrolled italic writing welcomed 'Girls. Girls. Girls.' Harry hoped that their guests wouldn't be too upset on their arrival to Boy Boy. When the words were invisible, a red arrow flashed on and off in sync. It pointed towards the second bright blue sign that continuously beamed 'BASHMENT' from the roof of the cab. It was the sole survivor from a Jamaican themed ska and rock steady party in one of the barns a few years before.

"Yeeeeeeeeeeeeee Hah!" The part time cowherd yelled from his vantage point. "It looks incredible, Barry! Well done, you old bastard! We have the technology! We have ignition! Fluorescent and neon plasma beacons? Check! Flag phosphorescence? Check! Zodiac Mind Warp? Check! Major Lazer? Check! We have all systems Go. Go! GO! Yeeeeeeeee Hah!" He repeated his wild western celebration and then clambered down. Knave vaulted back to earth too. They hugged again, enthusiastically thumping each other's backs while jumping up and down.

"Follow me." Barry commanded, breaking the clinch and they walked into the barn. Along the back wall was a curious object. It was five metres long, had single wheels at both ends and a tractor coupling in the centre. Along its length was suspended an enormous roll of transparent plastic sheeting. It resembled a gigantic tube of cellophane. "We use this to cover the more fragile plants if we get a late spring frost." Barry added for clarification.

"You'll go straight to global warming hell for that!" Kitson responded conscientiously before conceding, "Hopefully, our visitors tonight will be able to share some of their secrets regarding energy so that we can put a change to all that destruction?"

"Hear! Hear!" agreed the local councillor, looking forward to his resultant promotion, "And so say all of us! Now, we just need to fit two more posts above our seats to keep this free from the lighting rigs and attach the rest to the four corner flags and Hey Presto, we have ourselves a transparent roof to shield us and our modest mechanical welcoming committee from the elements." This was done. First they took a corner each and walked out a length from the roll. Then Barry whipped out his hunting knife and cut it straight across. They held it aloft and wafted it gently over the car. One holding, one climbing a nearby step ladder, they fastened the additional poles and sheet in place until it was taught and ridgid. They stepped back and admired their Heath Robinson work. The sky spots, neon lights and lasers were minimally distorted but, coupled with the increased intensity of the reflected glow within the canopy, the overall effect was perfection.

"Right! Let's get this party started right!" chanted the farmer pulling on his tweed jacket as he threw some waterproofs onto the back seat.

"You're not really going to wear that ridiculous garb, are you?" Kitson questioned, zipping his leather jacket up and placing his own rolled up wet weather leggings and jacket next to his friend's crumpled ones.

"Of course, I bloody well am!" retorted Knave. "If there's one thing that our great school taught me, it's that first impressions count! Besides, great men have climbed Everest and reached the Poles in this so-called 'garb'. I am simultaneously wearing the uniform of a pioneer, politician, adventurer, diplomat, party host, not to mention, style guru." Harry thought it wise to leave the development of Gortex and Lycra lecture for another occasion. "OK. Sorted?" The jeweller nodded so the delusional fashion icon continued, "So let's get this road on the show!" Barrington leaned over the cargo area, picked up the iPod, circled his finger on the dial and muttered, "Wallop! The Hacienda Classics Volume One Lack of Love Charles B slash Adonis." He pushed play.

The wall of sound almost knocked them off their feet. The bass and drums rattled everything in the yard. The bleeps of the 303 tweaked their souls. The tune catapulted them immediately back to their teen state. They leapt in the air with coordinated jubilation at the repeated "High!" lyric. They hopped into the front seats of the wagon, lowered the window so they could hear the full impact of the sounds, high fived and Barry slotted into first gear. As he began to move off, Harry looked over at the farmhouse, nudged his friend, who looked over too. They both metronomically waved slowly. The Knave family, his wife, kids and dogs, were assembled in the drawing room window. They were all very still. Another similarity was their collective open mouthed gawp. They could have been a photograph if Mrs Knave had not been very slowly shaking her head.

"They must be very proud." Harry commented.

"Shut it." Barry replied. Kitson did. He continued to wave his cheerio to the seeming wax work ensemble until they pulled out of the yard into the darkness.

The bright headlights located the first flicks of rain which were confirmed by the occasional swipe of the sensory wiper blades. They crawled up the hill. Barry sensibly navigated at a speed that would not dislodge their precious cargo of audio and optics. As they neared the crest of the hill closest to the farmstead, Harry exhaled in sigh. This was the venue of his first real kiss to the woman he now truly loved. This romantic thought brought on the first ripples of ecstacy down his neck. He shivered with the real and artificial love combination. Bliss.

"What the fuck?" Barry was distracted. A shadowy figure descended from the barrow on the peak. As the body broke the truck's beam, it was the farmer's turn to drop his jaw. Harry was better prepared for this alien presence. The red, yellow and green mirage that strode forward clasping a long twisted stick was far more familiar to him.

"I don't believe it!" He half whispered, above the sound, across to his shocked friend. "That's the same fellow that I met last year, just before I saw the plasma orbs! What in God's name is he doing here? Don't worry, Baz, he's a grumpy fucker but harmless."

"I'm cool," reassured Barrington, "And he's perfectly within his rights to be walking the ridge footpath, even if it is dark now. What a fucking weirdo." The rasta walked up to the driver's side and leaned inside the cab. Despite the landowner's first red and black impressions of being eyeballed by the seeming fires of hell, he levelled them and held the stare.

"Ya can' play bass!" The intruder bellowed, nodding back at the sound system. Knave was not to be outdone though. After many years of loafing, the two men in the truck possessed an extensive knowledge of reggae music. This ensured that Barry could reply in the correct vernacular, albeit that his attempted accent soundly more Welsh than Jamaican. He grinned.

"Ya can' play drum!" The result was instantaneous. As the Marcus Garvey devotee recognised a fellow DJ Scotty fan, his previously poker face broke into an enormous smile. He leant forward into the cab and grabbed Knave's hand and pulled him in an elbow to elbow greeting.

"Ya can' play (h)organ!" He laughed with a bass that matched the car boot's. He placed his arm around the aficionado of Kingston Town in a half hug and patted his back furiously. "Ya know, Man, I been waitin' fa ya all me life! Righteous!" Harry felt a twinge of jealousy that he had not received the same reaction with his blessing on their previous meeting, particularly after his faultless delivery in respect of Lord Jah. He pushed his emotions aside in the knowledge that he was in the presence of social genius, the company of the great mover and shaker, Barrington Knave. Harry felt a little more restored when the pilgrim looked across and registered his recognition with a nod. He then babbled.

"Blessing be upon ya from most (h)igh. Jah Rastafari, King o' Kings, beseech ya to bear witness to (H)'is all powerful force o' nature in unity. I and I. Blessing upon. Me know our path cross again." He waved towards Harry. "Me warn ya o' da prophecy back den. Dem Overlord come 'gain. Ya witness dat before, nah?" Harry nodded. "Dey bring us infinite wisdom an' knowledge so we ol' slaves can break down dem door o'ppression. A storm brew dis night and out o' dis darkness we will rise 'midst blindin' light and beat down Babylon!" He leant back slightly and banged his fist to his heart. Having critically surveyed Barry's choice of clothing with an appropriate, "Tchah!" he whispered with a smile, "Don't worry, Brethren. Me no hurt." He reached into his smock's pocket with one hand, clutched the puzzled driver's tie with the other, withdrew a large knife and cut the two silk tails off below the knot, adding, "Babylon Burn!".

"Point taken." Barry replied despite his total bewilderment, before adding after an awkward pause, "Well, God be with you too, Amigo, but we must be shuffling on now". He pointed forwards. The rasta looked up, waved at the heavens and decreed.

"As da great Lee "Chicken" Scratch Perry say, 'Dis is a Cold Weather.'" He paused then continued, "'So get your cloak an' (h)umbrella." Barry contemplated the meteorological prophecy and, with charity in mind, reached into his door panel pocket and produced a small pack umbrella with a red handle.

"Here you go, Pal-amino! You've already got the cloak so you'd better have this?" The rasta took it with a gracious bow, sprung the button and looked at the rain shield as it unfolded. It was tiny. It was mainly transparent but was decorated with small love hearts, a cartoon cat and the telling words 'Hello' and 'Kitty'. When the gigantic man looked at the object and then at the donor, Barrington continued by way of explanation. "Err. It's my daughter's. She would want you to have it on this wet night." The man broke into laughter, deep and rumbling. He moved off, uttering one last spiritual salvo.

"Jah Live!"

When he had meandered off into the darkness, Knave let out a sigh of relief. He wiped his brow. The drug's effect had been wildly accelerated by this more unusual and unnerving encounter on his farm. The music blared and the strobes flickered, which certainly helped too. All in all it had been a strange day for the farmer. He looked at the two long pieces of tie that lay redundant in his lap. He rubbed one of the many pheasant prints between his forefinger and thumb and sighed again.

"Judging by the Missus' reaction as we left this evening, I think I am in the house of hounds. I just praise Jah that he chose to destroy these feathered Agents of Babylon, rather than the springing teal tie she gave me one Xmas. That would've been my D.I.V.O.R.C.E." He sang the last spelt word in a suitably Deep Southern drawl. He clearly enjoyed the theme, so continued. "C'mon, y'all! We got ourselves a hoe down to Do si Do go to! Yippeee Yay Yaaaay!" The intoxicated adventurers tripped their spacecraft forward towards the next galaxy.

'Move it'

"Bugger. Buggeroon. Buggeroonie. Buggeroonical." Major Montgomery de Crecy Conrad-Pickles was bothered. He sat and stared at the printed orders in front of him. Monday mornings were usually a more stress free time back at his desk at headquarters. He could not believe that the top brass had fallen for his deceptions. The papers instructed him to lead a unit of men to intercept and capture his fictional communists and confiscate their plasma producing technology. What was more, they had already chosen the men from his company without his input. The main problem was that they were the very best on offer. Seasoned troops, all with combat experience. They would see through his shallow plan to create a smokescreen over the crop circle nonsense in seconds. If he had it his own way, he would have used a bunch of ill-equipped kids to lead on a wild goose chase of his imaginary Cold War enemies. On conclusion of the pursuit's inevitable failure, he could then report that the Red terrorists had escaped and his pathetic charade could have continued. There was no chance of him glossing over the truth now. In addition, they were sending two independent observers. His perplexion had forced him into the "Buggeroonical". He needed help immediately.

"Kitty!" he squeaked with panic. He cleared his throat and forced a deeper, more commanding tone, "Kitty!" The door opened shortly and the officer breezed into the office. She wore combat fatigues. "Captain Parker", he began formally, "You are no doubt aware of the contents of the documentation that you put on my desk prior to my arrival this morning? What. What?"

"I am, Sir."

"Then you know that our wretched generals wish us to foray towards a predetermined spot that they have calculated will be the next likely spot for a weapons testing experiment by our supposed enemy?" He tried to make his statement calm and calculated but Kitty detected a fear in his voice similar to that squeaked in his initial summons to the office. She decided that this was the moment to ascertain her own authority on the subject.

"Yes, Sir. The men are readying themselves and will be assembled", she glanced at the wall clock, "in approximately half an hour at 16.00 hours. The lads will be ready for your inspection and brief, Sir. There will be little need for detail in your address as I have already relayed the plan to Sergeant Major Grimley. He will have prepped his team." Conrad-Pickles' mood sank further. Grimley was ruthless. He had previous experience regarding the Sergeant Major, back in the days when they were cooped up in Scimitars in Helmand. A large patch of urine had appeared on Monty's desert camouflage pants after a particularly nasty exchange of enemy fire. The thuggish sergeant had delighted in reassuring his commanding officer that the wet stain would remain their secret. Monty had guessed from the smirk on the soldier's face that it would not.

"Thanks, Kitty." Montgomery exhaled sadly before he continued with a distinct lack of enthusiasm, "I guess I better get saddled up then. We've got some Commies to catch." He started to get up but was immediately interrupted so slumped back into his chair.

"With the greatest respect, Sir," Kitty commenced, "our chances of finding your Russian or Chinese insurgents are approximately zero." Major Conrad-Pickles glanced up at his subordinate. He smelt the all too familiar whiff of dissent. "The evidence that we have accumulated over several decades has never produced a single trace of your theory. Yes, a small segment of the data, maybe five to ten percent, have been proven to be produced by self confessed local artists but the vast majority of crop circle formations remain a mystery. We must go into this exercise with free minds. We may well discover more humanoid hoaxers. We may not. In my humble opinion, having viewed the unofficial film footage of circle formations, it is incredibly unlikely that anybody other than us will be present. That is also assuming that the algorithm data predictions regarding timing and location are correct too. We must be prepared for disappointment or ready to chronicle an act hitherto unconfirmed to our employers." Montgomery secretly hoped that a disappointing result would be infinitely more useful to him than one of scientific revelation. He really did not want to be involved in something more dramatic. This time he did get up, pushed his chair under his desk and addressed his assistant.

"Captain Parker. There is absolutely no evidence to suggest that you are correct. What. What? The theories that you continually press regarding previous sightings, crop mutation and plasma energy are totally unsubstantiated up to this point. However, we will just have to give each other the benefit of the doubt because, like it or not, on this very night, we may just find out." He paused surveying the combat clad woman then pressed on. "Whoever or whatever we encounter, I am going to need to get my kit on. I'll see you on parade."

"Sir!" The Captain saluted the Major. She had vocalised her beliefs and was ready for the big push with or without him.

As the yard clock struck four, the Major shimmied out of the Officers' Mess. He was a rare drinker so the double Cognac that coursed through his veins vastly emboldened him. He was dressed in green and black camouflage and had paid particular attention to the buffing of his calf length black boots. Polishing them always seemed to calm him during his frequent panics. He sighed at the fond recollection of his brutal teacher, Willy Waverling. Wilberforce would never have carried his own webbing though. Monty's own chafed his shoulders and pinched his softened sides. The man was ill equipped and under qualified for the guile and thrust of battle. His expertise was more limited to capture and torture. He walked gingerly across the parade ground, halted and turned towards the assembled soldiers.

"'Ten'shun!" screamed the Sergeant Major, "These 'orrible individuals are ready for your inspection, Sir!" Monty could not help but think that this man's theatrical decibel level would fill the Albert Hall rather than the five square metres required. He made his point pertinently by addressing the men with a more suitable volume.

"Stand easy now, Chaps," he lisped quietly.

"SIR!" bellowed Grimley as if to prove his impertinence. The men relaxed their shoulders and spread their feet at the command. Judging by the winks and grins amongst the ruffians, de Crecy Conrad-Pickles was under no illusion to whom the joke was once more directed. He hated all this macho clap trap. He was far more comfortable with his normal routine of a pen pushing job during the week and a penis pushing job at the weekend.

"Now listen, Fellas," continued the Major weakly, "My thanks to Sergeant Major Grimley for briefing you all about the importance of this sensitive and secret mission. It is imperative, despite our navigation on some minor public roads, that we raise as little attention as possible. Please remember that we are soldiering the unknown and that the capture of any would be assailants and their requisite equipment is of the utmost importance. We are being observed from a vantage point above our exercise by these two gentlemen," he turned towards the two additions to his unit and smiled at them. They did not return the formality so he continued, "and Captain Parker will monitor in person and record on camera our mission from the frontline." He stopped briefly as he surveyed the surveyors. In his long and distinguished army career, he had eyed up many uniforms. The two clipboard counsellors had more the air of psychotic killers about them than observers. Maybe it was their glazed cold eyes, drooping moustaches and sideboard hair that gave them away. That distinctive facial scrub was the reserve of two exclusive clubs. Those that frequented Soho bars and danced to "Y.M.C.A." or those of the Special Air Service and Boat Squadrons. Either way, it was an odd development that made the poor leader of men most wary. One of the grim men spoke.

"Thank you, Major," he began gruffly. Montgomery thought that he placed the accent at mid Welsh borders, not Old Compton Street. "We will be positioned at a high point on Milk Hill to assess your behaviour under duress and your conduct strategically, whether you engage aggressively or peacefully with the suspected enemy. On return to base tomorrow morning, we will interrogate any captives and examine any confiscated machinery and weaponry. Each of you will be expected to report to us for a thorough pumping in the debriefing room." Conrad-Pickles relaxed. Maybe they were members of the Soho Club afterall.

"Very good." The Major thanked the man after his mind had returned to the real task in hand. He then addressed the men again. "Best of British, Chaps. No itchy trigger fingers and minimal contact once we reach the drop zone. What. What? All clear?"

"Sir!" they responded in unison.

"Right then. Saddle up and enjoy the ride. It'll be a damned sight comfier than our little tanks. Come along. Get a wriggle on! What. What. On. On."

"Exactly, Sir!" The Sergeant Major rolled his eyes. "You heard the Major. What. What. On. On." The sniggering troops dispersed to the three awaiting jeeps.

The sun was low by the time they had trundled to the southern edge of Salisbury Plain. The gently undulating terrain was most familiar to all the party having endured years of training in hand to hand, rifle, machine gun, tank and helicopter manoeuvers. The yellowing heathland lulled some into sleep. Tin hats covered in plastic net camo provided pillows for their lolling heads. The men were savvy enough to realise that it could be a long night. When the Landrovers jolted to a halt near the escarpment, they awakened without a start. They mechanically tucked into various biscuits and bars in the knowledge that they would be on starvation duty until breakfast. They plucked grasses and shoved them in clumps behind the mesh of webbing and camouflage on their bodies and helmets. They painted dark vertical lines using oversized green lipstick tubes on their pale faces to follow the symmetry of their herbaceous disguises. Once ready, they waited silently.

Kitty sat atop one of the car roofs and surveyed the ridge. She was using her precious camera. Its lens produced far greater detailing than any of the other binoculars or rifle sights on show. Once the sun had set, the trees in the nearby copse blackened and she made one last sweep of the tourist path to be sure that any amblers had departed. All was quiet so she waved at the group below, circled her hand above her head a couple of times and pointed her finger in an easterly direction. They moved out shortly afterwards.

The convoy trundled along the dusty ground. Judging by the dark cloud formation that followed behind them, the land was just about to receive a drenching. As the first spots hit the windshields, one by one the cars turned left and crawled down the sharply inclined track towards the now faintly flickering village of Wilsford. As they reached the valley bottom the cars, first the Major's, then the Captain's and lastly the Sergeant Major's, turned right and the nobbled tyres drummed on tarmac for the first time since the parade ground. They sped through the darkness, slitted headlamps producing minimal illumination and wound their way north. The drab vehicles eventually came to a halt at the Broad Street junction. They paused. The Major was evidently lost. Or maybe he was just stalling for time to break up the careful chronology?

Kitty wasted no time. At least she appreciated the need to move fast and undetected. She indicated to her driver to overtake and turn right. He gunned the engine and whirred off into the night. The other two Landrovers followed suit and the train of trucks sped on. Kitty glanced at her phone. 22:10 hours. They were still on target. After turning left at the Altons junction, she looked up towards the dark shadow of the cliff, menacing in the early night. It was occasionally illuminated by the white moon as it passed behind the sporadic rain clouds. The pale light produced an eerie effect as it rippled on the ridged banks. As she gazed out across the heaving sea of grey wheat, she smiled. Somewhere out there was 'The Basket'. What an incredible experience she had enjoyed just a few short days before. And that boy! She shook her head and blessed the powers of fate that the sweet man had come back into her life. He would enjoy this crazy mission. She was sad that she was not sharing it with him but work was work.

After the Stanton junction Kitty nudged her driver and indicated to turn right onto the farm track and cut the lights. He did both. She adjusted the rear view mirror and inspected that the other cars had done the same. On confirmation she peered forward again up the twin tracks of compacted chalk that now glistened with the fresh rain. Halfway across the vast fields the track turned ninety degrees right and after another half minute it came to an end. The jeep then turned due north again by the same angle and crawled its way along a grass divide between the walls of the crop which swayed gently whilst the ground beneath guzzled up the enriching shower. At the base of the escarpment, the car turned left and Kitty waved the chauffeur to halt about thirty metres later in a small depression amidst the rolling geography. The recess, along with the small wall of wheat and larger bank, hid the three metallic hulks from all but air. The engines spluttered to a halt.

After a few seconds of muted equipment preparation, the soldiers clustered around the Major and Captain. The commanding officer looked decidedly ill at ease so Parker saluted him and took control again. Her address was whispered after checking her clock once more.

"It is 22:36 hours," she began, "so we have exactly twenty four minutes to settle into positions. Gentlemen," she indicated to the two poorly disguised Specials, "You are straight up the bank from here to the crest of Milk Hill. There is a cattle trough on the open ground which you should hunker behind. Good luck." She watched them move off before she continued, "We will walk in single file around the perimeter of this field. The Major will remain here in primary viewing position," she lied to ensure that he was as far from the actual drop zone as possible, "the Sergeant Major will be at the centre of our semi circle and I will be at the far end to achieve the broadest filming point. I need not remind you that the order to fire is strictly prohibited unless under extreme duress. If this occurs please be sure to remember everybody's positions to avoid crossfire casualties. To confirm this, please turn on your radios at 23:00 hours and call off one by one illuminating your torch briefly when you do so. After that, audio and light sources, including your phones, will be switched off until either the enemy are engaged and captured or the mission is over at dawn. Understood?" She looked around the group of men covered in waving straw and raw weaponry, registering each one's striped face nod in acknowledgement. "Right. Silence from now on. Grimley? You disperse half the men evenly before your post and I will take over from there. Hunker down then make this count please." Kitty watched the men walk off in single file behind their Sergeant then turned to Conrad-Pickles. "Sir! Best of luck, Sir!" The Major offered similar advice interspersed with his usual dose of drivel.

"Thank you, Captain Parker. Best of Blighty to you, what, what?"
Kitty saluted, turned on her heels and, caressing her camera to her
chest, followed the dark blur of moving soldiers. One hundred metres
along her route, a rustle in the grass indicated the whereabouts of the
first hidden combatant. She crouched on her haunches next to him
and indicated her appreciation of his field craft with a raised thumb.
He returned the gesture and she moved on, repeating the distance
and process a handful of times before she met the rest of the group at
the halfway point in the cosy womb of the great hill. The Sergeant
saluted her, she nodded at him, waved the remaining half dozen to
fall in behind her and carefully marched on around the bowl. Having
calculated the total distance to her own destination, she stopped and
patted each soldier in turn on the shoulder at even distribution
points. Twenty minutes later she was alone at her destination.

When her clock hit the hour, she turned on the radio in her helmet,
switched on her torch and pointed it across to the starting point. The
radio crackled into life and she heard the CO announce his name in
full. Major Montgomery de Crecy Conrad-Pickles. Kitty winced for
him. This announcement was not going to win hearts and minds with
his working class troops. She traversed her torch and one by one the
arc of men all responded far more helpfully with their surname and a
"Copy that", along with the requisite flash of their bulb. On
resolution, Kitty switched off her headset and torch. All was still and
quiet so she took a moment to test her camera lighting applications.
As she stared at the viewfinder, she revelled in the clarity and detail
in the green glow of the waving wheat on display. Mesmerised, she
settled in for her night's vigil.

It was around an hour since the Captain had completed her checks
when she became aware of a disturbance behind her. From far above,
over her right shoulder, she became aware of a sinister deep
vibration. The strange sound waves that grew steadily louder were
similar to the low hum of electricity, like those heard when standing
beneath vast pylons and lines. This bass buzz was metronomically

interspersed by muffled booms. Boom. Boom. Boom. It sounded like an accelerated artillery barrage when aubiable from distance on the Plains to the south. But this was no army night firing exercise and it was close. It was getting louder and deeper with every moment. Kitty looked over her right shoulder and up. Over the crest of the hill, one hundred metres above her, a pulsating light glowed from beyond. And what light! It glowed in the darkness, a strange combination of colour and fluorescence. This haze seemed to vibrate in sync with the deep boom bass. Sporadic flashes of green and red shot upwards and smashed then disappeared into the low clouds. Whatever it was emanating from was descending very slowly and the sound seemed to bounce off all three of the gigantic hills that formed an enormous hall of buzzing energy.

"The stupid computer algorithms must be wrong!" Kitty whispered to herself and thought quickly. "The landing site isn't in the crescent bottom of Milk Hill but in the neighbouring one below Tan Hill. Something is happening for sure but we have just predicted the wrong bloody place! Theoretically, our plan can still work but the soldiers will need to move fast." Having gathered her thoughts, Kitty broke her own protocall. She pulled out her flashlight and pushed the on off switch repeatedly, first in the direction of the Major then in a sweep around her distant assembly. The feeble light would never be detected by the unknown visitors behind the next hill. She then carefully laid her camera on a piece of tufted grass and sprinted to the hideout of her adjacent marksman. She crouched beside him, cupped her hands and whispered instructions in his ear. The action was hardly justified due to the ever increasing wall of sound behind her but it was the correct professional approach and an example she wished him to follow. Her message to him was to run the line and bring back all the troops to her muster point. The order was acknowledged and the man hared off.

Twenty minutes later, the agile men had reached the Captain. Time had been saved as all assembled had seen and understood Parker's torch revellee on the arrival of the strange sound and lurid luminescence. All except one. The Major was absent. There was no time to go and find him. Besides, his presence was hardly going to be of strategic advantage so Kitty pulled the men in a huddle around her. The instructions needed more than a whisper to be audible above the growing din.

"There is no time to reflect on the misinformation we have been issued with. We must adjust. The landing site appears to be in the same valley but in the next hill's recess judging by the sound and light energy emanating from the brow above us. We will not be able to fan out in our semi-circle again so we must all stick together. When we reach the heart of the next bowl, form a defensive circle and hide in the grass as before. This is actually happening, Gentlemen. Safety catches on unless I order to open fire. We are going to catch these powers on film or in person. Now! On me! Move it!" She sped off, resting her camera like a baby along her forearm as she ran with the agility of a cat in pursuit of a mouse. The men hunched their bodies low and forward as they hugged the terrain in pursuit of their natural leader.

Kitty looked up and down, left and right as she sprinted, assessing every contour of the land. Cows mooed in the barn way across the field. They crossed a concrete farm road that wound towards the summit. Once over it, she surveyed the bowl of fields beyond. She thought that something was amiss. There were no crops, just grazing pastures for sheep or cows. Most odd. A shallow ravine ran from on high to the base of the hill. She halted at its entrance and the soldiers formed a circle around her, laying themselves flat on the turf, automatics bristling outwards, toes touching inwards. Kitty pushed a gap between two men with her booted toes at the forward position, lay between them, unholstered her pistol and unstrapped her camera. Using it, she looked up the hill and started recording. The lights glowed on and off surreally in the artificially lit darkness but the source remained hidden by the brow of the hill above.

It was moving closer. The sound was reaching a deafening level and various new pitches skipped down the incline with the repetitive booms. A staccato clicking, a swirling spooky high note and a bouncing rhythm also rolled along on the music like tide. Kitty's mind momentarily wandered. The cacophony seemed like pure evil. She imagined a hunched green goblin, dancing on the spot to an orc orchestra. This naughty sound was finally accompanied by a deep and sinister whisper. It was in English! The dark tormentor from above was repeatedly whispering to the beats of the Tolkein tune, "Ecstasy. Ecstasy." One of the soldiers eventually broke the impasse with a poignant appreciation of the arts.

"Fuck my Old Skool boots! That's Joey Beltram's 'Energy Flash'! Hardcore! You know the fuckin' score?"

'All Day and All of the Night'

Delirium was an emotion that the school friends were most accustomed to. The drug ingestion was reaping rewards on their fevered bodies and slanted brains. The music shuddered and rattled the framework of their transports, both truck and transcendental. Harry's right knee rocked uncontrollably with the frantic beat and he rolled his shoulders and neck languidly with the haunting melody. His mind was a misty blur as he stared out into the darkness beyond the vibrating wall of randomly flashing light. He smiled to himself as he thought about the joy of love he was experiencing from a most unholy of trinities. A crop circle, a gorgeous girl and a chemical composite.

Barrington Knave was feeling odd too but masked it well mainly due to his inbuilt responsibility as designated driver. After his horrendous last LSD experience, now over twenty years previous, he had maintained the most important attribute for a long surviving bon viveur. Balance. During their slow descent of the rapid incline, he was helped in this matter of equilibrium by the tight grip he sustained on the steering wheel. His vice like formal handshake training was coming into its own despite the sweat that glossed his palms and trickled slowly down his back. Even the shudders that the dissolved pill delivered to his upper arms were shock absorbed by the taution in their fore. Technology also assisted. The four wheel drive low ratio setting to the car's computer ensured that the roll downhill was brake restricted, skid free and at a barely pedestrian pace. Apart from the occasional twist to the wheel to tack slowly back and forth to reduce the angle of descent, he was concentrating very hard on the wild fractals on the bed sheet flag which seemed to flap in slow motion next to his driver window. He beat away the mental image of his wife's shaking head and the rasta's bloodshot eyes within it and let the waves of ecstasy ripple through him. It had been an extraordinary day and he was now ready for the climax or anti, whether as a tale of the unexpected or just a chilled trip with his old buddy through the night.

The valley below twinkled through the light rain where a handful of visible villages nestled. The light breeze was slowly shifting the rain clouds and the breaks intermittently revealed the full moon above and its silver grey light below. These elements fascinated the deluded delinquents. The luminescence that naturally wallowed across the fields was mimicked by the breeze through the crop in the distance. It seemed to pulsate softly in gentle contrast to the bizarre bubble of extraordinary energy that enveloped their confused canopy. At close range the tiny droplets of water from on high flickered on their sweeping headlights and glowing theatre. The soft wall of water could be viewed in the distance moving slowly along with the mellow moonlight and wheat wobbles in bulging buttresses. Every few seconds the moon appeared. To the delusional men, the orb seemed to have a vivid rainbow of colours surrounding it which tickled the edges of the passing clouds before it disappeared again behind their wet caresses.

The hill gradient briefly levelled to near flat. An Ice Age scar had provided a convenient path for the last few thousand years of bovine commuters. The tight chalk paths that wiggled along it were scattered liberally with small black clusters of excreta pellets. Knave banked the car left onto the miniature plateau, drove sedately a few yards and allowed his hands a rest from their manacled endeavours by waving them out of his open window in the soft breeze and gentle shower. He opened his fingers wide and slightly backwards then clenched his fists. He repeated these actions a few times until his digits were stretched and cooled and then re-established their directional travail. A slight ravine opened up on the downward side and he angled the front tyres to its brink. He turned to his friend. His jaw lightly twitched in spasm as he explained his predicament.

"I'm buggered."

"Absolutely caked." Kitson corresponded accordingly.

"I feel like I'm a pink marshmallow on a stick over a warm fire. My outside is baked and my inside is mushed. How about you?"

"My body feels like it is being catapulted at a few hundred miles an hour from a medieval siege machine whilst my brain has been left behind. Much as I admire your ability to actually drive this old crate, I am bursting to get out and have a dance. If I don't do this very, very soon, I fear that I may spontaneously combust." Harry expressed his concerns with a wobbly grin and popping eyes. The severity of his request was not lost on the pilot.

"Understood, Old Boy. Not far to go now. We just have to shimmy down this wee gorge so we can gorge gorgeously. Bare with me, Buddy. Soon you will be able to release the ballistics." He rolled the car back over the edge and, when the back wheels had started the descent too, snaked it carefully left and right on the banks to once more minimise the angle and keep their cargo housed securely. The gully was smooth, bitten low by his sheep and soft hummocks of grass on rock dappled the crests. They too were nibbled raw. A minute of crawling descent later, the truck reached the bottom of the ravine. The ground began to flatten out in a smoother contour to the start of the valley bottom. They hovered approximately ten metres above the field. Barrington performed a tilting three point turn at nudibranch pace in appropriate technicolour. On completion, the tailgate pointed directly southward, providing the perfect viewing point of the field below, the grass walls around them and the heavens above. When the car stopped, Harry exhaled dramatically with a flood of relief and leapt out of the cab.

He stretched. He shut his eyes, stepped on tipped toes, arched his back and reached his outstretched hands up. He imagined fingernails firmly scratching him. An imaginary sensual journey along his shaking arms, down his tingling neck, across his muscled shoulders, parallel with his electrified spine, over his taut buttocks and along the back of his quivering thighs and calves which halted at his Achilles' heels. To hell with bodily weak spots, he thought, this was heaven. He shuddered with the bliss. He personalised those nails. Harry imagined Kitty's cat claws, raking his back in erotic passion. He felt energy rip through his frame and he opened his eyes. The lurid explosion of visual plasma and audio hypnosis meshed with these sexual undertones.

Something important caught Harry's eye. The first lingers of doubt flickered through his befuddled brain. There was an obvious disjoin between the plan explained over bestial cartography in the office and the current execution in the field. He put his point of concern to the farmer.

"Errr, Barry," he began, "Would you mind explaining why you have brought us to the edge of a field to view the formation of a crop circle which does not actually have a crop growing, whether to harvest for profit or for artists to vandalise?" It was a good point, well made. Barrington scratched his head in thought. Certainly, the two or three enclosures in the sweeping semicircle of the rolling hills were of the more pasturel variety. A small patch had been left as set aside too. A tangled mixture of meadow grasses and stinging weeds waved sporadically out of the darkness under the disco damnantions. The landowner did what he did best in moments of difficulty. Just as generations of Knaves had done with conviction before him, he rose above it.

"A minor technicality," he surmised, "My office work was not an exact science as you may have deduced."

"You dick." Harry was keen to highlight this important defect in the planner.

"Fret not, Amigo," Barry soothed, "We already know that crop circles are not always reliant on actual crops. Maybe it will be one of those 'ghost' images we researched? An energy imprint on the earth itself? Alternatively, the nearest wheat is only a couple of hundred metres away near my cattle shed." He waved his arm in the general direction of Milk Hill. "Don't worry about it! I feel the boogie in my bones! C'mon! Let's rave!"

Kitson placed his hands on the side of the truck and vaulted directly up and onto the hay bale between speakers and table, narrowly missing the flags, lights and balloons on the short obstacle course. Knave mirrored the route from his own side. His more imposing bulk necessitated a more considered climb than an athletic assault. On ascent, both men automatically turned, stood and faced each other, in a well practiced sequence, this time at opposite sides of the hay bale. They mechanically cocked their fingers into pistol shapes and held them in readiness at their hips. They stared at each other. Simultaneously they turned their faces slightly, maintained eye contact and spat imaginary chewing tobacco. They faced off again. Barrington raised one eyebrow. Harry tried to do the same but failed. They drew their fantasy weapons and fired.

This was a well rehearsed cue to dance. This they did with considerable commitment. Their former firearms were transformed into flattened fingers which whirled and spiralled in and out of the lasers in some sort of accelerated tribute to Tai Chi. Their arms were a seeming blur of constant palming, pointing and pushing as they pretended to throw an imaginary ball of energy between them. Their exaggerated gestures resembled a baseball pitcher and catcher in slow motion. Their waists twisted, they bounced on their haunches, spun on their toes and jumped high in the air. They were lost in their own world of dance, love, light and sound. The pent up excitement from the car's confines radiated up and outwards in a burst of laughter and happiness. The two friends then stopped, stepped forward and hugged. The embrace was held. A burning heat transferred from man to man. Both kissed the other's neck in a practiced signal of affection. They both basked in the sensation despite the damp clothing and wet chins and cheeks that were joined. After a minute or so, their hearts slowed a little, they parted, put an arm around their respective waists and shoulders and stared out across the gently sloping pasture.

Confusion is an emotion often experienced by the partaker of MDMA. Friends build a bubble of trust and they know its boundaries. Hugs to random strangers and kisses to their necks sometimes resulted in mutual appreciation and occasional tongue union. More often these advances would produce a reaction more in keeping with privacy invasion. Lessons had been slowly learnt. Mates don't slap. Dance moves were honed and perfected over time but newcomers would often stare, or, worse still, laughed. This was the environment that the boys had nurtured over many years of dedication to rave. It took a great deal to put them off their stride, leap and yell.

But this was one such moment of confusion. Their amphitheatre of trust and love was ruined by the growth of about a dozen shrubs. In a fraction of the time that herbaceous germination usually occurred, the plants in front of them grew from one to six feet high. Further hallucinatory alarm bells sounded within their fractured minds when the plants started moving forward directly towards them. It was of absolutely no relief that these miniature triffids all appeared to be heavily armed with semi-automatic weapons. One stepped forward and communicated in a tongue of distant and alien origin.

"остановить! руки вверх!"

The two friends gaped at the shrub that spoke in this obscure language. They froze. A few seconds later another plant joined the first. It waved its weapon at Kitson and Knave and addressed them with another foreign tongue.

"Tíng! Xiàsh ŏ u!"

Once more the boys did not move. Petrification seemed their best choice in these surreal circumstances. They certainly had not bargained on the crop circle creators being in situ so early. Or being plants. Or being armed. Or speaking directly to them in some strange planetary code. A third plant stepped towards the shaking lads. It shouted very loudly and Harry and Barry were relieved that this clump of yellow grass was also a psychic linguist.

"Halt! Hands up!"

The ravers did so. Despite the aggressive use of weaponry and language, they were relieved that communications had been established in their mother tongue. It was also of considerable comfort that the shrub appeared to be just a man disguised as one.

"Turn that infernal racket off!" the assumed Anglophile continued. He waved in the direction of the pulsating speakers. Knave obliged by lowering his hands and pushed pause on the small rectangular tablet that lay on the Formica surface behind him. "Now, put your hands up again!" He did.

The absence of sound created a silence most uncomfortable. Ears sang after the deafening tone and it was exasperated by the constant pitter of the rain shower on their transparent cover and the patter of its drips from the car to the ground. The boys were a little intimidated by this audio vacuum and greatly by the fact that a dozen men stood before them, pointing guns in their specific direction.

"Get down from that heap!" barked the lead man. When they had, they raised their arms again and stood in front of his raised muzzle. He continued. "I am going to ask you some questions and you are going to answer them very clearly. OK?" Two heads nodded. "Are you Russian?" Two heads shook. "Are you Chinese?" Two heads repeated the negative action. "Are you English?" Two heads nodded enthusiastically. "Are you here for the crop circles?" They nodded again. "Right!" the man bellowed, "Arrest these men! We're taking them in!" He turned to his platoon. "You four take these criminals. You two take their divisive equipment. You two go back to Milk Hill and fetch the observers. On route, inform the Major about the situation. The rest of you stay here and scan the area for any further evidence of these men's vandalisation." He looked at his watch. "It's 01:28 hours now. We'll rendezvous at our vehicles again by two thirty am. Right! Go!"

As the troops began moving to put his orders into action, a voice of defiance boomed in the silence. Barrington Knave was not to be outdone. The same bravado that had seen off the helicopter a few days before seized him once more. The euphoria artificially created by Ecstacy heightened his sense of bravery. He puffed up his chest and orally ejaculated.

"How bloody dare you!" he growled like an aggravated bear, "You are trespassing on my land! I have come here this night to greet crop circle creators that have previously graced my farm and left peaceful messages in my precious fields over my lifetime. You have no idea how bloody disappointing it is to discover that these visitors are none other than the British Army, stealing illegally onto my land in the dead of the night, and who have the sodding gall to try and pin the blame on me and my innocent friend. I am not having this. By trespassing, armed and dangerous onto my farm, you renegades are up to your necks in my farm silage. I am the landlord! I am a local councillor, for God's sake! I know people in high places! You are going to court martial and army jail for your invasion of myspace and vandalisation of my precious livelihood. I want names! I want ranks! I want...."

Barrington's rant was halted by the silent swivel of a firearm and its butt's fierce application to his solar plexus. He buckled to the ground. The farmer gasped for breath. He rested on one knee, one hand propped him up against the wet earth, the other clutched his winded stomach. He groaned. Then he smiled. The blow had actually stimulated the drug further and the corresponding rush of energy catapulted him back to his feet and he squared up to his assailant with his ham like fists clenched.

"Barry Knave! Stop!" The voice was higher than those previously exercised. "Sergeant Major Grimley! Stand down!" The vocals were cool with authority. "Gentlemen! Lower your weapons. Now!" The command was obeyed immediately. A shorter, slighter camouflaged figure stepped forward into the psychedelic glow from the lighting rig, brandishing a pistol.

"Captain Parker, Sir! I mean, Ma'am!" stuttered Grimley. His confusion was apparent and so he asked, "How do you know this man's name?"

"For two reasons, Sergeant Major. First, I have contributed to a file studying him and his father. This study included me photographing him at 'The Basket' site only recently." The officer removed a grass covered helmet, revealing softer features that were familiar to all assembled, for entirely different reasons. "Secondly, I know him socially. He is this man's best friend," she pointed at Kitson, "who happens to be my boyfriend."

"Kitty?" Harry stammered in disbelief. "I. I. I..... I don't understand. You said that you had a photography job to complete tonight." A mental penny dropped, "You lied to me!?" Harry's mind was thoroughly confused. He glowed at the mention of his status in her life but reeled at her clear breach of stated professionalism.

"My Darling Harry," Kitty's tone was firm but affectionate, "First and foremost, I must apologise. I'm sorry that you have been put in this extraordinary predicament. I had no idea that you two wonderful nutters would be here on this night. It just seemed implausible, no, impossible. You will explain later, I'm sure." She smiled lovingly and then continued, "But I have not lied to you, albeit I have only relayed a fraction of the truth. I am working tonight on a photography assignment," she patted the camera slung from her gun free arm, "but I am an officer for Her Majesty's Armed Forces specialising in surveillance. Captain Kitty Parker, at your service, Sir." Harry was dumbstruck. The girl of his dreams, his beacon of feminism, the love he had waited so long for, was a British Army officer. But it was Barry who piped up in the aftermath of her revelation.

"You crafty young fox! It was you taking pictures from the chopper of my chopper, wasn't it? I thought I recognised your face when you turned up at the farm on the bike with young Harry but couldn't place you. I guessed that I'd glimpsed you at Burningman but it wasn't there, it was only a few days ago when I waggled my wanger at you snapping pics through the window of the helicopter? You saucy little bitch!"

"Barry, please!" Harry interjected. It was his turn to feel the power of the drug and the rush of blood through his veins which emboldened his emotion to protect the girl. He was rapidly becoming accustomed to the fact that he was wildly aroused by the newfound professional status and uniformed fashion of his love. His dream girl had become even dreamier. "There is clearly much to discuss. Let's start with....."

Whatever Harry was going to say remained a mystery because, at that exact moment, a deafening buzzing hum blanked out all the other sounds in the world around them. Its deep tone rattled the assembled eardrums with a resonance similar to the vibrations from an aboriginal didgeridoo. The sound seemed to ebb and flow on the rolling cloud and waving rain. Everybody stopped and looked around them for the source of the thundering noise. Some of the soldiers squatted on their haunches and trained their guns across the surrounding hills and dark skies. Others slung their semi-automatics under their armpits and covered their ears instinctively.

Their darting eyes flashed across the fields, empty of all but wheat, the hills, inhabited by only grass, shrub and ridges, and the skies, full of cumulus, water and moonlight. It was the latter that initially changed. A wall of darkness descended from way up in the sky. The lunar light was suddenly eclipsed and the nimbus greyed further and then blackened. An awesome shadow moved steadily downwards along the bank behind them, upon the Milk Hill ridge to the east and towards the valley before them, in a vast circle about a half mile in diameter. The miniscule group seemed like a cluster of peas on a platter as an enormous domed restaurant cloche was lowered slowly over them. As the last edge of this phantom bell hit the Vale bottom, the group were plunged into darkness. The lights in nearby Stanton disappeared behind this veil of mourning. Only the pickup truck broke the totality of blackness around them. Its surreal mixture of fluorescence, laser, sparkle, search light and neon barely registered in the vastness of the dark and the accompanying ear splitting shudder of sound. The car's fizzled promise of pussy and party blinked slowly on and off. The tawdry joke suddenly seemed totally pointless in the vast void of emptiness.

The increasingly panicked soldiers tried to shout above the noise. Years of intense combat situations had developed their natural linguistic style into a most colourful complexion. Their full repertoire of filthy expletives was exhausted rapidly with questions regarding their current predicament. They waved their weapons at the abyss beyond them and thumbed safety catches on and off in anticipation of attack. Once more, their Joan of Arc rose majestically in command. Her voice was still, calm and dominant as they huddled in a ring around her. Captain Parker addressed her quivering cavalry.

"Gentlemen! Lower your weapons! Do not be afraid! Please listen to Mr Harry Kitson for one moment!" She nodded at her lover who calmly proclaimed.

"Indeed, Kitty. Fear is our enemy. Your guns are of little or no use to us now. We are in the presence of a natural power far beyond anything we could ever have anticipated. Revel in its ultimate glory and be official witnesses to the force of the universe! We are nothing. We are grains of sand in the infinite vastness of the desert beyond. Humble yourselves and bask in this most significant of moments. Be calm and under no circumstances provoke any reaction by using your ineffective artillery." Kitty's trust in him and Harry's soothing words seemed to have an immediately calming effect on the Captain's charges. Their tense shoulders dropped in unison with their lowered barrels. They gulped, shook, then settled themselves in for this most unique of theatrical displays.

Captain Parker was more proactive. She holstered her sidearm and hoiked her camera to her eye. The night vision revealed a familiar lurid green spectrum of crop, bluff and firmament. She then arched the lens around the huddle of men. She spoke their names into the microphone as she passed each and they casually acknowledged her by lazy salute or thumbs up on her traverse. They seemed extraordinarily calm given the circumstances. She felt the same way. Most peaceful. There were two obvious absentees from her cast of characters so she lowered the intensity of the night settings to avoid damage to her cornea, panned the digital device over the truck and onto the two civvies who had jumped up and resumed their hay bale vantage point. They danced to the pulse of the deep vibration. They grinned and waved at her. Maybe it was the depth of field in her apparatus as she zoomed in on the affable clowns but their eye pupils appeared large and black. Kitty thought to herself. Are they high on drugs? She would not be surprised in the slightest if they were. Idiots was a description that jumped to mind but she loved them for it, especially one of them.

On immediate recognition that their performance was far inferior to the main event, Kitty flicked the camera settings from 'Night' to 'Night/Heat' and swung the focus forward again. The screen was split into two separate functions. The new heat results were not surprising. The foreground revealed the flickering light sources of the pickup's accessories and the red core, with emanating yellow and green rings, around the individuals of the platoon. Beyond that was total darkness. All except one little crimson glow at the base of Milk Hill on the other side of their knolled enclave. She had entirely forgotten about the marooned Major! Parker imagined him cowering behind a bush, blubbing like a babe as he considered his impending doom. All alone, unloved and doing a job he loathed in total and inexplicable darkness. Poor sod. She wondered when they would be able to put him out of his misery and rescue him. She looked twice at her watch. Once in recognition, the second in disbelief. 02:15 hours. Where had the forty five minutes disappeared to? Was this some bizarre quantum leap? It seemed more likely that the old adage regarding time, flight and fun was true.

The still calm of dark and throb of sound was shattered by a distantly audible, "Incoming!" from one of the soldiers located near her right eardrum. Before she had time to react, her viewfinder blazed angrily as a fireball of white core, red rings with a correspondingly fierce heat tail whizzed passed her from right to left. She pulled her elegant face away from the viewfinder but left the recording on and held the camera steady. She swivelled her head in the direction of the heat detected. A perfect round ball of intense white light sped passed their observation post at a height of only ten metres. It was volleyball sized. It swept along at breathtaking speed across the field, illuminating the dull durum beneath it. It slowed then started to circle way across the wheat, not far from the three hidden army vehicles, and rose steadily to approximately fifty metres. It hung there. All eyes were transfixed on the beautiful sphere. Except one pair.

"Incoming!" yelled the familiar lookout, "Two bogies! Two o'clock!" Twenty something peepers wrenched away from the hypnotic sight before them and looked up and right. Two similar balls hurtled down the gradient between Tan and Clifford's Hills and swung seamlessly across the saucered valley in front of the strange audience of peaceniks and military. This brace of orbs seemed to be vying for the lead, like race cars on a long straight, before they too banked with pinpoint precision symmetry and circled slowly up to join the leader of the pack. "Bogey!" They all twisted west again. Another bright plasma rondure was rolling towards them. It was a little slower and noticeably larger than those before it, more like an inflatable beach ball. As it reached them, they all spotted another one, identically sized, break through the blackened dome behind. It followed its predecessor, mimicking its more pronounced and languid movements compared to the darting agility of the first three. The two larger balls mirrored the original paths and concluded at the same hanging point below Milk Hill.

"I can't believe it!" shouted Kitty. Her cry sounded like a whisper in the din but she pressed on, "It's incredible! The algorithms were correct! They are hovering exactly where the computers predicted. If only we hadn't followed the red herring cast by these two jellied eels, we would be right in the thick of it." She gesticulated at the goggle eyed double dance troupe behind her.

"It's just as well, Captain Parker," answered Sergeant Major Grimley, with a strange sweetness, "We would be of little use confronting these beautiful things. I don't think I've ever seen anything so mesmerising in all my years traversing our globe. Apart from my missus on our wedding night, of course." Kitty noted that the previously barking commander was sitting on the grass cross legged with a relaxed face and inane grin. She thought that it strangely suited him compared to the eye bulging, vein popping screamer she had been previously accustomed to.

Her train of consciousness was interrupted in another pleasant way. The thunderous noise stopped. A reticence of calm followed the storm. Even the rain seemed to lull. Then, one after the other, the spheres dropped vertically down and started swirling and weaving above the crop. Each seemed on it's own random course, dancing just above the grained ears. The avoidance of collision with the other plasma objects, sometimes with the narrowest of margins, always at incredible speed, made the sweep and dive of their actions seem like the most pristine perfection in an elaborate ballet. The humans watched the performance agog. Nobody knew whether it was seconds, minutes or hours that they were held hypnotised by the loping movements of this divine cast. As dramatically as the five had started, the intense baubles finished when they shot to the side of their round dance floor. They circled it in a clockwise direction. The two larger, slower balls on an inner trajectory, the three smaller orbs moved faster in an outer hoop.

As they watched these revolutions of brilliant white, each sphere left a perfect tracer behind it as it spun, then the centre of this distant circus was suddenly bathed in a milky pale light. On looking up, it appeared that the top of the dome had opened slightly and the moon's rays were entering the darkened amphitheatre. This lustre appeared to descend in a perfect pillar from cloud to crop. The transparent cylinder glowed eerily against the blackened backdrop. It suddenly pinkened as another, relatively vast, ball dropped through the opening above. It was like a spherical fire, burning red, orange and yellow, and was about ten times larger than its bright white precursors. It descended rapidly until level with the others, which span in a hypnotic vortex, and then hovered. A faint and distant melody began. Its notes soared then dived like mermaids in a lagoon. It sounded like seductive Sirens calling out to salacious sailors.

This effect was confirmed when a figure emerged from the shadows behind. The upper torso of a man seemed to drift on this crop tide. Major de Crecy Conrad-Pickles could be seen wading forward through the long shafts of wheat towards the epicentre. His arms were thrown aloft, apart in supplication and his head was tilted back as he stared at the heart of the crimson orb. He looked like a Baptist emerging from beneath a cleansing current. Montgomery appeared to be shouting and smiling intermittently. As he neared the perimeter, the large ball of roasting energy briefly pulsed, expanded in size, then instantaneously retracted to the sound of a bass 'Baa-oooooom'. The crop below rippled from centre to side and the Major first crumpled to his knees then disappeared in the wake of the shock wave.

"Holy Shit!" Kitty adapted her language suitably for the occasion and audience. She checked her camera. The split screen still was recording the lurid green night vision on the left and the heat sensors on the right. The latter was giving off readings that she had only seen when viewing the rear jets of fighter planes. "Man down! We must go and fetch him now! Prepare to move out!" The men looked at her with puzzlement. They were in no state of mind to start running around. Meditation, sleep or sex were more prevalent thoughts amongst the trained killers at that particular moment. They were hostages to bliss. Slaves of an unfamiliar yet all welcoming heaven. Kitty glanced in her view finder and focused nearer the core. Slowly a form was appearing atop the crop. At first just a shadow, then more distinct, like some gigantic force was pressing down on the wheat. "Look! It's happening!" she yelled with uncontrollable joy. The soldiers Ahhhh-ed as an image of concentric circles with random offshoots began to take shape. It looked like some intricately jewelled Art Deco motif or badge on a gigantic scale. Kitty looked at the right hand screen and scanned the crop beyond the recent linear application. There was a red glow where the Major had fallen. "He's alive!" she exclaimed, "Stand down for now! We can recover the Major when this is all over."

On her heat screen, Captain Parker suddenly saw a flashed white line streak from high above the action area. It narrowly missed her bunched hair and ended with a resounding 'crack' closeby. It's lightning fast arrival corresponded with a synchronised 'woah' of surprise from the two jesters on the truck as one of the searchlight bulbs exploded. Kitty was confused. Was the plasma energy in the field attracted to its less powerful cousins lashed all over the pickup? There was another crack. The 'Girls. Girls. Girls.' signage combusted and a shower of sparks fountained all over the rear of the vehicle. Helium balloons instantaneously popped angrily and a flicker of flame gently began to lick the corner fluorescent spattered flag. The fog in Parker's mind only cleared when the third crack corresponded with a whine and "Aghhhh!!!!" She looked up. The corner of the large speaker had disintegrated. Harry was clutching his left bicep with his right hand. The latter was covered in blood. She thought fast, reached up, grabbed, then tugged on her lover's thigh before she shouted above the confusion.

"Snipers! Run!"

'Rhythm of the Rain'

Kitty held Harry's good arm as she helped him down from the burning truck. Barry vaulted with surprising nimbleness from the other side and the three assembled under the cover of the front bumper in a low huddle. Kitty explained.

"There are two SAS marksmen on the ridge above the circle site." She began with the cool calm of leadership, pacifying the terrified twins. "They are under secret instructions to eliminate the cause of this threat. Just as these soldiers initially reacted, they think that you two are Russian or Chinese terrorists. They could not hear any of the dialogue that we had so have assumed that you are controlling those orbs. They are tasked with your elimination. My Uncle Max has told them to mop up immediately." The boys looked blank then Harry questioned.

"The same Uncle Max that took you out for Sunday lunch? I'm so confused. This is so strange." Kitty resumed her reassurance.

"It's too difficult to explain in full now but, in brief, my commanding officer, Major de Crecy Conrad-Pickles, has been feeding misinformation to deflect the more plausible scientific truths about crop circle formations. I have been under instruction from higher up the power ladder to investigate these matters more seriously. I report to Uncle Max but he is also pulling the puppet strings of those two nutters. When this incredible energy manifested itself, those crack shots assumed that you two had orchestrated it and, on seeing our unit sitting in submission to the spectacle, thought that you were holding them captive and thus opened fire to eradicate you. We must get out of this valley as fast as possible because they will not miss again. Those two are the very best at what they do but we have a geographical headstart on them. Barry. Do you know anywhere, away from here and your home, where we can hide?" Knave thought for a moment then answered with a grin.

"Yes! I have the perfect place in mind! It's about an hour's walk down the valley behind us." He gesticulated over the steep incline that they had previously laboured down in the vehicle.

"Great!" The Captain returned his confident smile, then turned to her lover. "Harry, Darling. How are you feeling?" She indicated the bloody hand that held his wounded shoulder.

"I feel fantastic!" Kitson drooled. "I think it has only grazed me. Motorcycle leathers to the rescue, me thinks!" He slowly removed the jacket with the aid of his caring nurse. He pulled the undergarments over his head and tucked them under his chin revealing his reddened shoulder. The bullet had missed puncturing him by millimetres. The glancing gash had already stopped bleeding. A congealed residue of blood coated the wound, defending it against alien invasion.

"Hankie?" Parker asked the question that she already knew the answer to. The little she had learned about Kitson, she knew that he was not the sort of chap that leaves home without this most versatile of gentleman's accoutrements. Harry produced the blue and white spots from his trouser's back pocket, perfectly folded. The Captain shook it open and then spun it into a long bandage that she wrapped then knotted over the wound. "Get dressed now," she ordered, "We must move fast. First we must make a break for the cover of this grassy knoll. They can't shoot at us there. I'll go first. This will give them time to see that it is me, not you, in control. I will then pretend to lead you out at gunpoint. Please, please, please make sure that you hold your hands above your heads and walk, don't run, to the lee of the hill. I will make sure that I am in between you and them as we traverse those twenty metres or so. Once there, we will need to sprint up the bank. I reckon that we will have a lead of about twenty minutes on them when we reach the top and they realise that we have escaped. Barry. I need you to think like a soldier now. You need to plan a route that hides us by the terrain for as long as possible please?"

"Affirmative, Captain!" Knave grinned again. "I already have. Nobody knows this terrain better than I. As long as we keep the pace up, we will be covered almost the entire way."

"Marvellous." Parker replied. She looked at the two men and waited for Harry to make the final adjustments to his redress. "Ready?" They both nodded. She checked her photography viewfinder. It was still recording. She held her pistol in her right and raised the camera with her left. She stood slowly up and backed away from the pickup bonnet, holding the weapon pointed in the direction that she had come from. She moved about three or four metres into the no man's land area and paused. No shots. Nothing. She waved the gun upwards. They responded to her gesticulation and walked with arms raised towards her. "Come and stand between me and them, slowly." They did. The brave use of her officer's body as shield paid dividends as the shooters disisted. "Now, maintaining the same position, walk sideways with me." They covered the remaining dozen metres to the hill's bluff within laboured and agonising seconds. They huddled together and looked back.

The straw bales in the car had ignited now. Electrical wires fizzled and cracked. Lights burst and shattered. Despite their peaceful countenance, Captain Parker was relieved to notice that the nearby soldiers had registered the inferno's danger and had wandered down the gentle slope towards the concrete road and illuminated crop theatre. They were all mesmerised by the continued galactic performance. Like the Major, they appeared to be drawn towards the circle in some form of hypnotic trance. Their weapons were slung by straps across their shoulders. One meandered lazily with his rifle behind his neck, his wrists draped over the barrel and butt in some supplicant act of crucifixion. Two of the soldiers were topless and strolled arm in arm across the pasture, their weapons now abandoned.

After briefly ingesting this bizarre spectacle, a far cry from any army manual, the trio of escapologists started their ascent of the steep incline. As the light of the fire below them and the cosmic light from afar were dissipated and obliterated, they stumbled up the bank ridges in the near darkness of the domed enclosure. The constant rhythm of the rain and vibrating sounds of the plasma creators were the only accompaniment to their laboured puffs and pants. Reaching the crest, they hunkered down out of the line of suspected fire. An explosion behind them directed their attention back down the slope. One hundred metres below them, the flash of light as the jerry can of petroleum exploded revealed a black oily mushroom of aftermath that billowed upwards.

"That's going to be an interesting story when I make my insurance claim," mused the owner. "'Yes, Mr Loss Adjuster'" he continued in the vein of an interview, "'All most unfortunate. There I was, minding my own business, viewing unidentified flying objects from my rave converted car, when the army, disguised as plants, popped up and started shooting at me. Luckily, they missed me but destroyed the truck.'" He paused then added after more logical consideration. "I might retract the fact that I was ripped to the tits on MDMA though. It might reduce the plausibility of my claim."

"I knew you nutters were high!" exclaimed the army captain. "Only you two could come up with such a ridiculous welcome party for our cosmic artists! And they didn't disappoint either! This has been an unbelievable night. Domes of darkness, plasma orbs and furnace hot crop circle creation. How the Major isn't dead having wandered into its centre is beyond me. I'm so jealous of you that I was on official duty now. I would have far preferred to get caked too. Having said that, I'm not sure that you would still be alive now if I wasn't working for Queen, Country and Universe!?"

"A good point, well made, My Love," glossed Harry, "We have been in the perfect state of mind to deal with this transplanetary conundrum and you have shepherded us through it all but for a minor scratch." He lent forward to kiss the girl. Pure love transcended all as usual for the hopeless romantic so he added, "My Heroine."

"There is no time for all that now, Soppy Boy," she interjected although, secretly, she wished there was. "Let's check out the lay of the land." She raised her camera above the parapet and rested it on the crest having focused the direction on the circle creation. Three heads followed it and six eyes trained on the field below Milk Hill.

The crop formation stood out in the milky light from the moon high above and the whizzing spheres around it. With a deep groan like rumble, the larger fire orb in the epicentre started to rise slowly upwards from whence it came. It bulged with power as it floated up the cylinder above it. It accelerated upward. First the larger plasma balls then the three smaller ones rotated clockwise and followed it. One by one they popped through the hole at the top of the dome and, on the exit of the last, the shadow base of the bell lifted off the ground. Within seconds its walls had risen to reveal the village lights beyond the fields. Another few moments later and the escarpments around them were on show again. Finally, the dark remains disappeared completely into the thinning clouds. The moon shone down imperiously. The rain stopped. The silence was awesome. All eyes returned to earth and surveyed the artwork, bathed in the perfectly white light. Three sighs collectively appreciated the immaculate beauty of the scene.

With a jab of her finger to the left and right, Kitty broke the ecstatics' spell and motioned with her thumb that they should get moving. Barry led the way. Hunched low they ran just below the crest of the ridge in a northwesterly direction until he found a gate. This they traversed at the hinge end on the farmer's insistent manual indication. This was his natural reaction to townsfolk's previous disrespect for the simple mechanics of his lovingly installed access points. They then jogged north along a shallow hollow until they reached a wall of earth, two metres high which snaked away across the ridge in both directions.

Barry recognised that they would be briefly exposed on the climb so indicated with a hand sign, using the baby and forefingers usually reserved for heavy metal music and VW Beetle fans, pointed to his eyes that they should watch and follow him. He darted up the bank, across the chalk track at its top and disappeared on the far side. The other two copied his actions and steadied themselves next to him just over the brink that was crowned by the snaking path. Below them loomed the dark nothingness of the ten metre high cliff from top to the ditch bottom of the ancient Wansdyke.

After centuries of this acting as the natural terrestrial barrier between conflicting peoples and kingdoms, the trio were strangely aware that they had just witnessed a force far more powerful than selfish man's. The beauty and power of the artistic message and its creators was humbling. The terror of the human hunters behind them reiterated the ignorance of humanity and its overwhelming desire to destroy itself and the environment around it. This drove them on. Survival was now key. Barry demonstrated the fastest method of descent with a measured bum slide down the bank. He dug his heels in near the base which drew him seamlessly to his feet. He used this momentum to run across the base then up the far bank, only a metre in height, to the tractor track at the edge of the pasture beyond. Kitty followed suit. Her feline agility sprang her to the farmer's side. Harry descended, tripped and rolled. He uttered a suitable expletive for their historic old English surroundings.

"Fuck!" Once he had composed himself, he rubbed his sore shoulder then, buoyed by the continued invincibility of narcotic, grinned and joined the fugitives. He then apologised for his lack of balance and loss of linguistic control in a manner more befitting a gentleman of his era, "I'm most terribly sorry."

Knave shook his head in mock despair then waved his compadres on. His route took them down into a massive bowl of pasture, the moonlight darkened its depths and highlighted the vast fields of wheat that crowned its sides and swept away across the Downs to the north. They scrambled down to the base of the saucer shaped decline. It opened out into a small valley that disappeared into the blackness beyond. They ran along it, once more shielded from the threat of rifled barrels. The ground was firm, the hungry earth having gulped up the recent rain. The only sounds were the pounding of boots and puffing of lungs emitted by the two middle aged men. The human cat moved silently. As they moved swiftly away from the hills behind them, the valley became shallower and the crop fields to their sides seemed to creep closer. The Captain stopped when she spotted a flat object protruding from the ground to her left.

"What's that?" she questioned.

"A pill box." The farmer's weazed his eventual answer.

"Let's get inside it now." The soldier's logic took over.

"No good," puffed the landlord, his hands on his hips, his body bent forward at the waist. "That hasn't been used since Blighty blasted at the Horrid Hun on their way to bomb Bristol. It's full to the brim with rain water. I use it to pump water onto the fields when we suffer drought. Besides, my house is just across that brow. We are far too close to my wife and kids to be having a fight at this OK Corral. Let's stick to my plan. It's not far now and far more defendable. C'mon." He straightened up and started to move.

"Stop!" ordered the officer, "We will use that old bunker to hide us briefly so I can survey the scene behind us." At her lead, they diverted towards the concrete roof across a slight upward roll of land. Once perched beside the rough edge of the cement, sand and stone circular promontory, she placed her elbows on the flat top, switched her camera to the heat setting and panned it back in the direction of Milk Hill. Barry interjected.

"You do that then. I've got some texts to do anyway. It's officially time for a Save Our Souls message!" He took his phone from his pocket and tapped the screen with remarkable speed for a man with such considerable fingers and thumbs. Kitty ignored him. This was no time to start playing with mobile phones. High boys really were an encumbrance of the greatest potential danger, she thought to herself. The first thing she noticed on her own screen was the soft surge of colour from the east as the first pulses of solar warmth hinted over the undulating horizon. The second was far more disturbing. Two small burning objects were moving at speed along the crest of the Ridgeway walk between them and the Knave homestead. "Damn it!" she muttered, "Those psychopaths are far closer than I anticipated. We are sitting ducks up here. I should have listened to your words of wisdom, Barry, we've got to get back to your gorge before they take a shot at us. Let's move."

Despite the pride in his fieldcraft, Knave realised that this was not the moment to gloat and refrained from forming the told you so words that jostled for position at the tip of his tongue. He had been married for fifteen years. He knew better. As they bolted from the temporary cover, a bullet whined through the air and cracked onto the stone slab that they had just vacated. Speed was of the essence. Stinging injuries and advancing years were cast aside as the three sprung back down the incline with the darting nimbleness of the conies in their burrows below. When they reached the depths of the dell, they banked left along its grassy belly. They passed a corrugated barn, vaulted a rusty plough, crossed a stoney track and carried on down the gentle slope. Two minutes later, they came to the tip of the pasture and disappeared behind the scraggy hedge and shallow ditch beyond. They huddled low.

"Nearly there!" Barry whispered between his pants, "There is the best hiding place, I know." He waved his hand northwards across the next field. "It's just a shame that we have two specially trained killers behind us so our location isn't any big secret. It does however provide the most perfect defensive position, even if we only have a pistol between the three of us. I should know. I used to attempt tactical assaults on my brother there, armed with only an air rifle. It's almost impenetrable."

Temporarily ignoring the idiocy of the man's confessed childhood game, they looked up the smoothly domed field beyond. At its peak, two long rectangular mounds broke the gentle contour. The familiar Wiltshire sign of ancient burial grounds. At the eastern edge of this particular cemetery rose a cluster of massive Sarsen stones. They jutted upwards like the jagged gnashers of some enormous giant. The light of the moon from one direction and that of the dawn in another played on their rugged surfaces in a magical way. It was awesome and was the reason why Kitty's question was delayed.

"Did you really shoot air rifles at your brother?"

"Sure," smirked the naughty scallywag, "But we always used skiing goggles for safety." He paused, then added, "That's nothing. We used to duel with a four ten shotgun. We'd take it in turns, using well waxed Barbour jackets, the aforementioned eyewear, jeans, gum boots and riding hats for protection. We would stand back to back, one with a BMX bike, the other with the weapon in three pieces and cartridges on the ground in front of him. On 'Go!', one would jump on the bike and ride like hell whilst the other assembled and loaded the pop gun before firing at his sibling. At thirty yards, it still stings, you know?" Kitty looked at the dope with a new found incredulity for his stupidity.

"Dear, dear." She summarised her thoughts with this repeated word and a slow shake of her head. She glanced up with pity as he pressed on.

"The good news is that it has trained me perfectly for the next part of our tactical retreat. Given that our pursuers are armed with canons of significantly fruitier design, may I suggest that we sprint this last hundred or so of exposed metres, in marginally different directions in a darting zig-zag formation?" Kitty was relieved that there was at least some reason in the man's clear insanity so nodded her head with eyes kept unblinkingly open.

They bolted from their inadequate cover and raced towards the mausoleum. In the growing light their passage bore more resemblance to three small sailing boats as they tacked this way and that in seeming competition for the fastest route to distant finishing buoys. Unlike a normal nautical traverse, the sailors were being shot at. The first bullet whined harmlessly but close to Knave's right lug hole. As it smashed into the earth before his eyes, he was reminded to dramatise his directional movements. As they reached their goal, a second missile zipped into the faceure of the ancient stone. It ricocheted and howled fruitlessly into the firmament. One, two, three disappeared safely behind the megalith entrance.

Barry was right. The five and a half thousand year old tomb was the perfect hiding place. The gigantic stones created a barrier to the entrance. The black cave opening was reached by a higgledy path behind them. It was guarded by three enormous stone slabs which created an open air porch. They assembled in this two metre square atrium. Knave pointed over the north most stone and the three looked down the rolling field. The curious manmade nipple of Silbury Hill loomed in the valley below them. Another pointer to the extraordinary happenings in the local vicinity many millennia ago. He turned on his phone torch and pointed it into the cavern. A tunnel of stone led through the centre and the back, approximately ten metres back, was just visible in the lights glow. Half a dozen black grave entrances led off the corridor, gated by huge stones stacked on top of each other. The two nearest were only a half metre back from the main entry point. Kitty stood and surveyed the immediate area with strategic defense in mind.

"Great work, Barry! This is perfection." Kitty purred and Knave swelled. "Our pursuers have only one route into this cave and to do so," she began to formulate her tactics, "they must either climb over these massive stones or drop into this forecourt from the grassy barrow above or take the path as we did. Whatever their assault plan, if I position myself at the entrance to this first grave on the right, I should be able to cover all eventualities with my trusty pistol. Let's hope that they see sense and realise that we are trapped anyway. For our sakes, surrender under those circumstances will be a great deal more pleasant than being shot! Remember that these guys are used to storming Afghan caves. You must hide together in the tomb opposite me, out of the line of fire." They both nodded and Barry added some more reassurance.

"At least we can be sure that they won't be using any bunker busters on a World Heritage Site. Can't we?"

"Ha! I wouldn't count on it, Barry. These guys are used to Terry Taliban and ISIS," Kitty countered, "who didn't even blink to consider the destruction of religious sites and the Hanging Gardens of Babylon. However, luckily they don't have the artillery for anything over dramatic on this occasion. I was at the briefing so I know this. Fret not. Harry. How are you feeling?"

"Terrific!" Kitson enthused, "This place is incredible. It is so fabulously spooky. It's making me rush all over again. I'm tingling from head to toe!"

"Thank God one of us isn't tripping the light fantastic and, luckily, is trained to use and is armed with a gun." Kitty rolled her eyes, "Right boys, quick! Into positions."

The two men scurried into the first opening on the left hand side and sat with their backs to the outer wall. Everything was dry and still, the floor dusty and the stones cold. Kitty stayed in the open air hall and trained her camera down the field in the direction they had come. She found the tell tale signs of double human forms moving down from the ridge towards their last huddle spot at the base of the field. When they reached it, they separated and stopped about one hundred metres apart, one in line with the sparse twinkles of the hamlet and farm at West Kennet, the other at the base of the valley they had just descended. Captain Parker lowered her photography equipment and poked her head out. She could now see the two Special Services men in the half light, without artificial aid. Her instinctive reaction on hearing the crack of a rifle drew her head back to safety as a bullet thumped into the mound behind her.

"They've stopped their advance for now," she whispered back towards the gibbering boys, "but are going to keep us pinned down while they formulate a plan or receive further orders. We will be safe here. It's day break so we should be saved by summer tourists within a few hours." She sat at the barrow's entrance, out of shot but able to peek briefly around the corner to check the besiegers positions. A voice quivered from inside the darkness of the tomb. It was Harry's.

"Does anybody here believe in ghosts?"

"What a load of bollox!" countered the farmer without consideration.

"There must be ghosts here?" questioned the high romantic.

"My father remembers the excavations back in the Fifties," started Barry, this time with more involved intellect, "When they unearthed four dozen bodies from these caves. There are thousands of these barrows all over the high grounds of Wiltshire and wealthy families were buried in them. This barrow is perfectly situated to be appreciated by visitors old and new to Silbury Hill, The Sanctuary, the stone avenue and circle at Avebury. The latter is just a mile or so away yonder. The Ridgeway was one of the ancient paths that ferried these pilgrims and traders. Interestingly, despite the superior size of the stone circle at Avebury, the artefacts uncovered at this barrow, pots, flints, beads and weaponry, show that the site had an inferior historical qudos to Stonehenge. Although smaller in size, the scale, precision and lintel design at the site near Amesbury is far superior architecturally. A recent ten square kilometre electronic excavation has revealed that far wealthier families, from as far away as Europe, travelled to be buried there. Can you imagine sailing across the Channel then? That's dedication to pilgrimage. Highly sophisticated weaponry and intricate jewellery finds, including large quantities of gold, show that Stonehenge was the Mecca of its day. There have not been wide reports of accompanying ghosts." He added dryly.

" It puzzles me," retorted Kitson, "Why can you be so open to the formation of crop circles and not to ghosts? Think about it scientifically. We are just dealing with events and happenings in space and time. It takes sunlight eight minutes and twenty seconds to reach the earth, a distance of over one hundred million miles. The sun is our closest star. Think of all the others and it presents infinite possibilities to what may or may not travel through space. We have just witnessed something tonight that to antiquated thought is totally inexplicable but to us makes perfect sense. How far that plasma energy has travelled to deliver its crop message and from where is a banana's thought and desperately needs investigating thoroughly. But the message of peace and art is clearly in direct opposition to the warmongering status quo that the human race continues to insist on. We will destroy ourselves if we do not listen to this reason or, at the very least, explore its possibilities." His monologue was greeted by a sarcastic slow clap from his closest male friend. Luckily his support network included a far more sympathetic and loving female one. She briefly checked around the Sarsen entrance and, on confirmation of that the two besiegers remained in situ, scampered back to her pre-ordained gunslinging spot across the grave's passage from the other two. She drew her pistol and crouched behind the stone wall with a clear view of the three potential assault routes. She looked across but could not see her friends who were still hunkered behind the opposite wall. She verbally scolded the sceptic and soothed her lover.

"Oh, behave, Barry!" His clapping stopped. "Go on, my Darling. You are, like so many extraordinary or inexplicable things, clearly fascinated by this subject. Tell us please? What is your experience of ghosts?"

"I have had a number of visitors to The Smithy who have seen ghosts. My godson was transfixed by one once. A clairvoyant friend refused to even enter the house. Some similarly minded guests even asked me if they could perform an exorcism for an old lady that they said was trapped inside. They performed their spell and proudly informed me that she had been released from her bondage."

"All very impressive, Dick Wad, but you haven't actually seen one there?" countered the unbeliever.

"No," continued Harry, "But I have seen ghosts elsewhere and both my father and grandmother reported phantasmic incidents in their lifetimes. I believe that you have to be in the right moment and place to witness this delay in terrestrial time."

"What Codswallop!" professed Knave.

"Barry! Shut up and listen!" commanded the officer.

"It was Christmas Eve when I was a child," began the wraith fan, "While I was living in Buckinghamshire. My parents' cottage back then was of very similar design and age to The Smithy. You know, creaky wooden floors and thatched roof stylee. I remember waking up and hearing footsteps coming up the rickety old oak staircase that wound up from the panelled parlour below. My tiny bedroom, which barely took my single bed and chest of drawers, had a clear view of the stair head and one metre landing to a bathroom, my parents' and my own bedrooms. I remember pulling up the bed covers to my chin when a man appeared at the top.

"He was dressed in a brown monk's habit, complete with rope belt, open sandals and a tonsure crowning his head."

"For fuck's sake! We already know that you have a serious fancy dress problem but this is ridiculous!"

"Barry!" Kitty shouted. "Please SHUT UP!"

"Thank you, Kitty Cat." Harry beamed at his all powerful goddess. "The monk looked into my parents' room. He then turned and walked to my door. I should have been terrified but a strange calm washed through me and I felt at peace. And here's the thing. I could see straight through the monk. He was definitely there but I could clearly see the rooms behind him as he moved. He softly walked into my bedroom and knelt at the foot of my bed. He prayed. He prayed for sometime. It was long enough for me to realise that I must be dreaming so I called out to my parents and asked them if I could get up and open my Christmas stocking that was bulging full of toys, toiletries and a token tangerine at the entrance to my room. My mother replied in the negative, explaining that it was 3am and I should go back to sleep. On hearing this discourse, the cleric turned to me, smiled and I heard him softly mouth, "Shhhhh." It was incredibly peaceful and calming. The experience felt just like the sensations we feel when we are in a crop circle. Just out of this world! After a few more seconds of prayer, he got up and walked out of my door, across the small hall and down the spiral stair. I listened to his footsteps until there was silence and slept. On waking, having savaged the stuffed sock, I asked my mother about the night before. She remembered my nocturnal question but saw or heard nothing else, despite being only a few metres away from the apparition. If I was more Christian, I would believe that it was the spirit of St Nicholas."

There was silence in the barrow. Even Barry was lost for words for a change. Kitty wanted to speak. She wanted to express her devotion and support for the man she loved. She wanted to thank him for being himself and having his whimsical fancy for all that is unexplained. He was so passionate about everything he believed in, whether naughtiness like bikes and drugs or strangeness like crop circles and ghosts. She could not wait to get out of this situation and hug, embrace and love his warming body, tender soul and momentous heart. But she couldn't because, at that very second, two hands stretched out silently from the darkened tomb behind her. One grabbed her free arm and twisted it behind and up her back in an agonising lock. The other gripped onto the wrist holding her pistol and squeezed a raw nerve that released her grip on the firearm instantly. It clattered with a sinister echo to the hard floor before a ghost from her recent past whispered in her ear.

"Boo!"

'I Walk the Line'

"Just hold steady there, you deceitful little Vipress!" hissed the familiar posh sounding voice that smelt of alcohol fused with tobacco. A calfskin two tone shoe appeared from behind and dragged her weapon across the floor. "Be still, you little bitch, or I'll break your puny little arm!" rasped the accomplice as he let her shooting wrist go, maintained the petrifying hold up her back and stooped to grab the pistol. She felt the muzzle nuzzle into her soft neck behind the ear. Her skin prickled.

"Uncle Max," Kitty wasn't sure whether she was pleased that the ghost was in fact her secret boss or not. On rapid second thought, she would have preferred the company of the spectre. "To what do we owe this pleasure?"

"Shut the fuck up, you treble crossing Minx!" the spymaster thundered.

"A high compliment indeed, coming from one so doubly backstabbing." Parker dared before she squeaked in pain as he levered the trapped arm further upward between her shoulder blades.

"Stop that now!" protested the girl's lover. Harry stood up to survey their surprise visitor. He darted from the boys' tomb doorway but the Military Intelligence man maneuvered himself rapidly so the girl was between them. He levelled the gun at Kitson's head.

"One more step and I'll blow your bloody head off." Harry halted at the order. "Now, Knave, you useless piece of farm manure, standup slowly and join your pathetic friend." Barry did so. "Good. Good.

Now, all three of you, go and stand against that far wall." He motioned towards the large menhir at the far side of the outside atrium and released his grip on Kitty's arm. They obeyed and turned to face the cave entrance. The spymaster stepped into the light. The sun's rays were just beginning to dazzle over the horizon behind them and shafts of pure perfection seeped through the stone cracks and hit the man. The school friends got their first view of their cunning captor. They both felt suddenly disappointed on surveying the garish plumes and jewellery, linen suit, peacock tie and pocket square on the wizened frame of the crackled man before them. He looked like he wouldn't be able to fight his way out of a soggy paper bag. Kitty knew better. She was suddenly very afraid. Uncle Max's next action confirmed her worst fear.

Maintaining his level aim at his captives, he removed his mobile phone from his inside pocket with his free hand and held it in front of his face. Once the object had activated on recognition of his slippery features, he pushed the fascia with his nicotine stained finger.

"I've got them. Get over here pronto." He cackled into the microphone before reversing the phone's journey to his breast pocket. Max redirected his vocabulary to his prisoners. "What a collection of halfwits I have before me. You," he waved the gun at Harry, "are the most air headed idiot I've ever come across." He mocked the innocent man's sentiments with a childlike tone, "'We must stand together and embrace the universe in terrestrial and extraterrestrial terms whether through our understanding of messages through ghosts or those in the crop circles formed from infinity beyond'. What a load of claptrap bullshit!" He laughed. "You!" He aimed the gun at Barry, "A renegade farmer with pathetic intentions to do some good for his community despite the fact that they have long rejected the so called theories that you evangelise about. Another fucking idiot. We have been watching you and your family for decades. How do you think I knew that I would find you here? I'll tell you how. Your own father was quoted in the newspapers as a child when they were excavating this archeological site saying, and I quote, 'This is the best hiding place ever!' When dealing with a man of the lowest intellectual level, it was easy to predict that you would run here. My twenty minute drive to the carpark at Silbury Hill then a ten minute stroll to this hell hole was far easier and faster than your sprint across the fields. Oh, and by the way, waggling your wizzened wanger at an army helicopter is about the most stupid thing I've ever heard and that's in stiff competition with the fool, that you call friend, standing next to you."

At that moment they were joined by the two cross country hunters. They now stood menacingly atop the great stones and trained their semi-automatic shotguns into the trap below them. In the now bright rays of dawn sunlight, their snipers' rifles jutted from their shoulder slings behind their helmets.

"Welcome, gentlemen," gurgled the covert commander, "You are just in time to watch the final show. Please cover these imbeciles for me." He pocketed Kitty's revolver and produced his bizarre smoking paraphernalia. Having ignited a cancer stick in its long holder, he continued his insulting speech. "Captain Kitty Parker." He sighed with seeming sadness. "What could have been. You displayed such perfect aptitude to become one of my very best, you saucy little trollop. The veneer of an artist, strengthened by soldiery and crowned with the deceit of spycraft at the very highest level. My finest protege was on target to be my most excellent undercover operative." Max noticed the pained expression that Harry shot at the girl. Kitson knew so little about her and her apologetic response was immediately manipulated by the cruel curmudgeon. "Oh, I'm so relieved that you maintained your little lie to the man that you started falling in love with. He didn't even know that you were a soldier? And now he finds out that you are a double crossing, nay, treble crossing spy too! I'm sure he must really trust his darling Kitty Witty Catty Cat now! How sad he must feel? Ha!"

"Actually, I don't care!" Harry stammered, "My love for Kitty and the knowledge that she believes in me and my beliefs, far outweighs her lack of time to explain her situation to me in full. A few hours ago, I discovered that she was an officer in the British Army and my love and respect for her accelerated demonstrably. Now I understand that she is even better than that, working undercover for Her Majesty's Secret Service. I am smitten with adoration and awe at her intelligence and guile. Even in those covert circumstances, she decided to support our scientific and logical plan to expose the crop circle phenomenon for the wondrous truth it is. She used all the resources available to her. She is the most incredible woman I have ever known. The extent of your loathsome underhand tactics, just strengthen that feeling for me. I love her even more now than before your revelations!"

"Ahhh, how sweet," lisped the loathsome locuter, "But, sadly, there won't be any time for that. You see, Captain Parker has indeed deceived far more important persons and plans than you and your meagre romance. The world is a complicated place and the powers that be really don't need the vast majority of ignorant people in this world being enlightened by universal hope, beyond the religions that we have already spoon fed them for thousands of years. No, no, no. We would never make any money if we had your peaceful solution. Sharing the truth about crop circles and their benefits to the world will just upset the applecart. We need fear. We need dependence. We need war. I'm with Major de Crecy Conrad-Pickles on that one at least. The longer your little theories are kept from the world, the better for business. Sorry to burst your pathetic little bubble."

"So what are you going to do about us?" braved Knave. "I am known all over these parts and people will listen to me! You are in big trouble, Mister Max, or whatever your real name is?"

"Most noble, gallant knight of the realm!" mocked Max, "You are deceived! You are clearly delusional! Nobody will ever know the truth. Do you not see? You can never leave this graveyard alive. Questions will be asked, for sure, but you will not be the hero you think. I suppose you may be criminally celebrated as a debauched pagan rapist murderer."

"I beg your bloody pardon?" Barrington was confused. "A debauched pagan rapist murderer? What the bloody hell are you talking about, you sick puppy?"

"Here's what the police detectives will deduce." Max mimicked the slow statement delivery of a stereotypical plod. "'Major Conrad-Pickles briefed us about the overall mission. On discovery of supposed terrorists or vandals, a fire fight broke out. Captain Kitty Parker pursued the two crop circle criminals from their burning vehicle across the hills to West Kennet Long Barrow. On departure, she instructed her unit to salvage the car equipment and investigate the field devastation before reporting back to HQ'. By the way, none of them will report any strange circumstances including our plasma protagonists. They will give corresponding statements, exactly as generations of soldiers and pilots have done before them to keep this nonsense from the general public. The extraterrestrial visitors or whatever the hell they are will never have even existed. Official Secrets Act and all that guff. Anway, as I was saying, or rather, as my Police Inspector was saying, 'At the scene of the crime, there was a struggle. Judging by her general state of undress on discovery, Captain Parker bravely fought off the men's intentions to assault and rape her. She shot Harry Kitson, Esq., dead with a round to his forehead before a struggle with Barrington Knave, Esq., ensued. He appears to have grappled with Captain Parker from behind and he managed to turn her gun towards herself. Unfortunately for both the local man and the officer, the final discharge was fired through her throat. The bullet went clean through Captain Parker's jugular vein and into Knave's chest and heart. He died instantly. She drowned in her own blood after approx a minute of struggling. Both men were found to have high levels of Class A drugs in their blood streams.

Captain Parker died in defence of her country and will be buried in Wootton Bassett with full military honours.'" He paused then leered, "Now, let's get on with this, shall we? The tourists will start arriving soon and we need them to discover your tragic little scuffle." He placed his cigarette holder back in his pocket and removed Kitty's pistol. He cocked it and raised the stub barrel to Harry's temple.

His aim was distracted by movement behind him in the distance. Looking skywards he saw two objects looming above the horizon. They were approaching rapidly but he was unable to identify them as they were partially obscured by the bright sun behind them. A rhythmical throbbing, like the sound of an Australian wooden pipe, accompanied the advancing aircraft.

"It's the plasma protectors! Welcome back alien friends! They've come to save us!" yelled Harry in triumph.

"It's two helicopters, you dick!" muttered one of the sentinels perched on the rock above. "It'll be our mob, come to pick up the pieces. C'mon let's get this done before they land." But as the two choppers roared closer, the distinctive navy blue and yellow colours of Her Majesty's 'POLICE' with corresponding crowned badge told a different story to the assumed military one. The two crafts hovered like imperious peregrine falcons above their trapped prey. The sound of the rotors was near deafening but a tannoyed voice spoke, at first with obvious information, from above.

"This is the Police. Lower your weapons and place them beside you. I repeat. This is the Police. Lower your weapons." The soldiers had no choice. Both specials put their shotguns, then their pistols down. They then unslung their rifles and placed them carefully on the top of their ancient stone vantage points. "Now, all of you, raise your hands high above your heads!" They raised their hands. Having realised that his plan was temporarily thwarted, Max lowered the pistol from Harry's cheek and placed it on the dirt before him. "Now," continued the megaphone instructor, "You two jump down this way and you four move out of the stone enclosure." The two SAS men vaulted from above and rolled in well practised unison to break their fall before resuming their feet. As Max, Harry, Kitty and Barry moved towards the winding stone and sand exit, the helicopters started descending to land in the field beside them.

Kitty was faster than most in many situations. Her clarity of thought and the speed to implement her decision did not let her down. The helicopters dropped out of sight behind the vast Sarsen stones. The man she hated most in the world for being a misogynist, bigotted, double crossing, homophobic, perverted monster had just admitted his intent to murder them. Her rage rocketed. As Uncle Max took his first step towards the path, she swung her small, yet heavily toe capped, boot directly into the man's soft genitals. He crumpled to the ground. As she stepped over him, she stooped to whisper in his ear.

"I told you I'd do that if you ever laid a finger on me again, you disgusting pervert!" Knave and Kitson grinned at her mastery as they followed her and imitated her actions. Both apologised profusely to the temporary cripple, albeit with a modicum of sarcasm, as brogue and biker's boot smashed into the man's solar plexus and ribs as they in turn stepped over their attempted murderer. The crushing loss of breath from injury to testicle, stomach and lung rendered Max defenseless for long enough for the trio to skirt the stones and reach the relative safety of the open ground in front of their police saviours. The haggard spy eventually regained his feet and composure before he followed them, dusting down his white suit with his hands then raising them over his head.

A line of firearm's unit, or SCO19, police officers stood brandishing their German machine guns, clad in blue overalls, body armour and dark helmets, visored for personal protection from identity, bullets and sunshine. A couple dashed to the tomb and recovered the assembly of weapons. The remainder formed a semi-circle around

266

the Special Services men and the suited spy before ushering them at gunpoint towards one of the loudly rotating choppers. As they moved off, Uncle Max turned and shouted against the din.

"This isn't over, you three cockroaches! I know people in extremely low places. You are going to rot in a holding cell for this! We will break you like fucking twigs. You'll see the extent of my powers then."

"I don't think so!" hollered Barrington Knave in immediate rebuff. "Wherever there is evil in the world, it can be balanced by good. Unfortunately for you, Scumbag, I know people in exceedingly high places. Cheerio now!" Barry waved and grinned. He puffed his chest out with the pride of a conqueror. As the three latest prisoners were pushed into the back of the flying machine, two policemen broke away and rejoined the three recently liberated who were braced against the gale of rotor blades. One policeman addressed the trio politely.

"Sorry to keep you, Mr Knave." Kitty and Harry looked quizicaly at their friend but he just continued to beam and puff out his upper torso. "Mr Kitson? Captain Parker, I assume?" continued the anti-terror officer, "If you'd be so kind to step this way?" He waved at the other helicopter, walked over to it, and opened the side door. He held his arm out to support the three as they climbed in, appropriately adding one, "Much obliged, Ma'am" and one, "Thank you, Sirs" as they ascended. He followed them in and shut the door behind them. The drumming sound was reduced from deafening to very loud.

The interior of the craft beheld a bizarre spectacle of human diversity. The pilot and co-pilot, with their vast array of buttons, switches and flashing lights, perched high up front and began their preparations for take off. In the passenger cabin, a brace of seats backed onto each of these flyers' more substantial thrones. A padded black and metal bench spanned the rear compartment nearest the tail of the plane. Across this sat down the five already known protagonists. On the far side by the window, the more silent of the SCO19 pair was making his machine gun safe. Next to him sat the familiar figure of Harry, his black leather outfit a spectacular camouflage of mud. His hair was tousled and his cheeks flushed. His eyes shone like black moons. Beside him perched the lithe khaki figure of Captain Kitty Parker. She cradled her beloved camera with her left arm and held the hand of her human love with her right. Her green eyes briefly gazed at him with adoration before she turned her attention forward. Barrington Knave's tweed three piece suit had seen better days but, despite his tie also being strangely decapitated below the knot on his neck, he glowed with the pride of an Olympic champion. He was flanked by the polite police escort who was also decommissioning his assault weapon.

Opposite them, on the two outermost seats by the windows, sat two dark suited men. Both wore white shirts, dark ties and polished black shoes. Both had neatly parted short hair and strange yellow lens aviator sunglasses. Each had one hand open on their seated thigh, the other gripped the butt of small pistols holstered under their armpits. They were only distinguishable by their slight hair and complexion differences plus their left and right handed firearms positions. These conveniently allowed them to cover the entire interior if they drew their guns, with their backs angled towards the glass. Their faces were set hard and unsmiling.

Next to each guardian sat a gentleman opposite Barry and a woman in front of Harry. The man carried an air of superiority and authority. His handsome demeanour was crowned with grey hair, slicked straight back and his piercing blue eyes twinkled in the morning light. His legs were louchly crossed, displaying high gloss patent black shoes with immaculate stitches to their leather and wooden soles. His black trousers were piped to the sides with a panel of silk from ankle to waist. His white dinner shirt had a moderate central ruff and his black bow tie was carefully and tidily knotted. His sumptuous maroon velvet smoking jacket, with similarly coloured silken lapels, fitted his slim septanagerian shoulders perfectly.

The lady was gazing out of the window in the direction of Milk Hill. She was seemingly lost in great thought. Her grey coiffured hair was bobbed to her neck at the back and waved gently sideways across her forehead. Her pale hazel eyes were fringed by modest mascara and arched penned eyebrows. Her lips were painted a luxurious purple. The contours of her face were elegant for advanced middle age but her puffy tired eyes belied beleaguering issues beyond this dawn appointment. Her ears drooped with the weight of black Tahitian pearl studs and her neck was adorned with a graduated strand of similarly large and coloured mollusc seeds. The padded shoulders of her dark blue wool waist length overcoat led to a sharp collar turned up to her high hairline and the garment was unbuttoned at the front revealing a sumptuously smooth Conservative blue ball gown from neck to ankle. A wide velvet purple sash was elegantly bowed across her midriff. Her crossed legs pointed in the same direction as her gaze, the ankles clad in saucy fishnets to smart kitten heeled purple shoes in a style that complimented the daring of her lipstick. Her hands were crossed in her lap. The left hand displayed a stack of white sparkling rings that hinted of a dedicated man's love.

This curious blend of police, biker, army, farmer, security and authority checked their seat belts as the craft rose steadily off the ground beside the barrow. It hovered above the site and was joined by the other helicopter which housed the prisoners. The gentleman broke the human silence, with a raised voice as he leant forward, shook Knave's hand with his right and covered their digital embrace warmly with his left.

"My dearest, Barrington! Bravo!" he began happily as he enthusiastically pumped Knave's hand. "Splendid work, my dear boy!"

"Thank you very much, Sir Percy!" grinned the land agent.

"You have always been most conscientious," continued the party attired man, "When it comes to matters of concern to my estates and the great of Britain beyond. You have excelled yourself this time, My Boy."

"Much obliged, Sir," Barry answered, "But I am only doing what you pay me for. As we discussed, your involvement in this escapade will help many aspects of your business, financial and political. But the real thanks must go to you. We would be in a total pickle if you had not been on standby as we had agreed. Your speedy reaction to my SOS text saved our lives! If you hadn't arrived, we would all be dead now so thank you from the bottom of my and these two's hearts." He gestured towards the soldier and jeweller. "May I introduce Captain Kitty Parker and Harry Kitson Esquire, Sir?"

"An honour to meet you both," the Knight of the Realm beamed as he proffered his hand to both in turn, "Barry told me, during our phone call and meeting a few days ago, that without your assistance researching this matter, we would never be at this critical turning point. We were delighted to receive your text, Barry, and be able to be with you directly from the smoking lounge at Chequers within twenty five minutes." Harry and Kitty gawped as the enormity of their friend's behind the scenes work became crystal to them. The lady lent forward. She was very familiar to them all. The Home Secretary cleared her throat and spoke with a soothing tone.

"I am delighted to meet you three too. Sir Percieval explained everything to me at our little soiree with the Prime Minister last night. Sir Percy briefed us in full. I am, and indeed the PM is, very interested in your combined work. It seems to me that, if everything he tells me is true, we can all help each other sort out some fundamental issues. Do you have evidence?"

"I have filmed everything, Home Secretary," Kitty answered, patting her camera, "But we can show you the reality first if we just fly over there now." She pointed to the crest of Tan Hill a mile or two away. "Once you have seen that, I can show you the footage of its actual creation on our journey home?"

"Splendid news!" continued the Home Office minister, "I will be frank. Our party political ratings are at an all time low and they never started high. We have been through the meat grinder in the House of Commons in the quest for a political resolution to the democratic wishes of our islands' people to leave the European Union. Our time is maybe up. If what you say is true, you may just save us! If the Party can deliver it effectively, this is the sort of news that will really stop people in their tracks and force them to think of the future. A future with a credible, forward thinking government at the helm. The implications of your findings towards health, energy and defence, far outdistance the importance of our borders and relationship with our neighbours. The global consequences of this interplanetary discovery could be our real legacy and set this Tory government up on the world stage, to have a real impact towards making our planet a better place. God knows, those climate change activists who camped in central London, could do with some kind of positive reaction. Give a dog a bone, if you'll excuse the non-vegan analogy? In return, you will receive our full support and funding to research this scientifically, unharness the existing military shackles, let farmers benefit wholey and profitably and encourage lay people to learn and be educated so that we can provide a stable future for this country, the globe and the universe beyond. This is our moment to triumph!"

With these rousing words, the pilot tipped the nose of the craft downwards and accelerated the copter back up the valley, away from the ancient curiosities of mound and tomb. The past disappeared behind them, the future awaited. Knave's crops waved like adoring throngs of jubilant crowds in the wake of their speeding procession.

The second helicopter veered away in the direction of some hidden interrogation room and holding cells. The remaining craft slowed and hovered beyond the Wessex ditch line above the escarpment and sunk towards the bowl. The triple hump of Clifford's Hill lay before them, the staggering sunlit beauty of the Vale of Pewsey glittered beyond. Below them lay the smouldering husk of the pickup truck. The wavering remnants of smoke curled slowly upwards in memoriam of the previous night's battle. The helicopter blades brushed the pyre haze aside as it moved carefully around the contour of Tan Hill towards the enormous field below Milk Hill.

The airplane crossed the tarmac track at a height of about fifty metres. Eleven pairs of eyes looked down from craned necks at the geography below. Apart from the cattle shed to the south, the saucer shaped field rippled continuously below them in the wake of the helicopter's blades. The shadow cast from the eastern ridge crept across its face and, as they reached the crop circle, the first rays of direct sunshine hit the art for the very first time.

Warning lights suddenly flashed and sirens sounded from the cockpit, the rotors seemed to slow and the craft rocked dangerously and began to drop.

"Get outside the circle!" commanded Kitty, "The energy column upsets the electronics!" The police pilot hit the stick left and regained full control at the fringe of the vortex. "Apologies to everybody," Captain Parker continued, "I should have warned him. Our army helicopters and some privateer aviators have experienced the same effects for years as we have collected our secret information and hushed up theirs. Apologies. That was a lesson we did not have to endure first hand. If you look down now, I think we can see for ourselves what effect crop circles have directly on some humans too?"

The perfection of the symmetry and design of the enormous crop imprint was breathtaking. The contrast between linear upright stalks and flattened weaves of pattern and geometric form on such a scale was awe inspiring. What was a surprising contrast was the small circle of seated soldiers, in various stages of demob, who grinned and waved at the aerial Metropolitan visitors. In the centre of the group was a naked man who lay on his back opening and closing his arms and legs in bodily star shapes. From the depths of his dark pubic bush, rose an angry erection. The Home Secretary shook her head and questioned the obscene spectacle.

"Who is that man? Or rather, who on earth are those men?"

"Err. That is my army unit, Ma'am," Kitty replied, before adding with a slight sigh, "And my commanding officer, Major de Crecy Conrad-Pickles, is the gentleman conducting the naturist exercises. Until last night, all these men were hardened battle troops. This clearly demonstrates the incredibly calming effect that this type of energy can have on human beings, however violent they may be."

"Conrad-Pickles? Did you say, Conrad-Pickles?" Sir Percy interrupted, "That family really has gone downhill since my generation and those hundreds of years before. Bedrock of our military since forever." He shook his head sadly. "How the mighty have fallen. Right! That's it! I've seen enough! Let's go home now please, pilot!"

The chopper rose in the air and pointed its snout back in the direction of the PM's Chiltern Hills country retreat. As it ascended, another interesting sight grabbed the passengers' attention. The top of Milk Hill was scattered with a few trees and bushes. Amongst them was a man of distinctive form. He wore a red, yellow and green hooded cloak and appeared to be shouting at them. Those not distracted by his wild bloodshot eyes and who were well versed in lip reading could clearly define the word, "Babylon!" as he wildly waved a gigantic gnarled staff and tiny pink 'Hello Kitty' umbrella at them.

"Our prophet of a new hope!" muttered Harry.

"A bloomin' nut job if you ask me," added Barry, "Nice umbrella though."

"Hello Kitty!" They both said in unison. The army Captain smiled at the boys and then noticed the Home Secretary's continued expression of shock. This was understandable given that she had just received a full salvo relating to the strangest behaviours in mankind and nature. The children's accessory's namesake decided that this was an appropriate moment to introduce happenings of an other worldly kind. She unbuckled her seat belt, stood before the cabinet minister's closest security guard and offered him her own seat.

"I'll swap you?" He looked at the questioner and then at his boss, who nodded so he got to his feet and settled between the two male school friends who grinned at him, a natural reaction given both their state and circumstance. He remained stoic and stared straight ahead at the woman he was paid to protect. Kitty wiggled into the seat between the window and stateswoman. She placed her camera between her knees and switched on the viewfinder. Once the image was clear, she pressed the search functions and found the moment in her footage when she was introduced as an army captain to Harry for the first time, by the side of the pickup truck, just before the arrival of the dark dome from the rainy heavens above. She snuggled up against the woollen coated shoulder beside her and the two all powerful girls pushed their heads together in a gesture of trust and mutual respect. "Now," Kitty whispered, "Are you sitting comfortably?" The Minister smiled softly in return and nodded again. "Great. Then your in flight entertainment can begin. May I present for your personal viewing, 'The Adventures of Barry, Harry and Kitty'?"

'The Honeydripper'

Monty strolled happily down the pavement of the third
arrondissement boulevard. The single lane road at its heart lay
mostly hidden behind the double avenue of modest trees and
bordered mature flower beds. The spring air was crisp and the first
green shoots were visible above. The lower herbaceous compliment
was bursting with fresh new colours. The short journey from his
favourite delicatessen to his home was always a joy, whatever the
weather. This street, like many in Le Marais, bustled with cafes,
brasseries and interesting boutiques. There was even an English book
shop which he loved to visit, even though his French was of a very
high standard by now. T'was in the blood of this de Crecy.

As he turned a corner south, he transferred the brown paper bag
cradled under one arm to beneath the other. Apart from the standard
fayre, rough pate, cornichons, rich butter, fresh coffee, requisite wine
and the obvious baguette that stuck out of the top, it contained some
more exotic treats. He was already looking forward to enjoying the
brioche loaf, lightly toasted, deliciously smooth foie gras and cold
half bottle of Sauterne after this day's work and personal sexual
punishment were complete. He smiled to himself. Life was to be
enjoyed wholeheartedly. He had learnt to free himself, quite by
accident, when he was arrested, naked, in the field in Wiltshire the
summer before. It was a blessing. Out of a negative, he built a
positive.

With this philosophy in mind, he looked forward and up. The
familiar sight of the twin towers of Notre Dame cathedral rose from
the centre of the Seine a block away. The once magnificent roof and
towering spire were a year gone but out of the ashes, the phoenix
would rise. He hoped that the replacement would represent

everything daring and wonderful about Parisian building projects. The proud edifice represented the heart of the Catholic faith in France but, in his mind, it far transcended that with its direct reach to every nation's heart and every international tourist. He further mused that the gigantic blueprint of symmetry and intrinsic artistic detail was surely appreciated by whatever universal powers looked down from the heavens above. These forces had touched him briefly and changed his life. He was happy. He prayed the world would trust and embrace the same omnipotent power. It certainly needed the improvement.

He dived down a little side street and the cathedral was lost from view. After a few metres, it opened into a charming old cobbled square, littered with the small cars and mopeds of local residents and shopkeepers whose premises lay behind the arched colonnade perimeter. He meandered under it and glanced up to appreciate its stone columns, curved lintels and red brick roofs. He passed two shops, one of vintage costume jewellery, the other a florist, then paused at his own door and fumbled with his spare hand for the keys. His shop front was nondescript. Black borders, a black board in place of the usual glass window and a large black door. The only identifying feature was the small brass placard beside the black wrought iron bell pull which read, 'M. & Mme. de Crecy - Sur Rendez-Vous Uniquement'.

Marriage had been a bureaucratic nightmare but a resultant romantic dream. Birth certificates had been produced and the couple had unanimously decided that Mister Monty and Mister Pascal de Crecy Conrad-Pickles wasn't terribly suitable. After much deliberation, Pascal became Mademoiselle Kinki. A few weeks later, the revised identity papers had arrived. They had skipped down to the registry office and signed the marital dotted line changing the mademoiselle to madame, Monty hoped forever. In the interim, they had moved from their modest flat of yesteryear into the current domain. The Major's dismissal from Her Majesty's Forces had been

276

smoke screened for reasons that the Prime Minister had insisted on. The Conrad-Pickles family still carried some serious clout in military and political circles. A combination of modest pension and substantial trust fund had enabled the out and out purchase of their new home and business premises.

The narrow four storey acquisition was perfect for all their needs including a rickety brick staircase which led down to a damp cellar that Monty intended to stock with a surplus of fine wines. The top floor garrett would one day be for guests, not that they had too many mutual friends yet, but was currently brimming with packing cases. A hallway of rippling wooden steps led from top to bottom of the house. The second floor contained their bedroom and bathroom, a work in progress that would clearly accommodate their more private sleeping and waking arrangements and its accoutrements. The salon on the first was a more regal affair with a vast gilt mirror and fox hunting prints on the walls. Their old chaise longue graced the window overlooking the outside square and a larger high backed sofa, complete with golden rope tassels and brocade, perched opposite. The only hint to their more depraved actions on the levels directly above and below were Monty's collection of willow cricket bats and Kinki's bullwhips which were artistically fitted and draped amongst the pictures. The tiny galley kitchen off the room was more than adequate for the cool storage of simple necessities, especially as the couple's more general habit of eating was out in the more important culinary establishments littered over the French capital.

The foot of the staircase at ground level was barred by a metal gate. Despite its suitably dungeon decor, this door's more practical function was to prevent clients from reaching their home above. They received all sorts. The entrance was modest and sparse. A small semi-circular mahogany table and rectangular mirror, for business cards, post and hair styling, were the only features beside the umbrella stand behind the door. A bathroom under the staircase provided clientele with an opportunity to freshen up after their treatment. A closed door opposite it led to their spacious work studio.

It was this hallway that welcomed Monty as he closed the front door behind him. He placed his shopping on the table and keys in his pocket. They were always careful not to leave these lying around for their sometimes strange visitors to snaffle. Security was not a dirty word in their household. Neither was domination. As he smiled to himself in the mirror, the salon door opened and the lady of the house shimmied into view. She placed a finger to her scarlet painted lips to indicate silence. Kinki wiggled her leather clad hips and bosom, which were enshrined in a most suitably business like skirt and bodice, in the direction of her faithful husband and willing slave. Her bright red stiletto heeled shoes tapped crisply on the smooth stone flags. He proffered his mouth to her which she bit and, on his gasp of pleasure, placed her finger on the orifice to reiterate her need for quiet. She nodded her head in the direction of the main door and Monty tiptoed to it and peered inside.

The blackened interior contained a couple of familiar objects from their previous flat. A dull red light emanated from a shaded standard lamp and the flicker from a number of vast black wax candles that were scattered around the room. Kinki's vast costume wardrobe centralised the far wall. In one corner, his beloved leather hobby horse was stabled awaiting the tack and ride of sex jockeys. Apart from the standard array of torturous paraphernalia that littered the walls on hooks, the ex army officer had invested in two new important pieces of kit. The first had a most unimaginative name, 'The Fucking Machine', but was of most imaginative design. A large chrome frame, which nearly touched the ceiling, housed an electrical motor which turned a small arm around and around at paces from steady to violent. This powered a six foot long horizontal rod, back and forth, over a distance of approximately ten inches. Various rubberised attachments could be fitted to the rod, dependent on the depth and width of the, hopefully, lubricated cavity the machine was servicing. It was an elegant piece of engineering only marred by the large red 'Emergency Stop' buttons and additional plastic sheeting that had proved useful on a number of more fountainous occasions.

But it was the modified massage table in the centre of the room that Monty was particularly proud of. It was this that the current client was enjoying. A man lay on his back in the centre of the room. He was wrapped tightly from head to toe in black latex and his neck, wrists and ankles were buckled to the table. His nose was covered by the grippy plastic but a hospital breathing tube was attached to his mouth which led to a pump that carefully regulated his supply of gas and air. Next to the slowly rising and falling clear perspex housed respirator was an electrical generator. One pair of black wires led to two of the three exposed areas of male flesh. At the cords end, red and black crocodile clips indicated the positive and negative electrodes. They were attached to the subject's heavily Vaseline glazed nipples which poked angrily above their PVC prison.

The other area of exposure, which proved the sex of the man, was under a construction of Monty's own architecture. He had to admit that the similar wires clamped to each of the man's meticulously shaved testicles were of existing scientific design. The cage and noose housing for the man's grotesquely enlarged penis, which dripped with oil, were all his own. Using an ever decreasing spiral framed wine decanter holder, a particular favourite of the connoisseur, an adjustable slip knot could be dangled from its top to pull the customer's member upwards whether flacid or hard. It worked a treat.

Monty checked the large school clock above the gym horse. It had been thirty five minutes since lock down. The spectacle made him feel horny. Not for the slab of meat before him but for the erotic aftermath with his beloved wife. The quicker the session could be resolved, the faster he could be spanked and violated upstairs. Happy days indeed were these. In correspondence with his thought process,

279

he cranked up the voltage a smidgeon and listened to the electrodes buzz. The man's body started shivering and shaking all over and the pump rose and fell faster and faster with his breathing. As a convulsion rippled through the black mummy, the protruding appendage jerked spasmodically and the testicles flinched violently as a jet of semen arched upwards, landing in a splatter against his black plastic belly.

This was the cue for Montgomery to switch off the electrical power. The body beneath him seemed to deflate in coordination with a vast exhale of breath. An aura of peace and calm emanated from the flesh beneath the wrappings. The breathing slowed and calmed with the passing seconds as the retired Major started to tidy up the mess. This began with the delicate mopping up of jissum, using surgical wipes which were dispensed by his black latex gloved fingers in a flip lid bin. The various electrodes were then prised open and dangled in a pure alcohol bath. The hangman's noose was then loosened and the shrivelled manhood tumbled, exhausted and dormant, to join the now prune like testes. He released the five bondage straps and then, starting at the skull, started to unravel the strip of body restriction. After the man's hair, forehead, nose and mouth were uncovered, he paused the unwind process and removed the breathing harness. The man sat up grinning as he carefully inhaled his first real air for nearly an hour. His seated body position enabled Monty to continue the bandage undress towards his most generous benefactor's waist. He addressed him with familial informalty.

"Was everything up to your usual standard of satisfaction, Uncle Max?"

"Indeed it was, oh, master of my pain!" replied the ex-spy with a smile that could have been friendly in appearance, if it wasn't mired by the nicotine stains of his crumpled moustache and rotten teeth.

"I will leave you alone for a few minutes to unwind, physically and mentally, then redress. Your clothes are in the cupboard. I'll be waiting in the hallway but feel free to use the bathroom to straighten yourself up if necessary." He bowed graciously and backed out of the room, shutting the door behind him.

The spy and soldier's business relationship had gotten off to a flying start when they had shared a cell that day back in August. It had been a long night. They had quickly realised that their current careers lay in tatters. Deals would need to be made if they were to get themselves out of the soup. The Major had admitted to his Parisian lifestyle without duress, explaining that his future would be a happy one there. The spy admitted that he knew all about the officer's depravities due to the extensive film footage collected by Captain Parker. Max had explained that the film was to be used to frame the Major, removing him from the crop circle investigations. Having initially cussed Kitty, they eventually conceded that the girl was in a class of her own and that they need not seek revenge as long as their own extensive connections got them out of the cell that night. Formalities became less so. A long conversation about pushing sexual barriers had followed, culminating with the curious double agent's demand for an exploratory visit to the gay city and its contraptions of pleasure, once Conrad-Pickle was out of his current pickle. A perverted plan was forged and dodgy details were exchanged.

Dismissed without his pension or funds in trust, it might have been Uncle Max that was in the relative jar of cheese or curry condiment. But he was far too clever for that. A lifetime of double dealing with Russians and C.I.A., Irish Republicans and F.B.I., Colombian drug lords and D.E.A., Afghan warlords and M.I.6., Radical Islamists and M.I.5., meant that his Swiss bank account already contained a multiple seven figure sum. He intended to live the life of Riley. Meeting the Major turned out to be the saving grace for many further innocents. The vile man that had maliciously and successfully caused so much hate and pain to so many, with such professional aplomb, was now unemployed. He was left with only his greed and selfishness but nobody to practice his torturous skill sets on. After his prison conversation with the Major, this was simply countered on his Parisian arrival by inflicting brutal pain and outrageous punishment on himself instead. He loved it. As a result, the ex-spy was probably happy for the first time in his life. Major de Crecy Conrad-Pickles (Retired) smiled into the mirror at this irony. He patiently waited in the hallway for Uncle Max's extravagant payment and departure before his own subsequent ravishment by Mrs de Crecy. Life was fabulous for Monty. It was for Uncle Max too.

'You're So Square (Baby, I Don't Care)'

The army had been kind to Barrington Knave. They didn't really have a choice given Sir Percy, the Home Secretary and the Prime Minister's insistence. He had received full compensation for their damage to his field. A bumper harvest last autumn had been supplemented by a sizable cheque from Her Majesty's Armed Forces. This one off payment included the first installment of an annuity that would enable him to work and travel spreading the good word of crop circles. It also provided a replacement for his discoteque equipment. Future barn parties were going to be far louder and much brighter as a result. Given the Forces forced generosity, Barry had deliberated long and hard about the replacement of his diesel belching pickup truck. It was time to say goodbye to tradition and embrace the future. Given his mission to save the planet from imminent self destruction, he persuaded the powers that be to let him drive the new hybrid. He justified the extravagance with his ambassadorial role clearly in mind. They paid up.

Given the new dimension to his already multiple job description, he was particularly proud of his new wardrobe. He had consulted his best friend Harry regarding the ensemble.

"Hmmmmm," Kitson had dug deep mentally as his forefinger and thumb rubbed his chin in contemplation, "Let's see. It's got to be a yokel farmer, responsible land agent, plus city slicker all rolled into one. I see tweed, naturally, a subtle hint of green and a predominance of grey. Smart but racey, casual but conservative, town but country." A few days later, Barry had jumped on a train to the capital and joined his friend after the resolution of his jewellery client appointments in Mayfair. They had sauntered north to Marylebone and found the perfect cloth at the appropriately named Dashing Tweeds. Having ordered a little more fabric than his previous version, accommodating for the subsequent riches in his life, they were recommended a tailor, relatively local to the farmer's home. They had then sallied forth from the cloth merchant, most content.

The pair had journeyed south again and made a bee-line for Jermyn Street. Like many men, they bolted like blinkered racehorses despite the fabulous retail distractions of Bond Street, Burlington and Piccadilly Arcades. Baby blue and white check shirts, ties that did not display aquatic bird prints and firm ankle high cavalry boots were quickly purchased. The latter were of the black variety. Harry had been keen to remind the countryman of his mother's repeated mantra.

"Never brown in town." He expressed this with an accent more like Pygmalion's Mrs Higgins than Mrs Kitson. After a roll down St James's Street to the Mecca of milliners, Lock, the men had emerged, one wearing his new brown felt trilby. The other sagely commented, "Fuck my old boots, Baz. You may actually cut a dash in that little beauty! You are now more than passable, whether entering my posh club or the jockeys enclosure at the Gold Cup. Even I'd put a bet on you." Harry knew how to make his pal feel swell. The men had rounded off their fabulous London liasson with a sumptuous lunch at the aforementioned members only establishment in Shepherd Market. It had been a marvellous day. Especially as the British Army had footed the bill.

A handful of months later, as he strolled through the corridors of Westminster, Barry felt empowered by his replacement threads. The suit was a masterpiece. The razor fronted trouser turn ups stopped perfectly above his shiny black boots. The jacket fitted his powerful shoulders with surprising elegance. He was particularly proud of the waistcoat for a couple of reasons. First, it had been tailored so that it smoothly followed the contours of his tummy. No bursting buttons anymore. Secondly, it had inspired him to take up sit ups. His rule was simple. Everytime he passed a barrow on his farm, whether walking or driving, he would stop and do twenty repetitions of the simple exercise. The muscular quest from one big barrel to a more defined six pack was hovering around the halfway number but he had thoroughly enjoyed winking at his wife before asking her to tighten the back strap of the third piece of his suit. He felt confident that his physical exercise endeavours might shortly be rewarded by a spontaneous lifting of the Sundays and Birthdays bedroom rule.

Barry cantered down the long arched corridor in the Houses of Parliament, occasionally checking the door plates for his destination. He was bullishly confident despite the intimidating political jungle about him. This was partially due to his clothes. They gave him authority. The, "You're a tiger, Barry!" routine in the mirror earlier in the day, also had some clout. However, the most important piece of his arsenal had taken months to develop. He was now armed with a solution. He had a product. It was with this in mind that he briefly noticed the plaque declaring an early Nineteen Twenties number before he took in its vast oak double doors, flanked by two men. Their black and white fashion was neither flunkey nor waiter but something in between. He declared his name and the pair simultaneously swung open their corresponding halves to the portal of power.

"Mister Barrington Knave, Esquire," announced one with a nose raised. Barry walked forward. A long rectangular table stretched out before him. It was inhabited by glasses and vessels of water, pots, cups and jugs containing coffee, tea and milk, numerous paper stacks and pens. White cards bore the names and titles of the dignitaries seated before them. With a numeracy skill honed on flocks of birds and sheep, Barry immediately estimated approximately three dozen human specimens. Another sweep of the room enabled him to quickly classify the game and vermin by their distinctive diversity of plumage. The tell tale indications of political, army green and airforce blue suits were rapidly honed to more specific identification by facial recognition garnered through meticulous study of the 'News At Ten' and an on-line crash course in medal honours.

It was a fearsome assembly indeed. Ministers and deputies from Foreign, Defence, Agriculture, State, Exchequer, Cabinet, Home, Health, Justice, Energy, Trade and Environment offices were interspersed by high ranking generals and marshals. Given the recent political parlance, it might be described as the National Security Council plus plus. At the nearest end, Barry could read his own name card. There was no chair for him. He would stand and be judged. At the far end were set three places. One contained his friend and client, Sir Perceival, who smiled kindly at him. The next was the Home Secretary who nodded on Barry's entrance. Lastly was the last Prime Minister. His face was set stern. Recent times were hard. He forced a smile as he welcomed and introduced the bearer of revelation and hope.

"Thanks for coming in, Barry," he began, "Ladies and gentlemen, it gives me great pleasure to introduce Barrington Knave. His dedicated service to this country, by privately researching then proving directly to me the extraordinary power that the crop circle mystery possesses, is thoroughly appreciated. I briefed you all before his arrival. I have witnessed the birth of a redress in power. Sir Percy and the Home Secretary flew over the plasma picture on Barry's farm only six months or so ago. We have since seen the corresponding film footage of its creation. That night was one the most memorable in my life. We had a Party party at Chequers. These two colleagues flew off in the night and returned with Barry and his friends a few hours later with their incredible revelations and evidence. It has resulted in a radical rethink of many of our policies. In political terms, your departmental support will be of fundamental significance to this development programme. In military matters, the sharing of historical and future information by our brave soldiers and airmen with enthusiasts, researchers and scientists will have a profound effect on progress within our society. It is now time to combine the strengths of public, political and military to harness this power to help save our planet. As your leader, I say that we make this our Party legacy.

"Needless to say, it might just save the Conservative Party. Our government can be the catalyst for change in this country, in every country, and whatever lies beyond. The message from beyond is loud and clear. We have ignored the intelligent array of dedicated believers in these powers for decades and covered up their and our own research in dark silos. That all changes right now. Working together, we can make Britain, Great Britain once more." A ripple of applause echoed around the wood panelled hall. As it died down, thirty or so heads turned slowly from the speaker to the solitary silent figure at the opposite end of the room.

Barry's commitment to the cause had begun, naturally enough, with a simple and practical approach. He had started with the farmers. They needed to be able to profit from the research and be protected legally for the subsequent trespass. Visitors should pay. He had analysed a cost structure based on frank conversations with the local community in both farm and research arenas. Early rising farmers were usually the first to spot new formations. All they had to do was give the location point, provide the easiest and least damaging route to the site, plus a safe place for visitors to park their vehicles without breaking any highway laws. When the crop discovery was made by others, for example Army helicopters, Airforce recce planes or public spotters, the location could be automatically noted, the farmer immediately notified and his directional and banking information registered. If the farmer decided to police the inevitable tourists, their payment receipts could all be checked on the spot.

With so many governmental departments set to benefit from the research, a percentage tax free subsidy would be credited to the farmer's account. A boon above and beyond the taxable income revenue from the tourists. It also provided further encouragement for the land workers to report each and every occurrence. Group bookings and season tickets would be available for dedicated researchers and concerned scientists. A database of all visitors, faculties, departments and laboratories would be available so that all the information individually collected could be shared immediately. These combined results would accelerate the process of understanding the crop circle phenomenon and implementation of its global saving benefits. The digital age of finance and connectivity would join all the various groups together. A unified quest for worldly betterment all started with the simple use of a Global Positioning System.

Barrington Knave was proud of this progress. Diligent hard work and creativity had made a great man even greater. He was doing something positive in the political sphere. The machinations of the Local Council seemed like a distant memory. The PM had already shown great faith in him and had suggested that his work might be more beneficial if he was closer to Westminster on more occasions. He had hinted that the safe Tory seat of Devizes might suit him perfectly? This was something that he needed to ponder on but he felt that it could be his launchpad for making the important changes that the country, nay world, needed. His well rehearsed speech was as clear in his mind as the air above Milk Hill on a clear and bright February morning. Barry pulled his mobile phone from inside his grey tweed suit jacket and held it aloft. He cleared his throat, puffed out his chest and smiled with all the confidence of generations of Knaves before him. He then declared,

"I've got an App for that."

'Let it be Me'

Art is the ultimate expression of love. On a galactic level, the creation of stunning images on the fields of planet earth, using tools and pallets thus far unexplained, gave Harry hope for the future. Violent wrenches in his heart resulted from witnessing the beauty in paintings, poetry, photography, prose and pottery. Jewellery, of course, was the only medium that transcended all art forms for the biased artist. The manipulation of metals that stay brilliant forever, coupled with the use of crystals of extraordinary strength and vividness of colour, continually took his breath away. Creating these eternal heirlooms, usually at the most romantic moments in somebody's life, gave Harry shivers of excitement. But Kitson was not dead as a result of these cardiac, respiratory or nervous system palpitations. On the contrary, he was very much alive.

His continued visits to fresh crop circles, usually with one or both of his fellow researchers and friends, had allowed him to raise his spiritual understanding even higher. People needed hope. Billions of people had attached themselves to religions over time for this reason. All those extraordinary happenings, the cyclones, tsunamis, earthquakes, floods, famines and eruptions needed justifying through a higher power. Science had accelerated this level of thought to far more plausible solutions concerning the Universe's creation and the powers and energies that controlled it. If people embraced this truth, he believed that the world would be a more peaceful place and the determined efforts to destroy themselves could be thwarted. The ebb and flow of space beyond our earth contained all the secrets to our creation and destruction. The crop art, whether formed by a secret human society or sent by life from far away, was merely a warning message. Either way, all that mattered to Harry was an examination of the macrocosm to discover the truth. That was his beautiful mission.

But to see the big picture, one must first understand the miniscule components that contribute to it. The sweaps of the brush, the mixture of the pallet and the powder grains of colour at its core. To achieve this clarity, Kitson had taken a long hard look in the mirror. He was initially disappointed. The years had been cruel. A sallow complexion, a face lined by worry and stress, eyes that seemed bloodshot and empty of passion stared back at him. He attributed blame on many objects and people for the hardships in his life. It then dawned on him that, just possibly, he had dealt with these inconveniences in life in the wrong manner. Harry decided that step one was to pull himself together.

The realisation that he had spent thirty years since his teens either drunk or hungover was an excellent starting point. The society that he had grown up in, come of age in, worked in and played in, dictated that excess drinking was fine. He decided that it was not. The constant drip drop of Class A narcotics in his lifestyle provided further doubts. Why not take away these false constructs and see what truth could be revealed without them? He did so. Bye, bye, booze. Cheerio, coca. A few weeks later, he took another long hard look in the mirror. Despite his fresh skin and bright eyes, he was still disappointed. This emotion was not due to the changes in his life. On the contrary, he was rising earlier in the morning, sleeping far better and for shorter, being more constructive and productive in the workplace. He enjoyed his and others company far more. Gone were the skulking demons of self doubt and personal despair. No, the problem lay behind the facade. He needed to bury the indiscretions of his past.

He did this by trusting in the truth. He discussed the frailties of his previously inebriated existence with friends and family.He apologised to one and all for his selfish behaviour. He began to understand the trap he had fallen into through earnest conversations with and examinations of people who drank or snorted too much. As he began to understand, he started feeling amazing. An energy was rippling through him that he hadn't felt since he was a teenager. He then realised that his future life would be twice as strong with the wholehearted devotion of another who fully loved and understood him, those warts and all. Kitty was the most incredible human being that he ever met in his colourful and rich life. He saw that they could be an inferno of love, passion, faith and understanding as a couple forever. He needed and wanted to tell her this.

But he also realised that the life altering events of the last half year or so would never have happened without the crop circle revelation. They were the catalyst of this change. After all, he was a nobody, relatively speaking. The billions of fellow nobodys were all at the mercy of the energy of the Universe. He now bowed to this higher power. 'God' was just a convenient word for the unexplained forces of nature on earth. The science to explain what lies beyond was truly awesome to him. The infinite possibilities of extraterrestrial power suddenly entirely justified the numerous different religious descriptions of the same ultimate power. Kitson put his faith into science and its voyage of discovery to reveal the truth. Through his love of art and romance, in his small way, he could be somebody at last.

There was only one way that he could express both personal and transcendental love. He wanted to pay homage to Kitty and crop circles simultaneously. They were one and the same everlasting future of truth to him. He already knew how to express this in eternal art. At their weekly workshop meeting, he explained all to his brother in confidence. His sibling was delighted that Harry was sober and in love. He was more confused by the artistic subject matter but, in the familial interests of their shared business and passion, he produced the meticulous digital designs a few days later. In the exploration of progressive art, the brothers had been amongst the first to embrace multiple software and technological advances back in the early Noughties. Using a surfing analogy, the board was streamlined by one and the other rode the wave, shouting loudly about it. They were a great team.

The render was tweaked and perfected. Virtual reality was replaced by substance. Harry 3D printed it in resin. The design was all he dreamed of so he committed the print to precious and, a handful of days later, the precision components arrived in 18ct yellow and white gold. The workshop manager looked as confused as Kitson's brother but dutifully cleaned up the vibrant metal, assembled and polished it. Harry waved goodbye to the jewel temporarily as it was posted to The Goldsmiths' Hall for testing, stamping and taxation. Hallmarking precious metals has been a legal requirement since around the time of Magna Carta. It wasn't a complicated procedure but nearly one thousand years had certainly influenced the accounting system as Kitson contemplated invoice number L55225/10833546 on it's return.

His diamond setter had added the white, pale pink, soft yellow and rusty cognac coloured stones. He too had raised his eyebrows at the extraordinary design before he gave the metal a final polish and cleaned every nook and crevice of the item in the ultrasonic machine. Having placed it in the rich navy blue velvet confines of its box, Harry just stared. It was the most meaningful object he had ever conceived. It simultaneously represented the most beautiful human and the higher power that he had experienced at first hand. The golden metal and intense colours sparkled in his bright clear eyes as he considered this trilogy of love. Tears welled in them as he considered how very lucky he was.

'With A Girl Like You'

Kitty nuzzled her cheek against her lover's back as she gripped him tightly around the waist. A warmth emanated from his body and she felt as one with him. In her mind she was still laying under their soft damp sheets after their earlier lovemaking. Harry made out that he was a simple man but she knew better. Her lust for him was stimulated by conversations that challenged their boundaries of art, passion and knowledge. Despite some clear personal differences, their Venn diagram of love inhabited a huge segment of their psyches, whether they listened to music at home, watched plays at the theatre or discussed the visuals at an art exhibition. He constantly aroused her and she basked in the knowledge that he shared this completeness of intellect and desire with her alone.

The journey west that morning was a beautiful blur to the army major. Her promotion had been an inevitability after her superior's spectacular fall the summer before. The more secret rise in her other employ had given her further access to all things confidential. She now answered to the very top at both the Foreign and Home Offices. Both employers needed to pay her their full attention, now that she was a public and private hero in the most exciting arena of the era. She was really making a difference to this world. But she was off duty now and Harry had promised her a new and spectacular location for her latest civvy photo shoot. The big black and green motorbike burbled along the little lanes passed fields of fresh sprouting crops and through woodland which glittered with acid green leaf shoots and carpets of lavender coloured bluebells. Life was a dream with this loving man. She knew he was different. He had entirely changed her perception of men after a lifetime of meeting and working with the cruelest, most selfish examples of the rougher gender. The sexual thrill of her brave gladiator coupled with their intellectual quest together through the realms of art and beauty gave her the purest joy. She knew that he would always be true to her, cherish her, understand her and love her without prejudice and judgement. He worshipped her unconditionally. And she worshipped him.

This journey had taken them along the closest, but by no means fastest, route on the northern fringe of their beloved Vale of Pewsey. After West Stowell, they had rejoined the familiar roads that led towards the Knave estate, passing the now distinctive hills of Martinsell, Golden Ball, Adam's Grave, Milk, Tan and Clifford's on route. The long line of swells and undulations resembled the silhouettes of pregnant women lying on their backs, their vastly engorged bellies and bosoms soaking up the life giving sunshine. Maybe this valley really was the womb of Mother Earth after all?

The landscape briefly became softer then more habitated when they arrived at the outskirts of Devizes but Harry indicated and turned right before the town centre. He throttled the bike out into the countryside again and up another steep incline. At the village of Roundway he took another lane up the slope and Kitty looked over her shoulder when they reached the crest. Her bird's eye view took in the aforementioned hills to the north, Salisbury Plain stretched languorously and hazily away to the south and little Pewsey was semi hidden amongst scattered trees between them in the middle distance. She sighed happily as she imagined their love nest, The Smithy, waiting for their rampant return somewhere beyond, sometime soon. Harry ignored the small cluster of cars which were parked higgledepiggerly on the chalky hummocked hill top. The Devizes dog walkers or doggers were not the focus of his mission. He continued in first gear along a rutted pot holed track for half a mile and then stopped the Harley at another parking area beside a charming little wood.

Having dismounted, the couple skirted the copse on the steep side of a modest valley. They chatted amorously, held hands and stole a kiss or two. The valley opened up as they strolled and within a minute or two they stood at the edge of a familiar local geographical feature, a bluff high above a huge plain of patchwork fields. This example disappeared in the direction of the distant Mendip Hills. Behind them was a large plateau with a modest ditch protecting it. Occasional trees dotted its crown but, beyond them, rolled endless downs towards the neolithic tomb of their previous adventure. They were at the furthest high point in the valley that had cemented their lives together. Harry touched on history.

"This is the ancient hill fort named Oliver's Castle. Like so many of the wondrous hillocks beside this valley, it contains stories of legend, mystery and intrigue. But I haven't really brought you here to take photographs of this extraordinarily beautiful place. I have ridden here with you, My Darling Kitty Cat, to show you a film." The spy was temporarily puzzled until he continued his critique. As an expert in the field, she already knew exactly where they stood. "In 1996, a man, supposedly called John Wheyleigh, was walking up here. He made the following film," Harry fumbled his coat from the front pocket of his black leather jacket, "Which is the first live footage of a crop circle formation." He pressed play on the YouTube clip which was repeated over and over again. She watched it, not for the first time. "This film was denounced as a forgery despite experts' confirmation of its authenticity and the filmmaker's mysterious disappearance. That was nearly a quarter of a century ago. You and I have witnessed this energy ourselves, my Gorgeous Girl. Thanks to your determination and strength, plus a little bit of Barry's string pulling and my utter belief in everything you do, you have brought this to the attention of those that can never ridicule it ever again.

"This film is where our journey together really began. I believe that we have been drawn together by fate, love and shared passion ever since it appeared. The six pointed circle formation which appears in seconds is crowned by whizzing and circling plasma orbs of light, like those we have been witness to. My romantic side believes that the two that swirl in tandem together, in perfect synchronicity, are you and I. I want to fly with you for eternity. I want to spend my life with a girl like you."

Harry reached into his leather jean pocket and pulled out a small blue box. Never letting his own loving gaze leave her eyes, he stooped on one knee, opened the box and held it between them.

"My Darling Love, you are the most exciting, intelligent, mysterious, sexy, charming, intriguing, powerful, feminine, elegant and all loving woman I have ever met. Please dance with me forever, together?"

Kitty looked inside the box. A miniature replica of the film formation gleamed back at her. The six points of the circle danced and sparkled with the warmth of the small pink, yellow and orange stones within an intricately woven mesh of a bright yellow gold. Two bright and white round diamonds hovered in correspondingly monochromatic metal above the crop formation. Never had such a delicate, tiny object meant so much to this pillar of feminism, the torch bearer for womanly beauty and power. She was temporarily at a loss for words, yet knew exactly what her answer would be.

'On The Sunny Side Of The Street'

The future Mrs Kitty Kitson and the forever Messrs Knave and Kitson
sat on either side of the long wooden kitchen table at The Smithy.
The two gentlemen perched on wooden chairs. The cutest bottom
had squeezed onto the bench seat by the window overlooking the
High Street. The warm looking ceramic floor tiles were cold to the
touch as the first flickers of dawn sunlight twinkled from the door to
the pantry and utility. One white wall was elegantly enhanced by a
series of gloriously feminine portraits. The half dozen photos were a
surreal mixture of vintage clothing, curvaceous flesh and textured
symmetry, using a straw woven background. They were signed 'Kitty
P'. Another wall housed a mounted landscape photo depicting a view
of the Pewsey Vale with vivid blue skies. A white and black card
decreed, 'Above Milk Hill - Harry Kitson'. The artists had been busy
between their hobbies and professional duties. Their home was
gradually transforming into a shrine to their eternal love and
devotion for each other, the nature around them and their circular
fixations.

Three cups of coffee steamed in front of them. Two black but the cat
had cream. The oil fired cooker burbled as it lazily stoked the boiler,
after their earlier baths, and filled the radiators against the brief
night time cold. Shelves of wine, port, whisky and gin decanters sat
empty in lines, unused for sometime now. Sobriety and going to bed
before the news had enabled Kitson to join the early pre-dawn risers
during this midsummer season. Farming and espionage had
provided the training for his world saving partners. The dynamic duo
of their fantasy Batman and Robin roles had now been joined by
Catwoman. The dreaming sidekick stared at his feline fiancee and
held her hand. He rubbed her engagement finger and the ring that

graced it with love and pride. They had barely finished their hot drinks and early morning vocal pleasantries when the simultaneous buzz, ping and dring of three mobile phones interrupted them. They looked at the devices and swiped onto Barry's app, 'Circum Navigator'.

"Ooooooo! Exciting!" enthused Kitty. "She's near Barbury Castle! Meow! Cats love castles. Purrrrrr. Purrrrrr."

"Holy Blazes, Batman! That cat has got this licked! A doddle. Straight up the A346. Atomic batteries to power!" added Harry.

"Turbines to speed! To the Batmobile, let's go!" ordered Barry.

They grabbed their accessories, crossed the kitchen to the pantry and back door. Having locked it behind them, they stood in the shadows of the graveled yard between the cottage and outbuilding. The brilliant sunshine yawned its early morning greeting on the quiet little lane behind them. As they moved into its rays and walked towards Barry's state of the art truck, Harry beamed at the glory of nature. He looked to the sky and smiled. He started humming, then sang.

"Grab your coat, don't forget your hat
But leave your worries, leave them on the doorstep.
Life's sweet, just direct your feet,
To the sun-sunny side of the street."

THE END

Chapter title playlist available on Spotify:

CIRCUM NAVIGATION guysh3p

Guy Shepherd was born in Buckinghamshire, England, where he lived until he was a teenager when he moved West to home near Newbury, Berkshire, and school in Marlborough, Wiltshire. After studying Comparative Religion at Manchester University, he joined his family diamond business in London's Hatton Garden. After creating a manufacturing jewellery company, Guy teamed up with his brother to form award winning fine jewellery company GUY&MAX. Guy maintains this vocation in London's Mayfair and at his home and art gallery near Pewsey, Wiltshire, The Smithy. It is from this base that Guy enjoys his hobbies of writing, walking, photography and crop circles.

Cover design by Max Shepherd

Printed in Poland
by Amazon Fulfillment
Poland Sp. z o.o., Wrocław

59858821R00186